I0614230

Amber Eyes

In Their Eyes Book One

by

Gabbi Black

This is a work of fiction. Names, characters, places, and incidents are either the product of the author's imagination or are used fictitiously, and any resemblance to actual persons living or dead, business establishments, events, or locales, is entirely coincidental.

Amber Eyes

COPYRIGHT © 2020 by Gabbi Black

All rights reserved. No part of this book may be used or reproduced in any manner whatsoever without written permission of the author or The Wild Rose Press, Inc. except in the case of brief quotations embodied in critical articles or reviews.

Contact Information: info@thewildrosepress.com

Cover Art by *Diana Carlile*

The Wild Rose Press, Inc.
PO Box 708
Adams Basin, NY 14410-0708

Visit us at www.thewildrosepress.com

Publishing History
First Scarlet Rose Edition, 2020
Trade Paperback ISBN 978-1-5092-3252-9
Digital ISBN 978-1-5092-3253-6

Published in the United States of America

Dedication

To Annabel Joseph—thank you for believing in me.
And for giving me Molly & Mephisto.
To Aidan—a better sister I could not ask for. I'm the
lucky one.

Author Acknowledgments

This book is the culmination of six years of work. I had an image in my mind of a woman in a kink club. I started to ask questions about her, and the next thing I knew, I had a book. Then, realizing I wasn't finished, I wrote another two. One image gave me more than a quarter of a million words. I wasn't sure what I had, and I was still in the early days of my writing career, so I reached out for help.

Beth from *A Novel Edit* provided an in-depth edit of the first thirty pages, and I learned there was a lot of work to be done. I tackled the book with renewed vigor then sent the book out to several contests. To my surprise, I won in the Erotic Romance category of the Orange County Chapter of the Romance Writers of America's contest. A month later, I won OCC RWA's *The Charlotte*. Still, I wasn't happy with the book. I worked with my freelance editor to make the book the best it could be. I sent it out into the world but couldn't find a home for it.

Then I sent the book to The Wild Rose Press. I had published a short story and a novella with them, so I already loved the company. I closed my eyes, pressed send, and didn't think any more about it. I think I was resigned to never finding a home for the book. Little did I know editor Josette Arthur would pick it up and see the promise. She saw the reason I wrote the story in the first place. Embarking upon a long journey, we set out to edit this story into the best book it could be.

I want to thank everyone who helped me along this journey, and I hope you love this book as much as I do.

She needs a firm hand.
He needs a challenge.

Temptation personified.

She leaned over the railing to watch the goings-on below, and Gage struggled to identify her expression. Grief? Loneliness? Wistfulness?

Some combination of all three?

As if sensing his gaze, she straightened, angling toward him.

She had caught him staring, and he wasn't the least bit inclined to turn away. Even in the dim light, her eyes were an amazing light brown. Like brandy—smoky and smoldering. Short brown hair with bangs fringed a delicate face with high cheekbones. Light pink colored her lips, and he admired their perfect bow shape. Something passed in her eyes, just a flash, but it spoke to him.

Unabashedly he shifted his gaze from her eyes and scanned her body. All-black clothing with stilettos at least three inches high complemented a lean shape with gentle curves around her breasts and hips. Wow, was he actually reacting to her nearness? Not just the subtle beauty, but her impression of a fawn waiting to startle at the slightest noise. A faerie who could disappear if he took his gaze away.

His fingers itched to touch, but that'd be against the rules. Admire? Yes. Touch? Oh hell, no.

PRAISE FOR AUTHOR

Gabbi Black

AND HER BOOKS

AMBER EYES

~*~

Winner of:
The Charlotte
Orange County Chapter, Romance Writers of America
2016 Contest

~*~

2nd Place Single Title Category
Toronto Romance Writers
2016 *The Catherine Contest*

Chapter One

Temptation personified.

She leaned over the railing to watch the goings-on below, and Gage struggled to identify her expression. Grief? Loneliness? Wistfulness?

Some combination of all three?

As if sensing his gaze, she straightened, angling toward him.

She had caught him staring, and he wasn't the least bit inclined to turn away. Even in the dim light, her eyes were an amazing light brown. Like brandy—smoky and smoldering. Short brown hair with bangs fringed a delicate face with high cheekbones. Light pink colored her lips, and he admired their perfect bow shape. Something passed in her eyes, just a flash, but it spoke to him.

Unabashedly he shifted his gaze from her eyes and scanned her body. All-black clothing with stilettos at least three inches high complemented a lean shape with gentle curves around her breasts and hips. Wow, was he actually reacting to her nearness? Not just the subtle beauty, but her impression of a fawn waiting to startle at the slightest noise. A faerie who could disappear if he took his gaze away.

His fingers itched to touch, but that'd be against the rules. Admire? Yes. Touch? Oh hell, no. Not without permission anyway, and something in her expression said *stay the fuck away.*

Looking into her eyes, he offered the smile Cara had always said was a surefire invitation for fun and games, the one that was both a dare and a promise. "I'm Gage."

Her brow furrowed.

Damn, she probably couldn't hear him over the house music. It wasn't obtrusive but a steady beat resonating through his blood. He stepped forward, and although her pupils dilated, she didn't step away. He leaned forward as much as was socially acceptable and tried again. "My name is Gage."

"Rielle."

"That's an unusual name. Is it short for something?"

Her brow furrowed again, and she slowly shook her head.

She wore no perfume, no chemical scent, but he caught a whiff of something fresh, subtle. He maintained eye contact as he sought a topic to engage her. Ironically, he wanted to ask if she came to Club Kink often, but the question sounded trite, the line lame. When he didn't speak, she turned back to the activities below, and he lost a chance to discover more about her. Missed an opportunity to make a connection.

An opportunity? Conversations there ranged from inane to deep to "wanna go fuck?" That particular proposition likely wouldn't get him very far.

Her body language screamed she was alone and wanted to stay that way. Her hands were on the railing, her long fingers gripping the wood as if she needed its support. She leaned forward, stare once again fixed on the show below.

That look was back on her face.

Longing.

She wanted to be down on the floor. Wanted to be part of the erotic scenes instead of watching them. As a sub or Domme?

Although some men claimed they could spot either quickly, he preferred to reserve judgment. Rielle might just be an observer, but that didn't ring true.

Club Kink was Vancouver's premier BDSM club, open to the discerning patrons who valued privacy while engaging in exhibitionism in a safe environment. The dungeon space contained all the equipment an experienced player could want while the gallery in the balcony allowed voyeurs an unobstructed view of the play going on below. Saturdays were always busy at the club, and that night was no exception.

Strapped to a spanking bench, one submissive squirmed while a Top caned her with a Lucite rod. The red welts were visible, stark against the white skin of the sub's sore ass, and a matching howl resounded with each strike. Lucite inflicted a hell of sting.

Another sub was strapped to a medical table while his mistress did some serious cock and ball torture. She squeezed the guy's balls, which was bad enough, but when she pulled out the urethral sound and lube, Gage winced. CBT was not his thing, so his gaze wandered.

The crack of a whip pulled his attention to the center stage, where he recognized the man holding the whip.

The man made a big production of selecting a woman and inviting her to the stage. He guided her away from the crowd and unlaced her leather bustier. As each tie gave way, the crowd grew. He was a showman, this guy. His chest bared, muscles on clear display, he pivoted, displaying the tiger tattoo on his back. A coil of interconnected whips made up the tattoo circling his biceps. What was his name?

It had been way too long since Gage'd come to play. When he was a club regular, he'd known many names. That was a lifetime ago.

Spike. The guy's name was Spike. *The hair*. Yeah, it shot out wildly in—surprise, surprise—spikes.

The woman's red leather garment fell away, revealing a beautiful, unmarked expanse of porcelain skin. From his vantage point, Gage noted the curve of the redhead's ample breasts. Her black leather micro-mini was so short her garters and stockings were in plain view. He'd bet she wasn't wearing any panties, either.

Red rolled her hips and stuck her ass as far out as her restraints allowed. When had restraints been applied? Probably while he'd been ogling. Next, she was helped out of her skirt, revealing a tempting sight. His hands tingled with the desire to touch the beautiful pale skin of that perfect bare ass. He didn't consider himself an ass man, but remembering Cara's always brought a smile to his lips and a jump-start to his memories of what he had done with that ass.

Spike pulled the woman's long auburn curls to one side, whispering in her ear. The woman shivered, and that frisson skittered down Gage's spine as well. Once, only once, had he submitted to being whipped. He firmly believed in knowing what damage might be inflicted should he lose focus for even an instant. A whip was one of the tools that injured easily, and he used it sparingly.

Even though he anticipated it, the first crack of the whip against the floor startled him. The music had been lowered to a mesmerizing beat, and the sound of the whip carried to the balcony.

When the first strike connected with that delicate skin, a collective gasp echoed from the audience, and a scream rang out from the woman. She strained against the restraints, and evidently realizing she was safely bound, relaxed into the bonds. There'd be a safeword, of course, between Spike and his partner, but she wouldn't need to use it. She probably wanted this pain as much as some women craved a gentle caress. With each lash, she moved toward an ecstasy Gage'd witnessed but never achieved himself. His high came from bringing pleasure through the infliction of pain.

The redhead's alabaster skin showed a crisscross of red stripes across her back and ass. He wasn't a man who obsessed about marks, but he appreciated a beautiful palette when he saw one.

He glanced more than once at Rielle.

Her lips were slightly parted, curling upward with each strike of leather on skin. She obviously yearned to be that woman whose back was bared to the crowd. Had she participated before? Personally enjoyed the magic Spike elicited?

With an extra flourish, Spike administered the final lash, then coiled his whip and dropped it at his feet. He moved closer to the woman, pressing his glistening chest against the fire of her back, using his body to support her as he unbound her. Her back showed vicious red marks but no blood. Blood play required permission from Kink's owners, so it was used only on special occasions. Some in the crowd still watched, but others moved away, looking for the next erotic scene. Before the house music cranked up again, Rielle sighed.

Longing. The sigh of a woman who wanted to be more than a voyeur to an erotic beating.

He'd been right. Without question, Rielle wanted to be that woman.

As her eyes drifted shut, her fingers tapped out the beat against the railing. Suddenly her eyes popped open, and she spun toward him, evidently having come to a decision. "Want to come home with me?"

He attempted to school his features, pretty sure he hadn't hidden his shock. A million excuses flew through his mind until he stopped them with an abrupt thought.

Two years.

"Yeah, I'll go home with you."

****

They walked four blocks to her home at a quick pace, given Rielle wore heels and Cambie Street inclined steeply as it wound southbound toward Robson. Vancouver's waterfront was at a lower elevation than most of the city and much of the housing south of Georgia Street. Did she live in one of the countless towers that dotted the skyline or in one of the few remaining houses downtown?

Words weren't exchanged, but his nerves sizzled. Anticipation might be a positive force, but he was out of his depth. At first he wasn't convinced this was a bright idea, then he mused over the alternative in his mind. He could make an excuse to leave, but he'd always curse himself for tapping out before the night had begun. She presented him a chance to step outside of his comfort zone, a chance to push himself, a chance to feel alive again. For two years he'd borne life, mired in grief, rarely finding respite. She offered him a chance to turn that around, if only for one night.

A brisk breeze came off the water, the buildings creating a wind tunnel. It didn't bite, but it refreshed. Club Kink's familiar comfort had embraced him like a long-lost lover, but it also confined, and on occasion, suffocated. An out-of-doors kind of guy, he loved the vibe from a stunning landscape including, when he twisted for a moment, the view of the North Shore Mountains, peeking out between the buildings. He preferred natural settings but appreciated the little park they walked past. It was an attempt to bring nature to the urban jungle.

Movement in the park caught his attention. The flash of a lighter illuminated two addicts cooking heroin, right there out in the open. A protective urge seized him, and he pulled Rielle toward him, encircling her waist with his arm. Clearly startled, she attempted to move away, but he tightened his grip. Meeting her gaze under the weak streetlamp, he indicated the park with his head.

She merely rolled her eyes. Maybe because he lived in the suburbs, far away from the poverty of the Downtown Eastside, his view of drug addicts and street people was skewed. Mere blocks from the park, Rielle indicated she lived in one of the soaring concrete-and-glass condo towers. The buildings were a literal and metaphorical barrier to keep out the unwashed masses. Unsure of what to expect, he was surprised when she guided him through the lobby, waved to the concierge, and led him up the stairs. He was in good shape, but climbing stairs was his least favorite form of exercise.

Since he walked up and down stairs all day at work, he preferred running when he got the chance to exercise.

"Short trip." He was grateful for the quick jaunt and hopeful his quip didn't fall flat.

She unlocked the door, lifting one of her shoulders in a laissez-faire movement. "I'm afraid of heights and confined spaces."

That explained living on the third floor and skipping the elevator.

Those were the first words she'd spoken since leaving the club, the most she'd strung together since he laid eyes on her. Wordlessly she dropped her keys into a bowl by the front door and emptied her pockets. Coins, a driver's license, and a debit card. She hadn't even carried a purse.

Flipping on the lights, she indicated he should go into the living room. As he followed her unspoken directive, she rummaged through the fridge.

Figuring he'd been given permission to look around, he moved toward the sliding glass door. The drapes were open, framing a good-sized balcony. Two lounge chairs and a small table, which barely took up any space, were centered out there. Spartan.

Looking around the apartment, he repeated the word. *Spartan*. The furniture was ultra-modern, made of chrome and leather. A state-of-the-art entertainment system was affixed to one wall, but no media was visible. No compact discs, no movies, no books. Nothing to give any hint of this woman's personality.

Rielle.

Sensing her behind him, he spun.

Her expression gave away nothing as she held up a bottle of beer and a bottle of water, arching a brow.

Tempting as alcohol was, he never drank and played. Were they going to play, or were they going to fuck? Or even better, were they going to do both?

He took the water and watched as she walked to the kitchen. Her smoking-hot butt gloved in those black jeans made his cock swell as he ruminated about the things he could do to that ass. Funny, when had he last been aroused to such an extent?

Upon her return, she uncapped her bottle of water, taking a long swig.

Her throat moved as she swallowed the cold liquid, and he suppressed his urge to step forward, pull her into his arms, and nuzzle her neck. Maybe even bite her, mark her. What the hell was that? How was she able to bring out feelings he'd thought long dead?

When her gaze finally met his, her eyes flashed.

She licked succulent lips, and he took a long pull of water, wetting his parched throat.

"This is going to be fun."

How was she so sure? Did she do this often and knew from experience? Or was her libido as revved up as his?

No matter. This was part of the game for her. She'd spun a web and he was ensnared.

Taking his hand, she tugged him down the hallway and into a dark room. Once inside, she closed the door and flipped on the light.

Impressive. He didn't doubt she was cognizant of exactly what flashed through his mind. He wasn't great at hiding his emotions, which, often as not, was a detriment in his job. A poker face would be far more suitable, but he'd learned to work around his limitations. He had other ways to exert his authority and used them when required.

Now, however, hiding his warring emotions was a losing battle. He tried not to show his surprise at the huge room with its covered window and matte-black walls set up as a dungeon. The display of a fairly complete collection of toys on one wall had his cock getting even harder. Surreptitiously, he shifted, adjusting himself. An intense desire to see what Rielle looked like draped over the spanking bench at the foot of the bed or restrained by one of the many hooks affixed to its frame embedded in his mind.

He arched a brow at her, angling his head at the device in the corner. "You said you didn't like confined spaces. What's with the cage?"

She waved her delicate hand dismissively. "Sometimes it pleased my Master to put me in the cage. When I needed punishment." She tapped her index finger against her lips, gaze lingering on the cage for an extra beat before she turned her piercing amber eyes on him. "You might think I need punishment."

Her seriousness provided him a moment's hesitation. Maybe he was in over his head because the notion of such a serious punishment with someone who had just specifically told him she didn't like confined spaces didn't sit comfortably with him. Neither did the term *Master*.

Cara had been his submissive for years, but their relationship had never progressed to Master/slave. Mastering her in the bedroom and dominating her in certain other aspects worked for them, but she'd always maintained her autonomy. A partnership in every meaning of the word and free will had always been hers for the taking. A simple "no" stopped everything. Not that she'd ever used the word, but it had been there nonetheless. His capacity to envision a relationship where one party had no right to say "no" verged on impossible. Several couples from the club had that kind of relationship, but he and Cara had never considered it. Was Rielle looking for that kind of relationship? Another Master? Or just a one-night stand?

Turning his mindset to Dominant, he scoffed at the notion he couldn't control the situation. This was a one-night stand and the situation his to direct. Time for him to start acting the Dom he was. The Dom he knew he could be. "Strip."

She stilled. Pupils almost blown in the near-darkness met his in neither defiance nor acquiescence.

Time spun out as he tried to read the unspoken message she was conveying. Did the command need repeating, or was she reconsidering bringing him there?

Her gaze dropped subserviently to the ground as she stepped out of her shoes. As she shimmied out of her jeans, her hips did a little roll as she pulled the pants down, eventually folding them and placing them on the floor. Was she purposely trying his patience? Possibly as it took an inordinate amount of time to remove her turtleneck.

Finally the offending piece of clothing landed on the pile on the floor, more haphazardly. His frustration level increased by the second. The show was by his request, but his cock didn't appreciate the wait.

She reached for the clasp on the bra.

"Stop."

She shot him a confused look and dropped her gaze again. "Yes, Master."

"Sir." This situation needed to be clarified there

and then, before they got started. "You may refer to me as Sir or Sir Gage. I am not your Master, Rielle. I'm your Dominant. In this room, you obey my commands."

"Yes, Mas...Sir," she quickly corrected. "Yes, Sir."

"I want to look at the woman who brought me into her lair. Turn around slowly." Again, that fraction of hesitation. Was she regretting this? Was there not enough dominance and strength in his voice?

How about the fact you haven't negotiated?

Every speaker from every lecture on consent he'd ever attended was shouting in his ear. As she executed a slow turn, however, he shoved those voices to the back of his mind. Regrets would undoubtedly come in the morning, but for now—in this exact moment—he was going to think with his cock. Amazing how hard he was, but disuse made him more easily turned on, right? Truthfully, he'd never studied anatomy, and his state of constant arousal around Cara meant he'd never been far from a hard-on. But in the past two years? A few masturbation sessions, but certainly nothing satisfying. Because when one had experienced heaven, why settle for a mere hand job?

Grasping the ends of her hair, her eyes cast down, she was fully on display for him, and his meandering mind returned to the room with laser focus. The high-end lingerie fit her like a second skin. It was white with little black hearts—a mixture of innocence and temptress in one package.

She was several inches shorter than he but taller than average. Her pale skin glowed in the low light of the room, contrasting with her dark hair.

Were her high and firm breasts courtesy of nature's

bounty or spandex? "Valentine's Legend?"

Her gaze shot up, and pupils widened. "Yes, Sir. Master enjoyed buying me gifts from that store."

"Enjoyed giving you gifts or enjoyed watching you wearing them?"

She pulled her lower lip through her teeth, hesitation clear. "His pleasure." She sounded less certain.

"You may finish undressing."

Another quick bob of her head, and the obscenely priced lingerie landed on the floor. Once, he'd scoped out the website and wisely decided that as lovely as the outfits were, he wasn't spending a week's pay on two scraps of silk, no matter how sexy Cara would've looked in them. Katriona's Kloset it had been, and she'd been pleased beyond words. She'd worn the lingerie any time she wanted to tease him when he was incapable of acting on the erection he inevitably sported. Her favorite escapades were at work. Giving him a glimpse while bringing him papers with an innocuous note meant to excite him tucked inside. At least she had the decency to get him riled up when he sat behind his desk.

Cara had been that same alluring mixture of naiveté and siren. She'd also had short brown hair, although hers had been riotously curly while Rielle's was straight. Cara's eyes had been dark brown while Rielle's were…he groped for the right word.

Amber.

An exotic brandy-colored amber.

Here a naked woman stood before him, and he was comparing her to Cara. It wasn't fair to either of them.

Once she finished folding her clothes, Rielle

dropped to her knees in front of him.

He suppressed the nervous twitch running through his body.

Her hands lay casually on her knees, and her head was bowed. It was the submissive's position, open to him.

An invitation.

"How may I service you, Mas...Sir?"

"Did I tell you to kneel?"

Shoulders drooped then rounded, allowing her to fold in on herself. "No, Sir." She hesitated. "Perhaps you might punish me." A peace offering? Or a concession? "You might let me serve you." Her tone held both hope and challenge, all the while she eyed the bulge in his jeans with pure appreciation.

"Are you telling me what to do?"

She shook her head violently. "I'd never—"

He took her chin between his thumb and forefinger and tugged it toward him, forcing her to meet his gaze. "Maybe I should put you on speech restriction."

"That might be best." Was that an acknowledgement or tacit consent?

Looking at the wall, he reached for a ball gag. "This, I think, is the way to go."

Her eyes lit with pleasure. Nipples tightened into hard peaks. Cheeks suffused with a flush of arousal.

"Before I do, though, we need a safeword."

"Sir, I don't need a safeword."

He raised an eyebrow. "Maybe you haven't been trained by the right Dom. With me, there's always a safeword."

Her eyes flashed with momentary defiance, then she dropped her gaze back to the floor. "Tort." The word was quiet and even hesitant.

"Tart?"

"Tort." *Was that defiance?*

Okay. Not what he might have expected, but everyone's safeword had meaning to him or her alone. If she chose to use some legal term, so be it. He snagged a piece of pale blue silk hanging from a peg. "Since you'll be gagged, this is your safeword. Drop it and we stop. Got it?"

She nodded, their hands touching as she took the silk.

He had a fleeting impression of soft skin, but that touch resonated in him. Hit him in the stomach and skittered down to his groin. He wanted to take her right then and there, but it wasn't the right time. She'd brought him back there to play, so he held the gag for her to see. "Stand."

This time she didn't hesitate. On her feet quickly and gracefully, she rotated away from him.

He inserted the ball gag and assessed it for fit, snapping it in place. With gentle hands, he eased her to face him and met her gaze. Her eyes were bright and clear, which was important to him. He didn't consume drugs or alcohol when he played, and he expected the same of his partner. "It's time we mark that lovely ass of yours."

She didn't react, but he hadn't expected her to.

"Bend over the foot of the bed."

Again, no hesitation. She lay down, pressing her chest into the mattress, her hands by her head. The footboard was the perfect height. She was on the balls of her feet with her beautiful, heart-shaped ass on display for him.

He gave her no warning as he used his right palm to smack her right cheek.

She went up on her toes and emitted a moan. It wasn't long before she settled again.

"Are the neighbors going to call the cops?"

She shook her head.

Ah, soundproofed. It would have to be considering what likely took place in the room.

The next smack was his left hand to her left cheek. He enjoyed putting his ambidexterity to good use.

A few more spanks and her ass bloomed a lovely shade of pink. Believing in symmetry, he had warmed up both sides, but with staggered, alternating hits. That way, predicting which cheek was going to be struck next was impossible. He liked keeping his partner on edge, not able to anticipate his next move. Pressing his hands against her warmth, he squeezed.

Another moan.

Fuck, she was responsive. But he wasn't finished yet. Not nearly.

An attractive paddle begging for use hung a few feet away—cherry wood with holes in a diamond pattern. It was going to sting. He tapped it against his palm several times before delivering the first blow.

Her hands shot off the mattress and moved to cover her ass.

"Hands by your head."

She put her hands back beside her head and grasped the comforter. Another hit, however, had her moving them down again.

Since he wasn't connecting much harder than he had with his hand, her reaction was a little puzzling. If a blow from the paddle connected with her hand, it would cause serious damage. She had to recognize that.

"I'm going to handcuff you."

Her hands immediately met at the small of her back, and her body relaxed farther into the mattress.

As he snapped on the cuffs, he stared at her. Was she dictating the terms of this encounter? He was doing what *she* wanted, what *she* expected. A little guidance didn't hurt, of course. As much as he was in charge, he still had to be aware of her pleasure.

This time when he used the paddle, she made some inarticulate sound of what he assumed was pleasure, loud enough for him to hear. He alternated a rapid-fire burst with more leisurely strokes. Again he changed hands intermittently. Her skin was now a deep red, and the marks bloomed scarlet where the diamonds had imprinted on her ass. She had to be hurting and would have bruises come morning, but wasn't that the turn-on? Would he be around to see them?

The final hit had a bit more force, telegraphing to her this part of the game was ending. He placed the paddle back in its place and thrust his hand between her thighs.

Almost flying off the bed at the contact, she rocked back on her feet and rubbed sinuously against his fingers. Arousal might be a physical reaction, but her swiveling hips spoke of desire, beyond the mere base need for something more tangible—something between the two of them that needed no words.

She was wet, and his cock hardened. Damn jeans weren't comfortable, but when he'd dressed that night, erections hadn't been on his mind. Sure, he sometimes reacted to the scenes, but it had been so long since he visited the club he'd forgotten how his body responded to the visual stimuli. When was the last time he'd had a boner, and wasn't that a depressing thought? He'd begun to wonder if he might ever have one again.

The fetish wear Cara convinced him to buy provided plenty of room for a hard-on. The mask she bought for him had been the reason he'd gone go to Club Kink without hesitation. Going that night had been a bit of a risk, but one he'd been willing to take. A million legitimate reasons for him being there existed, but the real reason remained unspoken and close to his heart.

Two years.

Adjusting his jeans with one hand, he continued to rub his fingers against her clit.

Her head thrashed back and forth, sometimes lifting off the bed. Still, she held firm to the silk.

When she tried to pull her thighs together, he forced them apart with his knees. She was so wet he expected her to climax within moments, but as time passed, it didn't happen. Why not? He was running through his repertoire quickly. How to push her over the precipice?

Finally, he slid one hand around her waist and yanked her up and against him. He placed his thigh between her legs and was rewarded when she continued to rub mindlessly against him. Her juices covered his jeans, but that was what washing machines were for. Her musky scent was strong, and his nostrils flared, taking in the potent and powerful smell. He got harder, if that was even possible.

Holding her tightly, he used his free hand to take her breast. First he palmed it, and then he tweaked the nipple. Hard.

In response, she flung her head back, narrowly missing his chin, and arched her back so her breast filled his entire hand.

"I want you to come," he whispered harshly in her ear.

She shook her head.

What?

Why was she fighting this? Unless this, too, was part of the game. He unsnapped the ball gag, letting it fall to the ground. "I want you to come."

Her breath came in ragged gasps. "I want you to fuck me."

"I don't have a condom." Damn, he hadn't planned on getting lucky tonight. Why was he doing exactly what he advised his students never to do?

"I can't get pregnant." She rubbed against him again, this time pressing her ass against his growing erection.

He was clean, and the invitation to fuck tempted him, but sex without a condom? Nope. *Never.* "I can't." His hoarse voice—laced with pent-up frustration— matched the unexpressed need as his balls grew heavier by the second. "Let me go down on you."

She shook her head again, frustrating him further. He had the distinct impression he was no longer the Top in this and arguing was pointless. They hadn't negotiated sex, and whatever happened, it had to be consensual.

"Uncuff me." The plea galvanized him into action, because he couldn't miss her need, her want.

He grabbed the key, which took entirely too long as she was already trying to escape the restraints. Worried she might hurt herself, he released the metal

Gabbi Black

quickly, and it fell to the floor with a clang.

Nimble as a cat, she dropped to her knees in front of him. She had the button of his jeans open and the zipper pulled down in a heartbeat.

Her haste to rid him of his clothes might have been comical if not for the near miss of rubbing his cock against the metal. Soon his pants and underwear were around his ankles, and he was in her mouth.

She took him deep in her throat without preliminaries. God, was there any better feeling in the world? Well, fucking her would be high on that list.

She was good. And this was going to be over soon. Her mouth was warm and wet, enveloping him and giving him pleasure he'd desperately missed. Again and again he thrust into her, reveling in sensations he'd believed beyond his reach.

She bared her teeth and raked down his length, giving him permission.

"I'm coming." He spoke through gritted teeth.

In response, she cupped his balls and sucked harder.

He could react only one way to that level of stimulation, doing what any red-blooded man would do.

He came, hard and fast.

****

Gage took Rielle up on her unspoken offer of a shower. She'd handed him a towel and washcloth and pointed to the bathroom. He came out with the towel wrapped around his waist, to find his clothes had disappeared.

"In the wash" was her simple reply when he asked where they were, as if that explained everything.

So he was staying the night. Or at least as long as it

20

took to do a load of laundry. Relaxing into a languid state, he followed her back into the dungeon and under the comforter. The room held a slight chill, and he pulled her against him, spoon-style. "You didn't enjoy tonight."

She shook her head. "Tonight was perfect, Gage. Go to sleep."

He wasn't sure he liked being told what to do, but he recognized her command for what it was. The discussion was over.

Had there been a discussion? There had been no negotiations, no meeting of the minds. He'd acted on instinct, taking his lead from her.

Of course he'd never had to negotiate before. He wasn't even sure he knew what to do, if it came to that. Which was the problem, wasn't it? Playing without consent was the equivalent of abuse. He supposed she'd consented when she brought him home, but still, they should've talked.

Except she clearly hadn't wanted to talk, and he hadn't known what to say. She'd told him tonight had been perfect, which confounded him. Perfect for him? Of course. Perfect for her? Of that he wasn't so sure.

Nothing to be done about it now. Negotiating the parameters of the relationship would keep until morning.

If they even had a relationship. Maybe she expected him to leave and never come back. Maybe this had been a one-night stand. He'd never had one before and was feeling a little empty, unsatisfied on an emotional level. He'd never received a blow job from a woman he hadn't been in love with, which made the night an exception in more ways than one. Maybe if he'd fucked her, he'd feel more fulfilled. Maybe if she'd orgasmed, he'd feel replete.

Sleep. He needed to let go and simply enjoy the comfort of a woman in his arms. Cupping her still-warm ass, he squeezed it, and she let out a moan of contentment.

Two years, he reminded himself. *Two fucking years.*

He owed her a lot. Pulling her closer, he let go.

****

Gage was normally a hop-out-of-bed-to-the-alarm kind of guy.

However, when a hand encased his cock, his awareness came gradually. The hand palmed him softly and with great care. A finger ran along the vein, with a hint of fingernail to entice him. He wanted to open his eyes. Actually, he *should* open his eyes, but that might break the spell. It had been so long. So very long.

The pressure on his cock increased, as did the speed of the motion. He was going to come, but that was what she wanted. She wanted to give him pleasure. Hers would come later, when they were both fully awake.

His balls contracted as he gave in.

"Cara." It was a whispered plea, a broken wish, a shattered dream. "God, I love you."

****

Black enveloped him, save the shaft of light the sliver of the door let in where it was open a crack. Gage's watch was unreadable in the dark, but his body informed him it was later than he normally got up.

Sunday morning.

Lying in bed a little longer before he had to get up

held great appeal. Reaching for Rielle revealed he was alone in the bed. He lay still for a moment.

Her breathing was barely audible in the silence. Not the deep breath of a sleeper, more like the breath of someone not wanting to disturb.

He rolled over to the far side of the bed, and there in the inky darkness, she lay on her side facing away from him.

On a pallet on the floor.

"Rielle?"

Instantly at attention, she scrambled up to stand by the bed. "Yes, Sir. How may I serve you this morning?"

"Why were you sleeping on the floor?"

"It's where I sleep when Master wishes it."

"Did I order you to sleep on the floor?"

Even in the dim light, her eyes widened. "No, Master, but I was restless, and I didn't want to wake you."

He slept deeply and doubted anything short of an earthquake would've wakened him. Except he'd been conscious, hadn't he? At least a memory flitted through his mind of…her giving him a hand job? Or had that been a recollection from the past? Should he say something or let it go?

The morning after was not his specialty. He was out of practice.

"Breakfast?" Her voice was soft, almost inaudible.

"That would be nice." Firmer ground, something concrete.

"What would you like, Sir?"

"Anything would be fine." Was there grit in his eyes? He rubbed his hands across them, only to find she hadn't moved.

Oh, maybe she required more direction. "Scrambled eggs and toast, if that's convenient."

Her head bobbed, visible even in the dimness. "Of course, Sir. It'll be ready in a few minutes."

With that, she was gone. Okay, how did this work? He'd assumed the Dom/sub dynamic existed solely in this room, because that was how it had been last night. Were they still role-playing, or was she simply being a polite hostess?

He stood and stretched, needing to piss. The light shone bright in his eyes when he left the dungeon, and the bathroom glare did nothing to spare his vision. A splash of cold water on his face left him refreshed. He took stock. Yep, he had in fact received a hand job that morning. After cleaning up, he put on his clothes that had been neatly stacked, waiting for him.

He'd worn a black silk shirt, black jeans, and black shoes. The rules at Club Kink dictated that if the club goers weren't in fetish wear, they wore all black. As he dressed, he caught a faint whiff of...vanilla? Did they make fabric softener that smelled like vanilla? Whatever it was, he liked it, so he'd ask her about it. On the other hand, due to allergies, the school had a no-scent policy. No, he'd better pass. He would, however, enjoy the memories the scene evoked—his mother's kitchen. Cara's kitchen.

Cara.

High after his orgasm, hadn't he whispered her name? He closed his eyes, rubbing his hand across his face. Yep, he had used Cara's name in Rielle's bed. God, what clusterfuck had he gotten himself into?

Rielle appeared unconcerned by the whole screw-up and placed his toast and eggs on the table as he arrived.

The meal looked appetizing, and his stomach rumbled at the smell.

She had laid out peanut butter, jam, and his favorite, marmalade. He sat, but the table was set for one. "Aren't joining me, or did you eat earlier?"

"I haven't eaten, Sir, but I didn't want to presume."

"I'd like you to join me."

She acknowledged his request and carried in a bowl of what looked like oatmeal from the kitchen before sitting next to him. She wore a short, light-blue silk kimono, which dipped dangerously when she leaned forward to scoot her chair closer to the table.

He itched to reach down and tweak a nipple. That might bring some color to her pale cheeks. They were as pale as…her *blonde* hair.

"You're blonde?" Didn't it usually work the other way, with women who weren't blondes pretending to be blondes? Was she wearing a wig this morning?

Without looking at him, she ran a hand through her long hair, looking self-conscious. "I'm a blonde."

"Why…?"

"I didn't want to attract attention."

She'd garner attention regardless of her hair color, but he understood her reasoning. Her hair was a pale yellow that many women tried to replicate using a bottle of dye. In the dim light of the club, her hair would've stood out. Might he have even noticed her if she hadn't been standing within two feet of him? No, she hadn't wanted to stand out. She'd wanted to blend in.

"Why were you there last night, if not to get fucked?"

She lifted her chin and offered him a rueful twist of her lips and an arched eyebrow. Catching herself, she dropped her gaze and demurely replied, "I wasn't planning to, as you so crudely put it, get fucked."

He was contrite about his language choice but not about the question. "Can we stop the role-play?"

Her head snapped up, pupils dilating. "You're displeased?"

He was treading on dangerous ground. "I was very pleased last night. And this morning." He eyed his toast, buying himself a moment. "But I'm not sure of the rules here. I'm trying to delineate between the play and the rest of it."

"I'm not...I'm not used to being anything but a slave to my Master."

"And I'm not your Master." His patience was fraying. "At the moment, I don't even want to be your Dom. I want us to have a normal conversation, on even ground."

She sighed, and it wasn't a sigh of pleasure. Wrapping her arms around her waist, she pulled in protectively upon herself. "I'm out of my depth, Gage. I don't know how to relate to you except as a submissive."

"Don't know how or can't remember?"

That brought her up short. "I've been a submissive for so long that..." She fluttered her hands. "I'm not comfortable as anything else."

"Last night, though, at the club..." Had she been anything other than submissive? Would he have come home with her if she'd shown any Domme tendencies? No, she'd been clear about what she wanted, but had also probably understood nothing short of a proposition

26

would've brought him here. He certainly hadn't planned on inviting himself.

"Try, Rielle, for a few minutes." He gathered his thoughts, choosing his next words carefully. "Why did you invite me here?"

"To get laid, I suppose."

"And you don't have any condoms?"

Her cheeks reddened. "Okay, I wasn't looking to get laid. I was looking to forget. I was looking for a way out of the loneliness."

You and me both. "Where's your Master?"

The bleakness overtaking her was instantaneous. Her face twisted, eyes shining with unshed tears. "He released me."

"Were you a slave? A twenty-four seven power exchange slave?"

She averted her eyes. "For the past four years."

"When did he release you?"

"Three months ago."

Rebound? "And what have you been doing since?"

"Waiting for him to come back."

Such a stark statement. *That* was the look he had spotted in her eyes the previous night. And why he found a kindred spirit in her. "Will he come back?"

She shook her head. "He's an important man. When it was just the two of us, it was fine. I mean, he kept me here, and I serviced him whenever he came over. But his new wife found out about me and pointed out if she could, so could his enemies. If he wanted the brass ring, he'd have to shed his proclivities. That's what she saw me as—a proclivity, a nuisance to be bought off. He signed the deed to this place over to me and began a completely vanilla existence."

"There's nothing wrong with vanilla." It didn't suit him, but he wasn't most people. "Much of the world is vanilla."

"But he could have chosen me." Her words were slow and plaintive. "I could've played vanilla and serviced him when we were alone."

"Why didn't he choose you?" An intrusive question, but he needed to understand.

"Because I didn't come from old money with powerful political connections."

Who the hell had she been with?

She gazed toward the window, displaying her profile. She was a striking woman, but also unbearably sad. "I know what you're thinking."

"I doubt that." His tone was wry.

"You're wondering how I got involved with someone like that."

"No, I'm wondering why you're pining over someone like that." He placed his fork on the table, mentally pushing away the plate that was mostly empty. "You're an intelligent woman. Why choose this life?"

Her amber eyes blazed. "Maybe I like what I can get. He gave me this condo and investments that produce enough income so I don't have to work. I don't have to do anything I don't want to."

He fought to hide his surprise, because his entire life he had worked and worked hard. He couldn't fathom lying about with nothing to do except look good and service someone else's needs. And now look where she was. Without that servitude, she was lost. "Why don't you go back to school? Or look for a job? Maybe volunteer?"

She considered briefly and shook her head. "I want

to be available to dedicate myself to my Master."

"Your Master released you. Or…" Was she…? "Are you looking for a new Master?"

Her mouth opened, but no sound escaped. She made a second attempt with the same result. Finally she simply said, "I want my Master back."

Like I want my Cara back.

"Rielle, you realize that's probably not going to happen. If he's gone vanilla by choice…"

"In his heart, though, he's a Master. It was his destiny, as it was mine to be a slave."

The word gave him shivers, and he was intimidated. What would it be like to be totally responsible for someone else? "Why did you go to Club Kink last night?"

Her eyes misted. "He used to take me there. He always wore a mask, but he liked the thrill of going out in public with the possibility of discovery. When we scened there, it was intense, and when we came home, it was explosive. Those are the times I remember most vividly."

"What about those private moments when it was the two of you? Those moments of shared intimacy?"

Her gaze sharpened. "The intimacy came from me serving him, not shared memories." She scowled. "You don't know what it's like."

"To be so involved with someone you lose who you are? No, I don't know what that's like. I know what love is, but it doesn't sound like that's what you had, and I'm sorry for you."

"Love leads to losing control. I might've been the slave, but at least I chose to be that way."

He didn't understand, and maybe he never would.

"I should be going."

She looked neither surprised nor disappointed.

He'd made the right decision. Whoever this woman was, they weren't compatible. They'd both been looking for an escape the night before, and in that sense, they'd both been satisfied.

When he stood, she followed suit. She trailed him to the door and held it open for him.

He stepped across the threshold. As she was about to shut the door, he pulled her against him and kissed her. He used her momentary surprise to thrust his tongue into her mouth. He plundered, imprinting the impression of her body against his so when he was alone once more, he'd have memories. He took without asking permission, but she again issued no complaints.

In fact, her arms twined around his neck, and she tugged his hair. There was a bit of ferocity on his part, and as she clung to him, probably a bit of desperation on hers.

He broke away, his breathing harsh, then he was out the door, and it slammed in his face. He held his breath until the bolt clicked into place.

Something deep inside him synced. *Over.* Whatever it had been, it was over. Time to put the one-night stand behind him and move on. Suppressing the bone-deep yearning, he spun and came face-to-face with a dour-expressioned old woman who raked him up and down with her gaze.

"Stay away from her, you hear?" She went back into her apartment.

He was more confused than ever, and he jogged down the stairs. Time for a long, grueling run followed by a really cold shower.

Chapter Two

Most days he loved his job. These two made it hard to remember that. Kane and Dane Nichols were the twin banes of his existence. They were so identical that even now, telling them apart was impossible. He repeatedly asked Ms. Nichols to do something to help distinguish the two—like a different haircut—but she was one of those defiant parents whose children did no wrong.

The previous day, Dane had taken Kane's chemistry midterm. Or at least, that's what Jenna Lee contended. Jenna was both vice principal and chemistry teacher, shrewd to the last, and Gage never questioned her. Her track record as a teacher was impeccable, and her new role as part-time administrator was increasing her value to the school. He relied on her more and more, but he had to deal with this situation himself.

Dane had taken chemistry the semester before. He was in the perfect position to ace Kane's exam while Kane would've had no trouble showing up for phys-ed class. Gage wanted the boys to take the same classes so they couldn't pull crap like this, but that wouldn't solve all their problems since both boys answered to both names and, to most teachers, were impossible to differentiate.

"This is a serious offense, gentlemen."

" 'Cept we didn't do nothin'," one of the boys—

maybe Dane—helpfully pointed out. "You can't prove we did anything."

Pivoting, he directed his attention to the brother who was looking at his fingernails as if they were the most fascinating objects in the world. "What do you have to say for yourself?"

The young man finally met his gaze. "I say whatever he says. Can I go back to class? Miss Lee's got a great...uh...teaching style, and I'm missing out."

Jenna Lee was, objectively, the most attractive teacher on campus. Thirty-two years old, firm body, generous breasts, and a nice tight ass. Of course, him noticing any of those things was completely inappropriate. On the other hand, he'd have to be blind to miss Jenna's attributes. She didn't flaunt them, and he found no fault in either her clothing or her demeanor. It wasn't Jenna's fault all the young men sported hard-ons whenever she was around.

He hadn't called Ms. Nichols because Jenna's suspicion wasn't proof. She'd dug up Dane's midterm from the past semester, but even the boys' handwriting was identical. Gage wouldn't have wanted to go to court with the flimsy evidence they had.

"Know this." He scowled at the boys. "You can't go through life playing games. One day you're going to need to know something important, and you won't have that knowledge because your brother covered for you." As expected, neither of the boys looked chastened, so he pointed to the door. "Don't do it again."

As the twins slunk away, they gave no further denials. He sent a carefully worded email to Jenna. As an administrator, she might appreciate where he was coming from. As a teacher, she was going to be livid at what she'd see as a weak response on his part.

He scanned his emails. Anything urgent? School was out in another twenty minutes, and he needed to circulate as the kids scrambled to get the hell out of the place on a rainy Friday afternoon. Then he'd dig back into his stack of work, trying to clear as much as achievable before he left to face another bleak night alone.

Friday nights used to be the highlight of his week. He'd leave work as soon as possible, anticipation propelling him home because he and Cara had the whole weekend ahead of them. Invariably she got home first and greeted him at the door, many times wearing nothing but a robe. How many times had they fucked right in the front hall? Often enough that they didn't display anything breakable in the foyer.

Then would commence a weekend of play. Sure, they had the odd vanilla engagement, but frequently they played the whole weekend. Cara had been his entire world outside the walls of the school, and making her the center of his existence never bothered him. Heck, she'd been the school guidance counselor, so a relationship existed at school as well. That one had been strictly professional, however. He hadn't supervised her and never handled her performance evaluations. As if that might have made a difference. Cara's ethical standards were as high as his own...except when she wore naughty lingerie to work and slipped little reminders into his lunchbox.

He rose, straightened his tie, and headed for the door, preparing to meet the onslaught who acted more like prisoners being released after years of captivity than students who had been in school for all of six hours.

He pushed Cara back to where she belonged—into the recesses of his consciousness and the unconsciousness of his dreams. Maybe someday he would be ready to move on. *Someday...*

He headed to find Jenna, bracing himself for the inevitable confrontation. Just another day in his life. The life that stretched on ahead of him, each day a duplicate of the last. Even his interlude with Rielle wasn't enough to bring him out of the unending pain and grief.

****

Sitting in his car, he debated for the umpteenth time whether he should go into Club Kink. It was Ropes Night, with Shibari demonstrations. The patience required to tie the intricate and delicate knots was more than he could handle, but it amazed him how quickly the subs fell under the spell of Master Kinto. The suspensions were spectacular, always a sight to behold.

To hell with it. No reason why he couldn't go in. He'd ended his two-year absence, and despite how the past weekend concluded, he'd enjoyed himself. There was no law saying he might not get lucky again. He was prepared this time, though. For the first time in twenty years, he had condoms in his wallet. Several, in fact, should the need arise.

He was once again sans mask. Risky? How many staff or former students might he run into? In all the years he and Cara had come here, they'd never met anyone they recognized. Or at least he thought they hadn't. Of course if those people wore masks...

He'd be in the observation gallery again. The owner of the club was a former student, so he could always say he was just checking in. In truth, he didn't care if he was spotted. He worked in the public school system and hadn't signed a morals clause, but he did comprehend the concept of moral hazard.

If someone accused him of deviant behavior, they'd have to own up to it themselves. The school board didn't go for anonymous tips, instead choosing to verify any accusations. It was a fine line he was walking, but dammit, he didn't care. He was sick and tired of being alone.

Decision made, he paid for parking and made his way over to the club. Paying the cover in cash, he allowed them to inspect his driver's license. At forty-three, he could hardly be mistaken for one of his teenage students, but lists existed. If one was on the "no-entry" list, one wouldn't make it any further. That list was fairly short, made up mostly of people who'd taken drugs and become altered while in the club. The rules were clear—no drugs and no getting drunk. Most people who came to the club were there for the natural high that came from that razor's edge between pleasure and pain. Giving or receiving. Others were voyeurs.

That night he was a voyeur.

The Shibari demonstration was already underway as he climbed the narrow staircase. The railing of the balcony was completely full. Unfazed, he bought a bottle of water. At over six feet tall, he easily saw over the group of women who leaned against the railing, hands clasped together and looks of awe on their faces. With a rustle of movement, one of the women's hands slipped up another one's skirt.

Kinky. The way he liked it.

He glanced up in time to see Master Kinto raise his

sub off the ground. She wouldn't have a single mark on her. That was the genius of Kinto's work. A line of rope bunnies always waited to play with him.

As he released her, the crowd dispersed. Several experts waited to help the amateurs who were trying rope play. Kind of boring. Maybe not the best night to have come.

Yet even then, he scanned for her. Would she be there that night? Would she be seeking a new Master or just someone to fuck? Why hadn't he been carrying a condom the previous weekend? He would've loved nothing better than to sink into her, balls-deep, and fuck her until dawn. He grinned wryly, his body reacting to the fantasy.

Did people come there to meet up? He'd only ever come there with Cara, and they always made it clear they weren't looking for company. He liked being with people whose interests matched his own. Chances were one or two kinky staff members worked at his school, but they didn't wear neon signs, and honestly, he didn't want to know.

"Gage!"

He spun, having instantly recognized the voice. "Mistress Gigi." Actually, her name was Marie da Costa, but Gigi sounded more exotic. At least that's what she'd told him when she confided she was opening Club Kink, about six years ago. Straitlaced as they came, Marie had been one of his first students when he was fresh out of teacher's college, twenty years ago. Even then, her keen intellect had been apparent. She co-owned the club with Master Dante, and while Dante was in the lifestyle, Marie had no interest in it. She had two kids, a husband, and lived in the suburbs. On Friday and Saturday nights, however, she was Mistress Gigi.

He'd run into her at Heritage Park when he and Cara were on a walk one lovely spring day. Marie had handed them a business card for her new club and invited them to come visit. Had she sensed their proclivities or simply been trying to drum up business? He'd never asked and she'd never told.

The busty, petite brunette pulled him into a hug. She'd tried to call him Mr. Clayton the first time he visited, but it hadn't felt right for either of them. Instead of Mr. and Mrs. Clayton, it'd been Gage and Cara.

"We've missed you." She beamed at him.

How to respond? "Well, without Cara…"

She pressed her hand to his cheek. It was such an intimate gesture, and he basked in the proffered comfort. "Two years, my friend. Two years. She wouldn't have wanted this."

Marie was right, of course. Cara would kick his ass, but she wasn't there to kick it, so he lived in stasis rather than trying to move on.

"Can I find someone for you to practice your rope skills on?"

He laughed. "Gigi, I have no rope skills."

"But with Master Kinto here, you would be an expert in no time."

"I'll pass."

"Fair enough." She pulled him toward the railing of the balcony and surveyed the room. "I see at least two women who might scene with you tonight. Still prefer spanking?"

Tempting as the offer might be, he shook his head. There was another ass he couldn't get off his mind. He took Marie's hand, pressing it to his lips. "I'll scene with you…"

She rolled her eyes and laughed, as he hoped she would. "If I ever indulge, it'll be with you." She eyed him carefully. "What's really going on?"

Before he could answer, she tugged him to the back of the balcony where her office was located.

He allowed himself to be led, not bothering to make even a token protest.

Shutting the door, she directed him to one of the plush chairs.

He sank in, gratefully accepting the bottle of beer she offered. She kept a secret stash back there for those long nights. "One. I'm driving."

She winked and dropped into the other chair across from him. They clinked the necks of their beer bottles. "*Salut*. Now tell me what's really going on."

Keen intellect and incisiveness. He shouldn't have been surprised, but he was. Were his emotions so close to the surface? "I met a woman here last Saturday night."

Marie's eyebrows rose, but she remained silent.

"I think she's a regular here, or at least she used to be. I…we…"

"Hooked up?"

He nodded.

Marie leapt up and slapped his back, nearly causing him to spill his beer. She did a little happy dance and dramatically flung herself back in her chair, fanning her face. "About bloody time."

He shrugged, not trusting himself to speak.

"So what's the problem?"

What was the problem? What right did he have to

ask questions? To ask for advice? Especially when he was never going to see the woman again.

"She's a slave, Marie." He purposely used her given name. "Or at least she was."

"Did you steal her away from her Master?"

He shook his head.

"Was it consensual?"

He nodded, shifting uncomfortably, despite the fact he hadn't done anything wrong. This was like the interrogation he'd gone through when his mother discovered a *Playboy* magazine under his bed. She'd explained about exploitation and that the women in the magazine weren't a true representation of what a woman could be. He hadn't understood what she meant until he met Cara. Then it had all made perfect sense.

"I don't get it. What's the big deal?"

And there was the crux of it. What was the big deal?

"She needs help. She's lost, Marie, without her Master. She admitted all she does is wait for him to come back, even though she knows he won't."

"Who is she?"

His gut churned as indecision warred within him. Marie would keep the confidence. "Her name is Rielle. I don't know her last name."

"I recognize her." She moved her head at an odd angle, as if trying to work out an unseen kink. "I can't believe she came here."

"You didn't see her?"

"I was off last weekend. We took the kids down to Seattle for a Mariners game." She continued to eye him. What did she see? "She was released about, what, two months ago?"

"Three."

Marie twisted her lips thoughtfully. "Sounds about right. Rumor is, he even took the eternity collar back."

"She'd been collared?" He didn't even bother to try to hide the shock in his voice. Sure, many people who came to the club wore collars, but eternity collars? The ones that required special tools to remove? "Where is he now?"

Marie eyed him warily. "This is one of those times when I can't—and won't—say anything. For my protection as well as for yours."

What the hell does that mean?

Shit. "Do I know him?"

Marie shook her head. "Probably not. You guys don't move in the same circles. But he's a man on the rise, on the cusp of becoming a household name. His reputation would be severely tarnished if it was exposed he'd kept a slave."

He shook his head. "But you know. Rielle knows. Surely other people know."

"You're not getting this." An eyebrow arched. "Gage, this man has the ability to destroy me. He's got that kind of power."

"What are you talking about? Here?" He gestured around the room. "You run a legal club, follow the by-laws, stay out of trouble. How could he destroy you?"

"He's one of those men. Up until now he's been a kingmaker. Now he wants to be the king."

Gage almost laughed at the absurdity of the whole thing, but something told him this was not the moment to do that. Marie was completely serious. "If he's so powerful, why release her?"

"His new wife is the daughter of one of the most

powerful politicians in the province. It's a marriage of convenience, well, more like a merger." Her brow arched. "Let's call them Mr. and Mrs. X."

Don't snicker.

"Mr. X has been quietly building alliances, making lists, figuring out how to take down people who might stand in his way. Mrs. X moves in influential circles and is already helping her husband prepare for the world of politics."

"This is ridiculous. People don't vote based on that kind of stuff anymore. We've had openly gay politicians—"

"This goes way beyond homosexuality." She took a long swig of beer. "You're naïve, Gage, and I love that about you."

"I'm hardly naïve." His hackles shot up, and he snapped back indignantly. "You have no idea what I've seen."

"At the school board? Or maybe a local politician? A deviant student? This is so much bigger than either of us."

Likely not to convince Marie otherwise, he deferred to her. "Where does she fit into this?"

"She doesn't. She used to come here, Gage, but never on a Friday or Saturday night."

"But you're closed during the week." After a moment of silence, the penny dropped. "You're not, are you?"

She averted her gaze. "We tried, but we were drowning in red ink, and we were going to have to close the club. Mr. X and some of his friends made us a proposition we couldn't refuse. Within months, we were in the black and have stayed there."

"But if city by-laws knew…"

Her expression shuttered. "I put everything into Kink, and I'm committed to it. But this is my family's future. I want to pay off my mortgage. I want to send the kids to university. That means knowing when to say something and when to keep my mouth shut."

"What are you going to do?"

"Nothing. Life is going to go on as it always has. Just because I've told you, doesn't change anything." She leaned forward and stared hard at him. "You're going to forget we ever had this conversation." Settling back, she gestured at his bottle. "Sure I can't interest you in another beer?"

He shook his head. "What about Rielle?"

She glanced at her desk for a moment before meeting his gaze again. "I won't ban her, but she shouldn't be coming here. It's not good for business, and it's not good for her."

"You mean her emotional health or her physical safety?"

Those perceptive deep-brown eyes narrowed. "Probably both." Her brow knitted. "That girl needs to find a new Master. I have several in mind, but these things are delicate, you know?"

No, he didn't know. A Master/slave matchmaking service existed? "Why is it delicate?"

"She has seen, and been seen by, some of the power elite. She needs someone strong to control her and keep her in the style in which she's become accustomed."

"She said he gave her the deed to the condo and has set her up with enough money to live off of." Frowning, he worked his way through the implications.

"In other words, he's bought her silence."

"She's a smart woman, and she'll not do anything to put her future in jeopardy."

"But you said her coming here was dangerous."

"Dangerous might be a bit of an overstatement, but not much. She needs to stay away. I need to talk to her."

He shook his head. "She'll know I spoke to you."

Her eyebrow arched. "So it was more than a hook-up."

"I didn't mean that. I didn't say that."

"I know you didn't. But now you know, you're going to get involved, aren't you?"

"It's none of my business."

She placed a hand on his. "That's where you're wrong, my friend. It is your business. You made it your business when you fucked her."

"We didn't fuck—" Too late. *Too fucking late*. He stood and Marie did the same.

Pulling him into an embrace, she hugged him tight.

When was the last time someone had held him? Just held him? When was the last time he had held someone? Aside from Rielle, of course.

"Cara's been gone two years, Gage. You need to get laid." Marie smacked his ass. "Pronto."

****

As he wandered through the city, he didn't stop to ask how she'd intuited he hadn't been laid in two years. Obviously she read his face. As soon as he protested about having bedded Rielle, Marie's supposition had been confirmed. His secret, however, remained safe with her.

Did anyone at school ever question? Staff events

occurred, of course, where teachers and staff brought their significant others. Several people on staff were single. Jenna, for example. He grimaced. One of the secretaries had tried to set him up with her sister, and he'd been as gentle and as firm as he could be under the circumstances. No one tried to set him up again.

Which left him at a distinct disadvantage when it came to meeting women. Internet dating was a thing, but he might wind up with someone associated with the school. How would it look if, however inadvertently, he found himself on a date with a parent or even a former student? Lines not to be crossed.

He'd been twenty-five when he started teaching, and soon he'd be overseeing the children of some of his former students. Time had moved forward while he stood still. Maybe if he and Cara had been parents, had kids of their own, he'd have had a reason to push past the grief. They'd talked about it often enough, but the discussion always ended the same way—the risk was too great.

Now Cara was dead, and he didn't even have a part of her. He'd had no reason to keep going. But he'd soldiered on, putting each foot in front of the other and telling himself he was okay with being alone. Lots of people were alone. Just because he'd been with the same woman for almost twenty years didn't mean he couldn't go on without her.

So why was he standing in front of Rielle's building and looking up at her window? Why was he walking toward the building? And why, for God's sake, was he opening the door?

The concierge stood to greet him. "How may I help you this evening, sir?" The young woman wore a uniform with a cap. This place was more upscale than he'd realized.

"I was wondering if you might ring someone and let her know I'm here."

"Are you expected?" It was a pleasant but firm tone. It was also ten o'clock on a Saturday night, not some obscene hour.

"No, but I'm hoping she'll see me." He put on his most genial smile.

Something stirred behind those blue eyes. Pity? Admiration for his gall?

"What's the resident's name?"

Oh, shit. "Her name is Rielle. She's in suite…313…?" Was that the number? He hadn't been paying attention on the way in or on the way out, when he'd been hoping to escape before the door was slammed in his face.

"Do you mean Ms. Reid?"

Rielle Reid? Sounded like the name of a porn actress.

"Yes, I believe it was Ms. Reid." He blundered on. It couldn't get much worse, right? "She's about five foot eight inches, blonde hair, uh, light-brown eyes…"

Blue eyes narrowed. "That would be Ms. Reid." She picked up the phone. "And whom may I say is calling?"

He swallowed his discomfort. "Tell her it's Gage Clayton."

She continued to eye him as she placed the call. An eternity passed before it was answered.

"Ms. Reid? It's Tarah, down at reception. I'm so sorry to bother you so late." She looked pointedly at him. "I have a gentleman here who would like to come up to see you."

A pause. "He says his name is Gage Clayton." Another pause, and Tarah laughed. "About six foot two inches, black hair with silver threads, and smoky gray eyes." A pause and another laugh. "Yes, Rielle, I'll have a good night. You do the same."

Comprehension dawned, and he rolled his eyes when Tarah hung up the phone. "You know Rielle." It was a statement, not a question.

Her grin lit her face, brightening it, even under her cap. "I'm familiar with all the tenants, but she asked me to call her as such and has always treated me with great respect." The grin diminished. "I care about her."

The threat might've been absurd, seeing as it was coming from a woman almost a foot shorter than him and about seventy pounds lighter, but he got the message. He had no doubt of her ability to hurt him.

"I care about her, too." And he did, what a surprise.

"Elevators are on the left."

He tipped an imaginary hat to Tarah, and she tipped hers back to him.

When he was at unit 313, however, he hesitated. Did he even have a good reason for being here? What would he say, and how would he explain his visit?

He'd raised his hand to knock when the door opened.

She was sleep-tousled and sexy as hell. Her sunshine-yellow kimono was haphazardly belted. Her hair fell in soft, unkempt waves.

"I've interrupted you—"

"You're here now." Her amber eyes focused on him. "You might as well come in." Without waiting for a response, she let go of the door and walked back into the apartment.

Deftly, he caught the door before it slammed shut in his face. He followed her into the condo, making sure to secure the deadbolt. A lone lamp emitted the barest amount of light, and he waited as she rummaged through the fridge. Now that he was in her home, words failed him.

This time, she offered no beer. She summarily handed him a bottle of water as she passed him on her way to the couch. Sitting gracefully, she tucked her legs under herself.

God, those legs went on and on. He wanted them wrapped around his waist. He wanted to spread her out across the couch and ravish her right here.

Wrong thought. His cock stiffened, straining against the denim. She was just that beautiful. His first impression of her had been bang-on.

Drinking her own water as if nothing was amiss, she continued to stare at the television, which was off.

Had it been on? Had he interrupted something? Finally, he ventured, "You must be speculating why I'm here."

Her gaze met his, wide in surprise. "Honestly, I hadn't given it much thought. I figure you will either tell me why you're here or you won't. You'll tell me what you want, or you'll take it."

"Take it," he echoed. What did she think he had come here to do? "What do you mean 'take it'?"

"Did you come to fuck me?"

He might not have put it so crudely at this moment, but "yes" slipped from his lips. "But I want more than that."

"So do I," she assured him.

47

"No." He shook his head. "You misunderstand me. I want to talk to you. Get to know you."

Her brow furrowed. "Why would you want that?"

"Because I want to help you."

She put her water bottle on the coffee table and unfurled herself from the couch. "I don't need your help. What I need is your cock, inside of me. Preferably sooner rather than later. We tried talking, remember? I'm better with a ball-gag than with words." She came up to him, and they were mere inches apart, but not touching. "You came here, and this is your game."

He put his bottle next to hers and reached for her, grasping her delicate wrist in his hand. His fingers circled it easily. When he pulled her toward the dungeon, she followed obediently. As they entered, the room seemed to have a more sinister vibe than it had the week before. Now he was aware who had paid for this. The ignominious Mr. X.

The illumination was from strategically placed wall sconces, made to look like torches. He hadn't noticed them before, but they helped convey a medieval atmosphere.

He had to take control, yet he took a moment. Her pulse beneath his finger was strong and fast, but it wasn't fear that kicked up her heart rate. The flush of arousal and the dilated pupils were unmistakable.

"Strip."

She complied. The kimono fluttered to the floor, revealing lovely alabaster skin begging to be marked.

"Against the wall, ass out."

She obeyed, selecting a spot where she could lean her cheek to the wall while displaying her pouting bottom. Her eyes were closed as she waited for whatever was coming next.

As if by providence, or maybe because he'd subconsciously intuited he was coming there, he'd worn a belt. He pulled it from his jeans, doubled it, and landed a blow right next to her head on the wall, missing her face by mere inches. Her eyes snapped open, a look of fear in her expression. It was transitory, momentary, and made him grow harder.

Belts could be triggers for some people, and again, they hadn't talked about this. He wasn't going to be too rough, but he wasn't going to go easy on her either. She hadn't let him in to be gentle with her.

The first blow was right in the center of her ass. She went up on her toes but didn't make a sound. The next hit was on the top of her thighs. This brought a startled cry followed by a low moan. Her hands, placed by her head, curled into fists.

He rained down blows at varying intervals, enjoying that she tensed while waiting for the next blow and relaxed when she thought it might not come. God, but she was responsive.

He didn't want to wait anymore. After delivering one final stinging blow, he commanded, "On the bed on all fours."

She didn't meet his gaze as she obeyed.

He watched her closely as he removed his clothes, taking time to fold them over a chair so they wouldn't wrinkle.

Her well-marked ass faced him, and she squirmed. Eventually she threw a glance over her shoulder.

"Eyes forward."

"Yes, Sir." Her reply was quiet, but she was quick to obey.

As he slipped on the condom, he faced a dilemma. Take her ass or her warm, wet pussy? He hadn't prepared her anally, so the decision was already made, and he grabbed her hips and pressed into her.

She keened as he seated himself, and he was pleased she was tight, enveloping him in a snug, intimate embrace. Fast and furious, this first time. He pumped in and out, and despite the condom, he felt the delicious friction that only came from fucking.

His cock going in and out of her pussy while her red ass was on display stoked the fire burning in his loins. The belt had left several nice welts, and the sight of them made him harder. Each time his thighs brushed her ass, the heat radiated from her skin. Grabbing her hair, he twisted it around his hand, yanking back and slamming into her at the same time. A moan of what could only be called ecstatic pleasure escaped her lips.

Two years.

He wanted to make it good for her, he really did, but as his balls pulled up, he couldn't wait. With one final thrust, he buried himself into her and let go his load. Cum shot from his cock, filling the condom. Bareback might have been better, but as he collapsed next to her on the bed, pulling her toward him, the sense of rightness overwhelmed him. When he slapped her ass, she gasped. When he gave it a little pinch, she moaned. His breathing was harsh in his ears, but his heartbeat was returning to normal.

Much as it pained him to let go, he rolled to the side of the bed, removed and tied off the condom, then dropped it into the wastebasket. When he turned, she'd rolled onto her back. Although she hadn't come, she looked satisfied. Her eyes were hooded, her lips slightly parted.

Shit, he hadn't even kissed her. He'd fucked her, but he hadn't kissed her. But kissing was intimate, and he wasn't sure he was ready to get in that deep yet. Because he could do something, he reached out, snagging her right arm and pulling it gently toward the head of the bed.

She offered no resistance as he secured her wrist with a strand of silk rope. Neither did she speak when he repeated the process with her left. She did give a little tug, as if making sure she was secure.

"Spread your legs."

Something flashed in her eyes before she complied. It hadn't been defiance. It'd been fear. Was she afraid of him? She didn't need to be, of course, but did he need to offer her reassurance? His actions would show her he was no real threat.

He lay over her, mindful of his weight. Without preliminaries, he took one of her breasts in his mouth. Using suction, he pulled the nipple into a hard point. Nipping it, he enjoyed the moans she emitted. As he suckled, he tasted something that reminded him of vanilla, but also something unique to her. She groaned when he moved to the other breast, but continued to flex her hips, seeking to rub against him. In response, he placed his hands on her thighs, holding her steady and making sure she was unable to find surcease from the longing strumming through her body.

She struggled, and he smelled her desire, musky and strong. He bit her nipple hard, careful not to cause too much pain. Some pain was okay, but he didn't want to bring her out of the trance of pleasure she was entering. Reluctantly, he pulled away from her oh-so-perfect breasts and moved slowly down her body. A lick here, nip there, a laving of her navel, and soon he had moved down to her pussy. When he licked her, she tried to pull away. Holding her hips firmly in his hands, he rumbled his approval as she bucked against him. He used his teeth to nip at her clit, and she tried to pull her knees together. As he lapped in earnest, however, she made an odd sound.

"Please." A broken whisper. "Please, stop."

What was he supposed to do? She hadn't used her safeword, but her plea sounded real to him. He pulled back and met her gaze that was wide with...panic? He narrowed his eyes as he took in her hectic color and her lip being tugged between her teeth so hard he feared she might draw blood.

Okay, he'd stop. But he wanted an explanation. "What's going on, Rielle?"

She closed her eyes and arched her back. "I want you to fuck me. Or let me give you a blow job. Or punish me in some way."

All things designed to give him pleasure in a way that bypassed her own.

"I want to give you an orgasm." *Why fight this?* "Then we can do any of those things."

She sucked in her abdomen and tugged on her restraints, letting out a low laugh that raised the hairs on the back of his neck.

"You're wasting your time, Gage." She opened her eyes and met his gaze. Her pupils dilated wide, and no amber was to be found. "I can't have an orgasm."

Stunned, he rocked back on his haunches.

Using his momentary lack of attention, she snapped her knees together and pulled her legs up toward her chest, trying to turn on her side. Clearly, she didn't want to meet his shocked gaze.

This woman had been a slave for four years and had never had an orgasm? Something was going on, of that he was sure. Desire waned, and the blood drained from his cock, leaving a shriveled limpet. He rose and released her from her bonds.

As soon as her hands were free, she pulled them to cover her face, rubbing it forcefully.

He stood at the side of the bed, watching as goose bumps rose on her flawless skin. No doubt she was beautiful, but hidden depths rested just beyond his reach. Did he have the right to push? To ask the questions? Demand answers? Beyond disconcerted, he snagged the comforter, but before he could pull it over her, she rolled, nimble as a cat, and presented herself on all fours facing him.

Giving him a "come hither" look, she reached for his cock.

Don't react. Don't get hard again because it would be so inappropriate, and you're a good guy... Responding, though, was inevitable.

Her eyes no longer held sadness. Instead, determination blazed.

Stepping back would end this, as she respected his boundaries as much as he respected hers. A discussion was in order, but with her lips mere inches from his now-reforming erection, rejecting what she offered was impossible. Despite the fact he'd gotten off not fifteen minutes past, his hard-on was back, his cock filling and angling upward toward his belly.

She arched an eyebrow, and all his qualms fell away. Taking a physical step forward, he pushed his misgivings to the back of his mind, surrendering to whatever she chose to give him.

The curl of her lips was Cheshire-cat like as his surrender was clear. Hesitation vanished as she swallowed him down. With rapt fascination he watched as she worked with diligence to make him hard again. Her warm and wet mouth quickly brought him back to full attention, and when she ran her finger down his perineum and took his balls in her hands, he bucked.

Heat ran hot through his blood, the burning extending from his torso outward to his limbs. Fingers and toes tingled, and he swayed, unsure staying upright was possible.

Angling forward, he rested one hand on her shoulder, steadying himself, while he stroked her hair with the other. The desire to grab it and tug was strong, but the moment wasn't right. Despite how the scene had begun, tenderness now enveloped him. This wounded soul offered him pleasure, and he was too selfish not to take her up on that gift. Reciprocating with kindness was instinctual. She might not want it, but she was going to get it. As soon as he got his rocks off, of course.

The sensations were more acute now that his dick was no longer encased in rubber. Fucking her had been nice, but the intimacy of this was undeniable.

Why not give in? She wanted this, right? Or he could fuck her again. She was wet enough, but to put on another condom when heat suffused through his body and tightened his balls? Rational thought fled as she took him deeper in her mouth. As she deep-throated him, he fucked her face, enjoying the scrape of teeth against his sensitive skin. Swirling him like a lollypop, she tongued his slit, nearly sending him flying. Desperate to hold out, just a moment longer, he ran through all the possibilities of how he would pleasure her.

Wrong thought.

Giving up the fight, he opened himself to the pleasure, orgasming, sending his semen shooting to the back of her throat. Whoops, too late to warn her. She swallowed, and it was clear she didn't care. His cock softened, and she gently kissed it, showing an odd and touching reverence. He was a bit sensitive after her voracious attentions. When she looked up, he met her gaze, hoping his pleasure was clear, because her smile was self-congratulatory.

His legs gave way, and he dropped to sit on the bed next to her. Hauling her into his lap, he pressed a kiss to her temple, pulling her close. "That was…" He searched for the words, pausing briefly. "That was fucking amazing."

Her lips gently curved up against his neck. "I'm glad you enjoyed it."

Now or never. "When you say that you can't have an orgasm…"

A noise of distress echoed in her chest, her body going rigid, skin turning to ice. "I am here to serve my Master and nothing more. My pleasure is not an issue."

To hell with that. "Let's be clear, here. I'm not your Master, and my pleasure comes from giving orgasms as well as receiving them. Got it?"

"Yes, Sir." Her response was stiff, stilted, and unenthusiastic, also with a tinge of suspicion. With gentleness, he eased her chin up so their gazes met. Wariness radiated from her, and he snagged her hand.

Hell, they'd never held hands before. Things that had been natural with Cara took on a whole new meaning with Rielle. Pushing Cara from his thoughts, he squeezed her hand.

"Is it that you can't have an orgasm, or you don't want to?"

Her pupils dilated, and she attempted to pull her hand away from him. "I don't want to talk about this."

"Why not?"

Her gaze darted around wildly. "Not in here. Not in this space."

Was this space sacred to her? It must have some kind of meaning. They should've finished the scene and exited the dungeon before beginning any discussion. Or maybe they should've had this discussion before entering the space. Where had his mind been? *Negotiations*. There hadn't been any negotiations. Even a safeword had been an afterthought.

It was midnight. No wonder he was flagging. Two orgasms hadn't brought him any energy either. He applied pressure to her hand. "Do you want me to go?"

Her headshake was quick, fierce.

"Do you want to sleep?"

Her head bobbed in affirmation. Having decided tonight's ending, they'd achieved a place of understanding. He wouldn't push her to talk, and she wouldn't push him out the door.

That had to be worth something.

Keep telling yourself that, and maybe you'll believe it.

****

Gage awoke with a raging hard-on. He'd been dreaming of mind-blowing sex, but with whom? Cara?

Rielle? The past or present?

The dungeon was plunged into complete darkness, and he had no idea of the time.

He needed to get a watch that glowed in the dark. Jenna always nagged him to get one of those fandangled new watches that counted his steps while working, his heart rate while resting, and most importantly, his distance and timing while running. Truth was, he never timed himself. He didn't run competitively. Time and distance had no meaning. He ran until the demons disappeared, if only for that day, that hour, that moment, that second. He ran until his legs ached, his lungs burned, and he couldn't go another step. Then he'd walk home, often limping, to take a lonely, long, hot shower.

When Cara had been alive, he'd jerk off often. Around her, he'd been like being a randy teenager again, and even though they fucked like rabbits virtually every day, it was never enough. She'd edged him as efficiently and effectively as he did her, and to say their sex life was explosive was an understatement. Given they were in their early forties, he'd anticipated a slowing. Whether it'd been because they had no children, or because of kink, that easing never happened. They'd had sex that last morning.

She'd died with his semen in her. That oddly comforted him. Repulsive as it might be to some, it gave him solace that she'd died with part of them united. Their time together might've been long to some people, short to others, but he had loved her as much as any man could. Now she was gone, and he faced a new set of temptations he'd never expected to deal with again. He could count on both hands the number of times he'd jerked off between Cara's death and Rielle's unexpected arrival. Contrary to popular belief, a man *could* go for extended periods of time without jerking off. Shocking, but true. He wouldn't have believed it, had it not happened to him. Thanks to Cara, he'd only ever associated arousal with desire—and without her, there'd been no desire.

Which brought him full circle to his current dilemma. The dream had left him horny as hell with no relief in sight. Even his trip down memory lane, including Cara's death, hadn't softened his cock in the least. And as tempting as it might be to wake Rielle and beg for her assistance in obtaining relief, he wasn't going to. Taking his cock in his palm, this time he purposely kept his mind on her.

A basket of contradictions, she confounded him. Her beauty, unmistakable and undeniable, wasn't what drew him. Although Cara had been beautiful, that hadn't been what had drawn him to her either. Her feistiness, her kindness, her generosity of spirit—those qualities called to his soul, providing him a mate. And despite barely knowing Rielle, he sensed many of the same traits. A wounded soul, she drew him, strong as a siren's song to a sailor.

Already painfully hard and leaking, he spread his pre-cum on his cock, and it only took a few deft strokes to bring him to an orgasm.

As the waves of pleasure receded, he took stock of the situation. First, he hadn't anticipated the amount of semen he'd ejaculate. Although wiping his hand and cock with the sheet was the only option, it felt sacrilegious as this was not his bed, and he doubted he'd be allowed to wash the sheets.

Secondly, his bedmate had fled their nest. Again. He held his breath until her deep, even breathing reassured him he wasn't alone. *Damn woman.* He reviewed their conversation. He'd asked her if she wanted to go to sleep. He assumed that meant sleeping together on the bed, but obviously she had other ideas.

He shook his head in frustration. If he hauled her up, she'd escape at the first opportunity. If this relationship was going to continue, there had to be a meeting of the minds. Was this behavior going to continue? She was enigmatic, but he was already protective of her. Marie's words of warning swirled in his mind as he eased back into sleep.

Chapter Three

Awareness came abruptly. The aroma of coffee wafted through the air, and the sliver of light where the door opened offered the promise of morning. Coffee was nirvana to him, and each morning he required a stop in the local café before heading to work. He freely admitted to extreme grouchiness before his first cup. Probably psychosomatic, but it was what it was. As he shuffled to the bathroom, he stretched, trying to work out the kinks. Some mornings, age would creep up on him, giving him a new twinge or ache.

He ran his hand through his hair—he needed a haircut. Cara had loved when he grew his hair out over the summer, but a close cut was a professional requirement, to his thinking. As time passed after her death, he'd spaced out his trips to the barber, opting for less to be chopped off. Now his hair was several inches long, and regrettably, it would have to be trimmed. Some men wore their hair long, sure, but reconciling that with his position didn't sit well with him.

A few strands of gray were visible, as Tarah so tactfully put it. In Rielle's bathroom mirror, his temples were almost completely gray.

He didn't even know Rielle's age. He guessed mid-twenties, but the truth was she could have been anywhere from twenty-four to thirty-four. She had an alluring beauty and skin so smooth it defied age. Did it matter? Age was just a number, right? As long as she was legal, did the gap really make a difference?

A hot shower washed away the sticky remnants of the previous night's escapade, but guilt nagged. Comparing Rielle to Cara was verboten. Rielle was her own person—her quirks and foibles unique to her, much as Cara's had been. Over time, though, he and Cara had begun to think and behave as one unit. Oh, she voiced her opinions freely and vociferously, but she'd yielded more and more power to him. Exchanged, or so they'd told themselves. In retrospect, Cara had ceded power to prepare him for her inevitable departure. She'd defied death so often her early death was a certainty. They'd been blessed and graced with more time than they'd earned in life. He wished her well in the hereafter. She'd been happy on earth but always looked heavenward, as if understanding instinctively her time with him was limited.

Shampooing his hair and cleaning the rest of his body was done quickly, brusquely, with an efficiency born of long practice. He'd spent far too long revisiting the past, and a living, breathing, exquisitely generous woman awaited him. Where this was going didn't matter because Cara's death had taught him that today was all that counted. Tomorrow was never guaranteed.

After drying off quickly, he donned his clothes from the neat pile. One quick glance in the mirror assured him all was well. He didn't linger because he didn't want to acknowledge the gray flecks in his stubble. That was the real reason he shaved every day, including weekends.

Following his nose, he made his way to the kitchen.

Rielle sensed him because she presented a steaming mug of coffee ready for him.

He offered a mock bow of gratitude.

"Milk? Sugar?"

He offered the same grin he'd given her the first night. The one Cara had assured him would bring him luck—most likely in the form of getting fucked. "Black is perfect."

Her eyes lit in pleasure, a blush stealing across her cheeks. "I'm glad." She indicated he should sit at the dining room table, off the kitchen, and he followed her unspoken request. As she pulled a plate, overflowing with pancakes, from the oven, his stomach rumbled, and she giggled. "Work up an appetite?"

"Yeah, I'm definitely hungry this morning."

As an offer of assistance would likely be viewed as an insult and resoundingly rejected, he held his tongue. Instead, he watched with rapt fascination. Today's outfit was an emerald-green, billowing blouse with long, white, wide-legged linen trousers. And bare feet.

Goddamn, aren't her feet cold?

Shit.

He was doing it again. Feeling protective and worrying about her. She was an adult—if she went without shoes or slippers, it was her choice. The apartment was temperate, which he appreciated. Even in the winter, he disliked warm spaces, finding them claustrophobic and nausea-inducing.

She placed the food in front of him, and to his immense relief, she joined him at the table set for two. She sipped her juice while he forked several pancakes onto his plate. The bacon was crispy, the way he preferred it. She served herself a pancake and a slice of bacon, taking the syrup from him when he offered it.

"Thank you." God, he was hungry. "Pancakes and bacon are my favorite."

"My pleasure." Her eyes shone, as they did whenever he praised her.

He'd have to do it more often.

The first few bites were made in silence, as he simply enjoyed the food. His breakfasts tended to be either eggs and toast or cereal. Cara always made special breakfasts for them on weekend mornings, as part of her service to him, she claimed. Once she died, no reason existed to keep up the tradition. What was the point of cooking a hearty fare for one?

"This is really good." The fluffy pancakes were heavenly, easy on his stomach, and suffusing him with contentment. Being cared for. Being served.

She waved her hand, eyes downcast. "You don't have to say that."

He snagged her hand mid-motion. He held it steady until she tipped her chin up, meeting his gaze.

Amber eyes widened as she waited for him to speak.

"I say what I mean and mean what I say, Rielle. I make it my business not to lie, if possible."

That caught her attention, and her head tilted, her golden hair shifting, falling down her shoulders. "There are times when you do lie?"

Tread carefully.

With extreme gentleness, he laid her hand against the polished mahogany, relinquishing her grasp on him. He needed the distance as she would undoubtedly sense his prevarication.

Worth a shot.

He shrugged with more nonchalance than his gut was happy with. "There are times when I might..." How to explain? "When people ask me how I am, I always say I'm fine. There are times when that's a lie. There are times when I am anything but fine."

"But everyone does that. We put on a mask for other people." Her left eyebrow arched, something he wished he could do.

He shook his head, searching for a better way to express himself. "I don't have a mask. I believe in complete honesty. It's just sometimes I miss my wife so much it physically hurts, but people around me don't need to hear about my grief."

"Maybe they want to." Her voice was soft, yet her gaze direct. "Maybe they want you to share your pain so they can help you deal with it. Maybe they want to share the burden to lighten their own heartache."

Her insight left him thunderstruck. He always assumed he had to be the strong one. Because of her position, Cara had many friends amongst the staff and students. When she died, he hadn't been the only one engulfed in grief. Her memorial, held in the school gymnasium because so many staff, students, and alumni attended, had been packed. Time to grieve privately had never been afforded to him. "I have to be the strong one."

"Is it because you're a Dom or because you're stubborn?" Her eyes widened, and she clapped her hand against her mouth. She pulled it away long enough to squeak, "That was impertinent of me."

It was impossibly incongruous, and he had to laugh. "I am both stubborn and a Dom. And the principal of a high school out in the Fraser Valley, so I must be the strong one, don't you see? Plus," he added with a touch of humor, "I'm not a switch. There isn't a submissive bone in my body."

"I'm aware of that." Her voice held reverence. "I'd never have asked you here if I hadn't been certain you could control me."

Seizing the opening, he narrowed his eyes. "You shouldn't be bringing strange men back to your apartment. I'm a good guy, but not everyone is like me. You could get in a lot of trouble, or you could get hurt."

She stood, bumping her hip against the table. Before he was able to offer help, she righted herself and snagged his coffee cup.

He tracked her progress as she went to the kitchen.

She reached for the coffee pot, held her hand mid-air for a moment, then let it fall to the counter with a soft thud. Her head drooped as her shoulders rounded. Her misery flowed off her in waves. "You're the first man I've ever brought back here." As if pulling herself up emotionally, she grabbed for the pot and this time lifted it, pouring him a second cup, which he hadn't asked for but definitely desired.

When she brought the mug back to the table, she retook her seat and met his gaze head-on. "I'm not a stupid woman. I understood the risks when I made the invitation."

"Were you feeling reckless?" He didn't necessarily want to know, but he had to ask.

Several moments passed before she shook her head. "I was lonely. I needed to be around people, you know? I wanted human companionship and was, in that moment, willing to take a risk to get it."

"Do you often go to Club Kink?" *Will you tell me*

22

the truth?

She shook her head. "My Master used to take me there, but I haven't gone since he released me."

She rubbed the base of her neck. Was she unconsciously searching for her missing eternity collar? Was she even aware she did that? "I probably shouldn't have gone, and that's why I wore the wig. No one recognized me, so it doesn't matter." She gave him a level look. "If I hadn't gone, I wouldn't have met you."

Good point. There was no fault in her logic, but her cavalier attitude disturbed him. "Promise me you won't go back there alone. If you want to go, I'll take you." And since he had no plans to take her, that solved the problem of keeping her out of the club.

"If you want me to stay away, I can do that. I wasn't comfortable there alone anyway." She pointed to his empty plate. "Would you like anything else?"

He shook his head, offering her a laugh. "I meant it when I said it was amazing. Will you let me help you clean up?"

Her eyes narrowed in indignation, and he swallowed a chuckle.

"Of course not. It won't take long." She took the plates into the kitchen, leaving him at loose ends.

He stood and stretched, turning toward the main living space. "Do you mind if I go out on the balcony?"

She met his gaze, her face an inscrutable mask— never giving anything away. "You can do whatever you like." She pointed to the television. "Feel free to watch something." She returned to her work in the kitchen.

Cara had loved cooking but was never a big fan of cleaning up, so he'd step out of the Dom role for a half hour and bring calm back to the chaotic kitchen. He swore she'd done it on purpose—the woman managed to use virtually every bowl and pot in the place. She'd rewarded him for his efforts, however, and Cara's creativity when showing her gratitude knew no bounds.

As had his. He'd never taken Cara or her generosity for granted. Their relationship had been built on mutual respect and intense trust. He'd have given his life for her, had it been possible. But it hadn't, and there he was again, thinking about her when he should be focusing on the woman he was with. Was this part of the grieving process? Wasn't he over the pain? He'd been honest when he told her the grief was a physical thing. When it was so visceral, he swore he could reach out and grab it.

After unlocking the glass door, he slid it back. The brisk autumn breeze hit him, and he quickly shut the door behind him. The air the previous night must've been warmer, or maybe it'd been thoughts of her that carried him through his walk from the club to her building. He snickered as he remembered Tarah. She could have sent him on his way, but he glimpsed something in her personality. She was clearly competent and protective of Rielle. He understood how that happened so easily.

Her protection of Rielle went further, though. Tarah viewed her not just as a tenant, but as a friend. Tarah was the first woman—or person, for that matter—who appeared to be a friend to Rielle, however peripheral the relationship. He'd doubted she had any at all. Even Marie, with her infectious laugh and vibrant personality, only viewed Rielle as a patron. Marie loved everyone—had affection for everyone. But not Rielle. Concern? Yes. Affection? Not really.

Rielle was a bundle of contradictions. Despite saying she'd been happy in a twenty-four seven slave relationship, she spoke for herself. She might say she didn't want to make decisions, but her decision to stay in the condo involved some degree of autonomy.

She was going to be a handful. Was he up for the challenge? Did she even want him? Did he want her? The answer was swift and definitive. Yes, he wanted her. He would be crazy not to.

The door opened, and she stepped onto the concrete. At least she wore sandals, but when the wind gusted around them, her blouse clung to her mouthwatering curves. Her nipples reacted to the cold, and he swallowed convulsively, dry throat working. His instinct was to cover her with his body, protecting her from the elements and all other intruders. As his arousal grew, he fought the urge to push her up against the wall, strip her, and bury himself in her. But she had dozens of neighbors who could see them, so he reined in his impulse. He wasn't an exhibitionist—it was antithetical to his work.

Another gust of wind swept across them, and her hair blew across her face. Her delicate fingers tucked it behind her ear.

Time to go back inside.

Reluctantly, he opened the door, indicating she go in ahead of him. With a final glance around the cityscape, he followed her into the condo. To his surprise, the bubble of intimacy followed them, something he'd not experienced before.

Hands clasped in front of her, she shifted from one foot to the other. "What do you want to do?"

You. Temptation and desire ricocheted through

him, but he tamped them down. They weren't going back into the dungeon until they sorted through some things.

"Talk."

The flash of discomfort quickly morphed into a more neutral look, as if she understood she had to school her features. "What do you want to talk about?"

He considered for a moment but pushed forward. "I'd like to keep seeing you."

"And I want to keep seeing you." Her voice strained against what appeared to be her own dry throat.

"We need a contract."

Her eyes lit. "You're going to be my Master?"

His "no" was met with a quick flash of disappointment. Time to cut his losses and run? His disappointment was sharp, like a knife to the gut. Okay, not giving up yet. But the terms had to be clear, and being her "Master" was off the table. Not open to negotiation.

She shook her head, vehemence radiating from her every pore. "No, I want this. I'll be what you want me to be."

He snagged her hands, guided her to the kitchen table, and held the chair for her. She sat and watched him warily as he sat next to her. "I want you to be you, at least some of the time. But I'm not comfortable with the idea of having a slave. If we continue this— whatever this is—you've got to have some say, some input."

"A contract."

Were her words a simple repetition or an acknowledgement? "Yes."

Evidently realizing this was nonnegotiable, she

69

rose, went to the kitchen, and retrieved a pad of paper and pen from one of the drawers. She placed them in front of him and headed back to the kitchen, pouring them each a glass of cold water and adding ice. She put them down in front of him before sitting again.

At least she'd gotten one for herself.

He wrote his own name, and the pen hovered over the page. "Is your name really Rielle Reid?"

Her eyes flickered before settling. "Would you like to see my driver's license?"

"No." His denial was quick. "I believe you."

"So what happens now?"

"We negotiate. We decide what will work, what won't work, soft limits, and hard limits." He let a beat pass before continuing. "Let's be very clear that complete slavery is a hard limit."

"I got that." Her touch of dry humor was reassuring. "When can I serve you?"

Of course *that* would be her first question.

An hour later, they'd completed a fruitful discussion. Some things had been easy—this was an exclusive relationship as neither was interested in sharing. They were both going to get tested, and birth control would be up to her. He was clean, so he hadn't had an issue with that one. Leaving pregnancy prevention to someone else always made him nervous, but he'd trust Rielle. Plus, she'd made an offhand remark that she never wanted anything to take away her servitude to him.

She was thirty-three, more than a decade his junior. During their conversation, at times she came across as immature, but at other moments, she made contributions showing a lot of personal insight. She wanted no limit on pain and punishment infliction. He put his foot down on that one. Somewhere in the middle had been the compromise. She claimed she was okay with humiliation, but what if she said that because of mistreatment in her previous relationship?

Surprisingly, Mr. X had not only been her first Master, but introduced her to the world of BDSM. Gage would've suggested starting with a less extreme form of D/s, but it was clear she didn't see things that way.

Although the man spent little time in the condo, Mr. X's demands on her had been extensive. He dictated what she ate (virtually nothing), what she wore (virtually nothing), who she could associate with (virtually no one), and how often she should be available to service him (virtually all the time). Although most of their time together was planned— certain evenings, part of the weekends—he had a nasty habit of showing up unannounced. Mr. X would place a call while on his way over and expected her to be naked at the front door, ready to do his bidding. Anything she might've been doing had to be put away quickly, lest he not approve.

And there was a lot he hadn't approved of. No wonder she'd been reduced to simply existing to please her Master. In addition, there had been what sounded like intense sessions. Gage couldn't bring himself to call them playtimes as they were so much more extreme than he could've imagined. More than once he questioned if she'd simply been brainwashed or had she truly been, as she continued to maintain, happy in her circumstances?

Her safeword was "tort," and she used "mens rea" for slow down. Club Kink used "red" and "yellow," but she seemed to want something more creative. Again, he hoped he hid his surprise at her suggestions. She still insisted she didn't need safewords. If Mr. X had ever done anything to push her too far, she would have borne it, believing it was meant to improve her as a slave or that it was a punishment she'd deserved.

He would arrive Friday night and leave Sunday night. For at least two hours Saturday afternoon and one hour on Sunday, the role-playing had to cease and she had to be herself, a concept clearly confusing to her. It was as if she had no idea who she was. And, although her time away from him was her own, he urged her to consider education, volunteering, or even working as a way for self-improvement. Was this a soft, or even hard, limit? But she yielded. Although she wouldn't tell him what she did, she agreed to do something productive.

Since she also agreed to be open and honest about her emotions and desires, he hoped she might eventually be comfortable sharing any extracurricular activities she might partake in. On Sunday, he'd provide his schedule for the week, including which nights he might have off. He lived more than an hour's drive away, so dropping in on a weeknight was impractical. If she chose to call him on nights when he was not occupied, she was free to do so, but it was not a requirement. She insisted he should call her on those nights, if he wanted to, and the compromise had been if she called, they would be in play, but if he called, they would be vanilla. She was annoyed to no end about that one, but he was too old for phone sex and wasn't going to scene from a distance. His gut told him he needed to be around her for that.

The final sticking point had been orgasms. He purposely left that one for last, hoping once she negotiated everything else, she might be more amenable to give on this issue. His hopes had been in vain.

"I told you, I can't have an orgasm."

The words daunted this time as much as they had the first. "Is this a hard limit?"

"It's not a limit at all." She met his gaze, and confusion clouded her features. "It's a reality."

"Did he forbid them?" Withholding orgasms was one of his favorite forms of play. Going around horny for a day often created more explosive sex when orgasms were again permitted. But four years? Had Mr. X cared for nothing except his own pleasure?

"He didn't forbid them." She gave Gage a look that transitioned from annoyance to desperation and back again. "I can't have an orgasm." Her voice carried the tone of a teacher explaining the concept to a first grader.

Was she serious?

"Some men would see that as a challenge, Rielle." His use of her name was specific, the message clearly received.

"I've never had one. I'm sure there's something wrong with me."

"Psychologically or physically?"

"One…both…who knows? In the end, it doesn't really matter." She straightened in her chair. "It doesn't make a difference. I can give you everything. I can keep you satisfied. I will give you everything I am and will endeavor to be what you want me to be."

"You mean, what *you* want to be." He scrubbed a hand across his face. "I can help you be the person you

73

want to be, but that has to be more than a slave."

She pushed back the chair and got out of the seat. "You think because I was a slave I was less of a person."

The flare of temper gave him a flare of his own—of hope. "I neither said nor believe that. I get the D/s dynamic, but the extremity of Master/slave is beyond me. I told you that, and I've tried to show you there are less all-consuming ways to have a relationship." He searched for the right words. "I want you, sweetheart, but that includes you being willing to take as well as give. You see, for me, part of the pleasure of power is being able to give a woman an orgasm." Choosing the endearment in the middle of negotiations might not be playing fair, but he needed her to see he wasn't just a task Master who'd make her life a living nightmare. He had to convey that theirs would be a respectful and fun relationship where both would contribute and both would get something out of it.

"I'm sorry you've wasted your time, because I suspect this is a hard limit for you." Her eyes shone, brighter than he'd ever seen, and she blinked rapidly. Was that disappointment and…a little sadness? Had she been coming to count on this as much as he had?

Was this a hard limit? Aside from his first fumbling attempts, he'd always ensured Cara received as much—if not more—pleasure than he did. She'd been…responsive. She rarely turned down sex when it was offered, and as often as not, initiated it.

"Let's put it in as a soft limit."

She wrinkled her brow. "How does that work?"

"We'll put it on the 'to explore' list." That list was fairly extensive. They'd used it as a way of sorting things they wanted to try together. He'd partaken in many of them already, but the promise of trying them with a new partner held a lot of appeal.

"Please don't hurt me."

"Physically or emotionally?"

She met his gaze head-on. "You have the ability to do both."

****

The negotiations ended, and instead of heading to the dungeon like she wanted, he insisted they go out to lunch and celebrate their new deal. She chose to wear sunglasses and her wig, which he had no complaints about. They were not going out to be seen, but rather escaping the confines of the condo.

Café Medina was still serving brunch, even though noon had come and gone. Luckily, they were able to go ahead of several larger parties and slip into seats at the last small table. Rielle let him hold her chair before he slid onto the bench. She ordered paella while he splurged on Les Boulettes. Silence descended after their order had been taken, she sipping her water and he enjoying his third cup of coffee. It wasn't uncomfortable, per se, but the charge between them, the tension from their discussion, still hung in the air.

"It sounds trite—" He cleared his throat. "—but tell me something about yourself. Something you've never shared with anyone else."

With her sunglasses removed, he had no trouble seeing the discomfort in her eyes. Was she going to refuse? Use her safeword already? He gave a little shake of his head.

Her expression shuttered, but finally she answered him. "When I was growing up, I wanted a chameleon."

He'd hoped for something a bit more insightful but kept his expression neutral. "Why?"

"They can change the color of their skin. They can blend in and become impossible to see."

"Did you want to disappear when you were younger?"

"Doesn't every child wish that at one time or another?" Expecting sharpness, he saw only neutrality, as if it meant nothing to her either way.

He reviewed his students, running quickly through faces and names. Sure, some kids endeavored to stand out, but other kids strove for anonymity—the shy and reserved kids who would've escaped his notice if he didn't work so hard to engage them. "Were you shy?"

She broke their eye contact for a moment, then met his gaze with steel in her eyes. "I—" She took another sip of water. "I wanted to survive my childhood."

As much as she tried to hide the pain, it was there.

"Was it that bad?"

Her mouth opened, as if to respond, but the food arrived. She dug right in, heedless of the heat.

When she gulped water to cool her mouth, he refrained from saying anything. She'd learned her lesson. "Rielle…"

Swallowing convulsively, this time she didn't meet his gaze. She swirled patterns in her food with her fork. "I don't want to talk about my childhood. Honestly, Gage, it's not relevant. You don't need to know."

Should he argue? *Look at it from her perspective.* She'd brought up chameleons, and it didn't take a psychoanalyst to understand her story was painful, her being forced to recall it cruel. Did he have the right to pry? Open and honest communication had been part of the contract, but this was a gray area. It was one thing to say she didn't enjoy water sports, but talking about her childhood? He'd let it go.

For now.

"You're right, Rielle. But know this." He leaned forward, elbows resting on the table, something his mother would scold him for. "You can tell me anything. Nothing is off-limits."

Slowly, dream-like, she nodded. "I'm sorry I was sharp."

His smile came quick and easy. "If that's sharp, this relationship is going to be a piece of cake."

She met his smile with a guarded one of her own, waving her fork toward her food. "This is good."

"I'm glad."

The food was delicious. The restaurant had been her choice, since he didn't live in Vancouver and wouldn't have had a clue where to go. It was Sunday, and much of the downtown core was closed, averting the chaos of the week. Would Club Kink be open that night, for that exclusive group Marie had alluded to? At least Rielle wouldn't be going down to the club, as he'd put that into the contract. If she wanted to go, they would go together—in gear.

When the waiter came by to see how they were doing, she checked with him before offering her thanks. She did that. Looked for cues from him, approval from him. Subtle, and most wouldn't notice it, but he wasn't most. It pleased him that she wanted to make sure he was satisfied, that his needs were being met.

"May I ask you a question?"

The tinge of uncertainty raised his hackles before he tamped down the reaction. "Of course." Nonchalant.

Calm.

"You mentioned you were married and she died..."

The relief was swift, his body relaxing into the reprieve. For a moment, he thought she was going to call the whole thing off. Silly, but despite their contract, he was never sure where she was concerned. She had an out, of course. A simple "I want to end this" was all it would take. That clause was specifically included for both of them to use at any time. And, like the safewords, supposedly there would be no hard feelings. Just a civilized parting of the ways.

Yeah, right. Bullshit.

Who was he trying to convince?

"My wife's name was Cara, and we were married for sixteen years." His voice dropped half an octave, and he didn't try to hide the hitch. "She passed two years ago."

"How...how did she die?" Her fingers tapped rhythmically on the table, the only discernible sign anything was amiss.

Was that a response to the topic of his beloved dead wife or a reaction to her forthrightness in asking the question? Should he ask?

Pressing a hand to his breastbone, a habit he'd picked up after his loss, he wished to somehow massage away his heartache. "When she was ten, her mother was diagnosed with an aggressive form of ovarian cancer. She died within months." Was Rielle truly interested or feigning interest? She seemed to be engaged, so he continued explaining. "Then, at eighteen, Cara received the same devastating diagnosis."

"So young."

Truer words had never been spoken. "It's

incredibly rare for a young woman to be diagnosed so young, but it does happen. She had aggressive treatment and recovered." His chest tightened at the memory, so he quickly moved to a happier place. "We met at the university, and I kept asking her out, but she always had excuses. I should've taken the hint, but I was unrelenting. When we started teaching in the same town, she finally had to admit it might be destiny."

Her finger stopped tapping. "Destiny? Does the world work like that?"

Did it? As a young man, he hadn't been convinced, but as time went on, his convictions had been tested over and over. "I was never a fatalist—I always believed I made my own decisions, made my own future. After meeting Cara, I wondered if the world worked in mysterious ways. She was a contradiction. The threat of the cancer recurring was a constant specter, but her spirit was strong. She embraced life and lived it to the fullest. No one knew of her illness, her secret."

"What happened?"

Rielle's question dragged him back into the present. "She was driving home from work one day, and a young girl ran out in the road in front of her. Cara stopped in time, got out of the car to ensure the girl was safe. One minute she was talking to the child's mother, the next, she collapsed. By the time the paramedics arrived, she was gone. A brain aneurysm. After all the cancer worries, she was felled by a burst blood vessel."

She placed her hand on his. "You must have been devastated."

He tamped down the emotions threatening to overspill. Always a dangerous topic, it had to be faced.

The twenty years they'd shared indelibly shaped him, as their time together was half of his entire life. She was an integral part of who he was today. "I was numb. We lived with the possibility the cancer might return, but I'd learned to mitigate that risk as best as I could. It sounds trite, but living was a risk, so why not loving?"

"And you loved her." It was a statement, not a question.

"Yes, I loved her."

Her eyes were soft and kind, shining a bit with dampness. "Do you have children?"

Swallowing the all-too-familiar lump, he shook his head. "She had a hysterectomy at eighteen, so pregnancy was out of the question. Cara was convinced there would be a recurrence of the cancer, and she insisted she didn't want to leave me alone to raise a child should we wish to adopt. It was like she knew. Understood in a way I couldn't fathom that her time was limited. We had our students, and that was enough."

"You were a teacher?"

"I was a math teacher and Cara a guidance counselor. I did my master's degree part-time and chose administration. I've been a principal for six years now."

Beautiful lips curled upward. "Discipline, eh?"

He rolled his eyes but met her grin. "It's a good thing my students don't know anything about my private life."

She eyed him carefully. "I'm guessing that's why teacher/pupil is a hard limit."

Grateful she understood, he inclined his head. "I have never, and will never, look at my students that way. I have no patience for men who skirt that line. My frustration is kids who grow up so fast and often have parents who are too busy to guide them through puberty."

A little V formed between her eyebrows as she stared at him.

"Teenagers need guidance, and not all parents are up to the task. I've had to deal with more than my fair share of bad parents over the years." He placed his fork and knife together on the plate. "Kids looking for attention at home can get into all kinds of mischief at school, and it never ends well."

"They're lucky to have you."

He laughed mirthlessly. "You want to think you're making a difference, but it's tough. Have I helped more than I've hurt? I would like to think so. I've managed to turn around a few kids but have also been forced to expel several students who wouldn't accept help." He gave himself a mental shake. This was a conversation he'd frequently had with Cara. She'd understood his doubts because she faced them herself. But here he was, showing Rielle a side he usually kept hidden. How could he be her Dom and cry on her shoulder at the same time? It was a line he'd walked with Cara, but their lives had been clearly delineated.

Seeming to sense his mood, she gave him a sly wink. "Can we go to the black room?"

And just like that, his head was back in the game. "That could be arranged."

****

The talk on their way back to the condo was light, airy, and filled with sexual innuendoes. As they walked by an alley, he fought the urge to drag her back there and have his way with her. The way her hand tightened in his told him he wasn't the only one with that fantasy. A brush of her finger on his jaw, his hand pressed to the small of her back to guide her, little touches, light flutters, all meant to excite and arouse with the promise of more.

By the time they were up the stairs and through the door, he was out of his mind, lust strumming through his veins. Rielle barely bolted the door before he had her against the wall. "Take that damn wig off."

"With pleasure." But it still took her a moment to unclip it.

He banked his ardor, wanting to rip it from her head. But that would be uncouth, and he attempted to rein in his raging hard-on.

As if she had all the time in the world, she slipped the wig from her head, placed it in the bowl with her keys, and ran her hands through her hair, letting it cascade down past her shoulders.

"Now?" It was a struggle not to growl at her.

"Now." She nodded.

He flipped her around, pressing his body to hers, capturing her between him and the wall.

Her hands flattened at the sides of her head. When he pressed his cock against her ass, she levered her hips, arching back against him.

He nipped at her earlobe as he continued to grind against her, encouraged by the moans she made deep in her throat.

Balling her fingers into fists, she flexed her hips, allowing him to press himself even deeper against her.

The scent of vanilla wafted and went straight to his head. He itched to strip and have her right there in the hallway, but memories of Cara flitted across his brain.

None too gently, he flipped her around and crushed her to the wall as his mouth pressed against hers. He nipped her lips and thrust his tongue into her mouth. Grinding their hips together, he whispered his command harshly. "Put your legs around my waist."

She did his bidding. It took a bit of maneuvering, but he was able to get them to the black room in a relatively short period of time. As he released her, she slid down his body with a sigh, soft and yielding. While she flipped on the torches and closed the door, he unbuttoned his shirt, silently giving a stern lecture about patience to his impossibly hard erection.

Standing before him, her hands clasped in front of her, she bowed her head.

Tempted as he was to draw out the undressing process, he wasn't going to. "You may strip."

She bobbed her head, relief flooding her features. Excellent. She was as eager as he was. With fumbling fingers, she unbuttoned the blouse, letting it fall to the floor as she undid the button of her trousers.

"Did I say you could make a mess?"

Her wide-eyed gaze flew to his. "No, Sir. I was just…" Her voice trailed off as she took in his look. Flushed, she bent over to pick up the blouse, then moved toward a walk-in closet.

Curious, he glanced into the space. This was probably part of the original master suite. A large number of fetish items hung on the racks, but no vanilla clothes. She must keep those elsewhere.

After placing the blouse on a hanger, she slipped from her trousers, also hanging them up.

As she pulled down her panties and unhooked her bra, he couldn't help but admire her lush curves and legs that seemed to go on forever. This time, he'd feel those around his waist as he drove into her.

With care, he removed his shirt and pants, and she hung the clothing up. For him, it was a practical matter. He needed to leave soon after their scene, and rumpled clothes wouldn't do. When he pulled down his underwear, his erection sprang free. She licked her lips, causing him to stiffen even further.

"You may service me." "Service" wasn't his favorite word, but throughout the negotiations, she returned to the word again and again. As a submissive, she thrived on providing for others, and he was about to be the recipient of her gratitude, her generosity with her body.

But will she ever give me her soul? Her heart?

Whoa. One week in and he was already looking at…forever?

Appreciation flooded her features as she dropped to her knees in front of him.

Moments later, he was immersed in warm heat, and the pleasure ricocheted around his brain. Already, her mouth felt like home, like a place of respite. She ran her teeth lightly along his cock, and the friction nearly pushed him out of his mind. Clever was the first word that came to his mind. Brave was another. She never worried about gagging or him taking advantage of their positions, of his size. Instead, she gave of herself freely, and tempted as he was to let her continue, he had other plans. "Lie on the bed."

With more grace than speed, she obeyed. Tamping his impatience, he moved to the headboard. Once she was lying on her back, she obligingly raised her arms.

The manacle he attached to one of her arms was

made of soft leather, padded with fur, and sturdy. She wasn't going to hurt herself if she strained—and he planned to make her strain. He planned to make her squirm.

He repeated the process with her legs and her other arm so she was laid out, ready to be feasted on. He tossed a condom on the bed and knelt on the mattress near the foot of the bed, a supplicant at her feet. And she was a goddess. Blonde hair tousled, cheeks flushed, lips slightly apart, she was ready to be ravished.

Placing a kiss on her ankle, he watched a shiver run through her body. His cock thickened. He ran his hands along her slender calf and nipped at the inside of her knee. Her sharp intake of breath told him she was not unaffected. He repeated the process on the other side, biting a little harder this time.

She tensed and, as the moment spun out, relaxed.

He took one thigh in his grasp and used his hands to create a delicious friction of warmth, massaging in long, fluid strokes. The muscles, previously tense against the manacles, relaxed under his touch. He and Cara had taken a sensual massage course for couples, and they had practiced religiously, enjoying the pleasure they could bring each other.

When he finally sensed her slipping into a state of bliss, he moved to the juncture of her thighs. He blew a soft, warm whisper of breath against her pussy, and she bucked. Undaunted, he began a thorough examination of her with his tongue. She tasted delicious, and her musky scent invaded his senses. Some guys didn't like going down on women, but he wasn't one of them. Cara had always let him know how much she enjoyed the attention, and he'd been happy to oblige. As he nipped at Rielle's engorged clit, he hardened painfully.

"Gage."

His gaze left her luscious pussy, and he looked into glistening amber eyes.

"I can't come."

He frowned. "Are you enjoying this?"

She pulled her lower lip through her teeth.

"So, to put it crassly, spread your legs, lay back, and enjoy it."

"You're wasting your time."

He raised an eyebrow. "You said you were enjoying this."

Her lips pursed. "But I want to bring you pleasure."

"Honey, if you think I'm not enjoying this, I have a boner to prove otherwise."

"Then fuck me." Another one of those damned broken pleas.

Okay, time to fight fire with fire. To put her in the right headspace. He slapped her lightly across her clit, and there was a sharp intake of breath. He hadn't hurt her, but he did now have her full attention. "I'll do this as long as it pleases me."

"Yes, Sir." She offered no other resistance, but resignation tinged her voice.

So he resumed his leisurely exploration of her nether lips. The scent of her arousal as he lapped up her juices made it was obvious he was doing something right.

Still, despite his best efforts, clearly a happy ending for her wasn't in the cards. No telltale clenching of inner muscles, no special mewls of need—nothing to indicate she'd climax soon. She let out little sighs of pleasure, but nothing more, so re-evaluation seemed in order.

Reluctantly, he pulled back onto his haunches. Releasing her legs from their shackles, he then fisted himself and finally slipped on the condom. Suspecting she was adequately lubricated from her own juices, he entered her in one commanding thrust.

As she pulled against the restraints, he wondered whether he hurt her, but she flexed her hips and took him in completely.

So fucking tight.

To slow things down, he resisted the urge to thrust, instead taking deep, steadying breaths. Soon she followed his lead, and they breathed in unison. In the dim light, he gazed into amber eyes.

Her pupils were dilated, and she stared at him unblinkingly.

"What are you thinking?" *Do I really want to know?*

"That I want you to fuck me...Sir," she added, as an afterthought.

He was about to make a comment about always doing what a lady wanted, but that would be out of character. He felt powerless despite the fact he was supposed to be dominating this. As he plunged back into her warm heat, he commanded, "Wrap your legs around my waist."

Like the last time, there was no hesitation, as if she understood what he really needed—her complete and total surrender, if only in that moment. He wanted to bury himself and get lost forever. He wanted to forget about work, grief, and everything else that consumed his waking moments.

This time, it was she who nipped his earlobe,

silently urging him forward.

He was rough, almost brutal, in his thrusts, and he wasn't going to be able to hang on much longer. When her inner muscles clamped around his cock, he let go, blissfully sinking into the orgasm.

****

After removing the restraints from her wrists, he carefully massaged her hands to ensure proper circulation. He pulled her into his arms, curving his body around hers protectively. Snagging the comforter, he then pulled it over their rapidly chilling bodies. Previously sweat-slicked, they now shared the quickly dissipating body heat.

He tucked her hair away, pressing a kiss to her shoulder. "You said you couldn't have an orgasm."

She twisted her head toward him but didn't meet his gaze. "I can't."

"But…" God, was he embarrassed? Best to plunge on. "I felt you contracting around me. I felt—"

"Kegels."

"Kegels?" Now he was confused.

She rolled her head, facing away from him. "I do exercises to strengthen my pelvic floor muscles. I do hundreds of Kegels a day."

"To keep…"

"My vagina tight. My Master insisted upon it."

Of course he did was Gage's rather uncharitable thought. He shouldn't feel a stab of jealousy, but he did. That he'd been the lucky recipient of that kind of pleasure was an afterthought.

"Will you consider seeing a specialist to see if this is a physical thing? Because I would say you want to have an orgasm, right?"

Her body went rigid, whatever pleasure that had seeped through it long gone. "Sir, I will do what you ask."

He was instantly remorseful. Since they were in play, she'd believe herself obliged to obey his orders. "You don't have to, and it wasn't fair of me to ask. You bring me pleasure, and I want to return the favor."

She pulled away and rolled on her back so she gazed up at him as his head was propped against a bent arm. "You bring me pleasure, Sir." Then more quietly, "don't ever doubt that. My pleasure is expressed differently than yours."

And that was the end of the discussion.

For the time being.

Chapter Four

Friday couldn't come fast enough as Gage planned all the things he was going to do with Rielle—to Rielle—as soon as they were together. His doctor appeared somewhat taken aback when asked for an STI panel, and he assured the doc he was practicing safe sex. Doctor Marco Raymond was five or so years older, but the man seemed wise in the way of sages from times gone by. The doctor also commented it was good he was getting out.

Apparently everyone was aware he'd been alone since Cara's death.

He wasn't ready to admit anything was going on yet and expressed gratitude for the doctor's discretion. The test results arrived in time for his weekend. Packing had taken a bit of time since he wanted to make sure he had everything. Her dungeon was pretty decked out, but he had a few toys of his own to bring.

He practically vibrated with excitement when he arrived Friday after work. Traffic had been relatively light because he'd been heading into the city while most had been escaping it. He used the key card she'd given him to get into the parking garage. Her condo afforded her two spaces, and she reasoned he might as well use the second instead of paying for parking elsewhere. Not finding any fault in her logic, he pulled his well-used and well-loved SUV next to a BMW that looked like it had been driven off the showroom floor the day before. Did she ever drive it, and if she did, where might she go?

It was none of his business. He'd told her their time apart was hers to do with as she saw fit, and he meant it. Making his way into the elevator, he hoped she'd followed his instructions. He shook his head in amusement—of course she had. She'd want to please him, and this was what he'd told her would make him happy.

Using the key she'd given him, he let himself into the condo. Relaxed, he made his way to the dungeon, anticipation beating through his veins. When he opened the door, everything was exactly as he'd dictated. Rielle lay naked on the bed, her hair fanned across the pillow. Her hands were placed lightly on her breasts, and she'd tweaked her nipples to attention. Her legs were spread open, inviting, beckoning him. He wanted to feast, but he had other things in mind. Going to the side of the bed, he decided a quick deviation might be okay. He took a plump, juicy nipple between his teeth. Her sharp intake of breath told him he was on the right track.

Laid out on the bedside table were the toys for the night.

He kneaded one nipple to a sharp peak and clamped it.

She squirmed.

He repeated the process.

She groaned.

"In pain, are we?"

"No, Sir." Finally, she opened her eyes. "Just a little horny. I've been lying here for an hour, thinking of the things you might do to me tonight, and I'm going out of my mind."

So she had obeyed his orders.

Mindful of the amount of time that would pass before the clamps were to be removed, he'd chosen to use the butterfly clamps, and secured them with the lightest pressure. They would stay in place, but not impede the blood flow and damage those fantastic nipples—mauve pert peaks he could spend a lifetime worshipping.

"I'll decide what I'm going to do to you tonight." He eyed her appraisingly. "Turn over, down on all fours."

With amazing agility, considering her nipple clamps were held together by a short chain, she flipped over, displaying her ass for him. Her beautiful, heart-shaped ass. He offered a silent prayer of thanks and gave it a couple of good slaps before reaching for the bottle of lube she'd placed on the nightstand. After taking a generous dollop, he placed it on her asshole.

The gel was cold, and she inhaled sharply. Ignoring her, he rimmed her with his fingers. With each swirl, he pressed his fingers farther and farther into her. She tensed, and he slapped her rear. Hard. "You have to relax, Rielle, or this will hurt ten times worse."

Or maybe she wanted that. She *had* selected a metal plug even though she had silicone ones. Continuing his ministrations, he inserted first one finger, then two. Reluctantly, he removed his hand and set about covering the plug with lube. He wasn't cruel, so he made it as comfortable as it could be—given he was sticking a large piece of metal up her ass.

When he first placed the toy against her, she tensed again. He tisked his disapproval, and she relaxed her sphincter a bit. Good enough. He pressed the plug into her.

She keened as the widest part of the plug thrust in, taking deep breaths to get her through the pain. *Well trained.*

When it popped into place, she let out an audible sigh.

For good measure, he slapped her butt cheek, and the sigh morphed into a groan. "You can get up now."

Obviously mindful she was both plugged and clamped, she rose carefully from the bed. She stared at his crotch with an anticipatory look.

Oh, what the hell. It hadn't been part of the plan, but their reservations weren't for another forty-five minutes, and the restaurant was around the corner.

"You may service me." That damn word again, but the sparkle in her eyes soothed over any irritation.

Her eyes lit. "Thank you, Sir, you honor me." Before he could react, she dropped gracefully to her knees in front of him, undoing his belt. She made quick work of the button and eased down the fly and his underwear.

Whereas he expected her to take him in her mouth immediately, as she had before, this time she took a different approach. She started at his balls and gently nipped the underside of his cock, right along the vein, until she made her way to the tip. Finally she took him in her mouth, and the pleasure sharpened, the sensations heightened. She held him in place with suction and placed her hands on that sensitive juncture where his buttocks met the top of his thighs. She gently kneaded his ass, possibly in return for his previous attention to her.

When he placed his hands on the sides of her face, she got the message and increased the speed of her head bobbing. She was good. He was large, and it had taken Cara some time to learn to deep-throat him, while Rielle had no difficulties at all.

Pleasure shot through him and then out of him. She rumbled her approval, causing him to convulse one more time. Certain she'd wrung every ounce of his semen from him and left his cock abused—but in a good way—he dropped his head forward, sweat beading on his brow. When she stepped gingerly from the room to go to the bathroom, he collapsed into a seated position on the bed. After returning from the bathroom, she applied a warm washcloth to his cock, and he groaned in pleasure. Her touch, which previously had been electric, was now as soothing as a mother's, and he was tempted to forgo his plans and curl into bed.

But reservations were reservations, and he still had plans for her.

"Show me what you're going to wear tonight."

Rising, she then moved slowly and carefully over to the closet. He rose also, pulling up his underwear and pants. By the time she returned, he was back to some semblance of order, even if his brain was still scrambled and fried.

He'd commanded she buy a new dress, hoping it would prompt her to leave the condo. Bronze in color, the dress had little spaghetti straps holding it up. With a shelf bra to hold up her beautiful breasts, it was adequately padded so no one would be aware she was clamped. The dress draped to her knees, but its light fabric moved when she walked, swaying gently and looking as if the lightest breeze might lift it.

She had a matching pair of sandals and a wool wrap for her bare shoulders. He planned to take a cab to the restaurant, so he wasn't too worried about her becoming chilled.

"You look fabulous."

Her eyes lit up. "My Master approves?"

He let her slip pass. "I approve very much." Why wouldn't he? He'd be the recipient of an amazing blow job, and now he was going to spend an evening in this alluring submissive's company. Plus, she wasn't wearing any underwear, her nipples were clamped, and she had a plug up her ass, but none of that was apparent from looking at her. He liked the thrill that came from knowing her secrets.

What about the other secrets?

Her squirming pulled him from his ruminations, making it clear she was horny as hell and would be in such a state for most of the night.

He extended his arm, and she took it gratefully. She'd twisted her hair into a slipknot, and he pressed a kiss to her cheek. "I'll be the luckiest man in the place."

If she dissented, she held her tongue.

****

Thanks to his having the foresight to make reservations, they were led right to their table. He held the chair for her, making sure his hand lightly caressed the fabric covering her naked ass. While he made his way to his seat, she shifted subtly, searching for a comfortable position.

In response to his twitching lips, she quirked an eyebrow, showing slight annoyance. Catching herself, her own lips curled upward. "Thank you for bringing me here like this."

Innocuous enough, but message received loud and clear. And what if she was uncomfortable? She needed to be reminded who was in charge tonight.

The waiter appeared to take their drink orders, and Gage ordered a bottle of the chardonnay.

Her smile was shy, and she looked pleased at his decision. She ordered chicken while he chose the fish.

Finally relaxing, he soaked in the ambiance. No kids, no teenagers, no complaints, no worries. *Nirvana.* Adult conversation and mature company.

She met his gaze, and her eyes were soft, luminescent in the candlelight. "How was your week?"

Should he compartmentalize his life, or would it be okay to blend the two? Was she asking because she cared, or was she simply being polite? No, she wouldn't have asked if she didn't want to understand.

"Pretty typical, which is a good thing. I like weeks where the worst infractions are catching kids smoking, skipping classes, and generally making nuisances of themselves."

"What does a bad week look like?"

He shuddered. "A principal's worst nightmare is something bad happening to the kids. A bus accident, a fire, a suicide, or—worst of all—someone showing up with a gun."

Her eyes widened in shock, and she leaned forward. "Doesn't that only happen in the States?"

"There have been a few isolated cases in Canada, but few and far between. Most of the time I don't think about it, but that doesn't make it less likely to occur." He took a sip of wine. "We try to foster a no-bullying policy, but stuff happens. Part of our school district is rural, so kids have ready access to firearms and know how to use them." He eyed her. "But this was a dull week—the way I like it. And you?"

She gave him a shy look, her delicate cheeks pinking. "I went to the clinic, as promised. I have the papers at home."

"And the other issue?"

"I told you I can't get pregnant."

Her wording was odd, but it was the sentiment that counted. Whether she was on the Pill or had an IUD, he didn't care. He liked the idea of going bareback with her.

He shifted in his seat, tugging gently on his pants to give himself a bit more room. "Although I appreciate that, I was talking about the other."

She appeared momentarily confused, but understanding dawned. "I didn't go to the doctor." Her body went stiff. "I didn't want to waste his time."

Annoyance coursed through him. He couldn't force her to get help, although he should've tried to work it into the contract.

Her gaze dropped to her lap. "You are displeased." The words were barely audible.

"Disappointed, which is a different thing." Hopefully she understood the nuance.

"I will endeavor to do better." She took a sip of wine.

He was saved from having to respond when their food arrived. Once the waiter departed, he grinned. "*Bon appétit.*"

"And to you as well." Her rejoinder was so quiet he barely heard. Was she regretting this?

The first few bites were consumed in silence as

each savored the delicious food.

It was she who first broke the silence. "Thank you for bringing me here."

"You didn't get out much, did you?"

She shook her head. "It wouldn't have been...appropriate. We also didn't..." She faltered. "We didn't spend much time outside of the black room."

He understood. Perhaps too well. "I want more than you had with him. I want you to get more out of life."

Evidently startled by his quiet vehemence, she dropped her gaze to her food. Had he pushed too far?

Finally, her chin tilted up in defiance. "I would like that, too."

He strained to hear her. "What did you do before?"

Her eyes widened, and for a moment, her eyes flashed fear. Then she became impassive. "This and that."

She attempted a taciturn demeanor, but he wasn't fooled. "Can you be more specific?"

Uncertainty clouding her features. "Gage, what I was before, who I was before, it doesn't matter."

"But those things made you who you are today."

"Are you not pleased with who I am today?"

"Rielle, you know I didn't mean that." He tried a different tack. "Did you meet him at the club?"

Amber eyes narrowed. "I don't want to talk about him, but, no, we didn't meet at the club. We met through work, and that's all I'm going to say about it." With an afterthought, she added, "Sir," in a hushed whisper. Low enough so other diners couldn't hear it, but clear enough to get her message across to him.

"I'm sorry I pushed."

"And I should be less sensitive about my past, but I'm not." She fixed a gaze on him, her eyes expressive. "I haven't lived a happy life." She took his hand. "But you make me happy. Can't that be enough?"

So much sentiment in such a short statement. It *was* something he made her happy. If maintaining her happiness required he back off, he would—for the moment. It disturbed him she wouldn't—or couldn't—talk about her past. "How's the chicken?"

"Delicious." She was surprisingly enthusiastic. "And your fish?"

"There's nothing like Chinook salmon."

She agreed. "No, fresh fish is the best." Her cheeks flushed. "Are we staying for dessert?"

"Eager to get home?"

As she shifted in her chair yet again, her lips twitched. "Whatever pleases you." The "Sir" was unsaid but clearly meant.

"I thought we might share some New York cheesecake."

"That sounds delicious."

****

They ate the cheesecake but didn't linger. A cab was hailed for the short ride home.

Tarah waited at the front door, holding it open for them. "Did you have a good time this evening?"

Rielle, whose arm was tucked snugly against his side, checked with him, and he gave her silent permission. She turned to Tarah. "We had a wonderful time."

"I'm glad to hear that. Have a nice night."

The young woman's words were genial and her

demeanor open, but Gage sensed something more. The ascent up the stairs to the condo was a bit slower since Rielle wore heels, clamps, and a plug. When they were inside, though, his patience strained. "What is up with Tarah?"

Her eyes widened in surprise. "Nothing. Why?"

"She seems…protective of you."

Ducking her head, Rielle placed her keys in the bowl. "There was an…accident. Tarah was working that night."

"Accident?" The word hit an ominous note.

She avoided his gaze and made her way into the main room, putting her shawl on the back of one of the chairs.

"You promised me honesty, Rielle." He tried to keep his expression impassive. "Of course you don't have to tell me, but it affects your relationship with Tarah, and it casts me under a suspicious light."

"I'll talk to her." Her response was quick. Too quick. "I'll tell her you're not like that."

He snagged her arm, turning her toward him and tipping her head so she was forced to meet his gaze. "Not like what?" He gave her a moment to answer, but unsurprisingly, she didn't. "What did you tell the paramedics?"

Her eyes widened in shock, confirmation he'd read the situation correctly. Something had happened, and Mr. X had lit out of there, leaving Rielle in trouble and Tarah to clean up the mess.

"I broke a rib, which probably might have been okay, except it punctured a lung."

His stomach lurched. "And how did you break a rib?"

"Falling in the bathtub?" It was a question, not a statement. A plea for him to stop asking questions. A soft request for him to let it be.

"Did the doctor call the police?"

She pulled back, and although he was loath to let her go, he did exactly that.

She walked toward the sliding glass door, looking out for some divine intervention, perhaps. "She wanted to. She thought I was being abused, and she wanted to call the cops." She wrapped her arms around her waist, still facing away from him. "I told her it was consensual. I told her I was in the lifestyle and things had gotten out of hand." She whirled back to confront him. "And it was the truth. I let him mark me. I let him punish me. The rib…was a fluke. He was rough, but he'd never intentionally hurt me like that."

"Because it might bring undue attention to the situation." Words forced out slowly between gritted teeth.

"I told you what came before doesn't matter, Gage." She looked at him pleadingly. "Don't let him spoil what we have."

And what did they have? A fine line existed between pleasure and pain. Could he ever trust her to tell him the truth? That was giving him sober second thoughts. "Tell me this—were there any other trips to the doctor? Any other serious injuries?"

Please, tell me the truth.

She shook her head.

"I'll talk to Tarah myself." He wasn't convinced by her denial.

Her look of surprise was more telling than anything else.

"Do you want to continue?"

"Please, Sir. I'll do anything. Please, Sir, don't leave."

Leaving had never really been an option. "I'll get us water while you go wait for me."

She bowed slightly and made her way to the dungeon. That she expected him to punish her was clear. What he couldn't figure out was what her transgression had been. She hadn't been honest with him the previous weekend about the level of violence in her relationship with Mr. X, but then he hadn't pushed. Her refusal to talk about her past was disconcerting and annoying, but not punishment-worthy. He could do it for his own pleasure, but somehow that was wrong. He wanted to wrap her in a blanket and hold her tight. He wanted to take away the pain inflicted by another. But coddling wasn't what she needed nor what she wanted. If she deemed herself needing to be punished, so be it.

Making his way to the black room, he tried to get into the right frame of mind. The night had started out with such promise, and it might still carry the musky whiff of anticipation. Her pleasure. His pleasure.

When he opened the door, he wasn't surprised to find her naked and kneeling. Various instruments lay across the bed—a paddle, a flogger, a whip, and a belt.

"Rielle—"

"Please." Her eyes were pleading, tears brimming in them, but not falling. "Please, Sir."

"All right."

Her face immediately relaxed.

"But you pick."

She took his offered hand, rising awkwardly from the floor.

He hadn't forgotten she was still plugged and clamped.

She studied the various implements, and turning toward him, took his hand in hers. "This would be my choice, Sir."

He was inordinately pleased with her decision. All impact play had elements of intimacy, but striking her skin to skin connected them in a way no paddling or flogging could. "Put everything else back in its place."

She bobbed her head and set about her work, handling each item as if it were precious china. To her, he guessed, they were priceless.

When she finished, he removed his suit jacket and handed it to her.

She put it on a hanger in the closet.

By the time she returned, he was seated on the bed. He patted his thigh, and she instantly complied, draping herself over his knees.

"Hold on." The lone warning he gave as he landed the first smack.

She gripped his pant leg and made a little whimper. The next blow had more force and landed at the base of the plug, undoubtedly pushing it a little bit higher. This time, she wailed.

He continued to rain down smacks even as she cried.

Never once did she use a safeword. Never once did she ask him to stop. Never once did she let go of his slacks.

Finally, he stopped. He ran his hands along both cheeks, admiring his handprints. He'd marked her, but not in any way that was permanent—not in any way that would cause true distress.

When he let her up, she was a little unsteady on her feet.

He snagged a tissue from the box and handed it to her.

She blew her nose, rather indelicately. "Thank you, Master." He noted the genuine appreciation in her voice.

"And why did I punish you?" This was not, to him, a rhetorical question.

"I shouldn't have evaded your questions. You asked me for honesty, and I didn't give you that. I'm sorry." It was a quiet apology, accompanied by another blowing of her nose.

"You're forgiven." He was grateful for the insight her words offered him. "Now come here." He was still seated, and she came to him, letting him guide her to the space between his thighs. Her breasts were at eye level, perfect for what he had planned.

He put his arm around her waist to steady her and removed one of the clamps. His lips immediately replaced it, and he sucked her nipple soothingly.

"Oh." A cry of surprise as well as a sigh of pleasure.

The blood rushing back to the sensitive nipple was painful, and he wanted to ease that discomfort. When he removed his mouth, she offered up the other breast, waiting for the same relief.

Had anything ever tasted sweeter? As he suckled, his hand slipped between her thighs. She was wet, slippery, and bucked against his hand when he slid two fingers inside. She made an inarticulate, strangling noise when he moved his fingers, thrusting them in and out.

Amber Eyes

She seemed like she was about to go over the edge, so he eased her away and stood up. "Lie on the bed," he bit out as he shed his clothes. Finesse flew out the window as she lay before him, legs open wide, hands on her breasts, offering them up to him.

It took forever to get naked, but it was worth it when she held her arms up to him. He eased himself over her and into her. There was nothing better than skin on skin, being enveloped by her warmth and wetness without the barrier of latex. She gripped him as he slid in and out, her heat enveloping and suffusing him. He felt the plug and marveled she could handle both of them, but she didn't look distressed. Instead, her expression was dreamy.

He swept in for a kiss. Her lips parted as he thrust his tongue into the recesses of her mouth. She parried with him, mimicking the fucking they were doing below. Each time he thrust, he hit her G-spot and mourned she couldn't fully enjoy this. Not that she wasn't enjoying herself—her little moans, groans, and nips of his tongue with her teeth told him she was right there along with him on the precipice of pleasure.

All at once, it was too much, and he fell over the cliff. His cock hardened that fraction more and let go. As sweat gathered on his brow, the warmth and ferocity of the orgasm rocketed through him, suffusing him with pleasure and then something ever more powerful. By coming inside her, he'd marked her in a unique way. Only he'd know, but it was something he could hold on to in those moments of confusion. For right now, she was his.

He collapsed on top of her.

Her breathing was harsh against his ear, and she

clung to him when he pulled away. Ever mindful of his weight, but with a bit of regret, he rolled onto his back, bringing her with him in a tangle of limbs. Reaching out, he pressed a hand to her ass, feeling the warmth that lingered.

He gave it a quick smack and pushed her from the bed. "Go clean yourself up."

"And remove my toy?"

He rolled his eyes, but the corners of his lips curled upward. "Yes, my little minx, and remove your toy."

"Sir, may I have a shower?"

"Of course."

"Would Sir consider joining me?"

He shook his head. "Sir is exhausted and is going to lie here."

She smirked. "Sir looks good lying there." She scampered away, leaving him with his thoughts. All good. The sex had been as explosive as he'd hoped. His planning had worked out nicely.

They had another forty-eight hours together, and he was going to make use of every minute of it.

****

It was no surprise that when he got up to go to the bathroom in the middle of the night, he was alone. Sleeping arrangements had been a huge point of contention the previous weekend, and he wasn't sure either of them was comfortable with the final decision. She had the right to sleep on the floor if she chose to, but had to be aware she was doing it expressly against his wishes.

He wasn't convinced for even one minute she was a restless sleeper. The bed was a California king, and although he was a big guy, there could be a chasm between the two of them, and he'd never know. No, she didn't want to admit the truth. Sharing a bed meant intimacy in a way that had nothing to do with sex. She let him draw her to him after sex, but never fully relaxed into the afterglow. It was like she didn't deem herself deserving of that level of comfort. Who knew whether this was because of Mr. X or some other person?

When he returned to the room, however, he was restless and fully awake. Evidently he wasn't going back to sleep, so he wandered back to the main room. His overnight bag still sat in the living room where he'd left it. He slipped on his jeans, a T-shirt, and a pair of sneakers, snagging the key on his way out. After stepping into the hallway, he locked the door and made his way down the stairs.

Tarah sat at the concierge desk, reading a book.

"Tarah?"

She nearly flew from her chair and scrambled to stand. "I didn't hear you."

He glanced down at his shoes apologetically. "I guess they don't make a lot of noise. I'm sorry, I didn't mean to scare you."

"Better than finding me asleep."

"Have you ever been found asleep?"

Her eyes shot arrows. "I have never been found asleep because I have never been asleep. I take my job very seriously."

"I know you do." He glanced around the lobby. "I was hoping we could talk."

Ice-blue eyes narrowed. "Talk?" When he nodded, she checked her watch. "I'm supposed to do rounds soon, might as well go now." She pocketed a ring of keys and a key card, indicating he should follow her. She led him to the staircase and down the stairs at a rapid clip, precluding any conversation.

When they entered the garage, the pace slowed enough for him to catch his breath. For a smaller woman, she moved fast. "How long have you worked here?"

"Six years."

He raised his brows.

"I got this job after high school. I know how lucky I was. Am," she corrected herself. "How lucky I am. I work five nights a week and take courses part-time during the day."

"What are you studying?"

"English." She eyed him warily, as if trying to gauge his interest in the topic. "I want to be a primary school teacher, but teacher's college is a lot of money. I'm saving every dime I make from here while trying to do my undergrad."

"Did you consider student loans?"

She inclined her head. "I don't want to owe money when I get out. I want to be free and clear."

Good logic. He and Cara had been married more than five years before they managed to pay off the last of their loans.

"Do you do volunteer work?"

"I help out with a preschool five mornings a week."

"When do you sleep?"

"In the afternoon. I'm lucky, because I don't need a lot of it." She never appeared anything other than alert and competent.

He required at least eight hours, so although

envious, he couldn't relate.

They finished the sweep of the garage, and she led him up the back stairs and out onto the street. It was dark, and the shadows menaced.

"Is it safe for you to do this by yourself?"

Her eyes widened with surprise. "Why wouldn't it be?" Her eyebrow arched and blue eyes sparkled. "I have a black belt, Mr. Clayton. Plus, this is a safe neighborhood. I vary my routine and check in with dispatch three times during my shift."

With grudging admiration, he admitted she was careful and professional. He expected no less. "I shouldn't have questioned you. And it's Gage, not Mr. Clayton."

Her sharp gaze appraised. "Okay, Gage it is." She swiped her key card to reenter the building. "Not that I don't appreciate the company…"

"But you're wondering why I came to speak to you."

"The thought did cross my mind." She leaned against her desk, casually glancing at the security monitors.

"Rielle told me you helped her out. That time…when you had to call an ambulance."

The younger woman's face shuttered. "She told you about that?"

He nodded abruptly.

"We've never talked about that night. She sent me a 'thank you' card with a bouquet of flowers, and it has never been mentioned."

"How bad was it?"

Her gaze darted around, as if worrying she might be overheard. "I got a call from that apartment, and I knew it was him, even though he didn't speak. I ran upstairs and knocked, but no one answered. I almost didn't go in, but I had a bad feeling in the pit of my stomach. She was in the front hall, lying on the floor. She was bent over and coughing up blood. God, it was awful." She seemed to pull herself from the memories. "I called an ambulance. They came and took her away. That's it. That's all I can tell you."

He considered his next words. "She trusts you, Tarah. She thinks highly of you."

Her face lit in pleasure. "And I feel the same way. I meet all kinds of people in my job, but Rielle, she's the best."

"You need to appreciate I'll never hurt her."

Sharp eyes narrowed. "I never said you would."

"But you thought it, didn't you?" He didn't wait for her to respond. "You're cautious, and I appreciate that. I guess I need to know she'll be safe."

"He doesn't come around anymore."

"She told me that." He pulled a business card from his wallet. "Will you call me if he comes back?"

Incisive eyes studied the card as if it would spontaneously combust. "It's not my business what she does, you know? I'm not here to invade people's privacy."

"Fair enough." She finally took the card. Excellent, progress. "How about you call me if there's ever any trouble with Rielle? Like if she needs anything."

That got a warmer reception and an acknowledgment. About to tuck the card away, she glanced at it. "You're a principal?"

"Of a high school out in Mission City, yes."

A look of longing flitted across her face.

"I'll give you a letter of recommendation when the time comes."

Those damn blue eyes narrowed again. "Why would you do that for me?"

"You kept your head in a crisis and got help for someone who needed it. You're protective of your own. Those are good attributes in a teacher."

She pocketed the card. "I have to check in with dispatch."

He held out his hand. "Thank you, Tarah."

She took it and applied the right amount of pressure. "My pleasure, Gage."

He contemplated a walk outside, but without a windbreaker, it was too chilly. Instead, he made his way up the stairs and quietly slipped the key into the lock. He shed his clothes, took a piss, and crawled back into bed. He was surprised to find he wasn't alone.

"I thought you had left." Barely a whisper, but as he pulled her into his arms, some of the tension seeped away.

"I'm right here." *But for how long?* "I'm right here."

****

Morning came a little too early, as far as Gage was concerned, but it was his own damn fault. He couldn't get too annoyed, because he was pleased about his tête-à-tête with Tarah. They were on the same page with regard to Rielle's welfare, so any lack-of-sleep hangover was worth it.

After a quick shower, he dressed in his casual clothes and made his way to the kitchen. He was handed a mug of coffee before he even asked. He bent down to place a kiss to her cheek.

Her eyes brightened. "Good morning." She purred the words.

"Good morning to you. What's got you in such a happy mood?"

"You're here." She acted as if it were the most obvious thing in the world.

It hit him how lonely she truly was. "We're going to go see a movie today."

"Okay. Sweater and jeans, or would you prefer a mini-skirt?" In other words, was he planning to grope her in the theater?

He named the movie they were going to go see.

"Jeans, it is."

Truth be told, he had zero interest in seeing the latest iteration of the franchise, but it was aimed at teenagers, and he needed to be familiar with the lingo. Some of his students expected him to be a Luddite, but he wasn't. He embraced technology and kept up with the latest trends as best he could. If that meant spending his Saturday afternoon in a theater full of teenagers, he'd suck it up and do it.

As he sat, she put a plate of pancakes in front of him. He inhaled deeply, enjoying the scent of fried bacon.

She was there. His Cara. Feeding him bacon, one foot running up and down his shin while her hand stroked his bulge. Cara's ministrations instilled a Pavlovian reaction with him every time. Bacon equaled either a blow job or hot sex. Or better yet, both.

He struggled to move from the past back into the present. *Lighten the mood.* "You're going to make me fat."

Rielle's expression was pensive, eyes penetrating.

She knew. Maybe not the specifics, but she understood he'd had a flashback of sorts. "Not likely." Her face softened, and her features relaxed. She was letting him understand she was okay with this. She placed a hand on his abs. "You're pretty hot…for an old guy."

"Old guy, my ass…ooh." His retort faded away as she rubbed him through his jeans. Suddenly it was less about reprimands and more about demands. Like the ones his body was making. As he hardened under her touch, he eyed the pancakes speculatively. There was always the microwave…

And just like that, she withdrew her hand and dug into her food. Her lips curled slightly, though, as if she recognized what he'd been thinking.

"Minx." He muttered the word under his breath, but the gleam in her eye suggested he wasn't hiding his emotions very well.

"Did you say something?" God, she was the vision of innocence, all blonde tousled hair, eyes liquid pools of amber, and her short kimono—this one in white.

"Nothing." He forced himself to stop staring at her. Either that or he was likely to explode. "I didn't say anything."

After the first few bites, he stopped. "This is really good."

"Cinnamon."

"Cinnamon?"

"Yes, you add cinnamon. It gives it that…sensual flavor."

Well, he wasn't sure he'd use sensual to describe pancakes, but the taste was definitely unique. He ate without another word, savoring the…sensual flavor, thinking about all the things he wanted to do to her today. He sipped his coffee and almost spat it out in surprise when something brushed against his leg. Startled, he glanced down, looking for the cat.

Nope, not a cat. Rielle's left foot, rubbing up and down his leg. Her gaze was on her plate as she feigned ignorance.

Naughty pussy.

"Rielle." He added an edge of steel to his voice.

Her gaze met his. "Yes, Gage." All innocence, yet a vixen lived underneath. Or a bratty sub.

"What are you wearing under the robe?"

Her eyes lit with amusement. "Nothing."

The words shot straight to his cock. "I'm so glad to hear that. Now stand."

She laid her cutlery at the five o'clock position and, with deliberate slowness, stood.

Little was left on her plate, so he had no compunctions about his next actions. "Hands behind your back."

She obeyed quickly enough but had been testing him. Pushing him. So be it. If she wanted to play, they'd play.

He rose swiftly and whirled her so she faced away from him. He pulled the belt loose from the robe and with a few deft movements secured her hands. He pushed her toward the dungeon, mindful her balance was a little off.

Once inside, he closed the door and flipped on the lights.

She gave him a look of mock protest. "You said we were going to see a movie…"

"We're going to catch the later show," he spat as he guided her to the bed, nudging her to kneel on it.

Without her hands to support her, she pitched forward and landed on her cheek. It was a soft enough landing, of course, but was effective in making his point.

"I'd paddle you for sassing me, but since that's what you want, you're not going to get it." For his trouble, he received an audible groan. He'd read her exactly right. He pulled down his pants as he admired her ass.

Grabbing the bottle of lube, he slathered a cold dollop across her asshole and ruthlessly, without warning, stuck two fingers in. Nice, the plug had loosened her up.

She let out a pleasured cry, pressing back against him.

He removed his fingers and slathered his cock in lube. He liked inflicting pain, but he wasn't a sadist.

When the head of his shaft brushed against her hole, she let out a yelp.

"You know how this works, Rielle. Relax, and it goes much easier for both of us." Actually, he didn't care how easy it was for either of them, because he wanted to be in her ass, balls-deep, as soon as humanly possible. It was tough to get his head past her sphincter, but she did relax as he massaged her lower back. Once it popped into place, he began the gentle process of seating himself properly, using her tied hands as leverage.

When his hips brushed her ass, he withdrew. She took a breath, and he thrust in. She whimpered, bearing up under the pressure. He withdrew again, she gulped oxygen, and he thrust in again. Pretty soon, they had a rhythm going, and he enjoyed himself more and more.

So was she, if her panting was any indication.

With one hand holding her waist, he flicked her clit.

She bucked against his hand, trying to evade him.

He rubbed his palm against her, plunging two fingers inside her pussy, continuing to rub her clit against his palm.

"Not fair." She spit out the words.

"Did you say something?" He tried to keep the amusement from coloring his voice, but it was a losing battle. God she was sexy as fuck.

"Nothing. I didn't say anything." *Huff*.

He did relent, however, and pulled his fingers from her and smacked her ass. "Smart Alec."

In response, she wiggled her ass against him provocatively.

Grabbing both her hips, he pounded into her. Her breaths were coming in shorter gasps now, and holding out any longer proved impossible. He stretched his arm around her waist, yanking her flush up against him. "Holy shit." A reverential shout as he came inside her.

"Fuck, yeah." Her whispered response came as she sagged back against him.

It was a long time before either of them caught their breath.

Chapter Five

"Have you ever had a threesome?"

Gage almost tripped on the pavement but managed to right himself. The theater was a few blocks from her place. The movie was predictable, but the audience loved it. So had she, as far as he could see. When he asked about the last time she'd seen a movie in the cinema, she waved him off, making some comment about having a good home theater system.

She hadn't answered his question.

And now she expected him to answer hers. *So be it.* "Yes."

They continued to stroll down the street, hand in hand. By mutual consent, this afternoon was a time-out from the play.

He couldn't punish her for her sassy mouth. Oh, but he wanted to. Nothing like mentioning a ménage to get his libido shifting into high gear.

"You can't leave it at that."

He could, but he wouldn't. Her questions tended to be incisive and purpose-driven. She didn't ask something for the heck of it.

"My wife has…had…a friend. I have no idea what Cara said to Alessandra, but Cara came to me and let me know Alessandra was interested in the lifestyle but was taking it slow. She wanted someone safe to introduce her to BDSM."

"An itch to scratch or real curiosity?"

"A genuine interest and, I think, a need to find her way to submission. Her job is high-stress and very intense. She makes major decisions with serious repercussions if she gets it wrong. She liked the idea of letting go of some of that control, that vigilance."

"And being with you did that?"

His chuckle rumbled in his throat. "She's a born submissive. There was nothing she loved more than serving me. And I, being magnanimous, would also let her serve Cara."

"Cara was a switch?"

Amusement suffused him with pleasure. "No, Cara was a submissive as well, but she let Alessandra serve her because it pleased me."

"This is like every man's dream, right? I mean two women…"

"You might think so. But with great power comes great responsibility. Sure, it was just for a weekend at a time, but I still managed every aspect of the dynamic."

"You mean sex."

Another chuckle. "Amongst other things. Sex was the easiest thing to manage. Cara and Alessandra were both up for anything, including each other."

"That must have kept you…amused."

"You mean going around with a permanent erection? Yeah, pretty much. Except while they could touch each other, only Cara could touch me."

"Doesn't sound fair."

"It was the way I wanted it. Alessandra's a nice lady, but she was my wife's best friend. I didn't want sex between us to make things weird for them."

Now she chuckled. "But sex between the two of

them wasn't weird."

"Nope," he assured her. "Just hot." They stopped for a red light, and he glanced around, making sure no one was within earshot. "What really got Allie off, though, were the corrections, the punishments. She loved the high."

"Sub-space." She said it quietly. Too quietly.

"Yeah." He pulled her toward him, tipping her head up. Seeing her eyes through the tinted lenses was impossible, but her face showed the sadness, the longing. "You've heard about it but never experienced it, have you?"

She pulled back and moved forward toward the intersection where the light had now turned green. "I did a lot of reading at first, you know? I wanted to be the best slave. I wanted to please my Master. Many things I read explained I could get something out of the relationship as well, but that I had to work for it." She hesitated as they hopped up onto the curb. "Now I think I…wasn't good enough, you know?"

Guiding her off the sidewalk where they would be out of the way of other pedestrians, he pulled off her sunglasses to force her to look him straight in the eye. "A slave might believe she is responsible for her Master's pleasure, but the same goes in reverse. A Master is responsible for a slave's happiness, health, and safety. He did none of those things for you." He let out a sharp breath of frustration. "Even when you're with me, you're focused on my needs and missing the point. What brings me the greatest happiness is to give you pleasure."

A flash of hurt flitted across her face. "I try—"

"I'm not criticizing. I'm saying that in a D/s

relationship with me, you can expect me to watch out for your needs as well. Alessandra wasn't my sex slave, but she was my submissive. I showed her the power of a submissive, and she loved it."

"Why did you never...I mean, why aren't you with her?"

"Because as loving and caring and gentle a soul as Alessandra is, I was never in love with her. Without Cara as the intermediary, it felt wrong. We both loved Cara, but we didn't love each other."

"What happened to her?"

He handed Rielle her sunglasses. Instead of putting them back on, she slipped them into her purse. "I see her occasionally in a professional capacity, but never more than that. I once offered to help her vet Dominants, in case she decided to go that way, but she never took me up on the offer. I don't know if she ever wanted the lifestyle beyond what Cara and I gave her."

"Is she a lesbian?"

"No." His laugh was genuine, his amusement clear. "What she had with Cara was special, you know? Alessandra wouldn't be interested in being with a Domme. Or at least I don't think she would." He resumed walking, Rielle's hand tucked in his, their fingers interlaced. "Alessandra is aware she can always come to me, and I guess that's what's important."

She sighed.

"What is it?"

"I wish I knew what it was like to have someone to depend on. Or, for that matter, to have someone depend on me."

The profound loneliness was back. He might be lonely, but surrounded by his staff, his students, his friends, he was never alone. Loneliness had prompted his visit to Club Kink, but all he had to do was show up for work Monday morning to get his fill of people. How was she surviving without human interaction?

"Are you hungry?"

"After all that popcorn? Are you kidding?"

He wasn't hungry either, but they needed to go somewhere quiet where they could talk. Once they got to the condo, she'd fall back into her role. He could try to force the issue, but things were still too fragile.

A gust of wind gave him an idea. "How about a hot chocolate?"

"That sounds perfect." She glanced around, probably getting her bearings. "There's a café on the next street."

He let her lead. It was a Starbucks, but it served his purpose. They took up residence in two of the oversized puffy chairs by the window, she with her chai tea latté, he with his coffee. He was amazed at the foot traffic in the area, given it was late on a Saturday afternoon.

He focused on her. "When I asked you last night what you did this week, I also meant what activities did you partake in. Aside from going to the clinic and buying the dress, did you even leave the condo?"

"Of course. I go swimming every day in the pool."

"Don't be obtuse." He growled, his patience being tested. "You know what I mean."

Her eyes flickered something dark. "This has been my life for four years, Gage. I can't turn it around on a dime because you tell me to."

"Because I ask you to." This was getting them nowhere.

A look of contrition crossed her face. "I'm not a

simpleton. I can see what you're trying to do." She broke her gaze away from him and looked out the window. "I'm out of practice, you know? Being out there scares me. People scare me."

"But you went to the club."

"Yes, I went to the club." She sighed quietly. "And I guess it wouldn't be so hard to get out more often, but still I'm afraid."

He shook his head sharply. "You went out today."

"Because I was with you."

His eyes narrowed. "Answer me honestly, Rielle. How often do you leave the building? I mean grocery shopping, trips to the library, coffee breaks, everything like that. How often?"

She swung her gaze back to him.

His breath was nearly stolen by her look of abject misery. And then it was gone. Replaced by something more diffident.

"I have a delivery service which brings the food. I have an e-reader where I can access all the books I want. I have an expensive espresso machine at home. I have everything I could ever desire. Why would I ever need to go out?"

"Are you that scared of him?"

"Yes." The answer was swift and stark.

"Why not leave? Sell the condo, take the money, and go somewhere else? Why not start a new life?" Impatience bubbled up in him. "Or are you still waiting for him to come back?"

Her hand shook so badly she was forced to put her mug down. "When I told you I was waiting for him to come back, I meant it. Do I want him to come back? Life's not that simple, Gage, and you know it. He was my everything for four years. My entire existence was for him. I lived for him. Everything I did was to please him."

"Why did he break your rib?"

"Gage—"

He leaned forward so no one could hear them. "Tell me or accept there will be consequences." And he wasn't talking about punishment either. He wasn't threatening to break up with her, but he was laying his cards on the table.

"I was…he caught me doing something I used to do and had promised to never do again. He had rules, and I broke one of the cardinal ones. I had sworn to give up my old life, but I hadn't." She swiped at an errant tear. "I learned my lesson."

Placing his mug on the ledge beside him, he took her hand. "The price was too high. You might have died because you, what, contacted people you used to know? You're a smart woman."

"How can you be so sure?" It was barely a whisper.

How was he supposed to quantify what he knew without equivocation to be true? "It's not any one thing, but it's a bunch of things. You're articulate, knowledgeable, and empathetic. You remind me of some of my brightest students with the most potential. I wouldn't have agreed to be with you"—*to be your Dominant*—"if I hadn't seen something in you." He squeezed her hand. "That's why I put it in the…agreement…that you need to do more with yourself. If you need my help, I can get you started. For instance, what did you used to do?"

She tugged her hand, but he held fast. He held on until it became obvious he was going to hurt her if he didn't let go.

"I walked away from that life, Gage, and I can't ever go back."

"So we start fresh. What do you like to do?" He strove to keep his tone as light as possible, worried he might further damage their fragile and burgeoning relationship.

"I see what you're trying to do." She sipped latté, avoiding eye contact.

"Is it so bad? Am I asking for too much?" If he was, he'd back off. Even if she only left the condo with him for the next month or so, it might give her confidence. Maybe, with time, he could coax her into doing more.

"I like words."

He almost missed her admission. *Words?* What did someone do with a love of words? "You mean etymology?"

She fidgeted and averted her gaze briefly but seemed to be slowly warming up to the conversation. "Yeah, I like to learn where words come from and how meanings have changed over time. I like seeing how they come together."

"Have you tried writing?"

"I'm not sure I could do that." Her response was quick and sharp.

"What did you study at the university?"

She closed her eyes. "Gage, please don't."

So she had done higher education. He wasn't surprised. *Back off.* Time to regroup. "Well, why don't we set some kind of goal? I mean, maybe you go to the library and get a book about the history of a language."

"I can do that on the internet."

"You can." He gave her a long level look. "But you are also able to walk the two blocks to the public library and sign out a book."

"I don't have a library card." She frowned at him with her bottom lip stuck out.

"Rielle." His tone carried enough warning to caution her she was pushing back a little too hard. "You take your driver's license to the library, and they issue you a library card. Then you go look through the stacks and find a few books you like. You sign them out, bring them home, and read them. Then you return them and repeat the entire procedure. You know, lather, rinse, repeat. The library is, literally, in the next block." He might not be from Vancouver, but even he knew of the iconic structure and how central it was to this area of town. He'd also parked in the garage more than once when coming down to watch a Canucks game in person. Cara had always bought tickets for his birthday.

Stop it.

The slight upward tilt of her lips was all he could ask for and pulled him back into the present.

"Okay. I promise I will go to the library."

The relief washing over him was tremendous. She was a tough negotiator, but this was in her best interests.

"Can we go home now?"

"Yeah." He stood, surreptitiously working out kinks that had formed during their intense discussion. "We can go home."

****

The walk back to the condo was made in silence as he let her accept her first assignment. He planned an excursion of some kind for her every week. Nothing too

125

extreme, but outings that pushed her and kept her mind sharp. Not that she needed much help in that department. She'd challenged him when he pronounced she was intelligent. Although he wasn't always able to quantify his feelings about people, he was good at reading them—he had to be in his job. He was able to spot potential a mile away as easily as he could spot trouble. Needless to say, he preferred the former to the latter.

A different concierge was at the door, and he greeted Rielle as "Ms. Reid" and gave Gage a cursory glance. Nothing like the warning glare he'd received from Tarah. They walked up the stairs in silence, and he used his key to let them in. He bolted the door and automatically helped her out of her wool coat. Summer was well and truly gone, and he mourned the loss a little bit.

Once she was out of her coat, he shed his jacket as well and stowed the coats. As she walked into the living room, she appeared...expectant? Uncertain? Uncomfortable? Some bizarre combination of all three?

"What is it, Rielle?"

She shifted. "I was rude to you earlier."

"Delineation." She needed to understand the difference in expectations. "We weren't playing. We were vanilla. We were equals. I'm happy to stay on as such—"

"No." She was quick to interrupt. "Not now."

"What do you want now?"

Just this once, tell me the truth.

"You." Blunt, simple, and heartfelt.

That he could do. He opened his arms, and she stepped into them.

She wrapped her arms around his waist, pressed her head to his chest, and shook.

He'd asked a lot of her today. Not simply leaving the condo—they'd done that several times already. But today he'd demanded even more honesty than when they negotiated the contract last weekend. He had a firmer foothold, but the ground still shifted. She held on to him as if he were her lifeline, so he offered what comfort he might.

Time spun out, and when her shaking subsided to shivers, he rubbed his hands up and down her back. Did she need a blanket?

She pulled her head back and met his gaze. "Thank you." It was a bare breath of sound.

He gently kissed her nose. "My pleasure, Rielle."

She opened her mouth to speak, but she didn't. Instead, she stepped out of his embrace.

Instantly his arms felt empty, his soul bereft. He liked offering comfort and strength—he was good at it. That was why he succeeded at work.

"What would you like for dinner?"

"I'm not hungry right now, but if you want something—"

She shook her head. "Not right now for me either." She started to say something, then stopped.

Sucking in his breath, he waited. Was she going to ask him to leave? He didn't want to, but despite the play, he'd expressly put an out in her contract. All she had to do was ask, and he'd go. Oh… "I want you to tell me what you want, Rielle."

Relief flooded her face in an unguarded moment. "I want you."

This time he understood. "Where?"

Gabbi Black

She pointed in the direction opposite from the dungeon, to a door he hadn't noticed before. They moved toward it, and when he grasped the handle, she placed a hand on his, stilling his motion.

He met her gaze and held it. "Trust me." He mentally willed her to have the courage, knowing what a leap this was for her.

Her wide eyes shone, and her lower lip quivered.

He longed to bite and then soothe it, and perhaps her fears, but this wasn't the right moment. A solemnity and an earnestness he'd not felt from her before enveloped, and he wasn't going to do anything to break the mood.

Eventually, she removed her hand.

He twisted the handle, and in the pitch-black room, ran his hand against the wall for the light switch, flipping it on. Together, they stepped into the room that was pure white and therefore pure light. One wall was lined with shelves crammed with books. Another wall's shelves were full of movies and music. An antique lamp adorned a desk with a laptop. The space was the antithesis of the dungeon.

In more ways than one.

Instead of a California king bed, a narrow single bed was pressed into the corner, so small it might've belonged to a child. White throw pillows and a coverlet provided contrast to the solitary color in the room—a brown worn-out teddy bear propped amongst the pillows.

This was *her* space. This was where Mr. X never stepped. Or maybe he had, that infamous night.

Shutting the door quietly, he met her gaze. "This is your room." The statement was superfluous.

128

Staring down at the floor, she was silent.

"You make the call."

"I want you to make love to me." She blushed furiously. "I mean I recognize you're not in love with me, but…"

He covered the distance between them, tipped her head up so she met his gaze, and laid his finger against her lips. "In this room, whatever the lady asks for, she gets."

Instead of words, she wound her arms around his neck and pulled his mouth toward hers.

Their lips touched, once, twice, and a third time. He took his cues from her—when to press forward and when to step back.

In return, she met each advance with one of her own.

When she wound her arms around his neck, he pulled her close. It was she who eased her tongue into his mouth, probing tentatively. He twined his tongue with hers, coaxing, encouraging, inviting. His hands were at the small of her back, but where he would've normally pressed her to him, he held her hips with loose fingers. When she grasped for the hem of his sweater, he obliged her by pulling it over his head. When she guided his hands to her jeans, he undid the snap and eased the fabric over her hips.

He'd stripped the night before, but now the action felt different. More intimate. How long had it been since a woman undressed him?

Although he disliked comparing the two most important women in his life, he couldn't help thinking that Cara had been a firebrand, while Rielle, although appropriately enthusiastic in the sack, never initiated anything. This gesture brought him hope more than any fantastic blow job she'd bestowed upon him. Her trust in bringing him into her sacred personal space spoke of a new level in their relationship.

Or so he hoped.

Rielle pulled her sweater over her head, mussing her hair. She unclasped her bra and was shy when she let it fall away. *Beautiful.* Not just the outer beauty everyone saw, but the inner vulnerability she showed him now.

He unbuttoned his jeans, waiting to see if she was okay with it.

In response, she shimmied out of her panties.

Soon they were both naked, in that tiny space of hers.

She grasped his larger hand in hers, pressing it against her breast.

He squeezed experimentally, watching the awe flicker across her face.

Make love to me.

Had anyone ever made love to her before? His other hand trembled slightly as he brought her closer. He slanted his mouth to hers and lazily explored her mouth. One hand supported her back while the other continued to hold her breast.

She lifted her chin, granting him access to the long column of her neck.

He nibbled his way down, nipping here, licking there, reading her silent signals.

When he took her breast in his mouth, she whispered the Lord's name in worship. Hadn't he done this the previous night? Taken her nipple in his mouth? This time was different. This time she was asking, instead of being told. Begging, more like it, as she held his head in place. It was okay, though, because they had all the time in the world. This room was a place of enchantment where time had no meaning and no world existed except this one.

"I need you." Her gasp grasped his heart and made his cock awaken.

You have me. He left the thought unexpressed. "Tell me, Rielle. Tell me what will make you feel good."

"I don't know." Her broken whisper nearly broke him. "I'm not sure."

He slid his thigh between hers, creating delicious friction. "Do you like this?"

Her breath hitched.

His hand cupped her breast and squeezed. "Do you like this?"

Her cheeks flushed.

"See." He held her gaze for a long, deliberate moment. "You do know what makes you feel good." His gaze met hers, and he looked as deeply as he dared, finding her vulnerable in a way she never was in the dungeon. She obviously wanted to ask, wanted to know, but had no idea how to form the requisite words. He could do this. He knew women's bodies. He *worshipped* women's bodies.

He gently nudged her back until the back of her knees bumped the mattress. He stretched behind her to push the comforter aside. After he eased her down, he removed the throw pillows and the teddy bear, careful to gently place them on the desk. He encouraged her to lie back. "Close your eyes, sweetheart."

Her eyelids fluttered shut.

He sat on the bed beside her and cursed the size of the mattress. He wished they were in the dungeon where he might make her more comfortable, but he understood her need to be in this space.

He gently cupped her cheek.

She nuzzled his palm, so trusting, so soft.

"The first time I saw you, you intrigued me."

Her eyes opened.

"Close your eyes, sweetheart."

She gave him one final, puzzled look and, at length, complied.

Using her momentary confusion, he moved his hands to her collarbone and made gentle, downward sweeps. Instead of touching her breasts, however, he eased his palms down the sides of her body, careful to keep the touch light, but not tickling. When he reached her hips, he secured his hands around her waist and pulled her up so her lower back lifted from the bed.

She had put her trust in him, so she let him do this gentle motion. Her back arched, and her breath came out in a long sigh. Slowly but surely, her body let go—releasing the tension it had carried for so long.

Letting her go, he watched as she sank bonelessly back to the mattress. Now he shifted, winding up at the end of the bed, that, thankfully, had no footboard. Taking her foot in his hand, he noted the slight curl of her lips, but she didn't laugh.

Excavating the memory of the exact pressure points necessary to bring pleasure, he cursed the elapsed time since he'd last partaken in that particular enjoyable activity. A bit of searching on the internet had led him to a guide of basic reflexology. Once he had a few practice sessions with a patient Cara, he'd become proficient.

Pushing away memories of his wife, he was rewarded with a moan when he hit the right spot.

"Don't stop."

The whispered demand made his balls tighten. And she had another foot to minister to. He worried she might be getting chilly, but it seemed her goose bumps were from arousal, not cold. By the time he finished with her feet, her toes curled with pleasure. Long strokes brought him along her slim calves to her knees. He snagged the skin behind the bend of her knee in his teeth. He nipped lightly, working the satiny smooth skin between his teeth, releasing it when the tension slipped from her thigh. He blew over the tender spot, finally placing a kiss on the erogenous zone.

Her fingers curled into the sheets.

Nailed it.

In turn, he massaged each thigh, mindfully keeping the pressure just short of therapeutic. He needed her aroused, nothing more.

At the juncture of her thighs, he used his shoulders to ease her knees apart and encourage them to fall outward. Her body complied. He had tried going down on her last weekend, but somehow this moment was precious, much more at stake this time. This time it was less about the goal and more about tenderness.

Telltale dampness wet between her nether lips when he did his first pass with his tongue. She tasted sweet and tangy, her musk of arousal filling his head. Arousal swirled within him, but he ruthlessly tamped it down. His focus had to be entirely on her.

He cupped her ass and brought her even closer. With each swipe of his tongue, each nip of his teeth, he sensed her desire building. When he sucked her clit, she bucked off the bed, forcing him to place his hands on her hips to hold her in place.

"Gage, please..." Her head thrashed back and forth, her body gathering for an explosion, but it didn't come. It *wouldn't* come.

He had one more trick up his sleeve. It took a bit of maneuvering, but he managed to lie on his back with her straddling him. Understanding, she guided herself, easing him in. She stretched to accommodate him and shifted so she was seated completely. He would've let her set the pace, but she appeared baffled, as if she'd never done this before. Instead of dwelling on the thought, he took her hips in his hands and set a slow, leisurely rhythm. He pulled her almost off him and pressed her back down.

Soon, she got into the swing of things and took over.

Using his now-free hands, he cupped her breasts, teasing her nipples to hard peaks.

She pulled her lower lip through her teeth, her eyes drifting shut again.

Watching her flush with pleasure, he responded even more, his cock straining. He couldn't get any harder, and his body begged for release.

He slid a hand to where their bodies joined and pressed his thumb to her clit, noting distractedly she was practically dry. She stilled her movement and opened her eyes, tears filling them.

Completely baffled, he pushed himself up, gathering her to him despite the fact they were still joined. "What's wrong, sweetheart?"

"You're hurting me." Another broken whisper and

his heart broke. Shattered into a million shards.

He slipped from her, easily, as his erection was fading a quick death. He lay on the bed and pulled her to him, resting her head on his chest. Goose bumps now caused by chill and not desire propelled him to pull the comforter over them.

She shook, her tears wet and cold against his chest.

Being so powerless in the face of something this monumental overwhelmed him. Wanting to speak but afraid of saying the wrong thing, he rubbed his hand up and down her arm, trying to create both warmth and comfort from the friction.

Slowly, ever so slowly, she relaxed.

"Can you tell me what happened?"

She tensed, sobbing, and for one horrifying moment, he questioned if he'd broken her emotionally as well as physically. He'd never had a woman tell him he hurt her. The image of her face when she said it still robbed him of breath.

Finally, she took a deep and steadying breath. "I wanted it, Gage. I wanted it so badly. I thought that you…in this place…"

He understood. "You were close, Rielle, of that I'm sure. I know women's bodies. You were close. The question is whether it's physical or emotional." This was a delicate and treacherous place to be. "If you're willing psychologically, it might be physical."

"You want me to see a doctor."

He pulled her even closer, if that was possible. "I want you to be happy, sweetheart. An orgasm is nice, but it's not the end of the world." He considered promising to try again, but that was fraught with dangers. She had been up in her head about having an orgasm. They both had. Maybe next time they could…what? He'd used about every trick in his arsenal to relax her. Had given her every opportunity to respond to him.

Maybe he should've used more words. Made love to her mind as well as her body. Maybe he should've distracted her, let her understand she was the focus.

Too many maybes.

Soon, her breathing evened, and she slipped into a deep sleep. He hoped it was dreamless, because nothing pleasant had come from that afternoon. It had started with such promise, and now he was confused. Rielle was devastated.

He had to take a piss, so he extricated himself, gingerly making his way to the bathroom. It was past seven o'clock, and his stomach growled. Should he cook? After cleaning up, he rummaged in the fridge until he spotted a frozen lasagna thawing. Obviously she planned to cook it, and although he couldn't fix her psychological problems, he could put a tray in the oven and turn it on. Setting the temperature, he waited for the oven to heat. Naked, he was grateful the blinds were closed. What a sight he'd made while sprinting to the bathroom.

When the oven pinged that it was at the right temperature, he put the pasta in and set the timer.

The package said an hour, so he opted to join her in bed. Maybe if he was there when she woke, she'd feel secure. Maybe *that* was her problem. To have an orgasm, she had to give up complete control. Except hadn't she done that for four years during the power exchange?

Fuck Mr. X and his fucking abuse.

How could anyone be in a relationship and show such callous disregard for the other person? She'd been a vessel for the jerk's pleasure and nothing more. Imagining the abuse clenched his gut, bile rising in his throat. Vomiting wouldn't help, though, so he pushed the images from his mind.

He crept back into the room, finding he needn't have bothered being quiet. Curled into a tight ball, she was in the fetal position. With a throw pillow clutched so tightly to her chest, he was amazed she could breathe.

Not wanting to disturb her, he tucked the comforter over her bare shoulders as he might for a child. Protectiveness was his predominant emotion as he donned his clothes. She had a core of inner strength but hid it so well most people never saw it.

Curious, and at odds about what to do next, he perused the media shelf. The odd collection of movies surprised him—black-and-white classics, romances, foreign films, and many documentaries. Unable to find a common theme, he settled on the word eclectic.

The bookshelves held much the same mixture. Although her e-reader was on the desk, she obviously loved the touch and texture of books. Amongst the fiction and literature were her old textbooks, obviously either well cared for or never used, because the spines were creaseless.

Well cared for. She used the books for the knowledge they imparted. The middle shelf of the middle section was oddly empty. While the rest of the shelves were crammed to the point of overflowing, a gaping hole stood out. Not that he was an interior decorator, but why a peculiar hole in that exact location?

When she moaned, he stepped back suddenly, a schoolboy caught doing something naughty. A person's library revealed much about them, and hers confirmed she was an educated woman, conversant on a wide variety of topics. He could quiz her about any number of subjects and undoubtedly, she'd earn an "A."

She didn't wake, and he exhaled the breath he held. Fifteen minutes had passed, so he pulled out the chair, and as he sat, his hip hit the desk, sending a file folder—and all its contents—flying everywhere. Cursing his clumsiness, he gathered the papers, hoping to put them back in correct order. She didn't strike him as overly obsessive, but she kept a meticulous home, so he assumed she'd notice the disarray.

Only when finished collecting the papers did he glance at them.

And nearly sent the stack tumbling again.

What the actual fuck?

Dropping his butt heavily in the chair, he thumbed through the pile. So what if he invaded her privacy? She'd *lied* to him. Well, maybe lie was too strong a word, but she'd definitely deceived him. Her entire life with him was based on a lie.

Even through the red haze of anger, things were a lot clearer.

****

She came awake suddenly, a quick intake of breath accompanying her eyes flying open. When her gaze settled on him, her features relaxed into a wistful smile. Wherever she had been in her dreams, it hadn't been a pleasant place. As she stared at him, however, her expression transformed to wary. "What's wrong?"

"Where are your law textbooks, Rielle?"

The flicker was so subtle he might have missed it, but he expected it, and she didn't disappoint. Despite so many aspects of her life being a mystery to him—as she was—certain reactions were now predictable.

Guilt.

The implacable mask descended, as if she had no cares in the world. "I don't know what you're talking about."

"Don't you?" He banked his fury. But barely. "Then you should have destroyed the actual degree." He held up the offending piece of paper. "And your certificate to practice from the Law Society of British Columbia." He held up the second piece of paper. "Nice marks, by the way. Were you at the top of your class?"

"Third." She clutched the comforter to her breast, as if ashamed of her nudity for the first time. "You had no right to go through my papers."

Her point was valid, but anger still tightly gripped him in its talons. "Tell me what you did with your law textbooks."

"I have to pee."

"Not before you tell me the truth."

He couldn't stop her, of course. If she dropped the sheet and left the room, that was her prerogative. But she had to understand he was a dog with a bone. A junkyard dog. One with no manners or sense of propriety.

"He took them away." She bowed her head as if it were too heavy for her neck. "Now may I go to the bathroom?"

Gage inclined his head and consciously unclenched

his jaw as she scooped her clothes from the floor, gathering them to her.

Silently, she slipped from the room.

The haze of red morphed into a dark crimson. Mr. X took away her treasured and much-loved textbooks. He could fathom nothing crueler.

Except breaking a rib and puncturing a lung.

The timer dinged, so he returned to the kitchen, turning on lights as he went. No shadows tonight.

He pulled the pasta from the oven to cool and set the table. Rielle's kitchen was well organized with everything in a logical place, so the task took relatively little time.

Still, she didn't come.

With a glance at the cooling lasagna, he went in search of his errant hostess. Placing his ear against the bathroom door, he didn't hear the shower. But that didn't mean she wasn't taking a bath.

He knocked. No answer. "Rielle, open the door."

Silence.

He knocked again. "Rielle." He fought to keep from making it a demand. "Please open the door."

More silence.

Knocking a third time, he added an edge to his voice. "Open the door."

The lock clicked, and she opened the door. She attempted nonchalance, but her body radiated tension, arms crossed, head bowed.

And something else, something more potent.

Fear.

She was afraid of him.

When he raised a hand, she flinched. His heart sank, and his stomach clenched. "Dinner's ready."

She wiped clammy palms on her jeans, leaving damp streaks. Wordlessly, she followed him to the dining room table, several steps behind.

He held her chair, swallowing frustration when she grimaced.

He cut two big pieces of lasagna, heaping them on plates. The bowl with salad was already on the table. He debated making garlic bread, but there was more than enough food.

When he placed the plate in front of her, she began to protest but caught sight of his face and obviously thought better of it.

They consumed the entire meal in silence, fraught and painful.

As she started to rise to take away the plates, he waylaid her with a hand on her wrist.

She flinched.

He should let her go, but they had to clear the air. He applied enough pressure to get her to sit back down on the chair. "First, let's be very, very clear. I will *never* touch a woman in anger. I never struck my wife, and I will never touch you that way." He paused for maximum effect. "Are we clear?"

"Crystal." She still didn't meet his gaze.

"Talk to me. Tell me what you're thinking."

Now she raised her chin, finally meeting his gaze. "He broke me that night, Gage. Figuratively and literally, he broke me."

"What happened?"

"I don't want to talk about it."

She spoke the truth, her expression of utter desolation proof. No tears sprang forth, of course, just a tremble through her body.

He was a bastard for pushing, but this was one of those times when he had no choice. "Rielle." He tried for an even tone. He wasn't going to order her, nor was he going to ask nicely.

"It was an ordinary Wednesday night. I was watching a documentary about..." Her brow furrowed. "I don't even remember which one. I was sitting there"—she pointed to the couch—"and then the key was in the lock.

"I knew something was wrong. Wednesday was...a night out with the boys. He'd never been here on a Wednesday." Her hands clasped tightly together. "I was dressed, of course, because he hadn't called to say he was coming over. I rose and started to strip when he grabbed me by the hair and dragged me to the dungeon. I thought it was part of the game, you know?"

Although he wasn't sure he did know, she continued without waiting for a response from him.

"He ripped my clothes, but that was nothing new. A gleam flared in his eyes, though, I'd never seen before. Figuring this was a rape fantasy, I fought back, you know?"

Gage did not want to hear this. He'd heard confessions of all kinds over the years, but nothing rivaled this, and nothing had ever hurt his heart so much.

"But he started hitting me. Beating me." Her shoulders hunched, hair veiling her face. "He threw me on the bed and forced himself on me. Into me. The fear...it was real. I assumed he was going to kill me." Her chin tilted downward so she was looking at her hands folded in her lap. "When he finished raping me, he threw me to the floor and kicked me. As he kicked me, he swore at me. Reciting all the things I'd done wrong. Then, with one swift kick, we both heard the crunch of bone. I'd never endured such pain in my life, and I closed my eyes against the flash of light.

"He stopped." She pressed her palms to her thighs. "He pulled me out into the hallway, locked the door to the dungeon, and left. It's funny, but he knew. Understood I'd never tell them about him. And I didn't." Her comment was unnecessary, but it confirmed what he'd surmised. "Because it was my fault."

"Rielle." Again, he fought to maintain an even tone and reveal nothing. Not the anger spiking his blood pressure. Nor the anguish tearing him apart.

Her gaze finally met his. "I was doing some legal aid work on the side. I did it when he was gone, and it was done by encrypted email, but it kept my mind occupied. I could only do so much to be there for him, you know?"

"As his slave." He bit out the words.

She tilted her chin. "The agency I worked for was supposed to keep my identity anonymous, but they didn't redact my name from a document. It fell on his desk, and…the rest is history, so to speak."

He tried to absorb what she was saying. "He's a lawyer?"

She stilled. "You could say that."

"He's a judge."

Apparently she was not surprised at his leap of logic. She waved her hand in an annoyingly dismissive gesture. "He's one of the top judges in the province."

"That doesn't make him above the law, Rielle. You should've said something."

"And then what? I had nothing. Literally nothing. I was naked when they took me to the hospital."

He struggled to keep the lasagna from reappearing. "And you convinced the doctor not to say anything? Isn't it mandatory to report abuse to the police?"

"For a child, yes, for an adult, it's less clear. I told her I slipped and fell in the bathtub."

"With footprints?"

Her gaze fell away. "Sometimes I think they get it—doctors, I mean. She understood if I reported him, he'd kill me." She took a deep breath, her hand moving to what he assumed was the affected rib. "They taped up my ribs, fixed my lung, and sent me home. When I arrived, my laptop had been scrubbed clean, and my law textbooks were gone. Needless to say, I never made that mistake again. He waited a week before returning, and I received a lashing like you couldn't conceive. He did things to re-exert his control but never touched the rib lest he reinjure it."

"You can still get him charged. Rielle, it's not too late."

Her eyes flashed defiance, then settled on great unhappiness. "You aren't getting this. The medical records have disappeared and the medical staff convinced I was never there."

"No one has that much power."

"I'm not willing to risk someone else's life to test that theory, Gage."

Fair enough.

"How long ago?"

"Two years."

She'd stayed another two after that? "You never told anyone, did you?"

Her expression answered the question, but she spoke nonetheless, drilling her answer home. "There was no one to tell and no point in doing it. I healed and learned my lesson."

At too high a price.

"How did you meet him?"

Her nose wrinkled in confusion.

"At the club?"

"In court." Her eyes were less focused. "I argued a case in front of him, and after the trial, he summoned me into his chambers. He made a promise to me in exchange for spending a month with him."

"That's blackmail."

A quick shake of the head. "I went willingly. What he offered me…it was what I always wanted, and he recognized it. He investigated my past and found my Achilles' heel."

"Which was…?" He waited, but no response came.

As if he hadn't spoken, she continued. "He took me to his condo in Whistler for a…lovers' retreat. He treated me with such respect and tenderness I thought I'd fallen into a fairy tale. He whisked me to his mansion in the city and bought me things. Clothes, jewels, the car—all of it without strings. He told me I could go back to my life at the end of the month, keeping the baubles and trinkets."

"He bought you."

A vehement headshake. "No. See, I had the upper hand. I was going to take those gifts and sell them. I planned to move out of my one-room apartment and own more than two business suits. I was going to crawl out of poverty."

"You were a lawyer, for God's sake."

145

"With over one hundred thousand dollars in student loans, Gage. Every spare penny I made went to making payments. I didn't want to be beholden to them for the rest of my life. I was used to being poor and hungry." Her shoulders rose in an oddly disconnected shrug. "He offered me a chance to see how the other half lived.

"The joke was on me, though, because at the end of the month, I didn't want to give it up. I'd fallen in love with him and told him as much. He explained I could stay with him and even have my own condo, if I agreed to a few conditions." She met his gaze. "He said if I loved him, I'd keep an open mind. He brought me to the dungeon and asked if we might try something. I wasn't sure at first. I was an independent woman who had everything she needed, but he showed me a different life. I was reticent but intrigued. I wasn't familiar with BDSM, so it was strange, but not scary.

"The first time we went into the dungeon, he flogged me. He went easy, as I've since discovered, but it was nice. Like he was caressing me. And the sex afterward? It was obvious he liked it." She feathered a hand through her hair. "He subtly broke down my barriers. He offered me security, told me what to wear, how to take care of myself. He encouraged me to show my appreciation by increasingly intense sessions in the dungeon. And I liked it. Not just sexually, but emotionally as well."

"When did you become a slave?"

"He collared me on our four-month anniversary." A ghost of a smile crossed her lips. "By then I'd quit my job, given up my apartment, and moved into full-time service. He wasn't married at the time, so he was here at least as much as he was at his house. I cooked his dinner, laundered his clothes, polished his shoes."

"More like licked them." His muttered utterance earned him a nasty look.

"I don't expect you to understand, but I had everything I'd ever asked for. All I had to do was be his exclusively."

He tried to comprehend what she was telling him. A piece was missing, but what was it? "Was it worth it, Rielle?" He gestured around them. "You have a home, you have money, but you don't have a life. You don't have real security. How can you say you're happy?" He had nothing against an M/s lifestyle. He knew couples who engaged in that kind of play, and they were happy. When it moved into the dark, though, all bets were off. This wasn't kink—this was abuse plain and simple.

She gave him a level, unflinching stare. "Happiness doesn't exist, Gage. It's an illusion, and all that matters is being alive. Despite everything, I'm alive."

She stood abruptly, removed the plates, and walked to the kitchen.

He didn't follow.

****

He stood in the middle of the living room, listening to the sounds of her cleaning up after their dinner. Time to get out and walk away. Pack his bag and leave. She was perfectly capable of self-destructive behavior without him sticking around for the show.

But she was also the woman who had almost come apart in his arms. The woman who had never experienced an orgasm. The woman who kept an old teddy bear on a tiny white bed.

Slowly, with each heartbeat, each breath, he fought that initial urge. He wasn't in too deep yet—he could still extricate himself if things didn't work out. For the first time in a long time, he'd spent an entire day without thinking about Cara. He had something to look forward to other than an empty house and a microwaved meal.

"Gage?"

He pivoted to face her, compelled by her soft pleading voice.

Wrong.

He was in way too deep. Because the idea of walking out the door tightened the band around his chest, robbing him of breath. "Yes, Rielle."

"What happens now?"

She read his silence as him having doubts—and she hadn't been mistaken. He took a deep breath. "Black room or the white room?"

Relief flooded her features, and she launched herself at him, barely giving him a chance to catch her. "The black room, please. Please, Gage, I need it. I need you."

Her words could be interpreted in several ways, but he chose the simplest. She needed him at this moment as much as he needed her. Tomorrow was another day.

"I'm going to get the bottles of water." His words were quiet, but the emphasis clear. "You know what to do."

She met his gaze with earnest anticipation. "Yes, Sir."

And like that, equilibrium was restored.

He snagged the bottles of water, meandering in his journey to the dungeon. He'd let her stew a little bit. Let her anticipate what was to come.

It was completely dark, save a bright light in the

corner, shining down on the St. Andrew's cross. The room's shadowiness left Gage both disconcerted and relieved. Oppressed and comforted. Freezing and burning.

On her knees, she faced the cross. Accusing her of topping from the bottom might have struck her as amusing, but this moment was too monumental because her intentions were clear. Her request shone as brightly as the light over the attached restraints.

Approaching quietly from behind, he placed a hand on her shoulder.

She rose and approached the cross with what appeared to be an odd mixture of reluctance and defiance.

Before securing her, he asked her, "Which rib?" and snapped, "Eyes forward," when she tried to glance back.

Instantly, she complied.

"I asked you a question, and I won't ask again. Which rib?"

She touched her side. "The fifth rib, Sir." Her breath was sharp. Perhaps being enveloped in sense memory, she was remembering having to take short breaths with the broken ribs. "But it's completely healed. You can't damage me."

"Not the point. You should have told me when we signed the contract." He'd asked before about injuries, and she'd denied them.

Her head drooped, and her shoulders bowed.

He counted down the seconds, waiting patiently, letting the seriousness of the transgression sink in. "I'll ask you again, Rielle, have you suffered any previous injuries?"

"Yes, Sir." Her spine straightened. "My rib was broken two years ago but is fully healed."

"Anything else I might need to know? Might want to know?"

She shook her head.

He had to trust her. Taking her left hand, he secured it to the cross. He repeated the process with the right and with each ankle.

She tested each one.

"Any preference of punishment?"

"Whatever pleases my Master."

Sarcasm or a true desire to please—to embrace submission?

Thank God his hands were completely steady. He let go of the emotions he'd stomached in the other room. They dissipated, leaving in their wake a calm and even tenor.

The whip it would be.

He'd take a couple of practice snaps to get used to the feel. If he couldn't get comfortable with it, plenty of other options existed. He hefted it, testing along its length for any nicks in the leather. No nicks. In fact, the whip was in pristine condition. Taking his first experimental snap, he hit the wall at the spot he'd chosen, despite the dim light. Three more snaps in rapid succession all landed on the same spot. The stuntman from Vancouver who supplemented his income by teaching weekend seminars on whipping had been a good teacher. His class had been completely sold-out and consisted mostly of middle-aged men whose wives had read *Fifty Shades of Grey*.

He and Cara had tried to read the book, finding it more amusing than entertaining, and neither of them finished it. At that point, they'd been in the lifestyle for more than ten years. A whipping had been Gage's tenth anniversary present to his wife—her sexy response was *his* gift.

He reverently laid the whip on the bed and removed his shirt, placing it on the back of the chair. He shucked his shoes and socks with an economy of motion, wasting no energy, as he'd need all of it. Clad in his jeans, he stood, snagging the whip, and padded across the hardwood floor toward the cross. He eyed the distance, reviewed the length of the whip, and did the appropriate calculations. He took his stance. "Count."

A bob of her head acknowledged the command.

The first lash landed perfectly diagonal on her back, feather-light.

"One." Her response was a little wobbly.

The next lash was parallel, but slightly lower, catching the upper curve of her ass. Again, a whispered touch.

"Two."

He strained to hear her. "Louder."

"Two." It was a little louder.

He needed to hear so he might gauge how much more she could withstand. The next three, easy brushes against her skin, were called out in a wooden voice, as if by rote. This wasn't working. She made it clear she *deserved* to be punished. He'd never pushed their dynamic this far, and yet obviously he wasn't pushing hard enough.

For whatever reason, she required this as much as her next breath.

Rielle needed this.

This he could do. This he could give her. He took

aim and let the whip slice through the air.

The whistle carried in the tight confined space of the dungeon, and the snap was crisp as it hit her back.

Her gasp rocketed through him.

"Six."

Seven was the hardest he ever let fly. The number came from her lips in a rush.

A livid red welt striped her back.

Oh God, what have I done?

The agony overwhelmed, but so did the knowledge, for this moment, he needed to tap into his well-hidden sadistic side. He drew deep, whipping again and again and again. Each crack reverberated against the walls, ricocheting back to him, despite the roaring of blood in his ears. Nothing existed, save the whistle, her count, and the deadened silence of the room.

On the twenty-third stroke, she broke.

It was sudden and violent. One moment she was counting, the next she moaned like a wounded animal. She pulled against her restraints. Finding she was secure, she arched her spine, threw back her head, and screamed. It was an otherworldly, primal scream that nearly brought Gage to his knees.

Her cries bored right into his soul. His gut churned, the hairs on the back of his neck standing at attention.

As if a dam had opened, sobs wracked her body. Great heaves and cries, causing her muscles to tighten and bunch. He was stunned at the ferocity of her reaction. When she cried out again, it galvanized him to action. Dropping the whip, he stalked over to her, bare feet silent on the floor. When he placed his cooler sweat-slicked chest against her heated back, she involuntarily sucked in a lungful of air. When she didn't breathe out right away, he splayed a hand on her diaphragm. "Breathe, Rielle." He held her skin to skin, and relief flooded him as she obeyed. He encouraged her to take more deep breaths.

There'd been no begging, no pleading, no safewording. Just a steady count upward. Until the moment, suspended in time, when everything went sideways. But hadn't he understood this was a risk? Everything he did with her ended unpredictably. Intellectually, he understood BDSM, but she was the embodiment and living proof it could be so much more intense than he'd experienced before. This needed to happen. Was it catharsis? For her? For him? For both?

He held on, her marked back against his cool chest, marveling at their closeness, their intimacy. The way she *needed* him. Her sobs eased, and the intermittent mewls caused him no panic, unlike earlier.

Once she was bonelessly relaxed, he unlocked the manacles at her ankles and massaged each in turn. Excellent, they were warm, and there'd been no constriction in blood flow. Releasing her wrists was a bit more complicated, as she sagged against him. When the final lock gave, he scooped her into his arms. Given her height, she was not a lightweight, but nothing he couldn't handle. He laid her gently on her stomach, admiring her nicely marked back, pleased to see no skin had broken. Tucking her hair away from her shoulders, he placed a kiss at the juncture of her back and neck.

If her little sigh was relief or contentment, he couldn't guess. With trepidation, he left for the bathroom, meaning to be gone a short time. Sub Drop was a distinct possibility, and aftercare required close monitoring. Still, he rooted in the medicine cabinet for a jar of arnica cream that was—surprise, surprise—unopened. She had no way of applying it herself, and even considering Mr. X might do it was absurd.

Palming the bottle of cream, he returned to the room, flipping on the torches in the dungeon, turning off the spotlight. In that bright light, he'd noted the little marks. Places where the whip had drawn blood in the past, but proper healing never took place. She'd assured him there were no other injuries. Obviously, their definition of injuries differed significantly.

She lay on her stomach, with her cheek nestled into a pillow, and her eyes closed. He sat, his thigh touching her ass, ensuring closeness. Making sure she was embraced by him, even as he put ointment on his fingertip and traced the first stripe. Carefully, making certain not to press too hard, he applied cream to every lash, even the whisper-light ones.

"What are you doing?" Her question, barely more than a whisper, came out mumbled.

"Making sure you heal."

"That's nice." Her childlike voice nearly broke his heart.

She didn't speak again.

****

Gage's body informed him it was morning even though he was still plunged in darkness. He had to investigate getting blackout blinds because he was restored here in a way he never was when waking at home.

Or maybe it was Rielle.

Damn woman was on the floor, again.

Shit.

Instead of getting his dander up, he gathered his clothes and crept to the bathroom. As he stepped under the hot water spray, he contemplated breakfast. He made a mean Southwestern omelet, if she had Tabasco sauce. Or maybe he should stick to simple, like French toast. With his face directly in the hot spray, his mind whirled into life. Memories of the previous night assaulted him, coming in staccato bursts, threatening to bring him to his knees.

He had whipped a woman. He'd caused physical pain to a woman. It was so different from anything he'd ever done with Cara. Once, just once, he'd cut her. She'd shifted as he released the lash and he pulled back, instead of letting it float, wrapping it. The size of the mark, little more than a paper cut, hadn't lessened his guilt. He'd fussed like a grandmother, eventually annoying Cara to the point she told him off. He'd thrown the whip in the trash, only to have her retrieve it. She'd insisted he whip her the next day. *Get back on the horse*, she'd told him, and he questioned in that moment who was really in charge. But she prevailed, he whipped her again, and the steadiness had been restored to their dynamic.

The past night had been his first time using a cross. He and Cara had had a playroom, not a dungeon. It had to look "respectable" because his in-laws stayed there when they visited.

The room hadn't been touched in two years. In fact, if pressed, he couldn't say if it was "respectable" or not. He'd closed that door and refused to open it. Maybe it was time to air out the room. Being with Rielle had put a perspective on his mourning, and it had been going on too long. Cara was gone and would be kicking his ass if she knew how much he missed her. He'd have desperately wished her to move on, had their positions been reversed. He certainly wasn't honoring what they shared by walling himself in with his grief. Rielle had shown him there might be another way.

Yet that realization came at a hefty price. He remembered vividly the amount of distress when she'd broken. His reaction had been both visceral and reasonable, and he appreciated, in his heart, he hadn't harmed her. Hadn't done anything irreparable. Being clear from the beginning, she'd wanted him as a Dominant and a Top. That meant meeting both her physical and psychological needs. And despite how things had ended the night before, he didn't regret it. They'd attained a new level of understanding, even though no words had been spoken.

Finishing his shower, he stepped into the spacious bathroom, grabbed a towel, and vigorously dried off. What was the best way to handle the morning after? Should he bring it up or let things ride? Wait for her to say something? And what if she asked him to do it again? Could he?

He exited the bathroom with no more clear sense that morning of where the relationship was going than he'd had the previous night.

After putting the coffee on, he rummaged around the kitchen again. Sure enough, he located fixings for an omelet. By the time the coffee was ready, the eggs were well on their way to being cooked.

Sensing her, he twisted, offering her a grin. "Good morning."

Her lips quirked, and she pointed to the cooking. "I should be doing that, Sir."

So *that* was how it was going to be this morning.

"I am capable of cooking, so I did." He pointed off in the direction of the bathroom. "Have you peed this morning?"

She blushed and nodded.

"You may set the table."

Doing it himself was instinctual, but she appeared uneasy. He'd prepared the meal the past night and was doing it again that morning.

Her face expressed her displeasure because probably no one had ever done this for her before in her life.

The toast popped, the eggs finished cooking, and the coffee completed brewing in perfect synchronicity. He snickered at the fluke because no way in hell could he have managed to plan it any better. His luck—or lack thereof—didn't work that way.

She wore a deep sapphire-blue silk kimono—a perfect foil for her pale blonde hair.

How many duplicates of this exact robe did she own? Actually, he probably didn't want to know. "How is your back this morning?"

"Well-marked, thank you, Sir."

She'd probably checked in the mirror, the little minx, accepting the stripes as a badge of honor.

He waited, holding his breath. Moments passed.

"Does Sir have plans for us today?" Her question was asked with a mixture of respect and curiosity.

"Sir does have plans, in fact." He offered her a slanted look, wondering if he'd received a reprieve and they weren't going to address what had happened the previous day. "Sir is glad you haven't dressed." It was a little weird to talk about himself in the third person, but well worth it.

Her face lit with eagerness that set off flutters in his chest as anticipation thrummed through his blood. But first, he had to ask, "Rielle, are you sore?"

"Oh, no, Sir. The cream you used worked well. It was kind of you to take care of me that way."

"That's good to hear, but that wasn't what I meant." At the flash of confusion in her eyes, he pointed to her crotch. "Are you still sore?"

From pale to hectic to crimson, her cheeks colored in the span of ten seconds. Was she going to safeword? Should he offer a break? No. She might not be honest with him if he let her out of this. And if she lied? She wasn't prone to lying to him, but she was good at leaving out relevant details at critical moments.

"I am not sore anymore, Sir." She closed her eyes, drew a breath, and her eyes snapped open, holding a steel and strength he rarely witnessed—from anyone. "You didn't hurt me, Gage."

Relief—on both counts. The memory of her whispered words that he was hurting her still caused his chest to ache. He inflicted pain all the time, of course, but in the black room, where it was done with intention and consent. Neither of those had been in place the previous day.

"I'm going to clean the kitchen while you go and lie on the bed." He purposely didn't specify which room, but he was perfectly aware which bed she'd choose.

"But you cooked, Sir. I should clean up."

"Are you arguing with me?"

Her eyes widened. "No, Sir, just trying to be helpful."

"Well, go be helpful by stripping and lying naked on the bed."

"Yes, Sir."

He rose and she followed suit. When she spun, he gave her a swat on the ass. A bit harder than playful, but less than a full spank. She flashed him a grin and sashayed toward the dungeon.

Cleaning took little time as he was well accustomed to doing it. As much as he wanted to, he didn't rush. Based on previous experience, when left to anticipate, she was even more responsive when the scene finally began. Lying on her back left her exposed, for sure, but the welts and stripes caused by the whip would be pressed down by her body weight, even though she was slight. Against the sheet, those abrasions would sing with pain whenever she shifted. Eventually, when the endorphins kicked in, her pliancy would increase, her willingness to agree to things previously off the list might be renegotiated. Never mid-scene, of course, negotiations were permitted only when both parties were clearheaded. A few twinges weren't enough to send her into subspace but might make her more amenable. Was he skirting the line? Possibly. The past night they'd had a breakthrough, and he had to capitalize it, find them a way to move forward.

He wiped down the counters and washed his hands. After a quick detour to his bag, he headed down the hall. The door was closed, and he entered quietly. She lay on her back, as ordered, her arms reaching toward the headboard, her breasts thrust forward. Her legs spread, she gave him a tempting view of her labia. He itched to touch, but he'd planned this scene carefully, and deviating from the script wasn't part of the plan. Improvisation was key to making changes on the fly if a scene started to go sideways, but he was confident he'd worked this one out in his mind long enough that things couldn't possibly go wrong.

He walked to the wall and pulled down several rubber straps, dropping them on the mattress. She squirmed. He adjusted the cuffs at the foot of the bed. She sighed. Clearly, she anticipated what was coming next.

"Keep your eyes closed."

He used the rubber straps to secure her left leg in the bent position—thigh touching calf. He attached the manacle, assuring she was well-secured. He repeated the process and moved to stand at the foot of the bed.

"Close your legs."

She couldn't, of course, as per his plan. Next, he used a strap across her pelvis to secure her middle to the mattress. He meandered back to the foot of the bed.

"Lift your hips."

She couldn't, of course, and he was pleased with himself. Next, he took her left hand and manacled it to the headboard. When she raised her right arm in anticipation, he tisked and she lowered it to her side, clearly uncertain of what to do next.

"Who is in charge here?"

"You, Sir." Her response came swift and uncompromising.

"Who knows what is best for you?"

"You, Sir." Again, she answered without hesitation.

"When Sir tells you to do something, you'll do it, right?"

"Of course, Master."

"Place your hand on your breast."

The uncertainty in evidence when he hadn't tied her right wrist was gone. The corners of her lips curled up as she cupped her breast. And they were beautiful breasts. Luscious, ripe, natural, able to fit into the palm of his hand, they were perfect.

Watching her tweak a nipple into a hard peak caused him to harden. But this was about her, not him. Just because he hadn't gotten off since yesterday morning didn't mean he couldn't wait a little bit longer.

"I want you to touch yourself."

Her eyes flew open, the denial on her lips.

"You have a choice, Rielle. You can 'mens rea,' you can 'tort,' or you can touch." He paused again for maximum effect. "Your choice."

She took a breath, formed a word, but nothing came out. She took another breath, tried to form another word, and exhaled.

"Think carefully about this. I'm your Master, and I know what's best for you." He cringed inwardly at using the word "Master," but he needed to get his point across.

Finally, she took another deep breath. "I can't." It was a thread of sound.

"There is no 'can't' in this room. There's 'mens rea,' there's 'tort,' and there's 'yes, Master.' " God, was this going to work? "I'm not going to wait all day. Do it yourself or I do it for you."

Her eyes widened, her lips curving upward. "Sir will touch me?"

"No." He used his principal's voice. "Sir will hold your wrist while you touch yourself."

She took another deep breath. "Give me another choice, please, any other choice. I'll do anything you want."

"What I want is for you to touch yourself." He raised an eyebrow. "Really, Rielle, it's not like you haven't done this before."

The penny dropped.

Oh, shit.

"You're thirty-three years old, were a slave for four years, and you've never touched yourself? God, were you a virgin when you met him?"

The rapidly forming tears that came to her eyes were more damning to him than anything else, and they lanced across his soul.

"Tort." She whispered the word, but it rang like a gunshot, echoing around the room. She pulled violently against the restraints. "Get me the fuck out of here now, you goddamn bastard." The ensuing struggle was so violent she shifted the bed.

"Jesus, Rielle, I'll get you out. Calm the fuck down." Unsure of where to start, he grabbed her left wrist and unlocked it. In response, she rained blows against his chest so hard bruising both of them was a real possibility. Grabbing her wrists, he yanked her arms above her head and barely missed being bitten on the neck for his trouble. "Christ, stop it!"

Another jerk and he feared she might break a bone or dislocate her hip.

He pressed his chest against hers, still holding her hands above her head. "I'm going to get you out, but you have to give me time."

She arched her back off the bed but with less force than before.

Placing her hands to the slats of the headboard, he curled them so she clutched it. "Keep your hands there, and I will release you." He eyed her. "And don't you dare try to kick me in the balls."

The disappointment in her expression assured him that was exactly what she planned.

It took more time than he wanted to undo the restraints, probably because his hands shook so hard.

She recoiled from his touch as much as she could, barely tolerating even the most necessary of contact.

With no small sense of self-preservation, he unclipped the bands first. When he was sure she was still compliant, he unhooked the strap across her waist. When she didn't buck off the bed, he unlocked the manacles at her ankles.

The manacles were padded, but her wrist and ankles had marks. Her thighs and hips had borne the brunt of her...whatever it was...and angry red marks where she had fought against the rubber striped her body. Her skin chafed, and she might bruise. He wanted to rub the areas to bring back circulation, but she was having none of it. She pulled her legs to her chest, rolled, and hopped off the bed.

Clearly not having thought this through, when her legs gave way, she face-planted into the floor before he could catch her. He winced at the bone-jarring sound her chin made when it hit the hardwood. Undaunted, she crawled on her hands and knees.

He sat on the bed, terror gripping him, and a band around his chest robbed him completely of breath. He didn't dare touch her again, but it was obvious she was going to skin both palms and knees if she continued to crawl on the floor. "Rielle, where are you going?"

She didn't respond, merely kept crawling.

To hell with this.

He pushed himself off the bed, passed her, and was out of the room with a few strides. In the living room, he yanked open his bag and stuffed his belongings in it. His suit still hung in the dungeon's closet, but he was willing to walk away from it to expedite his exit.

As quickly as the anger had taken hold, it let go.

What the hell was going on? Maybe she had some kind of mental illness. People in the BDSM community had the same rate of mental illness as did the general population, maybe a bit less. Mental illness existed in the general population, ergo, mental illness existed in the community. But being a slave didn't make someone mentally ill. She'd laid out the story—brief as it had been—how she wound up there. He hadn't pushed for details because he neither wanted them, nor did he believe she'd willingly give them. She had a right to privacy about her past.

And he had a right to walk out the door.

But his conscience wouldn't let him. He checked his watch. Tarah wasn't slated to start her shift for another ten hours, and he didn't have her home phone number, so that was out. If he called Marie, she'd come, but it wasn't his place to pull her into this…whatever this was. He was tempted to call Leandra, Cara's replacement in the guidance department, to ask her advice. He chuckled ruefully because Leandra was a member of the choir at the local church. She kept her religion out of the school, but she'd invited him to join her Christmas Eve service last year. Although Leandra was professional and discreet, asking her to intervene in a BDSM relationship was impossible. Okay, she was out.

Who did one call in a situation like this? Even as banged-up as she was, she didn't need medical attention, and he doubted she'd appreciate him calling the police. Likely he'd wind up in jail right along with her as she was put in the psychiatric unit.

Walk away.

I can't.

After dropping his bag back to the table, he strode to the dungeon.

Empty.

Whirling, he then stalked to the bathroom, where the door was tightly shut. He knocked on the door. He wasn't surprised when it neither opened, nor did he receive a response. What was the right approach? Pound? Order? Beg?

Or none of the above. If she made it to the bathroom, she was probably going to be okay.

He knocked softly and listened intently, ear pressed to the wood.

Silence.

"Rielle, I'm leaving." What to say next? "You can call me if you need me." He sounded reasonable, right? Still, no response.

His fist hit the door again but with less force than he wanted to apply. "I'm sorry." *What the actual fuck?* "Please talk to me. I need to know you're okay before I go."

A noise caught his attention. A sniffle? A sob? More silence.

As he could stand there all day and get nowhere, he shuffled back to the dungeon. Retrieving his suit, he cast his gaze around for the last time, still bewildered.

Maybe he'd wake up the next day and find this was a bad dream. Shaking his head to clear his mind, he strode back to the main room. He finished packing and pulled out his wallet. He dropped his business card on the table and fished in his pockets. After pulling out the mini-vibrator he'd bought, he dropped that on the table as well. The dungeon might have been decked out with every toy imaginable, but there hadn't been a single vibe. Now that lack was rectified.

Hefting his bag, he marched to the front door and came up short. He wanted to drop the keys and walk out, but that meant leaving the door unbolted. And he couldn't get his car out of the garage without the key card.

Oh, to hell with it.

He would mail them back to her.

Chapter Six

By Friday at one o'clock, Gage was at his breaking point. It rained all week—not all that unusual in the winter—but it was still just October. Everyone seemed on edge. He'd gone toe-to-toe with Jenna about Kane and Dane. Again. This time, she demanded they both sit in a room while Dane took the next test. She wanted absolute proof of which twin was which.

He empathized but was unable to justify punitive behavior against the twins without proof, and Jenna couldn't provide any. He'd never seen her so angry and hoped to never do so again. He finished supervising lunch and headed back to his office.

He checked his phone for the hundredth time and found no message. No personal calls at work, of course, but he could check messages and texts.

Not one word.

He'd started to call about a dozen times but hadn't been able to bring himself to do it. He'd gotten as far as packaging the keys, but the post office always seemed to be closed by the time he dragged his sorry ass out of the building. He worked later and later to avoid returning to his empty house, mocking in its silence.

His ass had almost landed on the cushioned worn leather chair while he contemplated a dubious cafeteria-bought salad when June knocked on his open door. He straightened and offered his warmest expression to his favorite secretary.

"Dorrie Duhamel is here to see you."

He tossed his salad into the trash can.

"Show her in."

There wasn't a single good reason why an RCMP officer was coming to see him. He'd met Dorrie when one of his female students had been filmed naked and drunk at a house party. The video had been posted on the internet and disseminated through the student body. Cybercrimes had come to work with the staff to get the computers sorted out as best as they could, in addition to obtaining evidence of the perpetrators. To his infinite relief, the culprits had been students from another high school. It didn't lessen the girl's trauma, but he didn't know how he'd have handled the parental backlash if three of his male students had been expelled and charged with making child pornography.

Corporal Duhamel had been brought in to help the female student. Kianda had graduated two years ago and opted to go to a university on the other side of the country.

Gage helped her secure a scholarship.

He encountered Dorrie occasionally in town but hadn't seen her in an official capacity in a year. He'd be happy to extend that time indefinitely, if possible.

But he couldn't, and by the expression on her face, this wasn't a social call. He offered his hand to the woman when she entered.

Dorrie's petite stature belied her imposing presence. Perhaps because she'd grown up with a big older brother and a tall, willowy sister, or perhaps even because she was a cop, her posture was always perfect, her blonde hair in a severe ponytail, her eyes bright even in the dull light of his office. Fifteen years her senior, he'd been her math teacher, and now she was one of the best cops in town. She'd completed her Bachelor of Arts in Criminal Justice in two years and been accepted into RCMP training soon after that. She was young, but her instincts were always sharp.

"It's good to see you, Gage."

"And you, Dorrie." He indicated she should sit. When she declined, he remained standing as well. "What's going on?"

Her gaze scanned the room. "I was always terrified of going to the principal's office."

"But you never were sent there, were you?"

Her expression lightened. "Nope, I was a good girl. I had to be good in order to be a cop. All I ever wanted was to be a cop."

"I had a visit from Kianda in late August, before she went back to the University of Ottawa. She's doing well, Dorrie. You did a good job." Small talk wasn't his specialty, but his acute senses picked up on Dorrie's discomfort. If it took her time to get to the matter at hand, as much as it irritated him, he'd wait.

"We did a good job," she corrected him as she studied the degrees on his wall. He hadn't chosen to hang them, but Cara had insisted, pointing out if not for his degrees, he wouldn't be in a position of authority. "But that's not why I'm here." She again glanced around. He was surprised she avoided his gaze. It was completely incongruous to him. Always assertive and sure of herself, this hesitant Dorrie concerned him.

After one more glance around, she straightened. "I'm here as a friend, Gage. I don't start my shift until two o'clock."

"Okay…"

"And the first thing I have to do is interview a man in an attempted murder case."

His stomach bottomed out. "Is it one of my students? Which one? Do I have time to call the parents?"

Finally, after what felt like an eternity, she met his gaze. "The man is you, Gage. What I can't figure out is whether you're a suspect, a witness, or someone who's completely innocent."

"Who was hurt, Dorrie?"

Her eyes flashed at his terse question. "I've already revealed way too much. When I start work in an hour, I'm supposed to come here, with my partner, and ask you to come down to the detachment."

"But if I were to be there in an hour, you wouldn't have to come here to get me." His chest tightened, his heart beating out a thundering tattoo, air being forced from his lungs. The dizziness almost—almost—forced him to sit, but instinctively, he understood showing surprise or weakness might be interpreted as guilt.

Relief clouded her features. She was taking a big risk coming there. If her superiors discovered, there might be repercussions.

Still, he found the words to express his gratitude difficult. "I'll be there" was all he could manage.

She acknowledged his comment, heading for the door.

"Dorrie." His voice hitched, rising slightly.

A moment passed before she turned back, hesitation clear in her expression, her blue eyes turbulent with stark confusion.

"Thank you." He gave her a direct look. "Whatever

happened, it wasn't me."

Without a word, she left.

His knees no longer holding him, he sank to his chair. What the fuck had happened? Attempted murder? The words didn't make sense in his mind. He was a principal of a high school, for Christ's sake. He lived a staid and boring life.

That brought him up short.

He *had* been living a tedious life. Until a few short weeks ago when a woman with a longing and pain rivalling his own had stepped into a BDSM club and changed his life forever. Did this…whatever it was…involve his amber-eyed vixen? *His?* His less-than-dramatic exit last weekend had severed that connection forever, right? He wasn't expecting to go back to Vancouver and try again, was he?

A masochist.

The goddamn Dominant with a touch of sadism at the right time was a masochist at heart. Even if he never crossed the Pitt River again to go to Vancouver with the intention of prostrating himself at Rielle's doorstep, his life had changed irreparably, and going back to plain and simple wasn't an option. He was in deep. Way too fucking deep. Marie had warned him, and he hadn't heeded her words. Now the hand was being called, and he'd bluffed. Even if Rielle wasn't the reason his attendance was required at the RCMP detachment in— the clock on the wall informed him he'd lost nearly a dozen minutes in his mental fog.

He had to get his shit together.

Before he could move, however, June popped her head in the open door and stopped short. "Gage?"

A response was required, but nothing came.

Nodding, he cringed inwardly at his apparent cowardice.

"You don't look well."

He didn't feel well, but that was beside the point. He had to get his ass in gear. "Can you page Jenna Lee for me?"

"Sure, no problem."

He appreciated June's discretion, because all of the problems he needed to handle hit his mind in disjointed bursts, hurting his brain, amping up the tension headache. Fuck, he did not have time for this now.

Prioritize.

What was most critical? How was he going to manage this?

"Look, Gage, I came on a little strong, and I can see your point—"

Jenna's words yanked him from his reverie, sharpening his mind and focusing him on the problem at hand. "Come in and close the door, Jenna."

She did exactly that. "What's going on?" Her astuteness always impressed him. It was the reason he'd pushed for her promotion and explained why he rode her hard sometimes. So she'd be ready to take charge in this exact situation.

Okay, maybe not this *exact* situation. He'd been thinking heart attack or some other medical issue. Maybe a car crash. But attempted murder…?

He rose, straightening his already straight tie. "I have to go down to the detachment."

She stepped toward him. "What happened? Which student?"

Ever the administrator.

"It's personal, Jenna, and I can't say anything more

because I don't know." He raised his hands to ward off the barrage of questions the sharp woman was preparing to pepper him with. "I'm putting you in charge for today. If I can't get this cleared up by tonight, I'll go on administrative leave, and you'll take over until the school board can name another principal."

Her eyes widened, pupils dilating so the dark brown iris was barely visible. "What the hell is going on?"

He grabbed his jacket, then shrugged into it. "I wish I knew." His voice caught, emotion clogging his throat. He was not going to lose it. He couldn't. Too much was riding on this. "All I understand is it's personal, and I will not let it shadow the school."

Stepping toward him, she visibly regrouped, steeling herself. "Call me tonight and tell me what's going on, but you need to take until at least Sunday night. No one needs to know except us, and if it falls apart, we'll say the hand off happened today. Take the weekend, Gage, and get this fixed." Catching him off-guard, she pulled him into a swift embrace, squeezing her tiny arms around him, robbing him of breath for the second time this afternoon.

The administrator might be all of five foot two, but her strength and steel were more than just mental. Dozens of things he needed to tell her swirled in his mind, but none of them mattered. If he was hit by a bus, Jenna had to pick up the pieces. This day's performance would demonstrate if his faith in her was warranted or if he'd overestimated her capacities.

Normally, he took his laptop with him, but it belonged to the school board, and he didn't want to be responsible for having to return it. God, what if he never came back? Despite his innocence, the whiff of scandal could taint his tenure there at the school. He'd been too cavalier with his personal life, and now a price was to be extracted.

****

Arriving ten minutes early, Gage let the surprised constable at the front counter lead him to one of the interview rooms. Interview, not interrogation. Dorrie had intimated he might be a witness. Except he was pretty sure he'd remember witnessing one person try to kill another person. It seemed pretty likely he'd have intervened.

When the door opened, he stopped pacing and stepped forward. Dorrie entered first, followed by a man. While she could pass for something other than a police officer, the man's entire demeanor shouted he was a member of the Royal Canadian Mounted Police.

"Gage, this is my partner, Corporal Colton Pritchard." Dorrie gestured between the two men. "Colton, this is Gage Clayton."

Unsure of protocol, he did what came naturally, which was to reach out a hand. Without hesitation, the return handshake was firm. And a fraction too long. Dominance? Pritchard's height matched his, but he carried about an extra twenty pounds in pure muscle. While Gage had a leaner runner's physique, there was no question the cop hit the weights a couple of times a week. The close-cropped haircut displayed sharp features, emphasizing the dark brown eyes. The cop was good-looking and undoubtedly knew it, but his hard edge raised Gage's hackles.

"Have a seat, Mr. Clayton."

174

Pausing a beat longer than socially acceptable, he finally took the seat indicated. He didn't want to appear reticent or, worse yet, belligerent, but he needed to make it clear he wasn't going to consent to being walked all over. Strength to dominance tempered with the right amount of humility. That façade he'd perfected. "Please, call me Gage."

Colton took the seat opposite, and Dorrie eased into the chair next to the man, handing him a file folder. Since she and Colton had the same rank, Gage catalogued each movement, each interaction, trying to determine who was truly running the show. The RCMP made a big show of all members being equal, but news reports still emerged of women and minorities being held back at some divisions. Dorrie always presented herself as competent, so her minor cue of letting Colton take the lead, as well as her submissive body language, told Gage more than all the words in the world ever could.

Colton pulled out a clear baggie labelled *evidence*.

Gage caught sight of what was in the baggie. He worked his throat, trying to swallow. "Is that blood?" Whatever bravado he'd accumulated left him, swept away as if by the violent wind in a Pacific rainstorm.

"Do you admit this is your business card?"

Colton passed the clear plastic to Gage, whose hand shook. "It certainly looks like it's mine. I have no reason to think otherwise."

"Do you hand out a lot of business cards?"

"Maybe five or six a month. More if I'm at a conference, less during the summer." And he did, but of course, he thought of the one he'd dropped on Rielle's kitchen table the past weekend. His gaze shifted back and forth between the two police officers, laser sharp. "Where did you find this?"

Colton met his stare, taking a moment before answering, a curl in his lips that was either a perverse smile or a pathetic attempt to hide a smirk. "It was found in the pocket of a woman nearly beaten to death."

If Gage had any color left in his face, it drained. The blood pumped from his limbs to his core so it could protect his organs. As his body prepared for the shock that fast approached, his mind spun out of control like a toy top. "Who?" It came out as a whisper, but he couldn't find the strength to put behind the word.

It was Dorrie who answered. "Rielle Reid."

A thousand questions bounced around in his brain, but one took precedence. "How is she?"

The two cops exchanged a look rife with meaning that Gage's muddled brain couldn't interpret. Rielle was hurt. Rielle had bled. It was attempted murder, so she wasn't dead, but that meant nothing. She could be at home cuddled up with a book, or she could be in a coma. He didn't want to go there, but speculation was all he had.

"You admit you know Ms. Reid?" The question came from Dorrie.

Caught in his panic, Gage belatedly realized the two cops were staring at him. No doubt noting every nuance, every micro-expression—anything that might give away if he was involved. Well, he wasn't, so they could go fuck themselves.

Was he supposed to be evasive? Ask for a lawyer? No, damn it, he hadn't done anything wrong. "I know Rielle." The calm he projected didn't hide his turmoil, but he needed to convey strength. Losing control wasn't going to get him to her any faster.

"And you've been to her apartment?" This time it was Colton.

"Yes, I have been to her apartment. I was at her apartment last weekend."

"What is your relationship with Ms. Reid?"

"We had a…personal relationship."

Colton arched an eyebrow. "Did you have sex with her?"

Gage wanted to be outraged—and he was to a certain extent—but this went deeper. No point trying to deny it either because Tarah would offer him up in a heartbeat. "Yes, Ms. Reid and I had a sexual relationship."

Dorrie shifted in her chair, and her evasiveness from earlier made more sense. "Gage, have you been in her entire apartment?"

His inclination, merely an hour ago, might have been to shift as well, but he held steady. "Yes." *Stay calm*. "Yes, Rielle and I had sex. Yes, she and I are both into BDSM. Yes, I've been everywhere in her apartment, but you're missing the point. I didn't hurt her. You're wasting your time with me because I don't know anything." Proud he hadn't lost his shit, he focused on Dorrie. "How is she?"

"Where were you at around midnight last night?"

"At home in bed, and before you ask, there's no one who can verify it." Hyperventilation or heart attack were two distinct possibilities if this ridiculous questioning didn't cease.

Or he might completely lose his shit.

"If you didn't hurt Ms. Reid, might you have any idea who did?" Dorrie sounded sympathetic, and although her eyes softened in possible understanding, it could have easily been a ruse.

He'd been focused on himself, not reasoning things through. "There's a man. He's a judge and he's her...ex-boyfriend. He hurt her once before, so maybe he did it again." Bile rose as his previous visions of Rielle beaten and battered flashed through his mind. The improperly healed whip marks, the broken rib.

"And the name of this judge?"

The emphasis Colton put on the word "judge" was unmistakable, as if he didn't believe the story Gage was giving them. If Rielle hadn't told him herself, he might've thought it merely a fantastical story. Any doubt whatsoever had disappeared the night he'd spoken to Tarah about the judge. The young woman's insightfulness and mental acuity left no doubt Rielle's story had been not merely true, but probably downplayed for his benefit. Was she being questioned? Was she lying to them? Why hadn't she identified her attacker? Protecting him still?

He nearly threw up.

The need to find her, the anger coursing through him, the visceral pain at the emptiness of his arms, was too much for him. Calm no longer an option, he laid his hands flat on the table. He took a moment to glance at his wedding ring and whisper a silent prayer to his dead wife, begging for her help.

Be here for me, babe. I need your strength more than I ever have. As hard as it was to lose you, this will be worse. You, I couldn't save. Rielle, I might yet.

Was it too late?

It didn't matter because the time for chitchat was over. He used a deep breath to center himself and as impetus to lean forward. On the exhalation, he shifted his weight to his palms planted on the table, and the momentum carried him to his feet.

The motion cut off whatever ridiculous question Colton might be preparing to ask. The man sprang to his feet as well, hand instinctively reaching for the butt of his weapon.

Uniformed RCMP officers carried both Tasers and guns, but since this corporal had one lone weapon visible, Gage assumed it was a handgun. Still, he was undaunted in his mission. The other man, who was about ten years his junior, was a cocky sonofabitch. Anger swelled.

Apparently Colton Pritchard didn't have the sense God gave him, because the man rounded the table even as the door opened.

The moment held in suspended animation. Gage was poised for a fight if that's what it took to get to Rielle. The entrance of the older man changed the dynamics in the room immediately, ratcheting down the tension, and at least momentarily, cooling Gage's anger.

"Mr. Clayton, how are you?"

"I'm fine, Gregory. How's your son?"

Sergeant Gregory Wilder was a handful of years older than himself, and they'd known each other for years. Mission was small that way, and most of the time it was fine. That day, he wanted to drop all the niceties and get on with the business at hand. Unfortunately, he had a reputation to uphold, although judging by the fact Dorrie and Colton knew about his proclivities, Gregory probably did as well.

"He's good. He graduated from the RCMP Depot,

and he's been posted to Northern Saskatchewan."

Gregory's son Cody had graduated from Gage's school five years prior at the top of his class. Cody told him in no uncertain terms he planned to follow in his father's footsteps, and apparently, he'd succeeded.

"You'll have to give him my best wishes." The inanity of the situation wasn't lost on Gage, but maybe now some fucking answers would be forthcoming. Gregory held out his hand, and he shook it automatically, albeit skeptically.

"Thank you for coming down here, Mr. Clayton. Your help as a witness was invaluable." He cleared his throat, clearly uncomfortable, but met Gage's gaze. "We won't keep you any longer."

He gave himself a mental shake because he was being shown the door, and as a smart man, he should get the hell out of there. But he couldn't, he just couldn't. "First, I want to know how Rielle is doing, and second, I want to know why I'm no longer a suspect."

When he glanced at the corporals, Colton's distinct displeasure was evident in the rigid position of his body. No longer a predator ready to strike, he stood like a sullen teen who'd lost his driving privileges after a petulant outburst.

Dorrie's expression remained confused, her clear blue-eyed gaze flashing between the three men. Since the cop was more than capable of taking care of herself, her discomfort again set him on high alert.

Gregory inclined his head. The salt in his hair was more plentiful than Gage's, and the man carried authority simply by existing. Although shorter than the other men in the room, he held his own. Still, his presence didn't shout testosterone-driven Alpha-male Dominant.

Normally, Gage couldn't stand that shit, but that day he wasn't willing to back down. Especially with Pritchard a mere step away.

"A suspect was arrested a couple of hours ago. I apologize, he was in another jurisdiction, so we weren't notified right away. We'd never have involved you had we been in full possession of all the facts. When he confessed…well, again, you have my apologies."

The sergeant's regret was genuine, but Gage wasn't willing to yield. He frowned. "The judge confessed?" This was way too neat. Too tidy. Like he'd been handed a present wrapped in a bow, but when opened, it contained a grenade about to explode.

Now it was Gregory's brow that furrowed. "Rielle's father isn't a judge. He got out of jail two days ago after serving twenty-five years for the murder of her mother."

Meager remnants of Gage's third cup of coffee threatened to reappear, and he barely kept from vomiting. Surreal. This was surreal. "You still haven't told me where she is or how she's doing."

Dorrie placed a hand on his sleeve.

Undoubtedly, it was meant to reassure him, to calm him, to keep the situation from spiraling out of control. The urge to twist away from her grasp was strong because no comfort she could offer rivaled the relief he'd feel when he finally found Rielle.

"We had to make sure you weren't involved in any way. She's at Vancouver General. They were running tests to see if she needed surgery."

Dorrie's words were spoken softly, but they hit him

with the force of a bullet. "Surgery?" Although it cost him precious time, he met each cop's gaze. Dorrie and Gregory were contrite, at least a little.

Colton's arms were crossed against his chest, chin raised in defiance.

He didn't give a shit. "She might be in surgery, and you're sitting here asking me if I had sex with her?"

He was halfway to the door when Colton waylaid him.

The man didn't touch Gage, obviously knowing what was best for him, but he did hold up a hand. "We were doing our job, and you'd expect nothing less from us. I'm sorry we made a mistake, but you tearing out of here isn't going to fix things. Let Dorrie call the hospital to get another update before you drive there. If"—he cocked his head—"that's where you're going."

Gage wasn't prone to violence, but decking the cocky cop would go a long way to alleviating some of his stress. Only a strong desire to stay out of jail kept him in check. He held Colton's gaze for one extra beat before turning his attention to Dorrie. "Can you do that for me? Call the hospital?"

"Sure, Gage, anything."

****

Dorrie had been true to her word. He now sat by Rielle's bedside, something that would've never happened without the corporal's intervention on his behalf. He had no memory of the hour-long drive to the city, parking his car in the garage, or even the trip to Rielle's hospital room. All that mattered was he was there now.

Staring at her, though, he choked down the panic again encroaching. If the nurse hadn't brought him there, to this bed, he'd never have guessed it was the woman he'd gotten to know over the past month.

She'd gone the proverbial ten rounds in the boxing ring—her face unrecognizable, her blonde hair dark and matted with blood.

A while back, there had been a bad bus crash involving a hockey team. Kids, really, all in their late teens. Absolutely tragic, half of the team had died.

The story that had twisted Gage's stomach was that two of the teens had been misidentified. Three days went by before the mistake was corrected. One family had been grieving, believing their son dead and planning his funeral. The other family was at the bedside of the teenager they believed was their son, praying for his recovery.

At the time, he questioned how that family hadn't realized. Rielle's grotesquely bruised face and battered body were injuries merely inflicted by another human being. What had the tractor trailer done to the young man? Now he understood how the error happened.

His emotions were all over the place, and although getting them under control was important for both himself and Rielle, he couldn't do it. Couldn't let go of the terror. Of the anger. Of the bitterness. He'd railed at the fates when Cara was taken from him, and the same level of rage simmered in him now. Whoever Rielle's father was, the fucking bastard was damn lucky he was in jail and beyond the reach of Gage's vengeance. He'd never, in his entire life, raised a hand in violence. To inflict pain? Oh, hell, yes. But in non-consensual violence? Fuck, no. It went against everything he stood for, everything he believed in. He preached non-violence to his students. He counseled about conflict resolution and restorative justice. He did not believe an eye for an eye was the solution, because violence inevitably begat more violence.

Those were all great principles, but in the face of such degeneracy, his impotence made him angrier, his need for revenge stronger. Suddenly he understood why some families sought the death penalty after a depraved and evil human being took the life of their loved one.

"Gage?" Tarah stood in the doorway, her gaze frozen on Rielle.

The young woman's complexion was normally pale, but this blanched-white pallor alarmed him. Rising from his chair, he moved slowly but surely toward the young woman, careful not to startle her. She might be strong in body and in constitution—given how she had handled the previous emergency—but this day was different. The violence and result were right there for her to witness. And the bond between the women had grown since the last occurrence.

Would this incident be one too many? Would Tarah back away and decide Rielle wasn't worth the stress? If Tarah's turmoil was half of his, she had to be tied up in knots.

"She's going to be okay, Tarah."

Her gaze shot from Rielle to him. "Really? Because she doesn't look like it."

Despite the worry, her words were also tinged with...sarcasm? Was she giving him attitude or showing bravado? Not for the first time, he quashed the desire to quiz the woman. To ask about Tarah's life and her connection to Rielle, and most importantly, whether she had any information about what had brought Rielle there. Judging by the woman's pallor, he suspected not.

"Why don't you sit by her and hold her hand? The nurse said she should be waking up any time now. It'll be good for her to see a familiar face."

Her all-too-knowing clear blue eyes narrowed. "What about you? Won't she want to see you?" The question was clear, but so was the underlying accusation. Did she know he'd walked away last Sunday? That he'd never planned to return? Rielle sharing his shortcomings to Tarah wasn't beyond the realm of possibility, but pretty close to it. While Tarah's open and honest manner invited confidences, Rielle didn't know how to trust. Whenever his mind went there, the realization gutted him.

Swallowing a lump in his throat, he guided her to the chair. "She's known you a lot longer, and I'd say you'll put a smile on her face first."

Her dubious look informed him what she thought of his bullshit. She sat, however, grasping Rielle's hand and holding it between hers as if she could infuse the unmoving woman with her warmth.

Rielle's unnatural stillness spooked him, but the slow beeping of the machine assured him she lived. That moment rivaled the shock of seeing Cara in the morgue after her death. He hadn't wanted to see her like that, so still, so cold, so…tinged with blue. Despite his desire to never plan for that day, Cara's realistic streak ensured she sat him down and laid out her wishes. If any chance of organ donation existed, she wanted that. The suddenness of her death had precluded that option.

Finally, Cara requested cremation. No open casket, no church service. Despite her faith, she understood he wouldn't be able to step inside their church, and as always, her insight was uncanny. Even from the grave, she protected him from having to face the unfathomable. God had taken the most precious of His servants, called her home, so to speak.

Gage's anger and pain overwhelmed, and at times, literally brought him to his knees. He'd survived the celebration of life and memorial at the school, but his patience and ability to cope ended in that instant. He'd gone back to work, trying to bury his pain and grief, focusing instead on his students. That morning, stepping inside a church would've been the last thing he'd agree to.

Now, if it meant easing Rielle's pain and bringing solace to him, he was damn tempted. Would God welcome him home? Or would the deity turn his back? Was Rielle's current state punishment because he'd shunned the church when he was hurting the most?

Desperate to push through that pointless line of thinking, he gazed from the immobile Rielle to the equally unmoving Tarah. Struck by how young she looked, he chided himself because Tarah *was* young. She might've been one of his students, and her vulnerability and uncertainty radiated. He wanted to reassure her, but he wanted reassurances himself, and they weren't coming.

As if in answer to a prayer, the nurse from earlier bustled in. She gave him a hearty grin as she passed him and moved her attention to Tarah, bestowing an even broader smile, if that was possible. "My name is Sheena."

The woman had a shock of auburn hair in corkscrew curls and moss green eyes. Short in stature and with an ample bosom, Nurse Sheena radiated calm competence.

Taking Rielle's slender wrist in her hand, Sheena measured her pulse while watching the monitor carefully. Apparently satisfied, she placed a hand on her patient's shoulder. "Rielle, honey, you've got visitors. You need to wake up now."

Save for the quiet beeping of her heartbeat on the machine, he doubted she was alive, let alone able to respond to the persistent nurse's urging. But something in the woman's demeanor ignited a spark of hope in his chest. Maybe Rielle would be okay. Maybe there would be an end to this nightmare.

Her eyelids flickered.

"That's it, Rielle." Sheena's tone encouraged, and she was rewarded with another flicker. "You're safe amongst friends. Now open your eyes."

The steel in the woman's tone surprised Gage, but he knew better than to question a skilled health-care worker.

Apparently Rielle held the same belief because her eyes fluttered open. They were swollen, her barely visible eyes bloodshot. How could she see anything? And how was she coping with the pain? Were they giving her the good stuff, or were they holding back, worried about a potential head injury?

Her mouth opened as if to speak, but she only managed to swallow. He was on tenterhooks as she licked dry lips and tried again. "Tarah?" It was more a croak than anything else, but he'd never heard anything so lovely.

"I'm here, Rielle." Tarah kept one hand on Rielle's but extended her other to him. He'd no choice but to grasp it, allowing himself to be pulled toward the bed.

"Gage is here as well."

Sheena unceremoniously stuck a thermometer in her patient's mouth, preempting further speech, but amber eyes locked gazes with him, and he took a punch to the gut. Not damnation as he expected, just quiet resignation. She held his gaze for another moment before returning her attention to Tarah. With the thermometer removed, her lips curled into the semblance of a smile, albeit a crooked one at that.

"Thank you, Tarah." Her eyelids with their impossibly long lashes fluttered shut. He'd never paid attention to such details until Cara had educated him. While his wife had lengthened hers, Rielle's appeared natural. They were blonde and delicate, contrasting with the ugly mottled purple skin around her eyes.

He arched an eyebrow, and Sheena waved off his unspoken question.

"She's going to be in and out of consciousness for a few hours, and we'll keep checking on her because she's on pretty heavy painkillers. If she does well for the next little while, we'll let her sleep for a few hours."

Rielle needed to sleep for a millennium, but the medical staff would have to check on her frequently, even if it disturbed her rest.

Tarah looked up uncertainly. "I have to get to work…"

He squeezed the hand he still held. "Give me your number, and I'll text you every few hours and give you an update." He met Sheena's gaze. "I'm staying."

She rolled her eyes with a snicker. "Dorrie's a friend of mine. Since she said you were a good dude, I'll let it slide. I'll be back in about an hour, but if she needs me before then, buzz."

He doubted Dorrie had referred to him as a "good dude," but he'd use whatever advantage he could get. "Can she have water?"

"Sure. There's a cup there." Sheena pointed to a side table and turned to Tarah. "Why don't you come with me, honey?"

She hesitated, her gaze traveling the length of Rielle's body, settling on her face. For a moment, he worried she might refuse to leave, but she pulled a notebook from her knapsack and jotted down her number. "I'm on until six tomorrow morning. Tell Rielle I'll come back tomorrow afternoon before my shift."

"She'll appreciate it, Tarah."

The young woman stared at him, as if trying to discern his motives while conveying a threat as well. If he hurt Rielle emotionally, there would be hell to pay. Unexpectedly, she placed her hand on his forearm and squeezed, offering unspoken support. Finally, she followed the nurse from the room.

He was alone with his thoughts. Dropping into the chair next to her, he enjoyed his first moment of sheer relief since Dorrie had confirmed it was Rielle who'd been attacked. Questions swirled around in his brain, but few answers followed. For the time being, however, he'd wait. He'd wait as long as it took to get answers from her. Hopefully he'd get enough information to decide whether they had a future.

****

Gage bristled when a pair of Vancouver Police detectives tossed him from Rielle's room, but he had little say in the matter. They wanted to interview her alone. If she insisted he stay, they might have relented, but she made no such request. Now he stood in the hallway with a sympathetic, albeit unhelpful, Sheena.

The nurse laid a hand on his arm, accompanied by what he supposed was a reassuring smile. "Gage, you need to let the police do their job."

He didn't return the smile but cocked his head. "So how do you know Dorrie?"

"She was here dealing with a patient, and we got acquainted. It seems like a big deal for the police to be here, but it happens from time to time."

At least the officers hadn't been in uniform, but like Colton, the man and woman's attitudes had all but screamed "cop."

Get over it. "When will she be able to come home?"

"She's seriously injured, Gage. The three broken ribs aren't a big deal, but the bruised kidney is of concern. Once they're sure she'll recover, she can look at coming home. If you need to go…"

He shook his head fiercely. "I'm not going anywhere."

Sheena grinned. "I didn't think you were. I, on the other hand, am out of here. I'll be back in twelve hours, but I hope you go home and get some sleep."

He wanted to say he'd sleep when Rielle was out of the hospital, but that didn't seem likely to be anytime soon. "I'll see you when you get back."

Sheena waved and headed out.

The next nurse, Korbin, introduced himself and left to do his rounds of patients.

Gage waited. When the two detectives stepped from Rielle's room, he pounced. "Did you get everything you needed?"

"She was able to answer our questions." The female officer's demeanor gave nothing away. Stoic like the Mission City cops.

"You've arrested her father?"

The male detective's gaze shifted back and forth between his partner and Gage. He scratched his nose. "He was arrested and charged with attempted murder. His parole's been revoked, so there's no chance of him getting out on bail. He admitted his culpability but claims Ms. Reid asked for it."

Gage gaped. "He says she asked him to do"—he pointed ineffectually—"do that to her?"

This time, the woman answered, holding up one hand in a placating gesture. "We're not saying anyone is going to believe him or that it makes any difference, but we had to ask."

"And what did she say?" During the awkward silence, his gaze shot back and forth between the two detectives. "She said she asked him to do that?"

"Not in so many words, no."

What the hell did that mean?

The male officer gave Gage a level look. "I recommend you talk to her."

He didn't miss the emphasis on the word "her." They weren't going to give out any more information now. He held out his hand. "I appreciate everything you guys have done. I'm sure it's a relief to Rielle that her father won't be able to hurt her anymore."

The officers shook his hand and took off, leaving him alone in the corridor. Why was he there? Was he an emotional masochist? Perhaps, but he was there now, and he wasn't going anywhere anytime soon.

Taking a deep breath, he reentered Rielle's room.

Her eyes were closed, but she wasn't asleep. When he sat, she opened her eyes. "May I have some water?"

Her voice was so hoarse he barely heard it. He filled the cup with cold water from the pitcher, then held a bendy straw to her lips until she took a sip.

She managed two more before indicating she was finished.

Putting down the cup, he pulled the chair as close to her as possible. He took her ice-cold hand, clasping it between his. "How are you feeling?"

She met his gaze, and the effort it took for her to focus on him was clear. Her lips almost curled upward but lost the battle. "I've been better."

"What happened, Rielle? How did this happen?"

Closing her eyes, she sighed.

Her misery ate at him. His gut clenched, nausea warring with anger. Despite the tic in his jaw and the frustration he was tamping down, his head was clear enough to see her emotional and physical pain.

"Can we do this later? Please, Gage."

He needed to know. "Just tell me one thing. Did you ask him to beat you?"

Her eyes opened, but it took some effort. "Did I ask him to beat me? No. Did I go to see him? Yes."

"Why?"

Her brow furrowed as if she had to consider the answer. "I had to confront him. He met someone while he was in prison and planned to marry her. I couldn't let that happen." Her voice hitched. "He killed my mother. I saw him beat her to death."

"So you went and confronted him? God, Rielle, what kind of logic is that?" His hands twitched. He wanted to reach out and shake her. The needless risk, the stupid notion.

A haunted expression flicked through her amber eyes. "She won't be marrying him now, will she?"

The coffee churned into acid in his stomach. "What did you do?"

She tried to pull her hand from his, but he held on tight. When she couldn't sever that connection, she closed her eyes.

He wanted to command her to open them, but it was neither the place nor the time. He'd wait for as long as it took.

"I…challenged him. I may have threatened to tell his fiancée about him."

"To what end? Whoever this woman is, she can't be completely ignorant. He's a convicted felon, for God's sake. Who did she think she was marrying?" The penny dropped. "And how do you know about her?"

She lifted her other hand to her brow, grimacing when the movement tugged on her intravenous catheter. "I received a copy of his parole officer's report saying he had concerns about my father's impending release, but the sentence had been served, and his time was up."

How had she received a copy of a confidential report? The question was rhetorical. "That was your deal with the devil, wasn't it? Information about your father in exchange for your submission?"

A little sound of distress escaped her lips.

Way to go, asshole. Time no longer held meaning, and there he was, challenging her, a few hours after she'd had the shit kicked out of her. "That was out of line. I'm sorry."

When she didn't respond, he clasped one of her hands but gently cupped her cheek with his other hand.

"You need to rest, Rielle. I truly am sorry I pushed."

She made another noise, letting her other hand drop back to the blanket. "I'm tired." The mumble was barely audible.

"I know you are, sweetheart." A lump formed in his throat, making it hard to speak. "Let it go for now. You're safe, and that's what matters."

"Thank you." A soft whisper.

He finally breathed a sigh of relief as she slipped into sleep.

****

The next two days passed as a blur. He caught naps and Saturday night managed a few hours of sleep, but it was fitful. He existed in constant panic, irrationally believing if he took his eyes off her, she'd die. She'd disappear. He'd lose her like he'd lost Cara. It was irrational in the extreme, but he couldn't talk himself out of the mindset.

There had been no further conversation as she was well-medicated and completely out of it. Korbin or Sheena was in every few hours, evicting him as they cared for Rielle. He also met the doctor—Lisa Giroux—and was impressed by the woman's gentle yet firm nature. She answered his questions about both Rielle's progress as well as her prognosis and kept a guarded but optimistic outlook. The tests showed she was going to heal without needing surgery, for which he was grateful. Looking at Rielle, though, he was still unable to swallow properly. The initial swelling had gone down, and she could open her eyes, but the purple color was still vivid even as it was beginning to turn that sickly yellow-green color.

He was looking out the window at the fading

autumn light on Sunday night when Rielle called his name, and he startled out of his reverie. In a heartbeat, he was by her side. She met his gaze, and he was pleased to see she seemed better able to focus.

"You're still here." Her voice was stronger than it had been.

"I am." He nodded, sitting in the chair he was intimately familiar with.

"You should go home."

He gazed intently into her eyes. "Do you want me to go?"

Her eyes closed briefly. "What day is it?"

"Sunday."

"You've got school tomorrow."

He'd spoken to Jenna, without specifics, and said he might need more time off. She assured him he could take as long as he needed, as he'd never taken so much as a sick day in more than fifteen years. But he was torn between responsibility to his kids and to her, a woman he barely knew. "I can take a few days off, Rielle. It's not a big deal."

Her expression was wistful. "But it is a big deal, Gage, and we both know it. I'm going to be okay."

He refrained from making a snarky comment about her false bravado. "The doctor says you should be out of here by the end of the week."

"I want to go home now." Her words were soft and tremulous.

Taking her hand in his, he pressed a kiss to her knuckles. "I get it, sweetheart, but you're in no shape to leave here." He didn't bother to point out she was completely bedridden, sensing that might cause more distress. "When the doctor says you can, we'll figure things out. For now, you need to rest."

Her lower lip quivered. "I hate hospitals."

Who didn't? He held his tongue. "We'll get you out of here soon, sweetheart."

"Okay." She turned from his gaze, also looking out the window. "But you don't need to be here."

"Do you want me here?" He held his breath.

"No. Yes." She closed her eyes. "I don't know, Gage. We didn't part on the best of terms."

An understatement if there ever was one.

"We don't have to talk about that." He gave her a moment to consider. "Unless you want to."

She shook her head. "I'm surprised you came. How did you find out about me?"

"You had my business card on you when you chose to go to your father's house. Hell, Rielle, they thought I did it. They thought I had attacked you."

"Your business...oh, I never even considered that. I had tucked it in my pocket because I couldn't bring myself to throw it out."

"Well, I'm glad you didn't, because they knew to call me, but I could've done without the police interrogation."

"If it'd been within my power, I'd have saved you that grief." Her eyes were unfocused as she glanced at him. "How did I get here?"

"Do you remember anything?"

"I...I remember going to his house and we talked. Or we argued. It was funny—he didn't even recognize me."

He squeezed her hand. "But you didn't leave."

"No, I didn't. I said I remembered what he'd done to my mother. I told him I remembered what he did to

196

me."

He swallowed past a painfully dry throat, and a trickle of cold sweat ran down his spine. "Did he…?" He couldn't form the words.

"What? Oh, no, not that. He hit me. A lot. He was about to do it again when my mother intervened. I'd broken his favorite ashtray. It was an accident, of course, but he didn't see it that way. When my mother stepped between us, he lit into her. I don't even know how many times he hit her, but eventually, she stopped fighting. He spun, backhanded me, and dragged me into the closet and locked me there. He went out for cigarettes." She swallowed convulsively. "When a neighbor came to visit, she saw my mother's body through the window. She called the police."

"How long were you locked in that closet?"

"Three days."

"And he went to prison."

"I remember when the police arrested him. He looked surprised, like he hadn't done anything wrong." She tried to smile but faltered. "I know what you're thinking."

"I doubt that."

But she persisted. "You think I have unresolved childhood issues that make me want to be…used."

He eyed her carefully. "Do you? Have unresolved childhood issues?"

"No." She said it with quiet certainty. "What I let you do to me was by my own choice. Safe, sane, and consensual. I knew what I was doing when I invited you to come home with me. I knew the rules when I submitted to *him* for the first time."

The infamous Mr. X.

"Did you even have a safeword with him?" He banked his frustration, because losing his temper would get him nowhere. When she didn't answer, he persisted. "How can it be consensual when one person sets all the rules?"

Her brow knit in confusion. "That's what it was about—he set the rules. He had the power. I let him." Her enunciation left no room for misinterpretation. "I knew where the door was."

"But the reports about your father would've dried up."

Her gaze darted around, confusion clouding her eyes. Was she seeking divine intervention? Then she must've recalled their conversation from Friday night. "It wasn't a deal with the devil. You must understand at first he offered me stability. Guess what happened after my mother died? I was put into foster care. Nice people, sure, but no security. I went through five homes by the time I aged out at eighteen. My grades were good, but not spectacular, and I got into university with no way to pay for it. Seven years' worth of student loans didn't daunt me. I didn't care because I was going to become a lawyer, and nothing else mattered."

"And?"

She swallowed and pointed to the glass of water beyond her reach. He held it for her, as he'd done many times over the past two days, and she sipped.

"Are you tired?" He was concerned, and stopping was an option, although he was reluctant. She was talking, being open and honest with him—perhaps for the first time ever—and he planned to press the advantage. Maybe if he understood this, he could better appreciate where she was coming from—why she made

198

the choices she did, had the reactions that often confounded him. Maybe, just maybe, he could anticipate her needs and react appropriately instead of being a step behind half the time.

A quick shake of her head. "I'm finally coming out of a fog, and I need to hold on to lucidity for as long as I can."

"Okay." He checked his watch.

"If you need to leave—"

He shook his head. "I was noting the time and wondering if you might be hungry. I can go get you some food." He offered her a grin. "I'm well-familiar with the cafeteria."

Now she shook her head. "I'm a little nauseous. Food is not appealing."

"Tell me if you change your mind, okay?" He traced a finger along her jaw. "Whatever you need, Rielle, all you need to do is ask."

She valiantly fought to hold back the tears, eventually losing the battle as one streaked down her battered but still beautiful face. His hand twitched, but she wiped it away quickly. "I'm sorry."

"You don't need to be." The pain in his chest increased, and he pressed a hand to his breastbone, attempting to rub away the ache. "You've been through a lot, sweetheart."

"Am I your sweetheart?" She met his gaze directly. "Why are you here, Gage? After what happened, I never expected to see you again."

Damn good question. His answer came swift and sure. "No matter what happened, Rielle, I never hesitated. You needed me, so I came. You were hurting, so I stayed."

"Like you would for anyone else?"

The question was tossed out casually, but he wasn't ignorant of her underlying meaning. "I care about my staff and students, but it never occurred to me to keep vigil by their bedside unless they had no one." He winced. "That didn't come out right. I'm not here because you're alone. I mean, is there someone I should call? I never thought to ask."

"There's no one, as you're well aware. Even before I was a slave, there was no one to call."

So much encompassed in a simple sentence. "He preyed on that, didn't he? Your loneliness, I mean."

Wetness pooled again in her eyes. "I felt cherished. I fancied myself in love with him."

"Fancied?"

Amber eyes flashed. "I know my mother loved me, but I hardly remember her. My childhood memories are of violence. Periods happened between the outbursts when we walked on eggshells because it was simply a matter of time before for the next eruption. I lived in terror each day. Why my mother didn't take me and leave, I'll never know."

"You don't have to talk about this."

Her unhindered hand pressed to her forehead. "I've never told anyone this. Except the policewoman who rescued me. I told her all of it. Her name was Arielle, but everyone called her Rielle."

"You took her name."

"When I turned eighteen, I left my old life behind. A name change appeared an expeditious way to do it. New name, new life."

"Same nightmares."

"Some things you can't outrun, no matter how hard

you try. And I tried, Gage. I assumed if I became a lawyer and obtained security, everything would be okay."

"What kind of law did you practice?"

Her face transitioned from passivity to sadness to resolve in a heartbeat. "I was hired by social services to represent children who needed protection."

"And you gave that up?" *Tread carefully.* This was the closest she had come to sharing her inner secrets. To sharing what lay beneath. Spooking her might be the equivalent to whacking a turtle's neck with a stick. Back into the shell, never to emerge again.

"I did it for four years, and it ate me up inside. Each case was like reliving my childhood trauma over and over. I considered getting counseling but told myself everything would be okay if I pushed through. I was on the verge of a nervous breakdown when I met him."

He squeezed her hand in support. He didn't want to hear any of this, but she was talking, and he wasn't going to stop her, no matter the cost to him.

"He saw it. It was a tough case of child molestation, and the mother was fighting to get the children back."

That didn't sound so bad to him. "Why were you involved?"

"Because despite physical evidence, she refused to acknowledge her husband was guilty. We had no proof she'd keep him away from her children once he got out of jail."

"You fought on behalf of the children."

"They didn't want to go back to their mother anyway, so it wasn't as hard as it could have been. He interviewed both children, and Gage, he was gentle with them. Careful and kind. He didn't re-victimize them, but he did get them to tell what had happened. It turned my stomach and broke my heart. The girls had an aunt who lived in Toronto, willing to take them, and happy to keep both parents away. She was going to get them into counseling and try to help them heal. Two heartbreakingly beautiful little girls who will never be normal."

"Why can't they be normal?"

"Because they've seen what cruelty and evil exists in the world. They've never known true security. Even if they recover, they'll never forget."

"And he offered to take you away from the misery and suffering." A statement, not a question.

She closed her eyes. "It occurred to me I might go into a different field in law. Nothing wrong with corporate or environmental or any other of a number of specialties, but I was burned out. I planned to take a couple of days off when he offered me a month. I hadn't had a day of rest since I turned eighteen, and it appealed. I could let someone else take the weight I'd been carrying."

"And you never chose to go for that counseling?"

Her brow furrowed. "No. I honestly believed I'd put the past behind me. And maybe I had, but the week before the case, I'd received a notice from the prison system that my father was seeking parole."

"And after he honed in on you, all it took was a bit of research to find your Achilles' heel."

"Yeah." Her jaw ticked with tension. "At the end of the month, I received a letter saying my father's parole had been denied. I wasn't so naïve that I didn't understand what was going on. My father was eligible for parole every year until his mandatory release at twenty-five years. Every year, like clockwork, the parole was denied." She swallowed. "You may think my former Master was a bad guy, but he made sure my new identity was never linked to my old one. If my father had ever decided to find me, he'd have a difficult time."

"So why go there? He tried to kill you."

A hesitation passed as she considered him carefully. "I told you, the parole report revealed he'd become involved with a woman while he was in prison. Twenty-five years locked in a cage does not rehabilitate that kind of evil, Gage."

"She is an adult, Rielle. She deserves to make that decision for herself."

"She has three daughters under the age of eighteen."

He sucked in a breath. Things made more sense. "And if he killed you?"

"Those girls would've been safe." The words were dispassionate, as if it were completely logical. As if she were simply recounting events rather than explaining a moment of temporary insanity.

He looked as deeply into her eyes as he dared. "Are you suicidal, Rielle?"

She seemed to contemplate her answer. "Do I have any special desire to die? No. Would anyone notice if I died? No."

I would notice. I would care. But he left the sentiments unspoken, instead letting her continue.

"It wasn't a death wish as much as an inevitability. I'm not sure how I survived."

He wasn't sure of that either, given the extent of her injuries. He still feared for her, though. For her mental health as well as her physical well-being.

"Will you consider counseling?"

Sharp eyes fixed on him. "There's nothing wrong with me. Nothing that talking to someone might fix."

"Do you want to keep seeing me?"

Her face lit in surprise, then fell with apparent uncertainty. "I do." Caution.

"Then you have to see someone. I'll pay, if that's the issue."

She snickered. "Money is not an issue, as you are aware. The question is why do you want to keep seeing me? What can I give you that you can't get elsewhere?"

Good question. "Are you saying no?"

This time she squeezed his hand.

She replied cautiously, "I'll think about it." Which sounded distinctly like a "no" to his acute hearing, but he'd let the issue drop. For now. Sheena bustled into the room, cutting off his next words.

"And how are we doing?"

Was she using the royal "we," or was she talking to Rielle?

Rielle was about to answer when a thermometer was stuck in her mouth. Her eyes showed part annoyance, part resignation.

Sheena was completely unperturbed as she adjusted the IV. "Ready to try a protein shake?"

Now that the thermometer had been removed, Rielle was free to speak, but Gage stepped in before she could make a rude remark.

"Sheena, that's a great idea. I'm not certain how much she'll be able to manage, but I'll make sure she gets some of it down."

She gave him a mutinous glare, but his brow arched, telling her in no uncertain terms who was really in charge. To his infinite relief, she yielded.

"Well, that's good news. Chocolate, strawberry, or vanilla?"

"Vanilla, please." Rielle shot him a look, daring him to say something.

He smothered his laugh.

Sheena, completely oblivious, headed out.

Then came the laughter, and after a moment, Rielle joined in. And it was a nice sound right until the moment she yanked her hand from his and pressed it to her ribs. "Ouch."

"I'm sorry." He didn't feel the least bit repentant. They needed some levity after the past hour. After the past day. After the past week.

Taking a breath, she closed her eyes. "You're not sorry, but we'll let that go." Her face relaxed a bit, and some of his own tension ebbed.

"What time is it?"

She spoke so quietly he had a hard time hearing her. "About six."

"You need to get going. You've got school tomorrow, and you need to go home and prepare for the week."

He wanted to argue with her, but she was right. His abrupt departure on Friday had left things undone, and although Jenna had held the school together, he still had work to take care of. Preparations to be made. "Do you *want* me to leave?"

Her eyes opened. "I don't want you to put your life on hold for me."

"I'll be back on Friday."

"You don't have to."

He stood, leaned over, and placed the gentlest of kisses to her lips. "But I want to."

Chapter Seven

Five days. Five days of trying not to worry, not to fret. Daily phone calls to Sheena and Korbin assured him Rielle was recovering, if slowly, and needing nothing. They wanted her to stay another couple of days, but she'd become recalcitrant. The compromise was Gage would pick her up, take her to the condo, and keep an eye on her. Sheena gave him the distinct impression Rielle wasn't happy about this condition, but he didn't give a shit. He needed the reassurance of seeing her for himself.

Long hours at work and long runs when he got home did nothing to assuage his worry. Dr. Giroux assured him Rielle would make a full physical recovery, for which he had been grateful. But what he and the doctor had never discussed was Rielle's fragile emotional health.

He arrived at the hospital on Friday night with a sense of trepidation and nervousness he hadn't endured since the night he convinced Tarah to call Rielle all those weeks ago. She'd let him in that night. Might she do the same now?

Sitting in a wheelchair, she waited for him, chin tilted upward. Tarah had brought her a change of clothes since Rielle's had been cut from her body when she'd first been admitted to the emergency department. She looked like a breath of wind could knock her over, but her expression dared him to say something.

He wisely kept silent.

It took a few minutes to get her to the SUV, and she managed with only a little bit of difficulty.

The groan she tried to hide was unmissable, but again he held his tongue. She was putting up a brave face, and he respected it—for now.

The drive to her condo took another few minutes, and he used his key card to gain them admittance to the garage. When she headed toward the stairs, he put his foot down. "It's four floors up from here. Rielle, you'll never make it."

"No one said you had to be here." Her voice snapped like a stretched elastic band newly released.

"You're getting into the elevator." He used a very reasonable tone. "You can go under your own steam, or I can carry you."

Even as he said it, the challenge daunted. She was a tall woman, and although slim, had some muscle to her. If she forced him to carry her, it'd be tough for both of them. When she didn't have a quick quip, he seized the advantage. "We're taking the elevator." He was using his dominant voice, but he didn't care. He had no doubt her making it up the stairs alive had slim-to-none odds.

As it was, she gripped her ribs, and despite the vivid yellow and green of the aging bruises, her face lost all color. It was telling that she let him guide her to the elevator without further complaint. When the elevator arrived, however, Rielle balked.

"Close your eyes and hold on to me." *Like a child, reassure, don't chastise.* "I'll be there to protect you."

She obeyed him and stepped into the car.

208

He pressed the button for the third floor and pulled her toward him. Because of her injuries, holding her was impossible, so he pressed his forehead to hers.

A shiver ran through her when the door closed, and she stiffened when the elevator moved. "Oh God." Her breathing sped up, and she grew even paler.

"You're safe, sweetheart. We're almost there."

To his infinite relief they ascended straight to her floor, and he was able to help her from the car because her eyes were still closed. "You made it." He tried to inject some pride in his voice, but she still trembled.

"Home." Yet another broken whisper that ate at him. "Please."

Needing no further encouragement, he guided her to the apartment. With deft hands, he held her and unlocked the door.

As she stepped in, she flipped on the light and took a deep breath, cringing as she did it. "Home." This time, she showed more strength and perhaps a touch of awe. As if she'd never expected to return here and was staggered she'd managed to do it.

"You need to lie down. Where do you want to go?"

Without hesitation, she pointed. "My room."

He understood what she meant. Guiding her to the white room, he contemplated the logistics of the tiny child-sized bed. What did it matter? She was safe. The rest was gravy.

Progress was slow as she could only take shallow breaths and short steps. When they entered her room, he reached for the light switch, but she waylaid him. "Maybe we can use the lamp?"

"Of course." He used the hallway light to guide him to the lamp, and flipped it on. Warm glow suffused the room instead of the harsher overhead light, and he saw her logic.

She wavered near the bed.

"Why don't you sit while I go get your pajamas?"

She let him guide her down. "I'm not sure I can get changed."

Her honesty tore at him. "Well, that's what Nurse Gage is for." He forced himself to be cheerful. "I'm here to make sure you have everything you might need."

She didn't respond but pointed to the closet. "You should find something in there."

Once he was certain she wasn't going to move from her seated position, he made his way over to the closet. Whereas the closet in the dungeon was full of sexy clothes and fetish gear, this closet contained plain, ordinary clothing. Jeans, shirts, blouses, skirts, and a few dresses. Not nearly as many clothes, but they were well-loved.

On one of the hangers was a pair of practical flannel pajamas that made his heart hurt. Pale green with white snowflakes, like a child's. Next to it was a nightgown which he selected, figuring it would be easier to slip her into it rather than trying to manage the pajamas. He tried to suppress his shock at the white gown. It would go all the way down her ankles, covering her to the neck, and the sleeves extended to her wrists. It was positively virginal and a vivid contrast to the kimonos she normally wore.

When he moved to her side, he crouched to unbutton her blouse.

She tried, rather ineffectually, to bat away his hands. Too much energy was expended, and her face took on a grayish pallor.

"Nurse Gage, remember? Let me do this, Rielle." Taking her silence as acquiescence, he continued to undo the buttons. A lone tear slid down her cheek, and he wiped it away. "I can see it hurts, sweetheart, but this will be over soon." She was due for another painkiller, and he needed to prioritize—

He sucked in his breath, and red-hot rage surged through his veins. Her face was nasty and ugly, but clearly that hadn't been the half of it. Her ribs were encompassed in white tape, a stark contrast to the vivid black and purple bruises which covered her entire body. There was barely a place on her torso that hadn't been hit. As he eased the shirt from her shoulders, he chanced a peek at her back and found as much damage. She cringed when he pulled down the shirt, and he saw fingerprint bruises on her upper arms.

"Oh God, sweetheart." He barely choked out the words.

"I didn't want you to see this." She ducked her head.

He spared a moment to tip her chin up so she faced him. "I'm glad you let me, Rielle, despite how painful it is for you. I want to take away your pain."

"You're helping." She rushed to reassure him, even as she took a deep breath and cringed.

He pulled her hands through the sleeves of the shirt and laid it aside. The hospital hadn't bothered with a bra, and he was relieved. He was able to slip the nightgown over her head, affording her some modesty. Not that he might ever forget what he'd witnessed. Some images were seared into his brain, and these marks were to be one of them.

He removed her running shoes and socks, debating how best to proceed.

"Put your hands on my shoulders," he encouraged. Guiding her to rise, he quickly undid her jeans and slipped them over her hips. They gave easily. She'd lost weight over the last week, something she couldn't afford to do. He loved her curves and was distressed as the jeans fell to the ground. Guiding her back to a sitting position, he then tugged her feet through the pant legs.

Now she was unencumbered, and all he had to do was get her into bed. It took some maneuvering, but he managed.

Soon she was lying on the bed, her face as pale as the white sheets beneath her head. Her eyes were closed, and she was breathing in short shallow gasps.

Helpless, he gathered up her clothes and folded them neatly, hanging them on the empty hangers in the closet. It occurred to him that when Tarah had come to retrieve Rielle's clothes, she might've stumbled upon the dungeon.

What must she have thought?

Maybe she'd found this room first, but he doubted it. Tarah would've been familiar with the layout of the condo and undoubtedly headed straight for the master suite. He'd bet his last dollar she'd never seen a master bedroom like that one before. Should he talk to her about it? She was working tonight. Maybe better to get it over with. Plus, he needed to express his gratitude. It'd been impractical for him to visit Rielle during the week, but Tarah had come every day without fail. Rielle said no one would notice her death, but she'd been wrong.

Tarah would've mourned. Marie, with her big heart, would've mourned. He would've been bereft, beside himself with grief and torment. He still couldn't put a finger on exactly how he felt about her, but it was more than compassion.

"Gage?"

He startled because he thought her asleep. "Yes, Rielle."

"Thank you." She didn't open her eyes. "I don't think they'd have let me out."

They wouldn't have. Her tests had been normal and the danger considered passed. But what came next was weeks and weeks of recovery.

"What are you going to do when I can't be here?"

"Sheena has a friend who does private care nursing. I've hired her to come in for a few hours each day to take care of me, cook a meal, stuff like that."

Relief washed over him. "That sounds good."

"She can't start until Monday."

"Well, you've got Nurse Gage until then."

She parted her lips, wetting them with her tongue. "I prefer Master Gage."

An image of her over his lap as he spanked her ass flashed into his mind, and he hardened at the image. Christ, he was going to get an erection two feet away from a woman who couldn't have been less able to respond.

"Sir Gage, if you please." He tried for a light teasing tone.

"Of course, Sir. That's what I meant."

"Rielle?"

"Yes, Gage."

"We don't need to…be in character right now."

213

She opened her eyes. "By tomorrow morning when I'm grouchy and refusing to do what you think I should, you'll come to regret those words."

"Are you going to? Refuse what I want you to do?"

"Try to give me one more fucking vanilla protein shake, and you'll find out."

Despite himself, he laughed. "Strawberry, it is." His laughter continued when she stuck out her tongue. *God, despite the horrible bruises, she really is beautiful.*

Her amber eyes were clear and bright, but she took a breath too deep and cringed. "Please don't make me laugh," she begged. "I can't handle it."

"One painkiller coming up. Aside from water, is there anything else you need?"

She shook her head, and he made his way to the kitchen. After snagging two bottles of water, he returned to her room. She couldn't even hold her head up, so he braced her against him, taking her weight, and helped her swallow the pill. They were still giving her the good stuff, but soon they'd downgrade her to less potent medication. He hoped the pain was manageable.

Ironic for him to worry about how much pain she might endure. He'd put her through her paces, but this was different somehow. When someone willingly submitted to pain, anticipation, endorphins, and control all mixed together to create an amazing experience. What she was going through now had none of those elements. She had no control and was holding on by a thin thread. He didn't know what it would take for that thread to break, and he hoped he never found out. As bad as things had been for her the last weekend they'd been together, that'd been mental anguish, not physical.

"Is there anything I can do?" He carefully laid her back down against the pillow.

"Could you read to me?"

He couldn't have been more startled. He'd been contemplating some kind of physical relief. Holding her hand, talking to her, maybe stroking her hair. They had washed it, he saw, and the dried blood was gone. Still, it was dull and limp. Nothing like the glorious mane he was used to seeing.

"What would you like me to read to you?"

He'd glimpsed every genre of book on her shelves and didn't even try to guess what she had in mind. She pointed to a book on the bedside table, and he picked it up. The cover held the name of the book and the author, whose name was not familiar to him. He flipped to the bookmark, pulling it from the book and laying it on the desk. He quickly scanned the page and chuckled ruefully. "Really, Rielle? Can't you pick something else?" He perused her shelf and listed off a dozen authors whose books he was familiar with.

"You asked me what you could do for me. You could read me this book."

Her eyes were glassy from the drugs, and he questioned how far he might get before she fell asleep. Still, if this was what she wanted, he'd do it—but only for her, he told himself.

Amazingly, she'd stopped right at the beginning of a very erotic bout of lovemaking. Still, he started to read. As he continued, however, he discovered virtually every page was erotic, with little activity outside of the bedroom. It was four pages before he got to the first spanking scene. As he read, he became aroused. The little upturn of her lips told him she was aware exactly what this was doing to him. Well, if this made her happy, at least one of them was going to get their proverbial rocks off.

By the tenth page, however, she slipped into sleep. Sheena had advised him that once she settled with the powerful narcotics, she'd most likely sleep through the night.

Joining her had never been an option since any movement on his part might bring her pain. He'd keep the door to the dungeon open. Rising, he flipped off the light. *Huh.* A weird glow in the room caught his attention. His raised his gaze, and his eyes widened. The ceiling was covered in stars and planets made of a material that absorbed light and glowed in return. It was kind of like a child's bedroom, decked out to keep away the monsters and other terrible things that might come in the night.

This must be her safety blanket. Some people used night-lights, but Rielle used constellations. Otherwise, no light permeated the room because it lacked a window. Claustrophobic. Yet she'd feel safe—or safer—with the glow. He left her door open so he'd hear if she called for him.

After grabbing the overnight bag he'd brought, he stripped out of his clothes. Time to rid himself of the remnants of the day. There'd been a brawl off school property, and the police had been called. The four young men had been surprised to find out the school would be involved. Parents, police, the young men in question, and he had held a conference. Two days of suspension and ten hours of community service had been the outcome. No one had wanted to bring the kids to the police station, but they needed to learn fighting was never the answer. After a bit of prodding and some intimidation from the police, the teens had admitted the whole thing was over a girl.

He was familiar with the young woman in question and wasn't sure she was worth fighting over, but shelved that uncharitable thought. Just because the girl went through boyfriends like underwear didn't make her a slut. But if it had been in his purview, he would've intervened. As long as she kept her extracurricular activities off school property, it was beyond his power to intercede. He hoped she used birth control.

Tension slipped into his shoulders. A shower was in order. Rielle's shower was completely decked out with multiple heads and jet sprays, and soon he was relaxing. Of course that got him thinking about her. How sexy she'd looked the night he took her out for dinner. How sexy she'd looked when she stripped for him that night. How she'd sighed when he removed the nipple clamps. How tight she'd been when he fucked her with the plug in place.

The memory of the erotica she coaxed him to read came flashing back. She appreciated he was going to get aroused and not be able to do anything about it. Well, he could now. He fisted his already-throbbing cock. If he couldn't have her, he could have the next best thing. Fuck, she was beautiful. Not as she was tonight, but how she'd been the night he whipped her. He'd made her happy that night. *He'd* been happy that night.

His eyes closed as he flashed back to what it was like to be deep-throated by her. A little scraping of teeth, sucking on his head, enveloping him in her intense heat. His balls drew up, and he let go.

Would he ever get to fuck her again?

He could hope, but he couldn't be sure.

****

Gage came instantly awake. A light came through the open door to the dungeon. There hadn't been another choice, so he'd sucked it up and tried to make the best of sleeping in there.

Now daylight crept down the hallway. Had she stirred? In an instant he was on his feet and about to walk over to her room when the woman herself groaned. He pivoted and headed to the bathroom. Opening the door, he didn't bat an eyelash when he found her on the toilet.

"Gage." Her gasp was indignant.

"You should've called me. How did you make it out here by yourself?" His tone was sharp.

"With some difficulty, now will you leave? I have to pee."

"Go ahead." He made no move to leave.

She grumbled something unintelligible and took a piss. "Bastard."

"You can't hide from me anymore, Rielle. Everything on the table."

"Can you draw me a bath?"

"What about your ribs?"

"You can tape the ribs again after the bath. Look, I haven't had a shower or bath in a week. Sponge baths suck, and Sheena said as long as I took care and supervised, I could have a bath." Her eyes gleamed. "Please, Gage, I want to be clean."

He couldn't fault her for that, so he ran the water. "How hot?"

"As hot as you can stand it. I need to wipe the filth off me."

He considered asking what filth she referred to but refrained. The dirt was metaphorical, not literal. As the room steamed, he gently removed first the nightgown and the tape. So he might have a clue as to how to re-tape it, he scrutinized the bandage.

Turning off the taps, he cringed after dipping a finger in the water. "Are you sure?"

"Yes." With great certainty. "Please help me."

He complied, helping her from toilet to tub. She didn't straighten, instead bending at the waist, taking those short, shallow breaths that scared him.

Putting her foot in the tub, she hissed.

"It's too hot, Rielle. Let me add some cold water."

"No." Short and sharp. "I can handle this. I need this."

He almost made a snarky comment about masochists, but this probably wasn't the right time to criticize or tease her. Instead, he helped her sink into the cocoon of warmth and security.

She closed her eyes, lying back against the tub, letting out a long sigh.

Snagging a hand towel, he rolled it, then placed it behind her neck, receiving a hum of gratitude in return. "Have you taken your painkiller this morning?"

As expected, her chin tilted mutinously. "I don't need them. I'm better."

He scanned her body, ending at her eyes.

"It looks worse than it is."

"Sheena said you'd fight me." He frowned at her. "Your impudence isn't a total surprise, but we're not debating this. You took a pill twelve hours ago. You know you're due for another one."

Her eyes shone with pleading. "They make me nauseous. They make me groggy, like I'm in a fog. I've been in that fog for the better part of a week. Please," she beseeched, "don't make me."

Forcing her wasn't an option, but she wasn't referring to physical power. He could order her, and tempting as that was, he didn't want to step into that role. "How about a compromise?"

Her look of eagerness was priceless.

"You take some extra-strength ibuprofen but agree to switch to narcotics if the pain overwhelms you. And before you get too excited, I'm not putting up with deception and lies. If I ask you how much it hurts, I expect you to be honest with me."

"You mean like a pain scale?"

That hadn't been what he meant, but this was something concrete he might work with. "So what's your pain level now? And be aware I saw how you barely got from toilet to tub."

"Let's say I'm at a five."

He scrutinized her carefully. "It's higher than that."

"But it's my scale." Her tone was petulant. "If I'm at a ten, then I'm dying. I'm nowhere near that."

"Have you ever endured a ten?"

She avoided his gaze, finally looking up through hooded eyes. That would be a "yes."

"Five, it is." He shook out two anti-inflammatory pills, put some cold water in a glass, and handed both to her. Without further complaint, she downed them.

Slowly her eyes drifted shut. The pain pills hadn't kicked in yet, but Rielle relaxed now she'd won the fight.

Uncanny how he'd been certain there would be a battle. How many more might there be over the next few days? And he hoped Sheena's friend was a battle-axe, or Rielle might clash—and win—a fight with her. Not everyone had his tenacity.

Whatever.

If the nurse pushed Rielle into rest, relaxation, and use of painkillers, he'd be grateful. He wasn't worried about addiction because Rielle would stop as soon as possible—of that he had no doubt.

She opened her eyes. "Can you help me wash my hair?"

Since he doubted she could lift her arms up to her head, he assumed he would be doing that. He examined and planned out the situation. "Please tell me we aren't going to shampoo then condition then—"

"No." He was pleased to see her lips curl upward. "I'm a pretty plain girl. I use a two-in-one."

Whatever that meant. His wife had used a myriad of concoctions to try to control her corkscrew curls. Rielle's hair was straight, but that didn't mean a lot of work wasn't involved.

He helped her slip farther into the tub to wet her hair. He eased her forward, put a generous dollop of shampoo on his hands, and began the laborious task of working it into her hair. Extending halfway down her back, her hair was heavy in his hands, and he added more shampoo to make sure he cleaned all the silken locks. She practically purred in bliss as he massaged her scalp. Finally she re-submerged, and he washed the last of the suds from her head. He wrapped her hair in a towel and let her head fall back again, using the roll to support her neck. Her eyes drifted shut.

"Are you ready to get out?"

"In a minute. Just give me a minute."

She could take all the time she wanted, but eventually the water was going to cool. "More hot water?"

"Mmm." That was agreement, right? Pulling the plug to empty some of the cooling liquid, he turned the hot water as high as he was able to tolerate it, letting the tub refill. When he was finished, he sat back down on the floor.

"Gage?"

"Yes."

"Aren't you cold?"

He was surprised. He'd worn a T-shirt and boxer shorts to bed for the sake of propriety, but he wasn't cold. "Sweetheart, there's enough steam in here for me to be sweating."

"Okay." The words came out on a sigh of breath. "Just checking."

"You're very considerate." He stretched to place his hand on her cheek. At that exact moment she shifted, and as he moved his hand out of the way, he dipped into the water and brushed her breast.

Her eyes shot open in surprise.

"Sorry." His face flamed as he mumbled. "That was unintentional."

He was pulling his hand back when she snaked up her hand. She grasped his wrist, guiding him back to her breast.

"Rielle." His voice was a little strangled. But when his fingers touched her nipple, it pebbled.

She arched her back slightly, but it was enough. Her breast fit nicely into his hand, as it always had. Her eyes drifted shut. "Make me feel good, Gage, please. It's been too long."

His cock hardened as he cupped her breast. Although his release the previous night had been nice, it was nothing like the last time they'd fucked. He'd been up to his balls in her ass, she moaning in ecstasy. This day, though, wasn't about him. It was about her. Maybe if he could bring her some physical release, she might be better able to manage the pain. Regardless, she asked, and he tried to never deny her when it was in his power to fulfill her requests.

He slid her breast against his palm, fighting for purchase because it was slippery, pleased when he got a good hold.

She moaned, her eyelids fluttering.

With his other hand, he tweaked her nipple. Hard. This time, the moan rumbled through her chest. She liked that, so he trailed his hand to the underside of her breast. He used the lightest of touches down her chest, mindful of the ribs. How many had been broken? *Three?* Had the fifth rib been broken again, or were these three different ribs? Did it matter? She had to be in agony.

When his hand passed her waist, her lips curled, her hips tilted upward, and her knees fell apart.

Excellent. He had access and permission.

At the first press of his fingers against her clit, she giggled.

That was not the response he'd been expecting.

She didn't open her eyes. "It feels weird, but nice, you know?"

He chuckled.

"Can you do it again?"

He complied, applying more pressure this time. As with her breast, he fought to get a good position, pressing his finger against her. Sweep after sweep and he was unsure if he was making any progress, when her lower lip slipped between her teeth.

A lovely flush made its way from her breasts to cheeks. It was such a treat to see some pink in her coloring.

When he pulled his finger away from her clit, she groaned. She moaned when he slipped two fingers inside her. The water was now up to the sleeve of his T-shirt, but he didn't give a damn. A subtle twist of his wrist and he hit her G-spot.

"Oh my God." Her voice was replete with reverence. "Please keep doing whatever it is you're doing."

He smothered a grin and redoubled his efforts to please her. He doubted she knew what a G-spot was, let alone that she could do this herself. Flashing to their last scene together, he cringed. He shouldn't have forced her. Holding her breathtaking naïveté against her had been cruel. *Water under the bridge.* He pressed his fingers to the rigid skin and rubbed.

Using his other hand, he clasped her ear in that sensitive spot she had, right where the lobe met her jaw. *Success.* She was being swept along with something that was greater than herself.

"Let go." He murmured the words in her ear, nipping at the lobe. "Feel the pleasure. Let it flow over you like warm water."

Her head shook, but she didn't open her eyes.

"Let go." He put a touch of command in his voice. To that, she responded by mindlessly pressing down against his fingers. "Rielle, listen to me. I know you can do this."

"I can't." Even as she arched against him, she whispered desperately. God, she was close. So close he could taste victory. Then she arched against him and let out a cry that was not pleasure.

His fingers fell from her, and as quickly as he could, he grasped under her arms, pulling her forward and allowing her to cradle her injured ribs. What the hell had he been thinking? He was so fucking obsessed with giving her an orgasm he put her in physical jeopardy. As a nurse, he sucked shit.

Her breathing was raspy and shallow. "I want to get out of here," she whispered.

"Okay." Keeping his arms beneath hers, he eased her out of the water and sat her down on the toilet. He grabbed a towel and gently, but persistently, dried her body. Afraid to put any pressure against tender skin, he used gentle strokes, meant to soothe. He needed to work quickly to get her dry so he could tape her ribs. He also didn't want her to get cold as the air was chilled with the steam gone.

Her head drooped forward, and her eyes were squeezed shut. *Fuck pain scales*. He grabbed the bottle of narcotics. That she didn't resist him when he placed the pills in her mouth told him everything. She gulped the water, and the band across his chest lessened a little. It had been squeezing tightly since she made that cry. That cry of intense pain had torn right through him.

"I'm sorry." He finished drying her.

She didn't respond.

He retrieved the tape. Well, damn. He was going to need help from her. "Can you cross your arms in front of you and lift them a bit?"

As she moved her arms to comply, he guided them. Finding another way, he draped her arms over his shoulders, carrying most of the weight. It was hard for him to see, but he figured he could apply the tape by touch. It took him longer than he liked, but as he scrutinized his work, he was pleased with the result. He wouldn't win any awards, but it should ease some of the pressure and pain.

"I'm going to put your gown back on."

She opened her agony-filled eyes. "First, you need to brush my hair."

"Okay." He pulled off the towel. Her hair was mostly dry, so he took her brush and ran it from her scalp to the tip.

"Gage, if you don't apply some pressure to get out the tangles, we'll be here all day."

"I didn't want to hurt you." The absurdity of the comment struck him. Taking a handful of hair, he held it at the scalp and brushed with more vigor. She winced but said nothing. Pretty soon, her hair was tangle-free. "How do you want it?"

"In a ponytail. There's an elastic in the medicine cabinet."

He located the hair elastic and secured it around her hair. He grasped her gown and pulled it on. She shivered, and he groaned inwardly. The relaxation and warmth from the bath were gone, and it took entirely too long to get her back into her gown.

"Okay, sweetheart, let's get you tucked into bed."

"Not bed." Her grumble amused him, even in the seriousness of the moment.

"If not bed, where?" God, let her not be thinking of

her pallet on the floor.

"The couch?" She opened her eyes and gazed into his. "Please, Gage, I'm tired of being cooped up in bed."

He hadn't noticed whether the couch was comfortable, but a blanket and a pillow could do wonders. He scooped Rielle into his arms as gently as possible and made his way to the couch. It was well padded, so he gave in to her request. He eased her down and held out his hands. "You stay here while I go get a blanket and a pillow." Taking her closed eyes as assent, he headed to her bedroom, hoping he might find the requisite materials to make the living room more comfortable than the chrome and leather might normally be.

He located a wool blanket on the closet shelf, and he grabbed her pillow. Her eyes were closed when he returned, so he put down the pillow and guided her to lie down. He placed the blanket over her, tucking it under her feet.

"Thank you." The words were quiet and laboriously uttered.

"My pleasure. I'm going to get dressed and make some breakfast." He took a step back. "Up for some food?"

"Not on your life." She mumbled the words and then placed her fingers to her lips as if she were about to vomit but needed to hold it in.

"One vanilla protein shake coming up."

She didn't smile.

****

His T-shirt was wet, so he hung it up to dry. He tossed on jeans and a sweater as quickly as he could, not wanting to leave her alone for too long. He needn't have worried, however. She was fast asleep. Her lips were pursed, lines of pain etched on her face, and her color was an unnatural gray. But she was asleep, and that had to be worth something.

He made himself a bowl of cereal using the last of the soy milk. A quick glance in the fridge told him some grocery shopping was in order. She used a service, but obviously they hadn't come during the past week or more. He tossed the rotting fruits and vegetables into the garbage and took his breakfast into the living room, needing to keep an eye on her.

He sat quietly and watched her. She lay on her side, and although he couldn't see the rise and fall of her chest, he sensed each breath. Each time, he waited to make sure there would be another one. When finished with his food, he relaxed. Her brow was no longer creased, and her breathing seemed less labored.

After going to the kitchen, he washed out his bowl and grabbed a bottle of water before moving back to the living room. He glanced around, at loose ends. He'd worked hard all week, often staying late into the night so he wouldn't have any work to bring home. Of course, he hadn't reasoned out that she'd be asleep this much. In retrospect, he probably should've planned this more carefully. He hadn't brought his laptop, a single report, or even the book he was reading whenever he had a spare moment—which was never. He'd been trying to finish that book since the beginning of school, and now that October was well and truly entrenched, he saw what a folly it'd been. Maybe by Christmas.

Amazing. This was the first time in more than two years that he'd prepared for Christmas without a heavy heart. Christmas had always been Cara's favorite time of year, and they had hosted many parties for family and friends. The past two years he hadn't put up a single decoration, hadn't hung a single Christmas light. Tactfully, no one in the neighborhood had said anything, but there must've been talk. Maybe this year he might dig into those boxes without feeling such anguish.

Okay, so it was a thought. That still left him with nothing to do at this moment. Well, she had a bookcase full of books—surely there'd be something of interest. In the end, he settled for the book he'd read to her the previous night. It had piqued his curiosity, and he started from the beginning. He expected erotic fluff, but he found himself becoming engaged with the book. It was being told from a slave's perspective, and he was drawn into her story. How she'd been introduced to the lifestyle, how it'd fit like a glove. How she was convinced she'd always been destined to be a slave. How much devotion she felt for her Master and how acute her suffering when they were apart.

The glimpses of the Master were from her perspective, but how had the Master handled the awesome responsibility of having to care for someone with such intensity? The love the slave had for her Master reminded him of his love for Cara, but subtle differences were notable. Complete devotion took love to a new and heightened level of danger. To put so much of oneself into the service of another…

Had Rielle been like this with Mr. X? She said she supposed herself in love with him, but had it been simple gratitude? The man had offered her security and stability like she'd never been privy to. He'd kept her father in jail. Was it any wonder she believed herself beholden to him?

As he left off his contemplation and began to read again, something in the room shifted. He lowered the book, catching the cat-who-ate-the-cream grin on her face. It warmed his heart. Ordering his body not to react, he held up the book in a helpless gesture, grinning sheepishly. "What can I say? I was intrigued."

"And?"

Was she asking his opinion about the book or what he thought about the story? Because they were two very different things.

"The book is well-written and the subject matter intriguing."

"That's an evasive answer." Her brow arched, the corners of her lips curling. "You won't spoil the ending for me. I've read it several times."

"A how-to manual?"

Now her lips faintly twisted upward. "You could say that."

"Was it like this for you? I mean, this is some intense shit."

"Or was I playing at it?" Her façade slipped. "I was a twenty-four-seven slave, Gage, and I didn't have a single hesitation about it. I lived to please my Master, and he lived to dominate me."

He pointed to the cover. "The couple in this book are married. Why did he never marry you?"

"I'm more than twenty years his junior, to start with. He'd have been judged as robbing the cradle or looking for a trophy wife. Also, I had nothing to offer him. He needed—needs—deep political ties. His wife was recently widowed from one of the richest men in

Canada and is the daughter of a former Premier of British Columbia. She has pedigree and endlessly deep pockets. He's wealthy, but nothing compared to her. She can support him all the way to the top. I had nothing to offer him." The desolation he'd come to associate with Rielle's reflections on her former Master wasn't as sharp today. Maybe the water was sanding the edges of the hurt like it did the rocks on the shoreline.

Arguing with her would be pointless. As a young lawyer saddled with student debt, she had no connections. But to be cast aside so cruelly when she believed herself so much in love… "Would you have stayed with him?"

She broke eye contact, gazing up toward the ceiling and the unseen universe. "At first, after the wedding, he kept coming around. I wasn't the 'other woman' because she didn't love him. She was with him because she wanted to be close to power. They used each other, whereas my devotion to him was pure. It came from the heart."

"What happened?"

"She suspected something and had him investigated. She pointed out if her investigator found me after mere days, what would his political opponents be able to dig up given enough time? She issued an ultimatum, and smart man he was, he took it. My only consolation is misery loves company. Two Dominants together never works."

He rubbed his forehead. He and Cara had been equals outside of their playtime, but she never tried to dominate him. It hadn't suited either of them.

"How are you so certain she's a Dominant?"

"His balls are in her claws. It would never, in a

Gabbi Black

million years, occur to me to do something like that to a man."

"Maybe she's a closet submissive."

That brought a snicker and a roll of the eyes. "She has brass balls."

"He said that?"

"While he was fucking my face. He kept telling me over and over how much he hated her for controlling their lives. When he drilled my ass, he ranted about how she emasculated him. When he whipped me, he recounted the nasty things he wanted to inflict upon her. I was a surrogate of sorts."

Gage flinched. If he lived a lifetime without learning those details, he'd be happy. His stomach clenched at the image of the ubiquitous Mr. X doing anything with Rielle. Doing anything *to* Rielle. But wasn't he guilty of doing the same thing? Hadn't he thought about Cara when with Rielle? Hadn't he made comparisons between the two? But it wasn't the same thing because he kept his observations to himself. And when he'd been inside Rielle, Cara had been nowhere to be found.

He sought equilibrium, holding up the book. "Does he love her?"

Her brow furrowed. "He doesn't just take care of her physical needs. He takes care of her emotional ones. When he goes away, he makes sure she's well cared for."

"By giving her to someone else?"

"You're missing the point. She can't function without structure and routine." A little V appeared between her brows; she was preparing an argument, to plead her case. "He makes sure her needs are met.

That's powerful, Gage. Please don't ever doubt it."

"Would you ever be with someone who isn't a Dominant?"

"That's like asking a fish if he'll ever live outside of water. He might, but he'll never try because it will probably kill him."

He tried to sort out the metaphor. "In other words, you could try to be with a regular man, but you would probably die?"

"Or suffocate from kindness."

"Is that how you see me? As being kind, I mean."

"There's compassion and there's kindness. You can care about someone without…you know what I mean."

Shaking his head, he met her gaze. "Are you saying my only worth to you is as a Dominant? As someone who tells you what to do and who to be?"

A long, pain-filled breath escaped. "That's too simplistic, Gage, and not fair. I don't know who you are to me. Right now, I don't know much of anything."

Instantly contrite, he rubbed his breastbone. "That wasn't fair of me."

Another sigh, this one deeper. "These drugs make me foggy, but I'm rational right now."

"Can you handle some food?"

Her brows furrowed as she pondered his question. "Not now. I'm going to put my head down again." Her head hadn't moved from the pillow, but her meaning was clear.

"Will you be okay if I go grocery shopping? Your fridge is bare."

Her hand waved. And like that, eyes closed, she was out again.

Directions to the closest grocery store he could obtain from the security guard. Fixing Rielle's life was a whole different kettle of fish.

****

It was mid-afternoon before she stirred again. She let him help her sit, insisting on walking to the bathroom instead of being carried. It took some time, but they managed. In respect for her efforts, he let her pee alone.

When they got back to the couch, he propped her up. She seemed less groggy—more lucid—but he couldn't be sure. He needed to get some liquids into her—and food, if possible. Negotiations took far too long, but as she sipped her mixed berry shake, immeasurable relief washed over him.

She was recalcitrant, but it was bluster to disguise the discomfort.

"Are you up for watching a movie this evening?"

With clear eyes and a bit of color in her cheeks, she managed a hesitant smile. "But first…would it be okay if we turn on the twenty-four-hour news channel? I feel like I've been out of touch for a year instead of a week. We don't have to leave it on for long." The words were said in a rush to assure him. "Just long enough for me to read the ticker at the bottom of the screen."

"Rielle, it's acceptable to watch the news, great, even. I watch it getting ready for work every morning and catch the national newscast before bed." Two constants in his life. His brow furrowed. "Why did you think it would bother me?"

She shifted uncomfortably, and not because of physical pain.

"He discouraged you from doing it, didn't he?"

"He said he didn't need an educated slave, just a slutty one."

"Jesus Christ. You're an intelligent woman with an innate curiosity. He knew you were a lawyer and yet still expected you to remain ignorant of world affairs?"

Her chin rose defiantly. "But I didn't listen to him. When he wasn't here, I watched the news. I didn't try to share my…insights…with him again."

He snickered but refrained from commenting. What else was there to say? Would they ever have a conversation without Mr. X popping up? The man was part of her past—a huge part. In fact, in this condo, his specter always loomed large over them.

"Will you consider coming home with me?" He blurted out the question before having the chance to reflect on the wisdom or significance of the request.

She stopped mid-sip. "You're asking me to move in with you?" She couldn't have looked more shocked if he'd told her clouds were made of marshmallows.

"Not so much you moving in with me as you spending some time with me. Maybe next weekend? I can come and get you Friday night and bring you home on Sunday." A plan coalesced in his mind.

The look of confusion became a look of terror. "I can't leave here, Gage."

"That's ridiculous. It's bullshit, and you know it." He met her gaze directly. "What are you really afraid of? I mean, we went out to dinner. We went to a movie. How is this any different?"

"It is and you know it." Her voice carried less conviction.

"What about me?" He demanded an answer, pushing his advantage. "What if I want you to come with me?"

"Are you ordering me to do this?"

What a quagmire he'd stepped into. If he asked and she said "no," there was an end to it. If he commanded her as her Dominant and she said "yes," would she come because she wanted to or because she believed she ought to obey? On the other hand, if he didn't push, she might remain trapped there until she died. Or until she got lonely again and ventured back to Club Kink, which would bring all kinds of hurt.

"What about we start with me asking and end with me ordering?" *God, let this not be a hard limit.*

"It doesn't make sense for you to make the trip twice..." She was getting desperate, scraping the bottom of the barrel.

"What's really going on, Rielle?" He stared at her, trying to divine the truth. When nothing came, he growled out of sheer exasperation. "It's an order, Rielle. It's nonnegotiable."

She bobbed her head, slowly at first, but with more conviction. "Yes, Sir."

Well, that was incredibly unhelpful. Was she coming as his submissive or as...someone he cared about? Because sex and playing would be off the table for weeks given the weakened state of her body.

"Well, your Master is proud of your courage, if not your honesty."

She appeared abashed. "I..." She took a deep breath and yet again winced.

He wanted to push, but he'd earned her agreement, and that was worth something. She handed him the empty container of protein shake, and his stomach unclenched a bit, the worry abating an inch. "Good girl."

As always, she preened under the praise. He disliked using "girl," yet it evoked the most honest reactions from her. Was that because of Mr. X? Something he had—or had not—called her? Or did it go further back? Something from her young childhood? Or maybe it was as simple as her understanding he meant it genuinely. It was sincerity in the face of her obvious attempts to please him. Preening was good; sulking was not.

"Now do you watch CNN or CNC—the Canada News Channel?" In other words, American or Canadian?

Both, apparently. She watched the chyron intently, and he didn't dare make a comment about anything on the news. Watching the ticker and the anchor at the same time was beyond him, but apparently she possessed that particular talent.

The lead-off story on CNN caught his attention.

Another school shooting.

This one in…Wyoming? The kid had brought a shotgun and a handgun and had gone on a rampage in the cafeteria at lunchtime. Eight dead, twelve injured, some critically.

When the gunman was surrounded, he'd killed himself. Heroes were emerging. Two teachers and the principal had run toward the gunfire. One teacher was wounded and not expected to live. The phys-ed teacher and the principal were both dead. But they had bought time, one student explained. While they advanced on the gunman, more students had escaped.

Because it was a rural school, little footage that normally accompanied such incidents was available. No shots of ambulances pulling away, parents being reunited with their children. The footage from the previous night was the parking lot with the principal's and teachers' cars. He wondered about that. Some colleagues or family members would have to come and get those cars. Maybe a police officer would drive them back, as a favor to the family. What if he faced that situation?

Oh God, please, no.

A student was being interviewed. Eerily calm, she recounted realizing escape was impossible and hiding under a table. Yes, she'd witnessed the principal trying to approach Mel, the student. Mrs. Lucerne had tried to reason with the gunman and had been shot in her head for her trouble. Still, the girl said, more students escaped. But it was sad because Mrs. Lucerne's daughter had given birth two days earlier to the principal's first grandchild.

Would she ever forget what she had seen? The teenager—God, she was young—shot the reporter a look as if the man was an idiot, which he was. No, she'd never forget. Her best friend had been shot in the stomach, died holding her hand.

As more footage of the makeshift memorial scrolled across the screen, his breath caught. Someone had created a cross for each of the dead and a heart for each of the injured.

As the camera panned, the disembodied voice pointed out nine crosses, including one for the gunman. Fewer flowers adorned his cross, but still…the woman who made the memorial pointed out the young man had been a beloved member of the community who volunteered at a local senior's home. They'd mourn his loss.

The tape broke as the station went live to a man and a woman standing in front of a very ordinary-looking, white clapboard house. The man had his arms about the woman, and her hands shook as she spoke.

"Our hearts are broken. Mrs. Lucerne, Mr. Jenkinson, and Ms. Larches were great people and amazing teachers. The students who died—" She stifled a sob. "—were innocents. The injured were innocents. We wish the best for the friends and family of those affected. We pray for our community.

"We don't understand what happened to our baby boy. He was a special young man who did many great things, but none of them will be remembered. We would do anything to undo what's been done. We would do anything to understand why this happened." She hesitated, as if trying to decide whether to continue. "About two months ago, Mel had been diagnosed with a mental illness but was taking his medication. We never had any inkling it wasn't working. Our son had come back to us. None of this excuses what he did. We"—she squeezed her husband's hand—"would trade our lives to bring back those victims."

She glanced up from the paper she'd been reading, pain etched in her haggard features. "We pray for the lost and the hurt and ask for privacy to mourn our own loss." She folded the paper neatly, then she and her husband supported each other as they entered their ordinary house on a very ordinary-looking street in what was probably a very ordinary neighborhood.

Jarringly, the anchor reappeared with a psychologist at the ready. The expert spoke of how the shooter was almost eighteen and possibly had schizophrenia. Gage's mind, however, was not on the expert. It was on the cross bearing the gunman's name. Might he be forgiving if someone had come into his school and massacred his students?

Pulled from his reverie, he realized Rielle's hand was on his shoulder. He'd leaned forward when he first heard the news. Had rested his forearms on his thighs and clasped his hands together tightly. Had kept fighting the sense of unreality. Now her gentle touch pulled him away from Wyoming and back to a brilliantly sunny Saturday afternoon. Her condo faced west, and the sunlight poured in. He rose to tilt the blinds while she shut off the television.

"I'm sorry."

He pivoted from the windows in confusion, bewildered. Her reactions were never what he expected. "What are you sorry for?"

"I asked if we could watch the news. If I'd suggested a movie…"

"Rielle, sweetheart, I needed to see this. Everyone in administration will be talking about this on Monday morning. Most students won't be, but some of them will be on edge. The teaching staff will be warier."

"But this happened in Wyoming."

"A school shooting doesn't respect international boundaries when it comes to bewilderment and grief." Sitting next to her, he pulled her hands into his. "Your hands are freezing." He scrutinized her carefully. "You're cold. Sweetheart, you should've said something."

She offered up a smile, but it faltered. "You were busy, Gage, and I didn't want to distract you."

"Never too busy for you." His response was

vehement as he hoped she understood the unspoken meaning. "Never too busy for you."

He cared. Perhaps too much.

Mindful of her ribs, he settled her into his lap, yanking the blanket over her. He tucked her head against his shoulder and took her hands in his. He blew a warm breath into them, and she exhaled sharply, eyes drifting shut.

Having her in his arms offered at least some reassurance. She was a weight, but it was a comforting one. A week ago she'd been in the hospital, and he'd kept vigil over her, willing her to recover. Now she was in his arms, and he wasn't letting go. Her breath was soft against his neck. It tickled, but he suppressed the giggle. He was a man, after all, and men didn't deign to giggle.

A glance at the windows revealed the sun was dipping behind the condo across the street. Five o'clock by his calculation, and his stomach growled, making demands. He planned rice, boiled corn, and cooked chicken. Bland, yes, but maybe something he might convince her to eat. She needed to build up her strength, and that wasn't going to happen by drinking protein shakes foisted upon her. He hoped the mixed berry flavor he found might tempt her more than plain old vanilla.

She stirred, pulling back to meet his eyes. The need and desire in the amber pools of liquid beseeched him, and he was powerless to resist. When she tugged him toward her, he settled his mouth over hers.

Just a brush.

But she opened to him.

Okay, just a nip.

Then she thrust her tongue in.

A taste? That won't hurt.

One taste wasn't enough, of course, because her desperation matched his own. He wanted nothing more than to press her to the couch and sink into her. He couldn't do that, however, so he settled for rubbing his hand up and down her arm, causing friction and warmth. The blanket slipped, but that didn't matter, as they generated heat of their own.

She snagged his hand, placing it to her breast where the nipple hardened instantly beneath the cotton nightgown. He wanted to get to bare skin, but she was completely covered. Virginal, he'd thought the night before. Now it was a pain in the ass. He massaged her nipple through the fabric, rubbing, creating heat.

This was a woman who couldn't have an orgasm, but her responses matched his own desperation. Nipple play always revved her motor, so he tweaked it. Super hard. In response, she squirmed deliciously, grinding her pussy against his crotch.

Jesus, just one moment. Please, God.

Dying was a real possibility if he didn't get relief. Not to mention blue balls.

Momentarily, their mating dance of tongues slowed as her breath hitched. She began again with renewed vigor, then she pulled back. "I want…"

His cock, already at full attention, straining against his jeans and leaking pre-cum, filled precipitously with more blood, ready to explode. Her legs opened a fraction, and he nearly lost it as her musky arousal, soaking through her nightgown, reached his sensitive nose.

Stop. Broken ribs and bruised kidney versus blue

balls.

The devil's choice if ever one existed.

"What do you want?" Keeping his voice steady proved challenging as his body begged for release. The sooner the better.

Her eyes sparkled with mischief. "Pizza. Deep dish delivery-style pizza with lots of olives."

He placed his hand on her thigh and tugged her a little closer, reveling in the friction.

"Pizza it is." The response was issued with gritted teeth. She knew. His raging hard-on was unmistakable.

The light in her eyes danced in the encroaching shadows. "I'd give you a blow job…"

He risked it, yanking her tight toward him, tugging lightly on her ponytail. "My little minx," he murmured into her neck, flexing his pelvis upward even as he responded. "Where's the number for the pizza place?"

The number on her fridge door was for a little restaurant she frequented, which used whole-wheat crusts and skinned chicken, but she instructed him to dig out the number for one of those places that offered greasy crusts and heaps of cheese. His mouth watered thinking about it. Since he was a fan of pineapple and she wrinkled her nose at that, he ordered them each a small pie. Let her enjoy her extra olives. He was grateful her appetite had returned, and he'd feed her anything. Within reason, of course.

While they waited for the pizza, she walked slowly to the washroom where she peed while he retrieved a fresh nightgown. Instead of tossing the used one in the laundry like any sane man would do, behind her back, he tossed it on the bed in the dungeon.

Once she was resettled on the couch, she insisted

Gabbi Black

he select a movie to watch. He went into her bedroom, tidied up a bit, and perused her movie collection. Eclectic had been an accurate assessment. She possessed every Michael Moore documentary, including *Bowling for Columbine*. Ruthlessly pushing aside his memories of the young girl and those grieving parents, he inspected her comedy section. While several ran along more sophisticated humor, he picked the classic *When Harry Met Sally*. He hadn't seen it in years, having watched it years ago with Cara, but now he wanted to form a new memory around one of his favorite films.

Her normally pale face was even whiter when he returned to the living room.

"Problem?"

She wrinkled her nose. "It's a long way to the bathroom and back."

"You wouldn't let me help you." He balked at her stubborn show of independence but had let her make her own decision.

"You were right, and I was wrong." She forced the words out slowly.

"I bet that hurt."

One eyebrow arched. "You'll never know."

He grinned. "But I do know, Rielle. You hate being physically dependent on other people."

Her acknowledgement was grudging, her eyes flashing defiance. "I wanted to give you a blow job. I've never wanted something so much in my life."

Out of gratitude, or from some physical hunger of her own? Did her reasons matter? The sentiment was what counted.

"Maybe tonight you can give me a hand job."

Her eyes lit with excitement. "Oh, I'd love that."

He bet she did and was about to say as much when the intercom ringing interrupted him. He informed the concierge he'd be right down, grabbed his wallet, and headed to the lobby. After giving the delivery driver a hefty tip, he rode the elevator back up to the suite. Dishing out the food took mere moments, and he asked her what she wanted to drink.

"Water, please."

He brought out her plate and water first, met by a mile-wide smile, gratitude shining. *Hmm. Note to self—extra olives and she'd be putty in his hands.* He made a quick trip back to the kitchen, then placed his own food on the coffee table and walked over to the entertainment system. No two ways about it, it was top-of-the-line stuff. Stuff he could never afford on his salary. She was accustomed to the very best, and he was unable to offer her that. Of course, she'd never shown a penchant for the material side of things. She seemed as happy with a movie and pizza as she did with filet mignon and *crème brûlée*. It was a series of contradictions he was only beginning to sort out. With each layer he unwrapped, he discovered more and more depths to her.

Once the opening credits rolled, he settled down next to her, careful not to jostle her too much.

"Thank you." It was simple and heartfelt.

Was it gratitude for the food, or for his nursing, or perhaps, for their relationship? "My pleasure."

****

Halfway through the movie he brought Rielle her painkiller. Twelve hours had passed since the last dose, and her restless motions indicated her discomfort. He also prepared a hot water bottle she gratefully held against her chest.

She cuddled up against him and promptly fell asleep.

After the movie ended, he nudged her awake. He carried her to the bathroom, and she made no objection. Nor did she complain as he carried her to her bedroom. When he tucked her into bed, her eyes barely stayed open.

"I'm tired of this." Her lower lip protruded, and she actually pouted.

He was momentarily stunned since she'd never done that before. He smoothed a few escaped strands of hair from her face. Sitting on the edge of the bed, he pulled the elastic from her hair, letting it cascade down across the pillow. "Promise me you'll call me in the night if you need me."

She closed her eyes without comment. In moments she was asleep.

Putting the pizza in the fridge took no time, and a glance at his watch had him deciding it was too early to go to bed. He hadn't grabbed another film from her room, and since he rarely watched television, the shows were unfamiliar to him. What did he usually do on a Saturday night? Watch a hockey game. He flipped to Hockey Night in Canada and watched the last twenty minutes of the Winnipeg Jets against New Jersey Devils. Happily, Winnipeg won by a commanding score.

Inexplicably driven by some perverse sense of curiosity, he flipped back to CNN. They replayed an interview with one of the victims' parents. Clearly heartbroken, they talked about their daughter and how she aspired to be a pastor. The girl's mother held tight to the cross around her neck. Her daughter's, she said. But the girl hadn't worn it to school that day because she had swim practice.

Through the tears, the mother's face took on a look of serenity. Yes, she knew the gunman. It was a small town, and everyone knew everyone else. Yes, she'd already reached out to his parents and offered her condolences.

He was stunned by the generosity of these people. How could they let go of such resentments so easily? Maybe they saw what he was finally acknowledging. Grief could eat you alive if you let it. Hadn't he railed against the fates over and over again after Cara's death? She'd been the religious one, while he'd been less convinced, but he'd gone along for her sake. After her death, he'd absolutely determined God did not exist.

Might he have grieved less if he'd been a religious man? He'd never know.

A bloodcurdling scream coming from Rielle's room rent the air.

He was on his feet in an instant, moving quickly to her room and flipping on the light.

The sheets were tangled, and she struggled against them.

One of her hands was stuck, and he moved quickly to free it.

Her eyes, wild and wide, shot open at the touch. He backed up a step.

"Rielle, it's okay." He tried for a soothing tone, banking down his own panic. "You're okay." He held his palms out in the universal "I'm not going to hurt you" gesture. When she didn't shrink away, he stretched for her.

Heedless of her ribs, she launched herself into his arms.

He sat by the side of the bed, holding on as tightly as she was. Her hair was damp, and he lifted it away from her shoulders as he continued to rock her gently.

It took forever until the sobs eased into whimpers that transitioned to quiet weeping. She pressed her nose to his chest, rubbing snot against his favorite wool sweater. Well, that was what laundry soap was for.

Finally, she eased away from him and leaned back to meet his gaze. "I'm sorry."

"What are you apologizing for? You had a bad dream." He succumbed to the desire to reassure. "You needed me and I was here." But what would happen when he wasn't there? "Can you tell me what you were dreaming of? What was the nightmare?"

Maybe she didn't remember? When she ducked her head, it was clear she did.

"Was it because of the news? Those kids…"

She shook her head. "No, it wasn't. This is one I have a lot." And she always had to deal with it alone.

"What was it?"

"You'll think it's stupid."

He snagged her chin, guiding it upward so she had to meet his gaze. She closed her eyes to try to sever the contact, but he held firm.

"It's the closet."

"The closet?"

She grew still. "My father locked me in the closet. For hours on end. It was a game he enjoyed because he knew how terrified I was. I begged and pleaded, but he never relented. Often, he sat outside the door and taunted me."

"How old were you?"

"Honestly, I have no memory of the first time it happened. Probably about two. The last time was the day he killed my mother. I witnessed him kill her, and then he dragged me to the closet. He locked me in there, and I stayed for three days—or so they later told me—until the police came. Until Arielle came."

Little wonder her strong attachment to the name.

"I had to go to the bathroom in there, and I was embarrassed when she found me. She swaddled me in a blanket and stayed with me in the ambulance. She stayed with me when they checked me over in the hospital and cleaned me up. I'm sure she was off-duty, but she never left my side. Aside from the black eye, I was dehydrated, but that was it. No lasting physical effects from my captivity."

"*He* knew about that, didn't he? That's why he locked you in the cage."

Her eyes opened, glassy and shimmering from her valiant fight to hold in the tears. "He used it arbitrarily, putting a blanket over so it was completely dark. I'm sure at times I deserved it, but other times…" A lone tear escaped. "He told me it was for my own good. That I needed to get over my irrational fears."

"Fears aren't irrational if they're based in reality. You had a terrifying first six years of life, Rielle, and the fact you survived is a testament to your inner strength."

"I'm not strong, Gage. I can't survive without depending on people, and that makes me weak."

How do I respond? Since words didn't come, he eased her back to the pillow.

She grimaced as she resettled.

"Do you need another painkiller?"

She shook her head. "It's more discomfort than pain. I'm sure it'll ease once I fall asleep. Will you…will you stay? Until I fall asleep? I never have more than one of these a night."

And how many nights did she have them? He was afraid to ask because the answer terrified him. "Do you want me to read to you?"

That brought a slight curl to her lips. "If you promise you'll get a boner."

"Minx." He was secretly pleased with the excuse to finish the book. He walked out to the living room to retrieve it, but by the time he was back, she was asleep. Since he wasn't ready to leave yet, he settled into the chair at her desk and found the place where he had left off.

The slave's Master departed town on business, leaving her with another Master for further training. Had handing Cara over to someone else been a possibility? Would he do that with Rielle? Of course not, he scoffed, even as he found himself intrigued. This new Master was strict and demanded servitude but also displayed moments of tenderness. What was the balance involved in such intense relationships? His curiosity was piqued again.

By the time he finished the book, midnight had come and gone.

She slept deeply, her arms cradling her ribs.

He pressed a kiss to her forehead, a sweep of tenderness engulfing him. He was in way too deep. But how could he leave her? He flipped off the overhead light, glancing at the glowing stickers. She had her night sky, and he had another night in the dungeon. He could jerk off again, of course. Nothing difficult about that. Except he didn't feel like it. He was... He searched for the right word and came up short. *Well, whatever.* He stripped off his sweater, noting the snot on it. He should go to the bathroom and wash it off, but he didn't give a shit.

Again he kept on his boxer shorts and a T-shirt. He slept in the buff at home, and it seemed a little silly not to do the same thing, but he had some sense of propriety. As he climbed into the bed, he conjured a memory, her smell being with him. The light scent of her body cologne. Her musky scent when she was aroused. Rolling his eyes, he snagged her nightgown and pressed it to his nose, inhaling the fabric as a man inhaled the scent of his coffee before taking that first precious sip. Instead of a jolt of energy from the caffeine, his body reacted with a languidness and possibly the fastest boner he'd ever had.

Then his memory took him to the way she appeared. Not as she was now, but how she'd been that first night, when he spanked her, paddled her, and she'd given him a blow job. And, just like that, the boner she teased him about strained farther. Laying the nightgown on the pillow next to him, he yanked down his boxers. With one hand he squeezed his balls while, using pre-cum as lubricant, the other frantically jerked his cock. God, prolonging it wasn't an option as he envisioned fucking her until she screamed out his name.

His orgasm seemed to go on and on as he coaxed every last drop of fluid from his now-flaccid dick. This was going to be the only relief he got for the next little while. Was that any different than it had been before?

He'd gone two years with only the odd masturbatory session, so holding on to the memories of her for a few more weeks until she was healed seemed reasonable.

Wiping his hands on the sheets, he reminded himself to do laundry even as he fell into a black and dreamless sleep.

****

Gage came awake with a bit of a start. Had she called out to him? He rolled out of bed and made his way to her room.

She'd pushed away the sheets again, curled up, arms crossed against her chest.

Hoping he had enough time, he took a shower.

Freshly shaven and invigorated, he stepped from the bathroom, and this time he heard her calling. Barefoot, he padded across the hardwood to her room.

She sat in bed, trying to rise.

He scooped her up, and she looped her arms around his neck, pressing a kiss to his cheek and inhaling deeply.

"I like how you smell."

He chuckled as he carried her across the condo to the bathroom. "It's leftover shaving cream. We don't wear scents at school, so I'm not in the habit of doing so on the weekend. I can find something, if you'd like."

"Nope." Her voice was so cheerful it eased some of the pressure around his chest. "I like a soap-and-water kind of guy, which you clearly are." She held his biceps as he slid her to the ground. "I like your muscles as well."

"I do work out occasionally, but I prefer running." He appreciated that she admired his physique. He wasn't vain, but a compliment from a beautiful woman never went amiss.

She ran her hands from his shoulders down his pecs, gently pressing his abs. "You have a great body."

"Well, thank you. Do you need any help?"

"Nope." Her grin matched her cheerful tone. "I'm a big girl and can pee by myself."

Now it was his turn to chuckle. "I'm glad to hear that. Are you up for some French toast?"

She considered and shook her head. "I could probably manage a shake. My stomach is a little upset this morning."

"Too much pizza?"

"I'm not certain." Her brow furrowed. "The nausea comes and goes."

"Did you tell Dr. Giroux?"

"She said it was a normal reaction to both the painkillers and the pain."

He was relieved to hear her having nausea wasn't a sign of something serious. "I'll wait outside."

"Could you get my pajamas? I need to get out of this gown."

Comprehending the sentiment, he was grateful to be given a task. "Happy to grab them."

When he opened the closet, however, he found several pairs including a deep purple lounging set, a satin ruby red short set, as well as a flannel mint green set with snowflakes. Since they were well into autumn, he chose the flannel set. A pair of thick wool socks and terry towel robe completed the ensemble.

She sat on the toilet, struggling to get out of her nightgown. With great care, he slipped each arm through the sleeve and pulled it over her head. The bruises didn't look any less vivid, but the other skin had a bit more color to it. She wasn't as ghostly white as she'd been that first night.

Getting her into the pajamas didn't take too much work, and he was pleased with the results as she held up her sock-clad feet.

When he tried to scoop her up, she waylaid him. "I'd like to walk, if that's okay. I need to keep moving."

He was amenable, keeping close at hand as she trudged to the living room. Her face was flushed from effort as she sat down, but she was visibly pleased with herself for that small accomplishment.

He walked to the kitchen, returning with a bottle of water, a painkiller, and a berry protein shake. Her nose wrinkled a fraction as she downed the pill and drank the shake.

He strode back to the kitchen and made himself some toast with marmalade. He rejoined her in the living room and sat in one of the chairs. "What would you like to do today?"

A tilt of her head gave nothing away.

"We could watch the end of *When Harry Met Sally*, because you slept through it."

She shook her head. "I've seen it a dozen times, so it's not necessary." A grumble of frustration escaped. "I'm not being a good hostess."

He arched an eyebrow. "I didn't come here expecting you to…host me." The lewd intention of the words was unmistakable. "I came here to spend time with you. To enjoy your company. Nothing more, so don't feel guilty."

Remembering his nocturnal activities, he rose. "I am going to do some laundry, though. I'll do your sheets as well." He pointed in the direction of the hall.

"In-suite laundry, right?"

"I would try to tell you not to do it, but I'd be wasting my breath, wouldn't I?"

His grin was quick and easy. "Laundry, I can do. Come up with some PG-rated activities? Not so much."

She chuckled as he stripped her bed. He moved to the dungeon, grabbing his sweater, her nightgown, and the sheets. His final stop was the bathroom to scoop up the second nightgown. The washing machine was simple to operate and soon chugged away.

When he returned to the living room, she was scrolling through the PVR. "There's an afternoon hockey game. Vancouver Canucks vs. the Anaheim Ducks."

"You sure you want to watch hockey?"

She rolled her eyes. "What are we going to do, play strip charades? Whip the whore? Strap the naughty nurse?"

He couldn't help it—he laughed. He appreciated she was showing a bit more humor than yesterday. "Okay, hockey it is. But I'm imagining whipping the whore as we speak." He was trying not to, however, but the images came unbidden and rapid-fire.

A knowing grin crept onto her face. Damn woman was making fun of him and loving every minute of it.

"I'm going to make you pay for that."

"I hope you will." She patted the seat next to her on the couch. "Game starts in ten minutes."

****

Despite her earlier protestations of "feeling fine," she soon fell asleep, and he eased her down, cradling her head in his lap. Her breath was soft and warm through the fabric of his jeans. It took more than a little

255

effort to concentrate on the game, especially when the hometown team was losing so badly. In the end, it was a rout, and he was thoroughly unimpressed.

When he attempted to extricate himself, Rielle stirred. "Sorry." He murmured the words as she gazed up at him with sleep-hazed eyes.

"It's okay. I need to get up. Too many liquids."

Again she insisted on walking by herself to and from the bathroom. She hid her face from him, but the effort cost her. When he tried to resettle her on the couch, she pointed to the table. "I want to sit up straight for a bit."

Dubious, he agreed. When she was seated, he pointed to the kitchen. "Pizza?"

Her face flooded with gratitude. "I like the sound of that."

The microwave was efficient, and soon they were digging in to piping-hot pizza.

"When do you need to leave?"

Glancing at his watch, he did a quick mental calculation. "I can stay for another hour or so, but then I need to go back. What time does the nurse arrive tomorrow?"

"About eight tomorrow morning." She yawned. "Tarah's going to stop by before her shift, in case I need anything. She's still got a spare key, so I won't have to get up."

"I don't like leaving you." In fact, the thought made him nauseous as his mind flitted through each scenario of things that might go wrong. He wasn't, by nature, a worrier. Then he'd met Rielle, and all bets were off.

"And I want you to stay, but that's not possible. I'll

manage." She placed a hand on his. "I'll keep the cordless close at hand in case I need it."

She'd confided she didn't own a cell phone and that was why she hadn't texted him.

"Keep it close because I plan to call every night."

Her expression shone with gratitude. "I'd like that."

"And you need to make sure you're packed on Friday so we can head to my place right away."

Her smile slipped. "I thought...I hoped you'd forgotten about that."

"Not a chance, Rielle, so don't make up excuses."

Her uneasy look assured him she was about to do just that.

"I'm scared, Gage."

"I know you are, sweetheart, but this is a fear you need to face."

An hour later he departed, hoping she wouldn't spend too much time obsessing over the upcoming weekend.

Chapter Eight

Rielle was ready to go when Gage arrived at her condo Friday night. She carried a small overnight bag, a purse, and a look of pure misery. When he ordered her into the elevator, they used the same procedure as before. She closed her eyes and held on to him. Now that he understood her claustrophobia, he was more empathetic but no less emphatic. No way was he letting her take the stairs, and she read correctly that was nonnegotiable. He assisted her into his SUV, pulling the seatbelt across her chest as gently as possible. Her cringe gave him a tinge of guilt because this ride out to the valley was going to be taxing on her physically, and possibly emotionally, but he held firm. They needed to do this. He needed to know if she could function outside of the condo. Because he planned on getting her to sell it and find a place where she could start over.

Asleep before they hit the highway, she dozed during the uneventful drive. When they pulled into his driveway, he gently nudged her.

"Already?"

"We're here."

"I'm sorry. I wasn't good company." She tried to suppress a yawn, failing miserably, but offered a sheepish smile.

The attempt warmed his heart, giving him hope. "I had the radio." His assurance mollified her, and he gestured to the house. "Welcome to my humble abode."

She giggled, glancing out at the house.

His front porch light illuminated the walkway, leading up to the rancher. Hard to see in the darkness, it was a simple house in a nice subdivision with most houses looking identical. Not much to differentiate it, except he'd made a life there with Cara. Had been ecstatically happy with her until she left him, miserably lonely without her, and ambivalent about bringing a new woman into his solitary space.

"Need me to carry you?"

"Let me stand up first, and we'll see where I'm at." She offered what he assumed to be a reassuring smile. "I'm much better than I was last weekend."

That was what she'd told him each night they talked. He wanted to believe her, but a weariness had permeated her voice each time they spoke. It was still present, no matter how hard she worked to conceal it. He kept his hands at her waist as she exited the truck.

She placed her hands on his shoulders to steady herself and met his gaze. "You haven't kissed me."

"Happy to oblige." He pressed his lips to her soft ones. It was short and sweet because even if she was healthy, providing a PDA for the entire neighborhood wasn't in the cards. Given the activity level on this street, chances were someone would spot them. He lived in a small town, and gossip was a possibility. Well, more like a probability, but for her sake, he'd risk it. Pulling back from the kiss, he checked her face for signs of discomfort.

"I'm fine." Obviously reading his mind, she added, "I can walk."

He grabbed her bag and offered his arm.

She took it, leaning on him to maneuver the walkway. Her breathing was heavily labored by the time they entered the house. "Whew." She exhaled. "I need to get into shape."

He wasn't impressed with her attempt at humor, but let it go. He'd have to pick his battles carefully. "Have you eaten?"

She shook her head. "Should I have?"

"Of course not. I wondered if you wanted to lie down while I cook."

"No."

Although her response was a little testy for his liking, he again let it go.

"I've spent two weeks lying down. I want to sit up, goddammit."

Opting not to argue, he led her to the kitchen table.

She sat a little gingerly, shifting to find a comfortable position, but closed her eyes in pleasure when she found that sweet spot.

Pasta would be quick and easy, and he put the pot on to boil. "We'll have grilled steaks tomorrow night. It'll be the last time I can use the barbeque before I pack it up for the season."

"Do you grill a lot?"

"A couple of times a month from April to October. I used to do it more when we entertained..." *Shit.* Another Cara memory.

"Gage." Her voice was whisper soft, compelling him to turn so he could see her lips. "I'm not the only one who lives with memories. Yours happen to be more pleasant than mine, but they're no less powerful. You loved your wife, and I'm probably the first woman you've admitted into her space."

"My space," he corrected, but it was only halfhearted because she was correct. "But you're right. You're the first woman I've brought here since Cara. I just…didn't think it would be so awkward."

Her amber eyes glistened in the light from the chandelier over the table. "I can empathize with what you're going through. You were the first man I let into my space after he left."

To Gage, it wasn't the same thing, but she was being respectful, so he wouldn't argue. When water boiled, he broke the spaghetti in half, then dropped it in the pot.

"I didn't make any plans for the weekend, Rielle. I want you to be comfortable here."

Her gaze went from the kitchen table to the family room with its big-screen television. "It's a nice and cozy house, exactly what I would've expected your home to be."

"It's not all flowered wallpaper and tea cozies." With an arched eyebrow he gave her a wicked grin. "I have a playroom. Not as decked out as your dungeon, mind, but a nice space nonetheless."

"Can I see it tonight?" Her eagerness was palpable.

"It's down the stairs." His reply was lame, but there was no way she'd survive the trip down there.

"Then tomorrow. Once I've got some energy."

That indicated how much she was flagging. "Dinner's almost ready," he assured her.

"Okay." She met his gaze, her lips tugging upward. "Will you give me a tour tomorrow?"

Chuckling, he stirred the pasta. "It's pretty boring. Three bedrooms, two bathrooms, walk-out basement…"

"And a playroom."

"And a playroom," he confirmed. "Other than that, nothing special."

She shook her head. "I've never lived in a real home, Gage. We had an apartment before..." She swallowed convulsively. "And after, there were foster homes, but they weren't all that nice. Not like this place." He noted reverence in her voice.

His heart ached for her, the little girl being shuttled between foster placements, never knowing the love of a parent, let alone the security that came from having a permanent home. "I'm sorry you had a rough time, Rielle."

A look of determination crossed her face. "That childhood made me who I am. I learned some tough lessons, but I survived."

But not thrived. Never felt secure enough to spread her wings.

He drained the pasta, adding the sauce. "Store bought, I'm afraid."

"Honestly, it's fine. Cardboard would be appreciated right now."

Pleasure suffused him. "You've gotten your appetite back?"

"With a vengeance. Even the nurse was surprised at how much I ate."

"But that's good, right?" He put the dishes of food on the table and sat.

"It is." Her fingers probed the underside of her right eye. Almost faded, the bruise was more of a memory but a potent reminder of how close she'd come to death. Now it was another of her unconscious gestures. "I don't want to put on too much weight."

No worries about that. If she regained what she had lost, he would be thrilled.

"You're beautiful."

Shit, subtle, buddy? He strove to compliment women on their intelligence, a witty comment, their choice of shoes…anything but their actual physical appearance.

Ducking her head, she took her first bite. Her eyes drifted shut, and she emitted a low moan. "This may be store-bought sauce, but it's still delicious." Her eyes fluttered open, her expression becoming more thoughtful. "I'm not used to someone cooking for me. Nor am I used to cooking for more than one person."

"You didn't cook for him?" Damn him for asking, but curiosity got the better of him.

"Sometimes." Her concession irked. "But he didn't keep me for my cooking skills. He wanted a slutty cock-slave."

If he was offended by the answer, that was on him. He asked the question and was a grown-up who understood the score, not some petulant adolescent with raging hormones.

Seeming to sense his mood, she reached across the table. "It's in the past, Gage."

Was it?

He hesitated, but nothing ventured… "But we've got a different kind of relationship, right?"

"Of course we do. I'm not your slave."

But she'd shown herself more than able at worshipping his cock. How fine was that line anyway?

As they both finished eating, he rose to clear the table. When she moved to help him, he gently brushed her aside, and she remained seated.

"Let's go for a drive tomorrow." He tried for casual, keeping his back to her, lest she see his poker face. "Fresh air and all that. I would love to take you out for dinner."

"But everyone would think you beat me up."

"We'll tell them you were in an accident and it was the airbag." *Like anyone is going to believe that.*

"A drive sounds nice." The long pause almost had him turning to her. "Aside from my trip to Whistler, I can't think of another time when I've left Vancouver."

He dropped the pot he was washing, and it landed with a *thud* in the sink, sloshing water everywhere.

He spun around, unafraid of facing her and letting her witness his dismay. "Wait, what? You're saying you never...how is that even possible? Didn't you go on field trips? Didn't your foster families ever take you on vacation?"

Her expression was thoughtful for a moment, and at length, she shook her head. "I never joined family trips. I'd go stay in another home for the duration. I was born in Vancouver, grew up in Vancouver, went to university in Vancouver, worked in Vancouver."

No wonder Mr. X had taken her to Whistler, far away from the concrete jungle she'd inhabited her entire life. Chances were he'd perceived her narrow confines and exploited her desire to get away from the suffocating restrictions of her existence.

"Never been on an airplane? Never taken a bus or train ride?" How was this possible? It was the twenty-first fucking century.

Her chin tilted defiantly. "I've been on the SkyTrain."

He rolled his eyes, not bothering to hide his

irritation at her flippancy. "Vancouver's rapid transit system doesn't count. Have you ever seen a cow? A horse?"

"I've seen a dog and a cat. I even saw a raccoon crossing the road once."

With her poker face, he had no idea if she was offering this information helpfully or with sarcasm. "That's not what I meant."

She met his stare, amber eyes flashing sparks in the light. "Why do you think I didn't want to come here? I took two tranquilizers to get up the courage."

"I'm sorry." The shame crawled into his bones, but he couldn't completely suppress the pleasure of seeing her riled up. So much better than apathy. "I should have listened to you more carefully. I should have respected your wishes."

I shouldn't have ordered you.

Her gaze broke away, toward the black night outside the window. Normally he didn't draw the drapes, instead opting for the comfort of the pink-tinged glow from the city lights. Tonight, he wished he'd pulled them shut, keeping out the outside world while protecting her from prying eyes. From the world and all its intrusions.

"I'm here now, and I haven't fallen to pieces, so that's something."

He wiped his hands on his jeans. Moving swiftly to her, he then dropped to his haunches and clasped her hands. "It means everything, sweetheart, don't doubt that."

She tugged one hand away, held it aloft for a moment, then ran it through her hair. Discomfort radiated from her every pore.

Was it because he'd lowered himself to her? Her uneasiness prompted him to stand, so he did, placing a kiss to her forehead before straightening. "Good girl."

She basked in the praise.

****

Lying awake that night, he reviewed the hundred or so little decisions he'd made once he decided bringing Rielle to Mission City was the only way to move her forward with her life.

Clean? Check.

Food? Check.

Entertainment? Check.

Separate beds? Double check.

He should've anticipated her annoyance, but her intransigency caught him off-guard. He hadn't been thinking about Cara when he'd made the decision, but Rielle somehow got it in her head this was about his dead wife rather than his concern for her battered and still-tender body.

When he escorted her to the guest bedroom, she begged him, pleaded with him, to stay with her. It was a queen-sized bed, she argued, plenty of space for both of them.

Finally, he put his foot down. This was for *her* benefit, and he knew what was best. She was to stop her bratty behavior, take her fucking painkiller, and go to bed before he was forced to do something drastic.

Her eyes lit at that threat.

No, he assured her, he wasn't going to lay a finger on her. But one more word and he'd put her on speech restriction.

Her eyes had gone as wide as saucers, and she hadn't uttered another word.

He wasn't a big fan of speech restriction—he liked verbal feedback when he played or engaged in a scene—but if it was the only way to deal with her recalcitrance, so be it.

Flipping over, he checked the clock. It was early still, but she'd been clearly exhausted, and wanting to encourage her to go to bed, he headed there himself. A half hour later, he still lay here, wide awake. About to stretch, he paused when he heard the sound.

A whimper.

It was so quiet he questioned if he imagined it, but it came again, still soft. If he'd been asleep, it never would have penetrated his unconsciousness.

Swift as a tiger, he rolled off his bed and made his way to her room. He contemplated knocking but didn't bother.

She was awake, and wide eyes glinted in the light coming from the hallway. The proverbial doe caught in the headlights.

He'd almost hit one, years ago when driving out of town one late night. Only his bright headlights and the deer turning at the perfect moment prevented absolute tragedy. He'd stopped, met the animal's eyes, and she'd leapt away. He was lifting his foot off the brake when two fawns leapt from the dark on one side of the road and crossed directly in front of him, following their mother into the brush on the opposite side of the road. A close call for all involved and a reminder that nature often clashed with humans and both stood to lose everything.

He flipped on the overhead light, and they both blinked at the brightness.

She was plastered against the headboard, her knees

drawn to her chest, arms wrapped tightly around them. She must be enduring a tremendous amount of pain, but she didn't move a muscle. Not as much as a twitch.

"What's going on, Rielle?" He sought an even tone, neither pleading nor demanding.

She continued to stare at him, bug-eyed.

"I haven't put you on speech restriction yet, so cough it up. What's going on?" This time he did let a bit of steel slip into his words.

Still, she said nothing.

He tried a different tack. "What scared you? The dark?" She didn't have her constellations. But she could have flipped on the bedside light. The quiet? She was probably accustomed to city noise, and the lack of sound in the country might be eerie.

Still, she remained mute.

Deciding this was getting them nowhere, he advanced into the room, pleased she didn't pull back any farther. Not that she had anywhere to go. As it was, she'd have marks on her back from the brass slats, she was plastered against them so tightly. For a fleeting moment, he wished he'd had kids of his own. Maybe that would've given him some insight into how to deal with this.

He perched on the edge of the bed, keeping a decorous space between them, taking her hand. He wasn't surprised to find it was freezing. "You need to talk to me." This time it was a gentle and coaxing tone.

A lone tear slipped from her lashes, and another joined it. "I hate my life."

It was whispered so softly he watched her lips to make out the words. Okay, at least he had something to work with. "What part, sweetheart?"

She scrubbed furiously at the tears that now fell with greater frequency. "I hate I'm scared of everything. I hate I have to sleep with a night-light. I hate I can hardly leave the apartment. And I hate I can't be the woman you deserve."

What the hell did that mean?

"Okay." He enunciated the word slowly as he continued. "We can deal with every one of those things. We were doing that, remember? You planned to go to the library. You arranged to go to a café." He let a beat pass. "There's nothing wrong with sleeping with a night-light—lots of people do." He didn't know anyone who did, but that was beside the point. Or maybe he did, and they didn't say anything. Who'd want to admit they couldn't sleep in the dark?

"As for being afraid, Rielle, there are ways to cope with that. There are therapists who specialize in this kind of thing. Some of them will even come to your home for counselling until you're ready to venture out. I have faith, though, because you've left that condo."

"Always with you." The edge in her tone was unmissable.

"Not the night you went to Club Kink." Two could play at this game. "You made it there by yourself."

Her eyes widened as if she'd never considered that.

"Rielle, you have to talk to someone about this. I can offer guidance and order you to do things, but that's not going to solve your problems."

"Why can't it? I meant to go to the library, I really did. Then I got the parole report and…"

He filled in the blanks. What she asked, though, stole his breath. A request for him to be her therapist, Dominant, and…lover? From a distance, no less.

Which gave him an idea. "I'll do it if you agree to move in here."

"I…" The look of terror returned with a vengeance.

"You don't have to decide tonight, but I need you to think seriously about it. You stay here, and we work on this every day. We set goals, make tasks, and move you forward into the life you want to be living."

"I…" Again, words seemed to fail her.

"For tonight, how about we leave on this light?" He flipped on the bedside lamp. "We'll leave your door open and my door open. You can call me if you get scared again."

He chose to take her silence as assent. He eased her toward him, so he could untangle the crossed and frozen limbs. First he uncurled her arms, then pulled her legs away from her chest. She let him, limp as a rag doll now all the fight had gone. Or all the fright had gone. He tucked her under the blankets, smoothing her hair back, pleased her forehead was cool to the touch. "Do you need another painkiller?"

She shook her head.

"I'm right across the hall, okay?"

She waved in acknowledgment.

He flipped off her overhead light and crossed to his room.

It was a long time before he slept.

****

Awareness came upon him in degrees. Early morning light slivered through the slit between the curtains, but he didn't want to open his eyes to greet it. His sleep had been fitful, as he'd kept one ear out for her.

Rielle.

He could smell her. He could taste her. He was enveloped in sense memory. What the…?

Oh, fuck. Fuck, don't stop.

Clever hands enveloped his cock, surprisingly warm given the chill in the air.

He should push her away. Well, ease her away. Because she had to be in pain, right? No, better to go with it. Maybe, just maybe, she needed this as much as he did. They would both pay a price later, of that he had no doubt. But, for now, he'd give himself up to the pleasure.

She took his balls in her hands and his cock into her mouth. He nearly bucked off the bed as, without ceremony, she deep-throated him. Teeth scraped gently along his length as she sucked him. Every time she did this, he lost his mind. The intimacy, the bonding…even if they couldn't air their problems, this bound them together in a way no words could. If a picture was worth a thousand words, her glow after he praised her carried him through the worst of this nightmare. Tousled hair from where he gripped it, lips swollen, body ravaged, showing off his marks like a painting…those were memories he clung to when she turned glacial eyes to him and gave him the cold shoulder. The warmth of her thawing heart was there somewhere, but she was vulnerable, and he had to find the fine line between Dominant and nurturer.

"Fuck, yeah." Ragged breaths matched his pounding heart. "God, Rielle, that's heaven." And it was. He wanted to reach out a tweak her tits, but she was too far away. She no doubt correctly figured he would've stopped her if he'd gotten hold of her, but now it was too late. Now he was about to let loose.

As if sensing how close he was, she drew a finger right along his perineum.

After that, his animal instincts seized him as the orgasm overtook him. He shot hot semen in her mouth, even as she continued to suck and swallow. The spasms went on and on, less powerful than previous ones, but potent nonetheless.

She nuzzled his pubic bone as the ripples lessened, and he sank back into the mattress, boneless.

Little licks and kisses along his flaccid cock provided him with a sense of comfort. Maybe, just maybe, this could be a new beginning. One where the chasm between the two of them wasn't as wide as a crater on the moon.

Reaching for her, he missed as she evaded him.

After springing off the bed, she fled the room before his eyes opened. Surely too fast for her injuries.

Was he supposed to follow her? Jump out of bed after the best blow job he'd ever had? And that said something, as Cara loved giving as much as he enjoyed receiving. It should have been sacrilegious to have Rielle take him here, in this room, but it wasn't. It fucking rocked.

The hot water tank rumbled to life, and the shower in the guest bathroom switched on. In that moment, he enjoyed the afterglow. That she initiated the intimacy this morning was a good sign because he never would have. And now? Well, fucking her in the shower was impossible. The shower was big enough, but her body wasn't ready, right? Obviously she must be better this morning, so maybe the previous night's fright had been an aberration. Well, probably not, but he could hope.

Today they'd go for a drive, and he'd show her

horses. One of his former students worked at a ranch, so he could give her a call and see if she could give them a tour. The fact Rainbow's older sister Kennedy happened to be a psychologist would be a bonus. He could feign ignorance if he had to. Well, his face would give him away, but hopefully it wouldn't matter.

The water switched off, and the image of Rielle stepping from the steam and using the towel to dry off stirred him. Still thinking about his limp dick, he visualized licking that damp off himself, sucking, nipping, even biting to leave his mark. Because he'd almost lost her to her father, the monster, and the grim reaper, the need to claim ownership gripped him.

When the bathroom door opened, he called out. "Do you need me to tape your ribs?"

A beat passed before she responded, voice a little strained. "They don't need to be taped anymore, thank you." Her response was a bit formal, but no big deal.

He was dozing lightly when he smelled coffee. Deciding a quick shower was in order, he made his way to the guest bathroom. The scent of her body cologne still hung fragrant in the steamy air. God, that woman liked her water scalding hot. He hoped she'd left him some hot water, given his tank wasn't super-sized. Well, he wasn't going to be in the shower for long—not with coffee calling him like a siren's song. He ought to feel guilty about letting her cook, but she seemed more limber the previous day when he'd picked her up. As he washed off the sticky residue of his orgasm, he enjoyed that extra moment of pleasure, basking in the memory.

He dressed quickly, craving coffee more and more. And, admittedly, wanting to see her in person and gauge her mood.

Without meeting his gaze, she pointed to the kitchen table, and he obliged her by sitting as she placed toast with marmalade in front of him along with his black coffee. She'd poured herself a bowl of cereal and now added soy milk.

"Thank you."

He understood her gratitude because he'd bought her favorite cereal and soy milk, hoping she might feel at home.

"Thank *you*." He almost added she didn't have to do this, but she needed to be comfortable at home in his space. He watched her covertly, looking for signs of discomfort, but none showed. "Did you take your painkiller this morning?" He wasn't surprised when she nodded.

"I've been up for a couple of hours. I didn't want to make any noise."

"You made a bit of noise when you were blowing me." His tongue was firmly planted in cheek.

Her careful contemplation wasn't the response he'd been hoping for, but he accepted it.

"Let's go out to a horse ranch today. One of my former students works there and has been pestering me to go visit her. Today would be the perfect day. She knows me, so she'll know I wasn't the one who…" He indicated the general area of her face, which showed marked improvement. "Maybe with a bit of concealer, we can use the airbag story. She's discreet—"

"You have to take me back to Vancouver." The words were spoken conversationally, as if she asked him to pass the jam instead of to be taken home.

"I thought we were going to see horses today." He eyed her carefully, desperately seeking some sign, some indication of how he'd misjudged the situation so atrociously. "Is this because of what happened last night?"

Her gaze never veered from her plate, stubbornly defying his unspoken command to look into his eyes.

"You laid out your terms, Gage, and I can't meet them." Finally, she raised her gaze, tipping her chin upward in what could be considered defiance but also might have been defeat. An imperceptible tremor ran through her, but it was gone so quickly he might have dreamed it. And where he might have expected tears—wished for some kind of emotion—there was resolve.

"Tort." She rose from her chair and left the room.
****

The drive to Vancouver was full of a heavy, uncomfortable, yet oddly resigned silence.

And why not?

What was there left to say? He'd put himself on the line, and she hadn't been willing to meet him halfway. Hell, she hadn't been willing to take a single step toward him. There'd been no negotiations, no discussion. A minute after she left the kitchen, she reappeared, overnight bag in hand. He'd begun to imagine he'd dreamed the orgasm when it dawned on him it had been her way of saying goodbye.

Pulling up in front of her building, he sought for words, but none were forthcoming. She didn't look at him when she slipped from the SUV. She didn't turn around once as she headed to the building. Instead, head held high, she walked through the glass doors and back into her prison.

Disgustedly, he put the truck in gear and tore out of there.

Halfway back to his home, he realized he still had her spare keys.

****

Instead of going home, however, he drove through the hills north of Mission City until he came to Healing Horses Ranch. Why was he there? Maybe because anywhere was preferable to home.

His tires crunched the gravel as he navigated the parking lot. As doubts assailed him, he almost reversed when his former student waved. He exited the truck and tucked his keys in his pocket. Uncertain of the reception he was going to get, he stuck out his hand. Instead of taking it, Rainbow stepped up to him and threw her arms around his neck.

He stiffened. It was an instinctual reaction. Teachers didn't touch students. He was breaking the golden rule. But she held on tight, and short of shoving her off, he had no choice but to return the hug.

When she pulled back, a grin lit her face. "Mr. Clayton, I'm glad you're here."

"Please, let's make it Gage, shall we? I'm here on a purely social call."

She cocked her head, indicating she saw through his bald-faced lie, but she let it go, continuing to smile. "Gage, it is." Clearly expecting him to follow, she walked around the side of the ranch house.

The massive horse ring contained several riders on horseback. Doubts surged. *This is a huge mistake.* "Rainbow, I need to leave. What if one of my students is here? Or a former student?" He backed away, but she snatched his hand, halting his escape.

"You'll show discretion." She was about to say more when a gregarious yellow Labrador retriever

276

bounded over.

Unable to suppress unbridled joy, Gage dropped to his haunches and held out his hand, knuckles up. The dog sniffed it for a fraction of a second before launching himself—herself?—at him. A smaller man might've been knocked to the ground, but he managed to stay upright and laughed when the dog gave him a thorough tongue bath on his cheek. "Cute dog." He met Rainbow's gaze as he ducked the industrious face-washing.

She giggled. Not in a childish way, but in the way of a woman who was thoroughly amused. "Tiffany is a special dog. You'll have to excuse the enthusiasm. The last puppy from her litter departed, and she's now unencumbered, free to do whatever she wants. For her, that means accosting anyone and everyone."

He scratched behind Tiffany's ears. "No more puppies, eh? You must be relieved."

The dog gave him a sharp *woof* as if she understood what he said. Another car pulled in, and Tiffany was off.

He stood and ran his hands up and down his jeans, wiping off the dog fur.

Tiffany waited with barely leashed patience until the door opened, and she barreled into the next victim. Or visitor, depending on perspective.

The young woman waved at Rainbow, who waved back before she turned, placing a hand on his arm. "I have to go, but I'll be back. Feel free to walk around. We're informal around here." Then she was gone.

He shuffled his feet and glanced around, trying not to make eye contact with anyone. Wandering over to the fence, he watched horses and their riders as they made their way around the ring. It was impossible to distinguish between patients and therapists. Over the years, he'd referred any number of students and heard good things, but he'd never visited himself.

"It's not just about horses." The voice next to him was soft but confident. "We start by getting clients to take care of the horses. Bonds grow, and eventually, the clients understand they're safe. After that, healing starts." The newcomer held out her hand. "Kennedy Dixon."

He returned the firm shake. "Gage Clayton."

"Oh, I know who you are." Her lips curled upward in a mischievous way until she took in his appearance, and then her expression changed. "Why don't we go into the house?"

"You must be busy." *Run now while you still have time.*

"My last client just left, and Rainbow has things well in hand." She eyed him with unabashed interest. "You're here now, so we might as well talk." It was a dare.

Watch out. She's good.

He followed her into the house, figuring they might go into an office, but she led him to the kitchen and poured them both a glass of water.

She spun toward him, hip against the counter, and waited.

His throat was a little dry, and he took a gulp of water. He, as a feminist, tried not to judge women by their appearance. Intelligence and enthusiasm were as potent as a sex bomb.

Yeah, right.

Kennedy Dixon was the most attractive

psychologist he'd ever met. Full and luscious breasts, legs that went on forever, a trim waist, and elegant face. Shiny chestnut-brown hair and dark-brown eyes completed a stunning visual.

And he wasn't the least bit attracted to her.

His imagination conjured a willowy blonde with amber eyes.

"I can help you, if you'll let me."

"I'm not here for…for myself." Annoyance stung at his slight stammer.

"Okay." His hackles rose at her open countenance. "Who are we talking about?"

How was he supposed to answer that? "I know a woman." He stopped for a moment, contemplating the wisdom of this, but her eyes bespoke compassion, and he believed trusting this woman was a safe bet. "I understand you can't force someone to get help, no matter how badly they need it. But what if they're only willing to take help from you and you're not a professional?"

She eyed him contemplatively, incisively. "There's a huge risk taking on someone with psychological problems. There's also a difference between psychological issues and psychiatric issues. Is this woman taking medication?"

Quickly reviewing the contents of Rielle's medicine cabinet in his mind, he came up blank. Nope, nothing. Plus, he'd been there the past weekend, and he hadn't seen her take anything. "I'm going to go with a 'no' on that one."

"Diagnosed psychological issue? Depression? Bipolar? Anxiety?"

His hands shot up in frustration. "She barely leaves

her apartment, so it's doubtful she's seen someone who'd diagnose her."

"Is she agoraphobic?"

"It'd be a logical conclusion, but I think some of her fears might be rooted in reality." He took a moment to reflect. "No, I know they are. She's…she's got reasons to be…wary."

"And compassion is a good thing, but it doesn't qualify you to help her."

Rubbing a hand across his face, he gave it a scrub for good measure. His whiskers reminded him he hadn't shaved this morning. "Maybe this was a bad idea."

"There's always therapy from a distance."

"I told her a therapist might come to her house."

"And do you think a woman whose fears are based in reality would let a stranger into her house?"

She let me in.

"There are female counselors, right?"

"Of course, but Gage, let me ask you this. How invested are you in this?"

He understood what she asked, and he didn't have a good answer. "Even if I wasn't emotionally involved, I would still be…involved."

"So you're in this for the long haul?"

His poker face—or lack thereof—gave him away.

"Give her my name and walk away."

What the fuck?

"You're that good?"

Kennedy arched her left eyebrow, exactly as Rielle did.

It punched him in the gut. Mere hours earlier, his cock had been down the throat of a woman he cared for deeply. Now he contemplated what to do.

"My skills aren't what matters here. You're having doubts about this, and you've lost objectivity. You can't help her until you help yourself."

Slowly, his brain caught up. "What the hell does that mean?"

"It means you need to look deep within yourself and determine if you're living the life you want to."

If she'd slapped his face, he'd have been less stunned. "I love my life. I have a great job, friends, family…" Even as he spoke indignantly, he faltered. He might have friends and family, but he'd shut them out for the past two years. He'd cut himself off since Cara's death, and Rielle was the first time he'd put himself out there.

"You can't be her everything, and she can't be yours." Kennedy slid her hand into her back pocket, extracting a business card. She opened a drawer, snagged a pad of paper and a pen, then placed them in front of him. She met his gaze directly. "The next move is yours. You can show yourself out."

****

Still fuming when he pulled into his driveway, he slammed the car door when he exited. Who the hell did she think she was? Kennedy Dixon had some nerve, and he'd reconsider carefully referring another student there in the future. *Walk away*? What kind of bullshit answer was that? His hands shook so hard he barely got the key into the lock of his house. His self-righteousness carried him right through the house and into the kitchen where he stopped short. Two mugs of cold coffee. His plate, her bowl. It looked terribly domestic.

It hit him in the solar plexus, and he dropped into one of the chairs. Kennedy read him perfectly. She'd seen him as the Dominant he was and had understood the only way to get through to him was by taking the hard line. Being a Domme to his Dom. And she'd been right, because the soft touch would've never worked.

He dialed the number on the business card. "Dr. Dixon? Gage Clayton. Can you see me this week?"

Chapter Nine

Saturday night, Gage prowled the confines of his home like a caged tiger. A horny and frustrated tiger, because this was the first Saturday night he'd been alone since spotting Rielle at Club Kink. Friday had been okay because he worked late, came home, and cleaned the entire house from top to bottom. He'd fallen into bed with exhaustion. That morning he'd run, leaving just enough time to shower before his appointment with Kennedy.

She insisted it was Kennedy, not Dr. Dixon. And none of her hard-assed traits had been on display. She encouraged him to talk about Cara. About his social isolation for the past two years. About how he'd been drawn to Rielle because he found a kindred spirit— someone as lonely as he.

Then, over the next hour, he talked about his time with Rielle. It was surreal, realizing so little time had passed since he'd met her. But with a minimal amount of prodding from Kennedy, he shared everything. He talked about his dominance, how he liked being able to control things around him. He disclosed his kinky side and recognized instinctively she wasn't judging him. Her easygoing nature made it easy to confide in her, and her professionalism was unmistakable.

During the next hour, she did the talking. She refused to say whether she'd called Rielle—he *had* left her number on that pad of paper. What she did talk about was what it was like to be a partner to someone with a mental illness. Not that she was diagnosing anyone in particular, she assured him, just letting him know what he might expect. Testing him. Ascertaining whether he was in it for the long haul. Mental illness could be managed with the right therapy. Could, in some cases, be cured, if the trauma was acute as opposed to chronic.

Knowing Rielle's trauma had been lifelong didn't give him much hope, but she'd once been a functioning member of society. If she was willing to work at it, she could be again.

Or so Kennedy intimated.

Completely wrung out, he shopped for groceries, acknowledging parents, greeting students, and doing all the things involved in the process. When he first started in administration, he went to the next town to get his groceries and do his shopping. One too many tubs of melted ice cream and he resolved there was nothing wrong with being a member of the community in which he worked. Often, he and Cara went shopping together.

Oddly, there hadn't been a pang of loneliness. One session with Kennedy hadn't solved all his problems, but it put them in perspective. Now, as he digested his single-serve microwave meal, a different pang rammed into him. He pulled out his cell phone and looked at it as if it could divine the answers to his questions. As if it could divine *his* truth. As if it might tell him whether to call her. Kennedy hadn't told him *not* to. In fact, she'd refrained from making any suggestions when it came to Rielle.

Trust yourself and trust her. If this is meant to be, it

will be. But be prepared to work hard at it. Nothing worth having comes easy.

Very Buddhist.

But he conceded her point. The first time he spotted Rielle, he'd instinctively understood she'd be a challenge. Was he up for it and was she worth it?

He held the phone with one hand and was picking up the remote with the other when the phone rang.

He dropped both.

Shit.

Snagging the phone from the floor, he checked the number.

Unknown caller.

"Gage Clayton."

"You're full of shit, you bastard."

Despite himself, he smirked. "Hello, Mistress Gigi, how are you this evening?"

"Fucking pissed. You said you'd keep her away."

Instantly on his feet, he moved to the front hall. "She's there? At the club?"

"Well, she was, you dick, but she's not anymore."

"What the hell does that mean?"

"Your pretty girl shows up here in full regalia. I mean, decked out and looking expensive and slutty. And all the guys are panting after her, but she only has eyes for Spike. They left together about twenty minutes ago. I thought you should know." During her monologue, some of her anger had drained away, but his heart beat a tattoo to the rhythm of panic.

"Where did they go, Marie? Back to his place? What's the address?"

"I can't give it to you because I don't have it. I'm not sure it would do much good, because he has access to a dozen private play areas. He might be taking her to do a private show at someone's house."

A cold dread enveloped him. "Is she in danger?"

"Probably only from herself. Spike has a good reputation in the community, but she's in over her head, Gage, and you know it."

He wasn't sure he did, but his gut clenched with tension and dread.

"What should I do?"

Wallet, keys, cell phone.

"Keep your phone charged, I guess. I'll call if either of them comes back tonight." Marie paused. "But I was serious about keeping her out of here, Gage. Friends of her friend showed up not ten minutes after she left."

"Fuck."

Shoes? Where are my shoes? How the fuck are they not at the front door?

Because he had come in the house through the garage, carrying the groceries.

"Yeah, that about sums it up."

"Marie…thanks for calling me."

"Go fuck yourself."

"I would if I could."

****

The drive to Vancouver was fraught with silence, much like the one the previous weekend. Had it been merely a week since she safeworded on him? He didn't even dare play the radio in case he missed his cell phone ringing. His SUV was too old for hands-free usage, and for once he regretted not doing something about that. It was illegal to drive with a handheld device in British Columbia, but he didn't give a shit. If she called, he'd take it, cops be damned.

But the phone didn't ring. For the nerve-shattering hour it took to drive to her building, the silence mocked him. Using the key card he kept forgetting to return, he pulled into the spare parking spot. Her car was there, but that meant absolutely nothing. Damn thing looked as new as the day Mr. X bought it for her.

Instead of going to the third floor, he jogged up to the lobby. This time he was noisy enough to warn Tarah, who rose to greet him. A moment of inspection on her part, as she took in his appearance, stole her look of delight at recognizing him.

"Have you seen her?"

She shook her head. "But I only started about an hour ago. Isn't she in the condo?"

Probably where he should've started, but logic played no part in his anxiety. "She might be." *Get your shit together.* He grimaced. "But I doubt it." He waved his cell phone. "I'm going to go up and wait for her. Call me the second you see her, okay?"

"Should I be worried?" The ice-blue innocent eyes were wide, her stance alert.

Tamping down panic, he feigned a nonchalance he didn't feel. "I'm sure everything's fine. I mean, she went out, right? That's a good thing."

"Of course." She eyed him warily, speaking slowly. "A good thing."

He waved before opening the fire door and heading into the stairwell. He took the stairs two at a time, even knowing he was on a fool's errand. She wouldn't be there. She was out there in a city with half a million goddamn people and had chosen Spike as her companion for the evening. He was going to throttle

287

her…after he was sure she was safe. He was going to punish her…after he was assured of her health.

The empty apartment mocked him.

He checked his phone to see if there had been any missed calls while he'd been in the parking garage.

No such luck.

Call Marie or go down to the club and ask around?

That made even less sense than sitting there waiting until she came home. No one at the club was going to furnish Spike's information upon request from some half-cocked asshole. And if friends of friends had missed her appearance, his presence and questions certainly would bring unwanted attention to both of them.

And anyway, she would come home.

She has to.

Tamping down his scruples, he made a systematic inventory of her condo, searching for any indication of where her head had been over the past week. Pointless, as everything was exactly the way it'd been two weekends prior. Neat as a pin, nothing out of place. Not even a novel on her bedside table. Had she finished reading that damn book for the umpteenth time?

The dungeon was exactly the same. Neat, tidy, well cared for. The equipment hung on the wall, waiting to be used. Would she bring Spike back there when they were done? Would she go trolling through Club Kink next weekend? How far was she going to push herself before she broke in two?

His bladder was making demands, so he took a piss, washed his hands, and splashed cold water on his face. His appointment with Kennedy felt like a million years ago.

Should he call her?

At midnight? If she wasn't convinced he was insane before, she'd be now. Plus, what would she say? Probably if someone was hell-bent on self-destruction, she was free to do so. That he'd done his part and walking away with a clear conscience was a viable solution.

Yeah, right, like that is ever going to happen.

Another glance at his watch showed it was five minutes later than the last time he checked. Fine, if he was going to be there for the "long haul," he might as well get comfortable. He stalked back to the white room and rifled through the movie selection. Then it hit him. As eclectic as her collection was, there were no horror movies. Not even any thrillers. Nothing in that collection didn't have a predictable ending. He pulled out *Titanic*. It was a good way to kill four hours. Even as he had made the calculation, his phone rang.

He dropped the movie and answered the phone.

"She's on her way up, Gage." She hesitated a fraction of a second. "He's taking her up the elevator."

"Thanks, Tarah."

He was at the door in a few strides and yanked it open, startling both himself and the couple on the other side.

Rielle looked devastated. Her face was tearstained, with rivulets continuing to fall. Mascara ran down, washing away the concealer. Her wig was askew, and she was unsteady on her feet.

"What the fuck did you give her?"

Defiant, Spike shot back. "I didn't give her nothing, man. She's one fucked-up chick."

Torn between taking care of her and giving Spike a

piece of his mind, he hesitated, and she took the decision out of his hands, making a mad dash for the bathroom.

For a woman with broken ribs and high heels, she moved with amazing speed. She slammed the door before he got to it.

Hand poised to pound, he refrained when the sound of retching reached him. He swallowed down the bile rising in his throat.

"Man, is she okay?" Spike apparently decided to stay.

Gage rounded on the smaller man and slammed him against the wall, pressing an arm to his windpipe. "What the fuck did you do to her? Did you drug her?"

Spike made an ineffectual effort to pull the arm off his neck. He cleared his throat, wheezing. "I told you, I didn't do anything. She came to Kink looking for me. She asked me to take her somewhere to scene with her. She was the one who stripped and asked me to whip her."

"And?" A growl.

"And nothing. I get in maybe five licks, and she starts howling. I mean, I didn't hurt her, but she's carrying on. She keeps saying 'Gage' over and over again." His brow furrowed as if the circuits in his brain finally connected. "You Gage?"

"I am."

"Well, I don't know what you're on me about. Those bruises on her are nasty. I mean, you did a number on her. And some of them are around her kidneys. I mean, you have to be careful there, you know?"

"Yes." He ground out the word like he was spitting

nails. "I know. I wasn't the one who beat her."

"Oh, okay." Spike cleared his throat again. "Can you let me go?"

Gage pressed a little bit harder. "You stay the fuck away from her. Are we clear?"

The shorter man managed a bob of his head. "I wouldn't go near her again anyway. I'm a sadist, and I only play with masochists. That girl is not a masochist. But she could have been hurt tonight. You need to keep her on a shorter leash."

"She's not a goddamn dog." Even as he said the words, however, Gage saw the truth of them. With one final shove, he pulled back, grabbing Spike by the collar and hauling him out the door. About to close the door, he spotted Rielle's neighbor, the old woman.

She sized up the two disheveled men and shook her little fist. "I told you to stay away from that girl." She returned to her apartment and slammed her door.

The men gazed at each other, and just like that, the tension dissipated.

He held out his hand to Spike who took it, if reluctantly. "Thank you for bringing her home. Do me one favor? Tell the woman down in the lobby Gage says Rielle is okay."

Spike appeared a little dubious about that but sauntered away with a backward wave.

Steeling himself for whatever he was about to find, he reentered the condo.

When he tried the bathroom door, he was surprised to find it unlocked. Maybe it'd been that way all along. The shower was on, and he was about to back away when he glanced into the stall. She was huddled naked on the floor, knees pulled up to her chest, arms looped tightly around them. Her head rested on her knees, shoulders shaking.

He didn't even bother to strip before he stepped in with her. He sank to his haunches. "Rielle?"

No answer. No movement whatsoever. No sign she even heard him.

"Rielle?" He placed a hand on her shoulder, expecting her to pull away.

She didn't, though. Instead she leaned into his grasp.

He was able to pry her arms away from her body and gently pull her to her feet. The water had cleaned off most of the mess from her face, and he figured they could sort out her hair in the morning. He switched off the shower and eased her to the toilet. After snagging a towel, he systematically dried her skin.

The bruises were healing and looking better than they had two weeks past. Welts were still visible, and he was able to touch contusions under the skin. One particularly bad one on her thigh caught his attention.

She winced when he touched it but didn't open her eyes. Her head drooped forward, hair veiling her face.

He tipped her chin upward and used a facecloth to wipe away the remnants of her aborted night. When he put the towel around her shoulders and it touched her back, she gasped. He eased her toward him so he could examine her back. Spike hadn't broken the skin, but some nasty stripes crisscrossed. He certainly hadn't pulled any lashes. Then Gage remembered the younger man's words.

She isn't a masochist.

The truth was there, hidden away, out of sight.

Rielle enjoyed pain, but not for pain's sake. She

enjoyed it because of what it brought both to her and her Master.

Gage hadn't seen that earlier, but it was clear to him now that the fog of worry and rage was dissipating. He applied the soothing cream, careful to not put any pressure on the marks.

A couple of times she stirred but otherwise remained catatonic.

He wanted to yell at her. Wanted to tell her how worried he'd been. He wanted to extract a promise from her that she'd never do something so foolish again. But the words wouldn't form. The pain in his chest ached, and he pressed a palm to his breastbone. Maybe a talk with Dr. Raymond was in order. What if this was a physical heart issue, not a metaphorical one? Except the pain had existed since Cara's death and only relented for a short period of time when he and Rielle had been on good terms. Was it possible for them to get back to equilibrium? Did he want to add that much stress to his life?

Like you have any say.

The heart wanted what it wanted, and his heart wanted her. So did his cock, but that organ was secondary again, as it often was these days.

When she was completely dry, he lifted her into his arms and carried her to the dungeon. He placed her on the bed, and she curled on her side. He snagged a pair of handcuffs, unceremoniously grabbed her wrists, and cuffed them together through the slats of the headboard. Ensuring she wasn't going to lose feeling in her arms, he rose.

She shook her hands, discovered she was shackled, and yanked harder. "What the fuck?"

He knelt, towering over her. "Don't struggle. Don't pull. Don't move a fucking inch. Clear?"

He didn't wait for an answer. He made his way back to the bathroom and cleaned up the mess. One pristine white towel had borne the brunt of the mascara, and nothing short of bleach was going to save it. Well, fuck it, she could afford to buy another one. He pitched it into the trash.

When the room was in some semblance of order, he stripped. His clothes were soaked and needed to go into the dryer because he hadn't brought anything with him except his keys, wallet, and cell phone.

Which reminded him, he needed to call Tarah. The woman might or might not have given credence to a guy with multiple tattoos, earrings, studs, and spiked hair when he told her Rielle was okay. He called, reassuring her that her friend was in fact okay. Whether it was true or not, who knew.

Having made the call, he reentered the dungeon. After shutting off the lights, he made his way gingerly over to the bed, mindful the room was pitch black. He crawled in behind her, then pulled her flush to him, cradling her body with his. Her back was fire against his cold chest.

"What are you doing?" It was a pathetic and weak whisper.

"Holding you."

She yanked experimentally at the cuffs. "And why am I cuffed to the bed?"

"Because I don't want to wake up and find you on the goddamn floor. Now I'm tired, so shut the fuck up and go to sleep."

He waited with bated breath for her response.

She sagged back against him and sighed her displeasure.

Relief flooded him.

****

Gage awoke in degrees. He was hard as a rock, and his body ached for release. Quickly he realized why.

A luscious ass was purposely rubbing against him.

He gave a quick, resounding smack on said offending ass.

Her back arched farther. "I need…"

"What do you need, Rielle?"

She pulled on the cuffs again, but it wasn't a real struggle.

He'd left the key in the lock should she go crazy again and he needed to release her quickly. Maybe crazy wasn't the right word, but it was the first word that came to mind.

A quick, sharp intake of breath accompanied her statement. "I need you to fuck me."

"Say my name." His tone brooked no opposition.

"Gage." A smile tinged her voice. "Your name is Sir Gage."

Well, that was something. He pressed his hands against her ribs, searching for tenderness.

"They are healing nicely, the doctor said."

"Doctor?"

"I called Dr. Giroux and asked her if she could come and check on me. She said she couldn't, but she'd see me in her office. I went to see her, and I went to the library. Now will you fuck me already?"

Her words were more powerful than any aphrodisiac he might have dreamed of, but he needed more. "Why did you go to the club last night?"

She stopped her sinuous movements against him, stilling completely. "I don't want to talk about that."

"Do you want to fuck?" She rubbed up against him, and damn if his cock didn't harden even more. "You want me in you? Tell me why you went home with Spike."

Her entire body went rigid, and he had a momentary flash he wasn't going to get to fuck her, which was going to be a disappointment to his stiff cock.

"I went looking for...something. I needed something."

"Which was?"

"*You.* All right? I went looking for you."

"You had my fucking phone number, Rielle. Your fingers aren't broken, and you know how to dial."

She sighed, and her head drooped forward away from him. "I needed to prove to myself that I could do it. That I could go out. That someone would find me desirable."

"All you had to do was call."

She shook her head. "You walked away. You sent a psychologist after me instead of you coming back."

"Did you want me to come?"

Another sigh. "I don't have an easy answer for that, Gage. But I talked to her, your psychologist. She convinced me to call Dr. Giroux. She approved of your library and café plan. I've emailed her or talked to her every day since you left."

His chest loosened. He hadn't realized how constricted and tight the band had been over the past two weeks. "Those are good things. I'm proud of you."

She let out a short sharp breath. "So I'm a good

girl?"

He gave her ass a resounding smack, then pressed a comforting hand against the blooming heat. "Yes," he whispered into her ear. "You're my good girl."

She pressed her ass against his crotch. "Now will you fuck me? Please."

He chuckled. "I like hearing you beg. Maybe I should hold out a little bit longer." Even as he said the words, though, his hand snaked around her waist. He grasped her thigh and pulled it back over his. He delved his fingers into her and found her slick and ready. The entire conversation had been a kind of foreplay.

He pressed his cock to her opening and entered her in one swift thrust.

She bucked against him, gasping even as her sensitive tissues stretched to accommodate him.

He brought his hand up to her breast, and she moaned as he tweaked her nipple. Even as he moved, he bit her shoulder. Yanked her hair. Bombarded her with as many sensations as possible. He was going to make this last as long as imaginable. He was going to have her screaming.

His body begged for him to pick up the pace, but he held back. Mind over matter. He ran his hand along her slick folds and pressed his finger against her clit. He wanted to piston in and out of her, instead of the steady languid strokes he made, but he was going to draw this out if possible.

Blue balls.

"Please, Gage, do something."

"This?" He withdrew completely. "Or this?" He thrust back into her.

A keening sound escaped her that might've been

either pleasure or desperation, but he couldn't tell which. He withdrew again and plunged back in again. When she made mewling sounds, he continued his assault with renewed vigor.

"I…please, Gage, do something to make this stop."

"Make what stop?"

She bucked back against him.

Am I hurting her?

Am I an animal for doing this now? To her?

As she ground her clit against his finger, the crying and fervent prayers to a deity continued.

Never had he been so desperate and she so aroused. Her smell invaded his every sense, down to the cellular level. Bonded them in a way he never conceived, more than any fluid exchange might.

When he seated himself to the hilt, a sound unlike anything he'd ever heard was yanked from her. As she contracted around him, he worried he'd truly injured her. Yet it wasn't a cry of pain, just of otherworldliness.

Figuring that was her way of telling him to finish up, he thrust with an intensity that robbed him of breath. His own release came as her breath thundered in his ears and his heart pounded in his chest.

"Gage?"

He stirred enough to reach up and undo the handcuffs, rubbing each wrist. Because the cuffs were padded, there would be few, if any, residual marks. Her hands were warm, and he pulled them down to her chest, imprisoning them with his arm.

"Gage?"

He nuzzled her neck. "Yes, Rielle?"

"I feel funny."

That got his attention. He pulled away so he could

ease her onto her back. "What hurts?" His hands urgently swept her body, checking for anything wrong.

A beat passed before she answered. "Not hurts. Just…funny." She snagged his wandering hand and pressed it to her abdomen. "Something happened."

He propped on his elbow, using his other hand to smooth her damp hair away from her face. He wasn't sure if it was still wet from the shower or damp from their exertions. He pressed a gentle kiss to her temple.

Still, she hadn't elaborated. "Can you describe what happened?"

He sensed her frowning and cursed the darkness. He almost stretched to flick on the light, but his grasp on her felt tenuous, and he didn't want to lose it. "Talk to me, Rielle." He tried to keep his tone gentle but prodding.

"It was like I left my body. Like my body took over and left me behind. Or got ahead of me." She made a noise of confusion and frustration. "I'm not making any sense."

He sought understanding. "I'm trying to get it, sweetheart." Suddenly, it all made sense. "Rielle?"

"Mmm." She still floated.

"You used those Kegels pretty effectively. I mean, God, the way you grabbed me, it was amazing."

She languidly rolled her head toward him. "But I didn't…I was too…"

"Occupied?"

"It was like my body…"

"Let go?"

She was slow to answer. "It was out of my control."

He pressed his finger to the frown line that'd

formed. "That's because you had an orgasm." He whispered it into her ear.

Her hand tightened around his and pressed it firmer against her belly. "But I can't have an orgasm."

"No," he corrected her. "You've never had one. Until now."

"Are you sure?" Her voice was barely above a whisper.

He wished he was sure, but he'd been pretty gone himself. "There are ways a man can tell, and damn, it sure felt like it to me."

"Could it happen again?"

Her voice was so full of desperation his heart constricted. How was he supposed to answer that? "Anything is possible. Even if you didn't have an actual orgasm, you said something happened. It felt good, right?"

Her hesitation had him holding his breath. "I've never felt that way. Like my body was beyond my control." She took a breath. "I want to try again, but I'm afraid that…"

She mirrored his own apprehension. So much pressure, and yet so much opportunity.

"We can try an experiment," he offered. "But let's be clear, Rielle, if you focus on the goal instead of the journey, it won't happen."

She brought his knuckles to her lips and pressed a kiss as gentle as a whisper from a butterfly's wings. "Even if it never happens again, I get to hold on to this memory."

He wanted to say something profound, but the words stuck in his throat. He cleared it, giving himself a moment to clear his head. "Will you let me make love to you?"

She let out a little sigh of pleasure. "I liked it when you did that, but in the end…"

It had ended in catastrophe.

"Do you trust me?"

"Implicitly." Not a moment's hesitation.

Now that he was well-familiar with Rielle's body, he wondered if it was maybe worth taking the risk right now. On the other hand, they had all the time in the world. Then it hit him.

I'm in this for the long haul.

Whatever that meant, whatever she wanted it to mean.

"Close your eyes."

She giggled. "Gage, it's completely dark, and I can't see anything."

"But still, close your eyes."

Even though he couldn't see, he knew she'd complied. He placed his hand on her diaphragm. "Breathe in. Deep breath, through your nose." Once she complied, he said, "Exhale through your mouth." He waited a beat. "And don't roll your eyes."

A little chuckle escaped from her, but she took another breath, following his instructions. And another. At least five minutes passed before she completely relaxed.

With his hand splayed across her abdomen, he made slow concentric circles, careful to caress, not tickle. He swept his hand up her chest, careful to brush—but not linger on—her breast. Goose bumps broke out on her skin.

"Cold?" he whispered into her ear.

She shook her head.

She rolled so she faced him, and he traced his hand along her jaw, coaxing her mouth to his. A little moan escaped her as their lips touched. Lightly. Once. Twice. The third time, he ran his tongue along the seam of her lips, and she opened for him. Indecision lingered for a moment, then he thrust his tongue into her mouth, sweeping and seeking recesses. He entered a kind of mating dance with her as she parried back. He sought out her breast, and she arched up, pressing her nipple against his palm. It hardened beneath his attention, and she moaned softly. Grasping her hip, he nudged her closer, pulling her flush to him.

When her hand grasped him intimately, though, he held it in place for one precarious and precious moment before gently moving it away. His cock wasn't impressed, but his mind didn't care. He'd had thousands of orgasms and, if the past was any indication, would have many more. This was about Rielle.

Appreciating the momentous pressure of the moment, his dick softened. To keep her hands from wandering again, he imprisoned her wrists and tugged them over her head. Instinctively, she clutched for the slats and held on tight. If he could've found the handcuffs, he'd lock her in place again, but her grip seemed pretty secure.

He left her mouth and took a leisurely journey downward. A nip here, a lick there, ending with a little love bite. The bite elicited the biggest reaction, as a shiver coursed through her. When he got to her breast, she arched up to him. He took his time, savoring, tasting, sucking. Nipping her skin caused her to buck against him again. As responsive as she was to all his affections, when he lavished her breasts—nipples in particular—with the most ardent of ministrations, it was the quickest way to get her engine revving.

He slid a hand to her hip, encouraging her to lie back down, while continuing to feast on her. He pulled back, and she moaned. He blew across the nipple, and she groaned. Pleasure suffused him when the slats shook. His cock stiffened.

He slid his hand from her hip to the seam of her thighs. With a bit of pressure, her knees opened for him, falling gracefully toward the bed. She was so aroused he smelled her, ruthlessly tamping down his body's demand to plunge into her. Instead, he palmed her nether lips, making wide sweeps, using her wetness to lubricate his fingers. He teased, touching everywhere except where she wanted it most. It was obvious by the bucking of her hips and her restlessness that she was close.

When he'd teased her sufficiently, he gave her what she wanted and pressed his thumb to her clit. It was a hard nub under his finger, engorged under the intense onslaught she was enduring.

"Please…" The whisper was suffused with passion and confusion. Her mind understood her body wanted something, but she wasn't sure how to ask for it.

In response, he plunged two fingers into her warm depths. At that, her hips came off the bed. His fingers tantalized and teased, easing in and out, creating delicious friction. He found the rigid flesh of her G-spot. He wasn't sure he'd ever touched anything more precious.

She flexed her hips down, pressing into his fingers.

He moved his fingers while ruthlessly grinding her

clit with his palm.

Her back arched, and her head moved back and forth, her breath coming in short sharp gasps. When she let out a prayer to a deity, he bit her nipple.

Hard.

So hard, he worried he might draw blood, but it didn't matter because she convulsed around his fingers. Her body clamped down so hard he pulled his fingers back on one of the waves. Quick as lightning, he seized her hand. She let him release the death grip she had on the headboard, allowing him to pull her hand down. He pressed her fingers to her clit and forced her to feel the pulses right along with him.

She attempted to pull her hand away, but he held firm. She needed to realize what her body was doing. Had to understand what it was capable of.

When his mouth left her breast and resettled to her lips, she welcomed him. Her other hand slipped from the headboard and came to rest on his head, her fingers running through his hair. "Fuck me." It was an achingly familiar whispered plea.

"Yeah, pretty amazing, eh?"

Her hand on his hair tightened. "No, I mean, fuck me."

"You—"

"I need you inside me, right now."

His body made no argument even as his mind sought purchase. "Rielle…"

She moved her mouth to his and pressed a kiss to his lips. "I want to share."

Suddenly, he understood. He rolled onto his back and gently pulled her astride him, mindful of her tender ribs.

She stroked for his cock, causing him to tighten painfully, and within moments, she eased him inside her. She was slick and hot, ready to go, so he arched his pelvis up as she sank down on him. Her sigh put them in sync. Unlike the last time, she took charge, setting the pace.

He cupped her breasts, and she emitted a long heartfelt moan.

Because he wasn't going to last long, he set a steady but quick pace, reveling in the heat encircling his cock. Jesus, how was he supposed to make this good for her while he was mindlessly wrapped in pleasure?

As if sensing his dilemma, she pulled his index finger into her mouth and bit. Her inner muscles clamped down on him. It wasn't the smooth continuous wave of an orgasm, but irregular and intentional pressing against him, encouraging him to share the mind-blowing sensation.

He let go.

****

As she lay in his arms, Rielle's breath was harsh against his chest. A sense of peace permeated and enveloped the room.

She relaxed, and the waning high of his orgasm encouraged him down as well. When their sweat-slicked bodies began to cool, however, he had to do something. He slipped from her with great regret, making sure, though, he still touched her. Not to excite, but to reassure. Not to arouse, but to comfort.

He lay on his side and pulled her to him so their noses touched and their breaths mingled. His hand cupped her cheek, and he sensed her smiling. He leaned forward and placed a kiss on her forehead.

"Thank you." Despite her quiet voice, the words were absolutely clear. "You'll never know what that meant to me."

He wanted to reply with something flippant, but it was neither the time nor the place. Instead he returned her happy expression. "It meant something to me as well, sweetheart. Don't ever doubt that."

Feeling goose bumps on her arm, he sat up, searching for a sheet, blanket, or anything else he might pull over them.

Damn darkness.

She chuckled and switched on the lights. The torches emitted a low glow that seemed less menacing than it had before.

Tonight was less about the dungeon and more about the bed, because his body wanted to go another round.

Slipping from his outstretched grasp, she stood. She gazed at him with a wink. "I have to pee."

"Thanks for sharing." He rolled his eyes but enjoyed watching her walk away. The curve of her spine where it met her ass was possibly the sexiest thing in the world. More shadows than light existed in the room, but the bruises contrasted starkly with her pale skin, and he took a punch to the gut. She might've died, and he'd never have appreciated such bliss was possible. He didn't kid himself—he was fucking proud. The first orgasm might have been an accident, but the second had been intentional. Now that he identified her sweet spots, it wouldn't be hard to replicate.

Denial of orgasms and forced orgasms were two of his favorite games, and he was already making devious plans. He closed his eyes with a goofy grin on his face.

"Gage?" Her voice was quiet but questioning.

He pushed himself from the bed and padded to the bathroom.

She held up his phone. "It was ringing when I came in, but stopped."

As he scrolled quickly, a cold dread enveloped him. A missed call from Jenna Lee at four a.m. on a Sunday could only portend bad news. Probably a break-in at the school, although in that case she'd probably have waited until daybreak.

"I'll check my messages."

"Of course." Rielle was quick to assure, to offer unspoken support. "I'm going to have a quick shower."

He heard her, but his mind whirled. Listening to Jenna's message didn't help as she implored him to call, stating it was an emergency.

Emergency.

His gut clenched. He and Jenna had lingo, an understanding. This word was to be used in the direst of circumstances. His unsteady hands hit the button.

It was answered on the first ring.

"Gage, thank God. You need to come down to the Mission City Detachment right away."

"What's going on, Jenna?"

"They won't tell me, but Katie Rhodes has been arrested."

He swallowed down a wave of panic. He barely knew Katie, as she was in the ninth grade, but an image of the diminutive girl with long dark brown hair and brown eyes flashed in his mind. Unremarkable except for her small stature. He doubted she topped five feet.

"Did they say why she was arrested?"

"No, but Dorrie Duhamel called me when she

couldn't reach you."

Cursing he'd left his phone in the bathroom, he let out a prayer of thanks it hadn't been ruined when he'd gotten into the shower with Rielle. This was unreal.

"Okay, Jenna, I'm on my way. I'm in Vancouver, so it's going to take a bit of time. Try to reach Katie's parents and tell Dorrie they can't ask Katie a single question. Not a goddamn thing. I'll be there in two hours, and we'll sort it out."

Jenna exhaled a shuddering breath. "Thank you." Her voice trembled.

"We'll get this sorted, Jenna, don't worry."

He ended the call and stood for a moment, staring at the phone. Who could he call at this hour?

"Gage?"

He whirled to see Rielle, wrapped in her ivory kimono, drying her hair with a towel.

"What's going on?"

In that moment, he was galvanized. "Do you have a suit that fits?"

"A suit…you mean like a business suit?"

"I mean like a lawyer's suit."

She swallowed convulsively, her throat working visibly. "Yeah, I'm still about the same size as before."

"Go put it on." He checked his watch. "And pack a bag. You're going to be gone for a few days."

Instead of arguing, she held up her hand in acknowledgement. "I'll pack my other suit as well, in case I need it. Otherwise…?"

"Whatever you need in order to stay with me for a couple of days. If you need more, we'll either come back here or buy it." He cringed at his naked form. He didn't want to take the time needed to be presentable, but showing up smelling like sex wasn't going to fly. "I'm going to shower. Can you get my clothes out of the dryer?"

"Yes." She stood tall, eyes alert and sharp.

"We need to be on the road within a half hour. Advise Tarah you're coming with me."

"I'll tell her." She stepped forward, placing a hand on his arm—initiating non-sexual contact for the first time in a while, much like the comforting she offered the day they'd watched the news of the shooting. "It will be okay."

Her eyes were bright and clear, no shadows, no hint of hesitation. Had he ever seen her so certain, so lucid?

Placing his hand over hers, he squeezed. "Thank you. I sure hope so."

Chapter Ten

They made the trip back to Mission City in record time, as they were the lone car on the road at five on a Sunday morning. A trip to the drive-thru at Tim Horton's wasn't so much a luxury as a necessity, since he'd had merely two hours of sleep. He was running on pure adrenaline, but that wasn't going to hold.

Rielle ordered black tea, and they shared a bagel with cream cheese.

He filled her in as best he could with the little he knew. What he couldn't explain was his gut reaction this was a bad situation. Kids got arrested, sure, but rarely would the cops call the school, especially in the middle of the night on a weekend.

Rielle made appropriate noises of sympathy and understanding, all the while picking at her clothes. The clothes made her look like a lawyer. The suit was professionally tailored in a dark gray. She wore matching pumps with her hair swept back in a twist knot. She'd started to put on concealer, but he'd stopped her, and she agreed to his request. Pearl earrings and necklace, with a simple brooch in the shape of a hummingbird, completed the ensemble. She was elegant, understated, and professional from top to bottom.

He felt rumpled next to her but wasn't going to stop at home to get a suit. His position in the community entitled him to authority. Not that he planned to throw his weight around, per se, but people needed to recognize he was a person to be reckoned with.

After pulling into the parking lot, he backed into a spot with ease and killed the engine. For a moment, they sat in silent contemplation. He snagged her hand. "No matter what happens, I'm proud of you."

"I haven't done anything yet." Her voice was dry but also contained a hint of nervousness.

He wanted to offer reassurances, but words wouldn't come. She was either going to handle this or she wasn't. He let go of her hand and opened the door.

They exited the vehicle together, the bite of the early morning air invigorating him. Although he wanted to pull her close to warm her, they walked together, side by side, each holding their drink. Steps before the entrance to the detachment, she faltered.

He spun back to her.

"I don't have a briefcase. I need a briefcase. I can't do this without a briefcase." She seemed unnerved, verging on unhinged, and her speech was rapid, panicky.

He pointed to the big-box store, whose blue sign was visible. "I promise to buy you a briefcase as soon they open. For now, you have to trust me. We'll get you a pad of paper and a pen. You have to do this, Rielle."

Oh God, please trust me.

Please do this.

Please let this not push her over the cliff.

Her head snapped up, and she nodded. And, like that, the crisis ended. They stepped toward the door, and he held it open while she entered.

The overhead lights nauseated, but the room was well-lit.

Jenna leapt to her feet. She appeared so relieved he was afraid she might embrace him, but she simply pursed her lips. Her gaze went to Rielle and back to him.

"Jenna, this is Miss Reid. She's an attorney." He inclined his head. "Rielle, this is Jenna Lee, my vice-principal."

The two women acknowledged each other but said nothing, likely hypothesizing the other's place in his life. Had he assured Rielle his relationship with Jenna was purely professional? Jenna didn't have any idea who Rielle was. Would the lawyer story fly, or was his poker face about to reveal the true nature of their amorous relationship to his brilliantly perceptive VP? He was about to ask Jenna for the rundown when the door to the restricted area opened. Dorrie Duhamel and—unsurprisingly—Colton Pritchard stepped out.

Introductions were quick, but he didn't miss the speculative look Rielle received from both corporals.

If she noticed, she didn't comment.

"Gage, we appreciate you coming down here," Dorrie began, her gaze meeting his. "We arrested Katie Rhodes last night at her residence. Neighbors called police when they heard a gunshot. Katie was sitting next to her father's dead body, holding a shotgun."

"Did she say anything?" It was Rielle who spoke.

"She told the responding officers she killed him. She handed them the gun, and they took her into custody." Dorrie's expression was neutral, but her blue eyes narrowed.

"Did she say why?" Processing this information

proved nearly impossible for him because, in his experience, petite brunette ninth-grade students didn't cold-bloodedly murder their fathers. In other places? Maybe…but not here. Not his kids.

A quick shake of the head. "We have no idea. The mother died of cancer when Katie was a toddler, and her father raised her. The neighbors were stunned, and none of them offered a single explanation."

"Was there abuse? Previous disturbances? Domestic issues?" Rielle peppered the questions in rapid-fire succession.

"None." Dorrie's spine straightened. "We've never been called to the house. We asked Jenna to check the school records, and apparently Katie's never had so much as a detention."

"I called the vice-principal from her grade school, and he said he'd no memory of her at all. She certainly never raised any red flags or got into trouble." Jenna seemed at a loss, as confused as the rest of them.

Gage let out a short, sharp breath. "Yet last night she picked up her father's shotgun and killed him? Does that make any sense?"

"There were no signs of a struggle, and he was sitting in his recliner watching television. There were no defensive wounds." Colton paused for effect. "She shot him—about three feet from him at the time, the techs estimate. We'll know more after the autopsy."

"Does she have counsel?" Rielle glanced back and forth between Dorrie and Colton. "Has she been read her rights?"

"They read her her rights, but that was after she confessed." Colton inclined his head slightly. "And no, she doesn't have counsel. I'm sorry, why are you here?"

Rielle made a show of searching her pockets, coming up short. "I'm sorry, I must have left my business card at home. My name is Rielle Reid. I'm Katie Rhodes' lawyer."

The look of shock on Colton's face was priceless, and while Dorrie's eyebrow quirked, she didn't miss a beat. "Well, we haven't booked her yet. She's in interview room two. I'll show you the way." Dorrie indicated the way with her head, her blonde ponytail swishing with the movement.

"I want Mr. Clayton to attend the interview."

"Third person could preclude admissibility." Colton's contribution.

"But not if the client accepts the third party and that third party does not have a vested interest," Rielle shot back. "Now I want to see my client, I want you to make sure the recording equipment is off, and I want the microphones cut."

"Of course." Dorrie was quick to assure. "We always do those things."

"I'm sure you do, Corporal Duhamel." Rielle's tone was entirely reasonable. "But sometimes mistakes are made. I want to make sure this is not one of those times."

Colton made a noise low in his throat. "She's already confessed."

Rielle pulled herself to her full height. In heels she was almost six feet tall, towering over both Jenna and Dorrie.

A flicker—just a flicker—of appreciation crossed Colton's expression.

For her moxie, Gage hoped, not her body.

Amber Eyes

"Well by all means, Ms. Reid, let's not keep your client waiting." Colton opened the door and held it for Rielle, then entered himself, forcing Gage to extend a hand to keep from being locked out.

So *that* was how it was going to be. He'd never met an RCMP officer he hadn't liked and respected, but Colton Pritchard was to be the first.

Katie Rhodes sat in the same chair Gage had graced mere weeks ago. Her arms were wrapped around her waist, and she was bent forward, shoulders hunched.

Rielle surveyed the scene and pivoted to face Colton. "How long has she been like this?" Her tone was icy, and her eyes flashed. Without waiting for a response, she barked out orders. "I want a blanket, a bottle of water, and a chocolate bar in the next five minutes."

Colton's face twisted, and it appeared he was going to argue. Then he looked over at Katie, finally seeing what was obvious to Rielle and Gage—Katie was cold and scared. He nodded curtly and left the room.

Having no idea what to do, Gage waited for Rielle to make the first move. Her hesitation was momentary before she crossed the room. She pulled up a chair alongside Katie's so they almost touched. Sitting, she placed her hands on her knees and leaned forward, mimicking Katie's posture. "Katie, my name is Rielle."

The three occupants of the room jumped when the door opened.

Dorrie entered with the requested items, handing them over to Gage. She gave him an odd look but left without a word.

He placed the water and chocolate bar on the table

315

and gingerly placed the blanket on Katie's shoulders, careful not to touch her.

As if in a trance, she reached for the edges and pulled them together, creating a cocoon. Still, she kept her gaze on some unseen place on the floor.

Rielle hazarded a quick glance at him while taking a breath.

Watching her inner struggle, he willed her to conquer the fear.

"Katie, I'm your lawyer. Do you understand what that means?" When she didn't answer, Rielle continued, "I'm here to protect you as best as I can. I'm here to make sure you're okay. Katie, are you okay?"

Without looking up, the girl made a quick curt bob of her head.

"That's good, Katie. I appreciate you letting me know." Rielle took the bottle of water, uncapped it, and handed it to the girl.

Katie took a long pull, swallowed, and then took another.

His anger flared as he did some mental calculations of how long she'd been alone and unattended. At a two-way mirror, he shot a withering look. Rielle demanded the recording equipment be shut off, but that didn't mean they weren't watching.

She took the bottle, recapped it, and put it on the table.

When she picked up the chocolate bar, Katie held up a hand to waylay her.

Rielle's expression warmed, encouraging. "Now, Katie, I need you to understand you can tell me anything. Anything at all, and I can't tell anyone unless you tell me it's okay. Do you understand?"

Katie bobbed her head, still avoiding looking up.

"One more thing, Katie. Mr. Clayton, your principal, is here. I asked him to come because it's important you have someone here who cares about your welfare. He's willing to advocate for you, to be on your side. Is it okay if he stays?"

Katie's gaze went to Gage's shoes. He pondered what she might divine from his well-worn sneakers. Then her gaze shifted back to that spot on the floor only she saw. Again, only a silent acknowledgement.

"That's good, Katie." Rielle clasped her hands on her lap. "Now I am wondering if you can tell me how you're feeling."

He waited patiently. Should he sit? No, better not since he didn't want to bring undue notice to himself.

Suddenly, the young woman turned her head and looked up at Rielle. Her face was hidden from his view, but he watched as a tiny hand stretched out and, with hesitation, touched Rielle's cheek. Without makeup, the bruises were a sickly yellowish green, well on their way to fading. Katie's touch was feather-light. "Who hurt you?" The barest of whispers.

Without missing a beat, Rielle answered, "My father. My father hurt me."

Katie leaned toward her. "My father hurt me, too."

Gage's stomach dropped. This was the part of the job he hated the most—being faced with a child who suffered at the hand of a parent. He'd had no idea Katie was hurting.

"Katie, can you tell me how your father hurt you?"

Katie glanced over at him and back to Rielle. "He tried to take my baby away from me."

"Where's your baby now, Katie?" Rielle's question

317

was soft and coaxing.

Pressing her hands against her abdomen, Katie's fingers curled. "Inside me. I'm pregnant, and my father wanted to take my baby away."

"How was he going to do that?"

Katie took a breath, shakily exhaling. Her voice was soft, as if she understood the magnitude of her next statement. "He was going to take me to the doctor on Monday. He was going to make me say a boy at school got me pregnant, but that was a lie. He knew it was a lie."

Rielle chanced another glance at him, and he gave her whatever silent support he could convey.

"Okay, Katie, you're doing great. Now can you tell me who the father of your baby is?"

Katie's arms wrapped back around her waist, and she bent, doubled over.

Rielle moved quickly to rescue the slipping blanket. She put it back on Katie's shoulders, and as if it were the most natural thing in the world, put her arms around Katie and drew the young woman to her. "I need you to say it, Katie."

An unnatural wail escaped Katie's lips.

It was quiet, but Rielle tightened her grip. "You can do this, Katie. You need to do this." She was right, but it didn't make it any easier when the words finally came.

"My daddy."

Gage's rage reared up again, and for one unguarded moment, he was grateful she'd shot the bastard. Child molesters and rapists were the scum of the earth as far as he was concerned. Momentarily distracted, he almost missed Rielle asking her how long the girl's father had been hurting her.

Katie flinched but took another breath. "I don't remember…I'd just started school."

"High school?"

The young girl's brow furrowed. "Kindergarten."

The coffee he'd drunk threatened to reappear.

Rielle, however, was in her element. She was poised and confident while being nurturing and caring. "You're doing a great job, Katie. I'm proud of you." Her hands tightened. "Now can you tell me what happened tonight?"

Katie let out another noise he couldn't define, and that hurt his soul, but he was relieved to see Rielle wasn't fazed. Seconds bled into a minute, and then another slipped by.

Finally, Katie took another audible breath. "At dinner he told me we were going to go to the doctor on Monday. I didn't know why, but he said I was pregnant and…" Her voice trailed off. "When I got upset, he told me to go to my room and wait for him. That was what he would say. 'Go to your room and wait for me.'" Katie shuddered, and Rielle's hand on her shoulder twitched, tightening. "I'd always hope he wouldn't come, but he always did. And the thought…of there being a baby…I went and got his gun."

Rielle's presence silently offered strength and support to the young woman in such obvious pain.

"I went downstairs, and he was sitting watching the television. When he saw me with the gun, he laughed. He told me he was all I had and to go upstairs and wait for him." Katie met Rielle's gaze. "I couldn't let him do it. I just couldn't."

And with that, she broke. "I killed my father. I shot

Daddy. Oh God, what am I going to do?" Tears slipped unheeded down her cheeks, and her hands flew to her lips. "Help me. Please, help me."

Rielle held out her arms, and Katie collapsed into them. The older woman moved her hands up and down the teenager's back, making soothing sounds. She held on as the young girl cried.

Time spun out, and eventually, Katie's sobs eased into sniffles and hiccups. She wiped her nose on a corner of the blanket, glancing with trepidation from Rielle to Gage and back to Rielle. "But you won't tell anyone, right?"

She pressed a hand to Katie's cheek. "That's right, sweetheart."

Gage came up short. Of course she was going to tell the police. This horror story would prove mitigation, right? Surely they wouldn't charge Katie once they understood what had happened.

"Gage?" His attention focused on Rielle and what she was asking. "Can you get some tissues and more water?"

Relieved to be given a task, he left the room, encountering Dorrie and Colton as they emerged from the room next door. "Were you listening?" His voice hitched with unrepressed anger.

Dorrie shook her head. "No audio and no video. And neither of us can read lips. Whatever is going on in there is private."

Somewhat mollified, Gage spoke. "Can we get some tissues and maybe another bottle of water?"

"I'll get them." Dorrie exited, leaving the men. Gage felt protective of Katie and Rielle. Like an alpha wolf, he attempted to assess Colton for any weaknesses.

It was masculinity as toxic as it came, yet he wasn't going to be the one to relent, to break. Katie—and Rielle—were counting on him to keep his shit together. To not blow his lid and deck the ever-cocky cop. "What happens now?"

Colton gave him a once-over. "We talk to our boss about which charges we're going to recommend to the crown prosecutor. We'll get the forensics reports, but it looks like a cut-and-dried case of murder."

Suppressing the shiver running down his spine, Gage tamped down the sense of unease. "Aren't you going to talk to people? Ask questions? Look for a motive?"

"Are you saying there's more to this than meets the eye?"

Groaning inwardly, too late, he saw the trap. "You know I can't say anything."

"And we don't share our investigative techniques with civilians."

Gage wasn't sure there could have been more derision in the word "civilians." He was about to respond when Dorrie returned, handing him the requested items.

"Gregory, our staff sergeant, said to tell you he's on his way in and is hoping to talk to you and Ms. Reid." Dorrie's eyes demanded clarification of Rielle's role.

Gage wasn't going to yield on that one. Let them speculate about her as well as his relationship with her. He had nothing to hide nor to be ashamed of. He took the water and tissues and walked back into the interview room. So they'd called in the big guns, and Gregory was coming in. Gage wasn't sure if this was good or not. Two weeks ago, the man had been the one to call off Dorrie, and more importantly, Colton, during their interrogation of him. If the older man arrived, might saner heads prevail?

Katie, eyes closed, rested her head on her hands lying on the table, the blanket covering her.

Rielle stood in the corner opposite of the mirror, gazing into it.

Quietly, he put the tissues on the table, stepping to her and passing the water bottle.

She nodded gratitude and drank.

He waited until she consumed the entire bottle.

"Why did you tell her you wouldn't say anything? I mean, you have to tell them what she said."

"And once I get her permission, I will. But for right now, she needs to trust. I have to prove I won't betray that trust." Her eyes flashed.

"And if they charge her with murder?" His voice was hushed but his tone stern. "What then?"

"First, I talk to the crown prosecutor, then I come back and work with Katie."

"Not to point out the blatantly obvious, but it's not like she's going to be able to hide her condition for long."

"Of course not." The "duh" was implied, not spoken. "The first thing we need to do is get her a doctor. She's had no prenatal care, and I'm worried about her physical health."

"And her mental health?"

A withering look was her response.

He waved his hand, indicating he realized the ridiculousness of his question. Katie's trauma was profound, and he couldn't imagine how she might ever move on, even if she didn't go to jail. As he was about to speak, the door opened.

Dorrie stepped in, and seeing Katie, quietly approached Rielle and Gage. "Gregory is here. So is Zachary Finnegan, the crown prosecutor."

Gage didn't miss Rielle's eyebrows moving upward.

"Will you stay here with Katie?" Rielle was speaking to Dorrie, not him, surprising him. Did she not trust him with the young girl? Or was something else afoot? "Stay with her. I don't want her to be alone. But don't talk to her."

"If she wakes up, I'll come and get you. We could move her to a cell so she can lie down…"

Rielle shook her head. "No, she's resting here, so let her. I don't want her to spend a second longer in a cell than absolutely necessary." She met Gage's gaze. "Let's go talk to Mr. Finnegan."

He didn't know Zachary Finnegan personally because he'd graduated from a rival high school, but the man was said to be tough but fair. Young and ambitious, the hometown boy had returned from law school ready to get to work and improve his community.

Once handshakes and introductions were taken care of, they sat in a conference room—he and Rielle on one side of the long table, Colton, Zach, and Gregory on the other.

Very adversarial.

Zach spoke first. "I want to believe your client didn't wake up yesterday morning and decide to shoot her father for the fun of it. To kill him because he wouldn't let her go to the mall or date some pimple-faced kid."

Completely unfazed, Rielle offered a smile. "I'm pretty sure Katie had good reasons for doing what she did."

"Care to share?"

She didn't miss a beat. "Not at the moment. Cards on the table, Mr. Finnegan."

Now it was Zach's turn to smile. The expression twisted Gage's gut. "Ms. Reid, you are well aware this is serious. The RCMP is suggesting murder because there appears to be premeditation and no defensive wounds on the victim."

Acknowledging Zach's point, Rielle placed a hand on the table. "We know there are lots of reasons to kill. I need to consult with my client, and this might take some time. I don't want you to be in a hurry to file charges."

Zach checked his watch. "You've got a few of hours. After that, no promises. We're both aware she must be charged or released within twenty-four hours. Clock's ticking."

"That sounds like a threat." Gage spat it out.

"You're here as a courtesy, Mr. Clayton, so keep your opinions to yourself."

He bristled at Zach's rebuff, but held his tongue. When Rielle stood, he followed her.

The three men opposite also rose.

"I'll talk to my client, Mr. Finnegan. I'll call you."

Zach shook his head. "It's my day off. I'm going to do some paperwork while sitting at The Springs. Not drinking alcohol, of course. Why don't you text me when you're ready to talk, and we can do it in person?"

Rielle held out her hand, and he shook it. Without

another word, she left the room, Gage following dutifully behind.

If he wasn't so in tune with her, he might've missed the tremor in her hand when she reached for the door handle to the interview room. Before she could push it open, he pressed his hand over hers. "Okay?" He whispered it even though no one was within earshot.

She twisted her head, doubt flickering in her eyes. Then, as if taking strength from him, she squared her shoulders and blew out a breath. "I'm okay. Let's take care of Katie."

He wasn't sure she was being honest with him, but he nodded, releasing her hand.

She opened the door.

Dorrie sat across the table from Katie, who was eating the chocolate bar. The police officer rose to greet them. "She woke up a few minutes ago. I took her to the washroom, and we came back here. I didn't ask any questions, other than asking if she needed to use the facilities, and she hasn't said a word." Obviously Dorrie had taken Rielle's threat to heart.

"I appreciate you giving us some time. We'll be out when we're ready."

Dorrie left, and Gage took her seat, letting Rielle again sit next to Katie.

"Now, Katie, you remember I told you I'm here to protect you?" Rielle's voice was calm and reassuring. As if coaxing a wild feral cat to accept food.

Katie nodded.

"Okay, I need to ask you some hard questions, and I need you to answer as honestly as you can."

The young girl nodded again.

Thus began a three-hour odyssey into the life of

Katie Rhodes. Rielle was thorough, taking notes on a pad of paper provided by Dorrie.

After each painful revelation, he prayed it might end, but then another level of depravity Dennis Rhodes had achieved was unveiled. Gage listened, offering silent support to the two women as they struggled through the morass.

When it was over, they all needed a break.

Dorrie escorted Rielle and Katie to the women's washroom while he made a pit stop.

When he exited, Gregory waited for him. Before Gage could speak, he held up his hands. "I know you can't tell me anything. Jenna made a run for coffee and sandwiches." He pointed to the bag of food and drinks on the wooden bench.

"Is she still here?"

Gregory shook his head. "The woman was exhausted, so I sent her home. I told her you'd call if you needed her."

"Thanks, I'll do that."

"So that's Rielle Reid."

Gage aimed for a poker face but knew it was a failure. Instead of speaking, he held his ground.

Undaunted, Gregory continued. "I'm glad to see she's doing well. We still feel bad about what happened."

Sizing up the older man, Gage asked, "Do you see her as anything but competent because of who she is?"

Gregory considered the comment. "You mean do I see her differently because I'm familiar with her personal life? No. Like I don't see you any differently because of…well, you know."

He did know. Every person in that room was aware

he and Rielle engaged in BDSM. Well, everyone except Zach Finnegan, but Gage wouldn't count on him staying in the dark for long. Instead of saying something, he took the bags of food and the drinks.

He organized everything, and when the women returned, Katie docilely accepted a ham sandwich, and Rielle took the tuna, leaving him with the roast beef. Katie drank apple juice while Rielle drank black tea, and he consumed yet another coffee. Words weren't exchanged as the food was consumed. As the meal wound down, he collected the trash. He was about to stand when Rielle spoke.

"Katie, you remember when I said I would protect you?"

"Yes." The teenager's earnest look bespoke her true immaturity and need for love and guidance. Thank God Rielle was there to provide it.

"Well, now I need you to trust me."

Wariness crept into Katie's expression. "Okay." She drew the word out.

Rielle placed her hand on Katie's. "I need to tell your story to the police. To the crown prosecutor."

At Katie's look of confusion, Rielle clarified, "The lawyer who decides whether we go to trial or not." She took a breath. "Look, Katie, I'm going to do everything in my power to take care of you, but now I need you to trust me."

Katie's expression lightened a bit. "I trust you, Rielle." Her gaze went to Gage then back to Rielle. "I didn't want everyone to know about…you know."

"I know, sweetheart, and I wouldn't tell if it wasn't absolutely necessary. But it is, Katie. For your sake, you need to let me tell some people."

Katie squeezed Rielle's hand. "Okay." She managed to whisper the word, but it rode a hitch in her voice.

"Now I'm going to need to go talk to people." Rielle caught his gaze. "I'm going to leave you here with Mr. Clayton. If you need anything, tell him. You can trust him, too, okay?"

Katie's response was another bob of her head.

Rielle stood, taking her notepad and pen.

Gage rose, and they walked out of the room together. "Are you sure you can handle this?"

Rielle offered what seemed a genuine expression of serenity. "I handled being a slave for four years. Colton Pritchard and Zachary Finnegan don't scare me."

It was the first time she'd referred to her slavery in a teasing way, and it blew away much of the tension from the past few hours. Gage pressed a kiss to her cheek. "I'm more proud of you than I can say."

"We're a long way from a resolution, Gage."

He took in her words. "I know, Rielle, but I have faith in you."

She held out a hand to him, which he instantly grasped. "I'm going to go see what I can sort out." With that, she was gone.

He sorted trash from recycling, tossing them into the proper bins.

Back in the interview room, Katie sat, hands on her lap, and stared into the mirror. "Are there people behind that?"

"Sometimes." He answered slowly, acknowledging he'd need to tread carefully. "But Rielle asked them not to record what you said. What you said in this room was for her. The police can't listen in to a conversation

328

between a lawyer and a client."

Her gaze fell to him. "Am I her client?"

"Yes."

"But I didn't hire her. I can't pay her."

"That may be true, but there are lawyers who do things because they want to help other people. Rielle wants to help you."

"Why would anyone want to help me?"

Her tone was so soft and confused Gage's heart broke. "Katie, what happened to you...it was wrong. You know that, right? What your father did to you was terrible, and none of it was your fault."

She glanced from him to the mirror and back again. "I knew, you know. But I never said anything. I didn't want him to get in trouble. He said if I told, he'd go away. Now he's gone forever."

No big waste. Gage refrained from voicing that particular opinion. "But you're still here, Katie, and that's what counts."

"I'm in trouble, aren't I?" Not waiting for an answer, she continued, "I'm going to jail, aren't I?"

He longed to reach out and comfort the girl, wishing Rielle was there to guide him. "I honestly don't know, Katie. But that's why Rielle needed your permission to tell the truth. It might make a difference as to whether you go to jail. It might make a difference as to how long you go to jail. Regardless," he continued, "Rielle and I will be here to help you."

"Why?"

"It's my job to take care of my students."

Katie's eyes narrowed at him dubiously, and Gage was a bit chastised. Okay, so he didn't come running to the rescue of every student brought down to the detachment, but these were extraordinary circumstances requiring extraordinary effort on his part. "Let's say I want what's best for you."

Seemingly appeased, Katie nodded.

Time had no meaning that day. He surreptitiously checked his watch. It was only four thirty, yet it felt like he'd been there forever. His nerves were frayed with worry for both Katie and Rielle.

Rielle.

She hadn't hesitated when he'd asked her to come, but eighteen hours prior, she'd been under Spike's whip. If this caused him whiplash, he couldn't conceive what she was enduring.

"Mr. Clayton?"

"Yes, Katie."

She squirmed a bit, and Gage offered his most open expression, hoping to reassure.

"I want to have my baby, but I don't think I'd make a good mother."

Easy to see how she might feel that way. "Well, you've got some time before you need to decide what to do. In the meantime, we're going to take you to the doctor. Do you have a family doctor?"

Katie shook her head. "I've never seen a doctor."

Of course not.

A doctor might've seen what was going on. As long as Katie attended the requisite immunization clinics, the school would never have needed her to get medical attention. That would have to change.

"We'll find you a good doctor, Katie. I promise."

"Will he hurt me?"

"No, he—or she—won't hurt you. The doctor will be there to take care of you."

He wasn't sure if she believed his assertion but was appeased when she inclined her head.

She pressed a hand to her stomach. "It doesn't feel real, you know?"

That, he understood. "I know, Katie, I know."

"Can I go to school tomorrow? I don't want to fall behind."

"School tomorrow is out, but I'll arrange things and make certain you don't fall behind. I'll talk to your teachers."

Would the judge lock her up or let her out on bail? What would the school board think about an accused murderer attending school? If she didn't get bail, would they let her study in jail? How was she supposed to do that? Did they allow tutors in jail?

Taking a breath, he tried to clear his mind of possible scenarios. Until things played out that day, there was no point in begging trouble for the future.

When the door opened, he was immeasurably relieved. He felt awkward and unsure whether his words had any effect on the young girl sitting next to him. Surely he hadn't made things worse, but it was hard to tell. Her demeanor was the same eerie calm that had been present since Rielle departed.

He stood as Rielle entered the room, Dorrie Duhamel by her side.

"Katie?" Rielle's voice was soft.

Katie nodded.

"Dorrie needs to take you out of here. She's going to take your fingerprints, check to make sure you don't have anything with you that might hurt you, and she's going to give you a bed for tonight. Just for tonight." She rushed to reassure Katie, as the young girl's panic was quickly becoming evident. "Tomorrow we'll go in front of a judge and ask that you not have to stay here anymore."

Katie's eyes widened. "I'm going to jail?"

"I'm going to do everything I can to make sure it's just for tonight." Rielle pulled Katie into a tight hug, propriety be damned, and Gage was proud. He wanted to embrace them both, to offer and receive solace, but he couldn't, and that hurt.

"You need to trust me."

"I'll see you tomorrow?" The young girl's voice was soft, pleading.

"I promise." On what seemed like impulse, Rielle pulled Katie into another tight embrace. "You'll be okay. There are people here to take care of you. They know I'll be asking you tomorrow how you were treated." The look she sent Dorrie was full of warning, and the woman acknowledged the sentiment.

Katie stood and accepted Dorrie's invitation to leave the room. Well, invitation was the wrong word. Command was more like it. Before she stepped out, she gazed back at Gage and Rielle.

"Thank you." Katie's simple thanks was quiet and heartbreaking. Then she and the corporal were gone.

He moved to Rielle's side, desperate to hold her close, knowing decorum dictated he wait until they were away from prying eyes. "What happened?"

"Home, please, Gage. I want to go home."

He didn't want to drive back to Vancouver. In a moment of clarity, he understood her meaning. She wanted to go to *his* home. Well, that he could do.

When they stepped out from the interview room, no cops hovered. No prosecutors either. No one to waylay them as they left the cop shop. Stepping out into the brisk dusk air, he extended his arm to her, and she gripped it, using it to steady herself. In her other arm, she still clutched the notepad to her chest as if it were a shield. And maybe it was. Like her briefcase was her proverbial safety blanket.

She allowed him to tuck her into the truck, and by the time he made his way around the vehicle, her eyes were closed, her head lolled back. As he started the engine, she let out a long sigh.

"Deep dish pizza with extra olives?"

He was favored with a low chuckle but no other response.

****

By the time the pizza arrived, she'd stripped, showered, and was in her favorite mint green pajamas with little white snowflakes. She clasped a cup of hot tea while sitting at his kitchen table.

"Should I be worried about how much caffeine you've ingested?" He was only half teasing. An unreality existed that just a week ago they'd been ending their relationship in that exact room, and now they were unified, dealing with the horrors of the world.

"I'm either going to sleep or I won't. I'm either going to relax or I won't. Caffeine will have little or no say in what happens."

He inclined his head as he dished out a couple of slices for her.

She didn't even wait for him to serve himself before she sank her teeth into the cheesy, greasy, doughy concoction.

His worry eased as he served himself and joined her at the table. Her two slices were consumed before he'd even finished his first. When a groan of contentment escaped her lips, he ventured to speak. "I'm so proud of you, Rielle."

Her gaze met his, and something passed over her expression. "I haven't done anything yet to earn that praise."

He shook his head. "I won't let you say that. Katie Rhodes needed help today, and you stepped up to the plate." Her face formed the mutinous expression he'd seen before as she was about to deflect his words, so he continued. "You might've folded under that pressure. No one would've blamed you if you needed time to regroup, but you persisted."

"She's still spending a night in jail."

"Which I'm sure you did everything to prevent."

She gave a grudging acknowledgement. "We weren't able to get her in front of a judge today, but we will first thing in the morning. Zach's not going to oppose bail, and we've agreed to an ankle monitor instead of cash, which she probably wouldn't have anyway."

"Will she be able to come to school?" He ruminated over the idea in his mind. "Would that even be feasible? I mean, where's she going to go?"

"We've arranged for her to see a psychologist tomorrow. Dr. Denise Lang, do you know her?"

"One of the best child psychologists in town. We often use her for consultations in the school district. She's a good diagnostician. She's also very young and relates well to the kids." Now that a plan was taking shape, his anxiety ratcheted down.

"Well, she's going to meet with Katie before the bail hearing, to assure Zach that Katie isn't a homicidal maniac." A ghost of a smile passed her lips. "Once bail is set, she'll be placed in the care of social services. They want to take her to foster care, Gage." Her eyes were wide and solemn. "You probably don't know what it's like…"

"I've had a few kids under the care of social services. We can watch out for her and make sure they take care of her."

She raked her hands through her hair in frustration. "It's not enough."

"Will anything be enough? We can't undo what happened. All we can do is make sure Katie isn't traumatized any more than necessary."

"Which reminds me, we need to arrange for her to see a doctor. I've requested a specialist who deals with rape victims, as we'll need to document…well, you know. And we need to get her in to see an obstetrician. Dorrie gave me a couple of recommendations for both as she's dealt with rape victims before."

Unadulterated rage washed over him at what Katie was enduring. What so many girls and women had gone through before. "Can you be there? I mean, if Katie wants you to be?"

"Wild horses wouldn't keep me away, Gage. For the next few days, my sole job is to be by Katie's side. I'll also talk to Dr. Lang about arranging ongoing counselling." Her expression was bleak. "She'll never be normal, but maybe, with a lot of professional help, she might be able to come to terms with what's happened to her."

He snagged her hand. "How are you going to cope with this? I mean, Katie needs your help, but you can't do this to your own detriment."

She seemed to consider his words carefully. "Today, I felt...like I haven't in a long time. Useful. Someone needed me for something other than sexual servitude, and it was overwhelming at first, but it started to...fit." She shook her head. "I didn't think I'd ever be a lawyer again."

"You were too young to retire." He chose his next words carefully. "Look at it as having taken a break. Now you're fresh and ready to start over."

"Do I deserve a do-over?"

He balked. "Of course you deserve a fresh start. But that doesn't mean you don't still need help with your own unresolved issues." He hadn't planned on bringing this up so soon, but she seemed receptive, so he gave it his best shot. "Kennedy Dixon's farm is not far from here."

Her reaction was not what he expected. Instead of defensiveness, a telltale upward curl of her lips emerged. "Didn't take you long, did it?"

He offered a sheepish smile. "What can I say? I care about you."

She squeezed his hand that she still clung to. "I know you do. And I appreciate you waited a whole hour before bringing it up." Her eyes held a bit of mischief in them, and her lips twitched.

On impulse, he leaned over to press a kiss to her lips. It was chaste, holding a promise of much more.

When he pulled back, she made a little sound of distress. "I need to go to bed, before I drop. Tomorrow's going to be a long day."

He squeezed her shoulder. "I'll clean up while you get into bed. In the morning, maybe you can drop me off at school, and you'll have use of the truck should you need it. You can drive, right?"

"Yes, Gage, I can drive."

"Well, there's a rumor not all city folk drive. Plus, I'm not convinced that BMW has been out of the garage."

She cocked an eyebrow. "I drive it for twenty kilometers every month, like I'm supposed to. But yes, it doesn't have more than a couple hundred clicks on it. Maybe I can go into the city later this week and get it? Along with a few other of my things."

He liked the sound of that. "If you can survive until Saturday, we can retrieve them then." He held his breath.

"Saturday sounds good." She released his hand, rose, and stretched. Leaning down, she placed a kiss to his cheek. "Come to bed soon. You're looking as tired as I'm feeling." Then she was gone.

In her wake, however, a wave of desire swept over him.

Come to bed soon, she said. As in come to *our* bed soon? There had been no talk of sleeping arrangements, and the room she'd used the previous weekend had been cleaned, sheets laundered, everything put to rights. Sex was out of the question, but sleeping with someone? For the whole night? That held almost as much appeal.

Almost.

Cleanup was simple, and within a few minutes, he headed to the bathroom. The steam from her earlier shower had dissipated, but her scent lingered. He'd yet to put his finger on the exact scent of body spray she used, but he liked trying to guess. He loved the mystery and allure that came with the not knowing.

When he stepped into his bedroom, one of the bedside lamps was on, casting the room in shadows. She was already in bed, covers pulled up. He stripped out of his clothes and slid in beside her, cradling her against him, spoon-style. She extended a hand to switch off the light, and he stopped her.

"I don't mind sleeping with the light on."

"With you next to me, I don't need the light."

He was moved almost to the point beyond words. "I'll always protect you. You know that, right?"

Instead of responding, she cuddled closer to him, burrowing herself under the blankets. It wasn't long before her breath evened out and even less time after that before his did.

Chapter Eleven

By Friday, almost everything had been resolved. Or at least as resolved as they might be, given the circumstances. Katie wouldn't be going to jail.

Rielle and Zach spent the week going back and forth. First Dr. Lang had seen Katie, and Denise was adamant the teenager was a threat to no one except herself. Her pregnancy, however, kept suicidal thoughts in check. Denise's greatest concern was for Katie after the child was born. Her report made it clear Katie had been defending herself and her unborn child from a threat she perceived as being real and imminent.

Dr. Renée Grantham, an obstetrician and gynecologist, examined Katie and confirmed the girl was pregnant. DNA tests would be conducted, but everyone agreed it was a foregone conclusion Dennis Rhodes was the father. She arranged to take Katie on as a patient.

Katie had met with Dr. Kennedy Dixon. Although equine therapy wasn't appropriate, the young woman had been enthralled by Tiffany, the comfort dog. She'd endured two intense sessions with Kennedy, and it was arranged they'd meet weekly, at least until the baby was born, and probably for a long time afterward.

The biggest surprise had been Katie's living situation. She'd been put in an emergency foster home for two days and then moved in with Jenna. Jenna had been expedited as a foster parent because of her previous vetting through the school board. Cara's friend Alessandra had been the supervising presence from social services and been prevailed upon, convinced Jenna would be able to provide a stable environment for Katie. He'd questioned whether it would feel odd to be dealing with his former submissive, but as always, their relationship had been completely professional. If Rielle recognized Alessandra's name, she hadn't mentioned anything.

Satisfied Katie wasn't a threat to society, was telling the truth about the sexual molestation, was willing to accept help, and had a good living situation, Zach negotiated.

Parole until she graduated from high school and an expunged record if she stayed out of trouble. Regular meetings with her parole officer and mandatory counselling for at least a year, longer if Dr. Lang recommended it.

What Rielle accomplished in a week stunned Gage. Each day she dropped him off at school by seven thirty and picked him up at five thirty. Each day she'd been dead on her feet. Each day he cooked a simple meal that he coaxed her to eat before she fell asleep, usually by seven o'clock. What she lacked in stamina, she made up for in dogged persistence.

By Friday night, he worried she might be broken, physically and emotionally.

She'd come home, gone into the bedroom, crawled under the blankets—fully clothed—and gone to sleep.

Eventually she'd wake and be hungry, so he put her plate of lasagna in the fridge and made his way to the television. The Canucks were playing, and he lowered the volume enough so he could hear her if she called for him.

In truth, volume wasn't necessary as his Canucks were being routed yet again. Not an auspicious opening to the season. It was the middle of the second period when she came into the room, stark naked. She didn't even give him a chance to move before dropping at his feet to a kneeling position.

"What the hell?" He said it in a reasonable tone, the best he could do.

Her gaze swept up at him through hooded lashes. "I need you, Gage. I need this." The tone was plaintive, but not whining.

He fought back another epithet. She needed dinner and to sleep for the entire weekend. He questioned whether she even comprehended what she needed, but if this was what she wanted, who was he to argue? But still…

"Please, Sir." She blinked, pupils dilated in the dimly lit room. "I think I did a good job this week."

He reached for her, but she scooted out of range. "You did."

Her gaze continued to hold his. "And maybe I've earned a reward?"

"Whatever you want. Within reason." *Careful, she might want the moon.* She wouldn't, though. She never asked for more than she believed she deserved.

"I want this." Her chin rose before her look morphed to coquettish, and she batted her eyelashes. "And you do, too."

Well, the body was willing, even if the mind was a step behind. From the moment she walked in, his body reacted to her nudity. He should've been able to control himself. Would have, if he'd supposed it possible to feed her and coax her back into bed. But that stubborn lift to her chin said this was nonnegotiable. She'd told him she needed this. Maybe, if he was honest with himself, he did as well.

When he flipped off the television using the remote, her eyes lit and her smile widened. "This is going to be fun," she whispered reverently. They were the same words she'd used that first night they got together.

He knew her much better now. Now he appreciated, without a shadow of a doubt, it'd be good. "Stand."

Instantly, she was on her feet, ready for inspection.

Since she'd spent the past week covered from head-to-toe in her pajamas, he hadn't been able to examine her body. He ran his fingers across her skin, tracing the faded bruises. The ones on her face were mere shadows, and to the best of his knowledge, no one challenged her about them.

He stood, pressing his hands above her waist, against her ribcage. "And how are they healing?"

"Not even a twinge this week, Sir."

He'd still be careful, but other things they might do that wouldn't jeopardize her recovery flitted through his mind. He slid his hands up to cup her breasts. She rolled her shoulders forward, and he enjoyed their full weight, their plumpness. When he pressed his thumbs against her nipples, she made a noise of supreme contentment.

"Follow me." He didn't wait to see if she was going to comply. Of course she would. She wanted this even more than he did. He led her down the carpeted stairs to the basement. To the right was the main room that led to the walk-out patio. Autumn-colored leaves already blanketed the ground, waiting to be raked.

To the left was the room that always remained locked. He'd grabbed the key on the way down and now fumbled putting the key in the lock. His cock twitched as she breathed warm air against his neck. Her nervous anticipation matched his own.

The past Saturday, during his cleaning frenzy, he'd come down there, unlocking it for the first time since Cara died. Swamped by pain, he'd fought through the discomfort as the good memories bombarded him. His love for her would never leave him, but as time passed, it was less of an ache and more a warm glow in his heart. He owed Rielle for that. Her presence gave him the incentive to keep moving forward. Even if she never came back, his life was better for having known her.

Now, as he led her into the space, the feeling of peace infused him with calm. Well, peace mixed with anticipation mixed with a raging hard-on, but still, the sense of rightness was unmistakable.

Her breath hitched as she took in the space.

"It's not a dungeon…"

"No." She moved to the wall, running her hand against it reverently. "I love it. It feels…welcoming."

Not exactly the description for a playpen of pleasure and pain, yet her statement rang true. Painted gray with slashes of scarlet and black, the walls held avant-garde paintings of Rubenesque nudes mixed with playboy-style pinups. The room had been created tongue-in-cheek, but he and Cara had mixed their styles and sensibilities to create a fun space in which to play. The paintings came down when the in-laws were staying, but when he'd been alone with Cara, they'd come out to play.

Although Rielle took in the entire space in one sweeping glance, her focus was the bed. At first glance, it was just a king-sized bed with a headboard and footboard with colorful fabric draped in artistic arches.

In reality, it was a place of both torture and pleasure. The fabric attached to the boards with loose ends easily released and were designed to hold someone in bondage. He made a show of releasing them now, letting them flutter to the mattress.

"But first…" Walking to the wall, he removed two rather unwieldy paintings to reveal manacles.

"Clever." Her reverence was clear.

"Face the wall." He issued the order, and she was quick to comply. He took his time attaching the restraints, pleased when she pulled against them as if testing them.

He walked over to the bed and pressed a knot in the wood that released a hidden compartment. A lot of his toys were new, having been acquired a week prior. Although he tried to tell himself she was out of his life and never coming back, his heart hadn't been in it. He'd continued to hope. Waited for the phone to ring.

Now he extracted the paddle. It was oak, made custom for him with an engraving of a rose in bloom. "Count." His order came, even as he laid on the first spank.

"One." The word was pushed out through gritted teeth. "Sir doesn't believe in pulling his punches."

He simply smacked her again.

"Two." She continued to push matters. "Not taking it easy, are we?"

He stepped forward, grabbed a handful of her hair, and tugged. Not hard, of course, but enough to catch her attention. "I said 'count,' not give me a running commentary."

"Yes, Sir."

He released her hair and smoothed his hand down the length of her spine. In response, she shivered.

"Now we're going to start again."

She groaned but said nothing.

He used the paddle to spank her.

"One." She obviously concluded continuing to critique his technique wouldn't end well for her. Two, three, and four came in rapid succession, but she managed to keep count. He gave her a moment before he laid into her again with five, six, and seven. He stepped forward, delving his hand between her thighs.

She tried to close her legs, but he ruthlessly forced them apart. "Tut, tut," he admonished. "Sir wants you to keep your pussy open for him." Before she had a chance to respond, he thrust two fingers into her. She bore down on him, and he grinned. Her desire was mixed with potent arousal. "You're pretty. Are you wanting some relief?"

She moaned low in response, trying to rub against him. When he withdrew his fingers, she let out a groan of protest. He stepped back and delivered four quick smacks. The final one was the hardest, causing her to go up on her toes and pull against her restraints. It wasn't anything she couldn't handle, but she'd forgotten to count.

I'll let that slide. "How much do you want it, Rielle?"

"I—" Her breath hitched. "More than anything."

She let out a long, shuddering sigh. "As soon as I can get it."

He wasn't inclined to make her wait long because he was so hard it bordered on painful. Removing his clothes with deliberateness and speed, he draped them over a chair. When he was naked, he walked over and gave her a couple of smacks to get her warmed up.

"Please." Her plea went straight to his cock, bringing it to attention even more. "Don't make me wait."

Since she merely echoed his own sentiments, he didn't prolong the situation. He positioned himself behind her and entered her in one thrust. Her gasp matched his own. She arched against him, giving him the chance to reach around and grab her breasts.

Already sensitive from where they'd been rubbed against the wall, she pressed her nipples against his thumbs with wanton abandon. "Please fuck me." Her whispered whimper was just as arousing.

Letting go of her tits, he stroked downward and splayed one hand across her abdomen while the other pressed against her clit.

She tried to buck away, but his hold on her was too strong.

He withdrew almost completely and pressed home. Again and again until his legs wouldn't hold him any longer.

Prolong this. Think about hockey and how badly the Canucks are losing at this very moment. Think about—

Just like that, it was over, and he spilled into her. Pulse after pulse coursed through him as he let go. Let go of tension, let go of stress, let go of everything. "I'm sorry," he whispered harshly into her ear even as he nipped the lobe.

"What for?" She was clearly confused.

"You didn't come."

"But I can't…" She clamped her mouth shut abruptly. But she had, she obviously realized. A week ago, in fact. She was used to denial, and the words had come out without thought.

He swept her hair aside, kissed her neck, nipped her earlobe again, and gave her shoulder a love bite. "I have an idea."

She shivered in response. "I like ideas."

Ten minutes later, she wasn't looking happy.

Oh, she'd been eager enough when he'd unshackled her and led her to the chair. She'd sighed when he'd pulled her arms back to tie them to the chair. As always, she'd tested the restraints and found them to her liking. She adored being secured, he'd learned. When he tied her legs to the chair, she tried to close them but hadn't been able to. That caused her to squirm.

When he gagged her, she'd given him a look of appreciation. When he brought out a pillow, she looked at him quizzically. He doubled it and placed it at the small of her back, and she'd begun to clue in as to what he planned. Now her expression was mutinous.

Grinning, he sauntered behind her to the bed and selected his weapon of torture. When he flipped it on to test it, her head snapped back. She tried to speak, so he came up behind her, placing his cheek next to hers. "Did you say something?"

"Mrph, urmf, humph!"

He laughed, glad he'd chosen to gag her.

It added to her misery she couldn't communicate.

He rounded in front of her, producing the offensive weapon. "This"—he held out his hand to show her—"is a vibrator. Am I to guess you never made use of the one I left you?"

Her eyes shot daggers, and she didn't speak, but he already intuited the answer. Of course she hadn't used it. She probably tossed it in the garbage the first chance she had.

Now, however, with her hips thrust forward, her arms and legs bound, she eyed him with wariness.

He grabbed a scarf that he now secured in her hand. "That's for if I'm hurting you. Only if you're hurting." His warning was evident. "Clear?"

"Humph."

Good enough. Reaching between her legs, he found her slick and warm. "Your mind might be saying 'no,' but your body is begging for this."

She shook her head and tried to move her hips. It was a heavy chair, and it wasn't moving. She could struggle all she wanted, but she wasn't going anywhere.

He leaned forward and kissed her forehead as he pressed the vibrator against her clit.

A strangled noise escaped from behind her gag as she attempted to pull away.

"Breathe through your nose, Rielle." It took a couple of seconds, but she obeyed. She still tried to pull away, but he ruthlessly continued to hold the vibe against her.

Her thighs quivered, and she struggled to roll onto the balls of her feet but was too well-secured for that to happen. Her pelvic muscles were strong but no match for his restraints. Finally, slowly, her struggles lessened. She wasn't pulling as hard, and her eyes drifted shut.

"You may think you can wait me out." He grinned wickedly. "You're wrong. I've got all the time in the world."

Her eyes opened to stare into his, and it was clear he read her exactly right. As a reward for her impudence, he increased the speed of the vibrator.

Her eyes narrowed.

"Oh." His exclamation was all innocence. "Did I not mention there were different speeds?"

Her eyes shot daggers, but he smirked. Then he pressed the vibrator against her clit. Again. She let out a muffled howl of indignation, but he arched an eyebrow. "The sooner you come, the sooner this will be over."

Defiance transformed to doubt in a heartbeat. Her lower lip trembled, and her eyes shone. Undaunted, he snagged her chin between his thumb and forefinger, tipping her head back. When her eyes drifted shut, he placed a kiss on each cheek, each lowered lid. "You can, sweetheart." He let a beat pass, lowering his mouth to her ear. "And you will." His words were spoken with absolute certainty as he bit her earlobe.

She took two deep breaths through her nose, nostrils flaring. But he had become familiar with her body, and it was tensing, poising itself for something more. She might not recognize the signs, but he did. The rosy hue of her chest, the flush of her cheeks, the hardening of her nipples.

Patience rewarded, as her body drew up, he doubled down. He leaned over, taking her nipple in his mouth. With perfect synchronicity, he pressed harder and bit down at the same time.

Her head snapped back, but this time in the throes of ecstasy.

Dropping the vibe to the pillow, he thrust his fingers into her. Was there any headier sensation than feeling a woman climax? Nope, none. He continued to stroke her G-spot, coaxing every last spasm from her body.

What had been tense became lax. What had been taut slackened.

Breathing that had been harsh was now soft whimpers and whispers.

He grasped the vibrator, switching it on. Her head snapped up, and the look of anguish on her face was comical, but he bit back the laugh. Instead, he gave her the sternest look he was able. He leaned forward so a couple of inches rested between them.

"Again." He pressed the vibe against her clit.

She shook her head and tried to speak, but it came out as garbled snatches of speech. Her abdomen convulsed as she tried to pull her hips away from the unrelenting torture. She was sensitive, but not sore.

This was uncomfortable—physically and psychologically—but he wasn't hurting her. He'd stop if that line was crossed.

This time, the orgasm came much faster and harder. Without a doubt, she was absolutely stunned by the ferocity of the waves of pleasure.

Her eyes were closed, but he saw into her soul. When two tears leaked out, he took the scarf from her boneless fingers and touched the silk to the wetness. Tenderness overwhelmed him, and he pressed a kiss to her forehead.

"My angel." This whisper wasn't broken. Instead it

held reverence. "My precious good girl." Normally he didn't like to use that particular term, but she always responded to it.

Now she did, opening her eyes to meet his gaze.

Liquid pools of amber shone up at him, and his chest constricted. He was pleased she kept eye contact with him as he untied her legs. As he used long powerful strokes up her calves and thighs, her eyes drifted shut again.

Her head lolled forward, and he moved around the back to loosen the bindings. He released her arms, and her hands tightened into fists. Using the persuasive power of massage, he encouraged her to open them, and she complied.

When she was completely unbound, he gathered her into his arms. She looped her arms around his neck as he carried her the few feet to the bed and slid her from his arms onto the mattress. She didn't open her eyes as he pulled the comforter over her, instead snuggling deeper into the pillow. The little sigh she exhaled was the exquisite personification of contentment.

Moving away from her was agony, but he had to. He scooped up his clothes and made his way upstairs. A quick detour to his bedroom to grab his robe, then he went to the kitchen and set to work making a couple of sandwiches. He hummed a tuneless song as he put together ham and cheese. He added a side of olives for her and tucked two bottles of water into his pockets.

He padded back downstairs and found her much as he had left her—in a blissful slumber. It was past midnight, and she needed sustenance. He put the plates on the floor, sat next to her, and pressed his face to hers. "Wake up, sweetheart."

She stirred but didn't open her eyes.

"Not a request, Rielle."

She pulled her hands up to her face, trying to push him away.

"Get up, or I'm putting you back in the chair."

Eyes snapped open, and she struggled to move. "I'm up. I'm up," she assured him. "No need for the chair."

Despite his best efforts to suppress it, he grinned. That was going to be her Achilles' heel. Worse threats existed, but clearly that one was going to be very effective. Helping her sit up, he used his position to cop a feel, pressing his hands to her breasts.

She moaned, closing her eyes. "Are we going to go another round?" She sounded resigned and would've, he had no doubt, found the energy for whatever he had in mind.

He was pleased when she was relieved at being presented food. In fact, when she spotted the olives, her grin was downright grateful. She immediately popped one into her mouth, savoring it as she bit down. "God, thank you. That was good."

"You were pretty good yourself." He was inordinately pleased when she blushed.

"Sir, I…"

He leaned forward and pressed his lips to hers, delving his tongue in and cursing when he tasted olives.

She nipped his tongue and giggled. "That'll teach you to kiss me while I'm trying to eat."

"I guess I'm going to have to learn to love olives." He pulled back to gaze into her eyes. "In fact loving olives might be the easiest part of this proposition, but here it goes." He dropped to his knees and took her hands in his. "Rielle, will you become my submissive?"

Her eyes widened in shock. Maybe he'd pushed too hard, or maybe he'd chosen the wrong moment. She pulled her hands from his, leaned forward, and cupped his cheeks. Slowly, she returned his smile, but she still had a look of wistfulness on her face.

"What's wrong, sweetheart?"

"Can I tell you something?"

"Of course, you can tell me anything." He pressed a thumb to her frown line, trying to ease her brows from the furrow they were in.

"I just...I love you, Gage." She took a deep breath. "I just had to say that."

In here, in this room, a myriad of emotions flowed through him. It was right. It was time. "I love you, too, Rielle."

"Are you sure? Because let's be honest, I'm a lot of work."

Of course, yet he had no doubt in his mind. "Yes, I'm sure."

"Is it really that simple?" Her brow furrowed again, as if she couldn't believe such happiness was in front of her and all she had to do was step toward it.

"It is." And it was. He blinked for a moment, comfort suffusing him. Although he'd sworn not to think of Cara when with Rielle, he sensed her presence in the gentle caress of Rielle's hand against his brow.

"I think she would have approved."

He swallowed the lump in his throat. "I know she'd have approved. So...a June wedding?"

Rielle grinned. "Fuck no, I'm not waiting that long. How about next week at the courthouse?"

"How about Christmas with close family and friends." Her happiness slipped, and he added quickly, "Mine will love you. You'll never have to feel alone again. And we'll invite Gigi and Dante…"

"I'm not going back to the condo, you realize." She leaned forward and kissed him. "Can we bring the St. Andrew's Cross?"

He quirked an eyebrow. "We can bring whatever you want. In fact, why don't you sell your place? Move in here. Start fresh."

"We'll have to hire a contractor to demolish the dungeon."

"Or not." He chuckled. "I'm sure Mistress Gigi and Master Dante can find someone looking for a fully decked-out dungeon."

About the Author

Even though Gabbi Black is a firm believer in happy endings, she makes her characters work for it in every romance she writes, no matter what the genre. From contemporary to BDSM, they are penned late at night in her home on a beautiful British Columbia mountain surrounded by magnificent trees and every conceivable woodland creature—including bears. She also writes gay romances as Gabbi Grey.

~*~

Visit Gabbi online at:
www.gabbiblack.com

Also Available
from The Wild Rose Press, Inc.
and major retailers.

For the Love of Max

By Gabbi Grey

Ironworker Dodge Vasilius has been in love with LGBTQ social worker Maxine Reeves since he first met her at a party when her date abandoned her. She's way out of his league. Except she's finally left the abusive jerk. Dodge is just checking to make certain she's safe. Because making a move on the newly single Maxine would be classless...right?

Also Available
from The Wild Rose Press, Inc.
and major retailers.

Falling for Two
By Melanie Hoffer

The party was supposed to be easy. Wear a mask, dress sexy, and get laid. When a stranger walked in, everything changed. I didn't expect him to look at me that way or touch me so perfectly. I also didn't expect to meet him again months later, working at the same company and leading the biggest project of my career. Luckily, he doesn't remember me until one slip of the tongue throws me back in. Nathan Richards isn't exactly single, and his roommate and boyfriend, Clark Peterson, has other…interesting ideas.

Thank you for purchasing
this publication of The Wild Rose Press, Inc.

For questions or more
information contact us at
info@thewildrosepress.com.

The Wild Rose Press, Inc.
www.thewildrosepress.com

www.ingramcontent.com/pod-product-compliance
Lightning Source LLC
Chambersburg PA
CBHW051130030726
47504CB00004B/799